The Chessmaster

William Wilkin

Bell Street Publishing, LLC

Bell Street Publishing, LLC

Published by Bell Street Publishing, LLC,
7360 Middlebrook Cir
Nashville, TN 37221-6545

ISBN: 978-09903164-3-5

First Published in the United States,2019

Graphic Design: Matthew A. Stone & William Wilkin

Contents

Acknowledgements

I owe an immense debt of gratitude to several people who have contributed substantially to this book's artistic integrity.

There are my two sons, James Wilkin and Matthew Stone.

James contributed a number of graphic design suggestions that are incorporated in the cover design and interior of the book.

He exhibited attention to detail and artistic consistency far beyond my capabilities.

My wife, Lou, contributed in both obvious and subtle ways to the completion of the book. She is a Spanish teacher and has extensive experience editing and correcting texts—both student and professional. Any remaining grammatical and spelling errors must not be accounted to her. They proceed from my eccentric ideas about the value of deviating from standards occasionally to accurately portray a state of mind or emotional content. A subtle way that she supported the completion of this book was her endless patience with those eccentric ideas.

In addition, she was willing to endure the many, many times that I worked into the early morning hours pursued by my characters who insisted on telling their stories at the most inconvenient hours.

She has always been emotionally constant in the shifting winds of our lives throughout the long thankless years of the struggle to bring these stories to print. Bravo Lou!

Booksellers

I found myself waiting at the entrance to my home in London. Minerva had promised to come and pick me up to go to Diagon Alley. I had almost given up waiting when I noticed her coming out of our favorite alley. She signaled me to follow her. When I caught up just inside the alley, she gave me a nice kiss and asked how Stiffie was doing.

"Oh, we've entered a new ice age. She has gone back to never talking to me. I suppose that's good."

"You bet it is."

"But it's kind of spooky running into each other a couple of times a day and never saying a word."

"Just keep up the good work." Minerva said and took my hand. I gritted my teeth and prepared for the inevitable gut-wrenching pain of being stuffed through the space-time continuum in ways that nature had never intended.

We arrived just outside the Leaky Cauldron and Minerva continued to hold my hand so that I could enter with her. This morning the Cauldron was particularly quiet. It was too late for the breakfast trade and well before lunch. Tom, the barkeep, just waved at us as we passed through. We were going to "Flourish & Blots" so that we could talk with the proprietor about getting some new textbooks for my new English classes.

We stopped off at Gringotts so that I could pick up some money in case old Mr. Petitfour wanted a down payment on the books that I wanted him to acquire. When we arrived, the bookstore had only one

1

other shopper in it browsing the Muggle bookshelf. I'd first discovered it the previous summer when I'd been there getting the books lined up for the next term. Most wizards don't like frequenting Muggle businesses, but they sometimes want books published by Muggles.

The books there have a strange mixture of topics. There are books on chess openings next to books on French Cuisine and cartoon collections. I guess humor is pretty universal. There were several Calvin and Hobbs collections and Petitfour claimed that they were good movers. The copy I picked up and glanced through had been handled a good bit— probably by the Weasley twins.

But this day I was there to get Petitfour to bring in my new textbooks. I gave him my list. He just looked at them and shook his head. "You'll never get anyone who isn't required to buy these to even glance at them.

"Now, you take this one, *English Literature: With World Masterpieces* by Macmillian (**Hardcover**- Jun 1991). Who would ever pick that one up and glance through it? Besides it's written by a Muggle."

"Sure, I know that good literature doesn't have much following among wizards."

Petitfour looked at me with his eyebrows furrowed and said, "Now, there's a lot of interest in good literature among Wizards. Just look at this author Gilderoy Lockhart. He's got at least half a dozen books on the Wizarding Best Sellers list." He picked up a book off a prominent display and handed it to me—*Gadding with Ghouls*.

I opened it and glanced at a few pages. Petitfour said, "You won't find better fiction or at least more entertaining fiction than this in a Muggle book."

I glanced at the Foreword of the book and said, "But this claims to be non-fiction."

"Oh, yes. It claims to be non-fiction, but it's got all the hallmarks of fiction. Everything is too neat. Nobody whom the author likes has anything bad happen to them. Lockhart never has a problem beating the pants off vampires or werewolves or whatever he's up against."

"Hmmmm."

"If you like, you can meet him in person. He's scheduled to appear here for a signing on August 28—just in time to catch the back to school trade. The kids buy their school books and the Mom's buy their romantic fiction to fill their time when the kids are off to school—like the latest Lockhart book."

"Then he's a heart-throb for middle-aged witches?"

"You might say that. He's on the cover of Witch Weekly more than anyone else. See here." He picked up a slick magazine from a rack. It had a picture of a man with a beaming smile full of perfect teeth and blazing blonde hair. I glanced at the article that was an interview with the author about his latest book. I handed the magazine back and went off to see if I could find Minerva. She was thumbing through a copy of "Transfiguration Today."

"You ready to go?"

"Yes, but I want to buy this first. I'll just be a minute."

"I'll be at the Muggle bookshelf looking for a copy of *A Brief History of Time.*"

"Don't waste your time with that Muggle superstition." She had a twinkle in her eye as she said it, but I decided to give her a hard time about Prof. Hawking after we left the shop.

"Did you buy anything beside the magazine?"

"No. Did you?"

"I wanted to buy a copy of *Gadding with Ghouls* but they were sold out.'

"Oh, don't waste your time with Lockhart. He's worse than Hawking if you ask me. I don't think he did half the things that he claims to have."

"Who, Hawking?"

Minerva spluttered for a second and then realized that I was kidding her. "I'll let you in on a little secret. I think that Lockhart is going to be a professor at Hogwarts this year."

"Really!" I was surprised indeed, "Why would Lockhart have anything to do with Hogwarts? It doesn't seem like his style. And why would Dumbledore have anything to do with Lockhart?"

"Oh, Dumbledore is desperate to find someone to take the Defense Against the Dark Arts class this year."

"Right. I forgot for a second about the bad luck that seems to affect that post. But why would Lockhart want it?"

3

"I think that he's looking for material for his next book. Dumbledore would be a great source for magic adventures that could be.-.-. uh.-.-. adapted to Lockhart's history."

"Lockhart must believe his own publicity if he thinks he can take that job and come away unscathed." By this time we were approaching Fortescue's ice cream stand. We stopped for one, and Minerva complained about ruining our appetite for lunch.

"Oh, come on. We've not got that much time until school starts again." She reluctantly agreed, and we shared an ice cream sundae. It was made with Bott's every flavor beans. We were lucky. There weren't any ear wax flavored beans.

We had lunch at a nice Italian restaurant in Diagon Alley that I'd never been to before—Schiaparelli's. We just had a salad, a little pasta and a little red wine. I asked Minerva why we'd never eaten there before.

"Oh, you know. I just like patronizing Tom's place." While we were there, we ran into Madame Malkin, who had come for some quick takeaway. She tried to convince me that I needed a new wardrobe for the new term.

"I haven't seen you in my shop in more than two years. You really need new robes."

I wasn't buying it or new robes, "I was in your shop not that long ago with Minerva. Why do I need new robes?"

Minerva interrupted, "Oh, Marianne, he's a man. He's not going to buy new clothes until they wear off his back. I tried to get him to get some new clothes at the end of last term. It's hopeless."

Malkin clucked her tongue and gave up for the moment. I knew that I'd not seen the last of her though—or Minerva—on that topic.

▽

Minerva dropped me at my rooming house. I spent the next couple of weeks reading things other than English Lit doing some writing. Once in a while Minerva and I would have lunch—sometimes at a wizarding restaurant and sometimes at a Muggle place that I knew. Once, Minerva disapparated us to a small French village on the Atlantic that was solely a wizarding village and treated me to lunch. It had one restaurant and it was quite good. I had a little better French than Minerva did, so I repaid Minerva for my meal by conversing with the staff. The seafood was great.

The summer disappeared like a magician's rabbit. The day of Lockhart's book-signing came. I'd had forgotten about it, except that Minerva reminded me a couple of days before it was scheduled to happen—on the 28th.

The day of the big event Minerva picked me up especially early. She insisted that we meet at 7AM. I tried to cross-examine her on it, "But why do you want to leave so early? We'll get there more than an hour before the 'Blot' opens."

"No, we won't. If we stop for breakfast at the Cauldron, we'll be lucky to get there half an hour before the opening."

"Right. Why would you want to be early at all?"

"We might beat some of the crowd."

That didn't seem logical. The rabid people show up early. Why wouldn't we want to avoid them? Then it hit me, "You're a Lockhart fan?" She didn't say anything, but I followed up, "Yes, you are, aren't you?"

Minerva colored a little and said, "No. No. I just want to get the ordeal over with as quickly as we can."

"Then why go at all. I wasn't dying to see this signing."

She had nothing to say. We arrived at the Cauldron and had breakfast. Minerva seemed to be in a hurry, hardly tasting her chipped beef on toast and tea. We arrived at the "Blot" at least 45 minutes early. There were more than fifty people there already—mostly middle-aged matrons along with a few men who were apparently husbands. The wait for the store to open was interminable. However, even bad things eventually end. Petitfour opened the doors and we flowed in like a rising tide at the Bay of Fundy.

Minerva picked up one of Lockhart's books and got in line to get an autograph. The line was moving quite slowly. Apparently everyone wanted to talk with Lockhart at some length. I told Minerva that I was going to do some browsing and see if my textbooks were selling. There were lots of students and parents there as well. I saw a few that I recognized, including the Weasleys.

And then I saw something that froze the blood in my veins. There was a head of blazing platinum blonde hair. I froze and started thinking desperately. Did I have my Glock? No. But then I realized that in the crowded store I wouldn't use it even if I were sure it were the Deatheater. I wound my courage up like a clock and ventured closer. I finally could see the back of the figure and realized it wasn't tall enough to be the Deatheater that I'd met before. I released a breath that I'd been holding for what seemed like hours. Then I walked up to the figure and got in front of him. He looked vaguely familiar but I couldn't place the face.

Then someone approached who solved the mystery for me. It was Draco Malfoy. This was a relative, probably his dad. I approached him and started to introduce myself. Draco interrupted me and told his dad that I was a Hogwarts professor.

Mr. Malfoy said, "Surely you're wrong Draco. This is a Muggle or more likely a Squibb. Ah, yes, a Squibb. That would make you, sir, the new teacher at Hogwarts."

"My name is Professor James Wendt. And you are Mr. Malfoy, the father of Draco?"

"Yes, I am. But I must say that I was disappointed to hear that Dumbledore had appointed a Squibb to a teaching post at Hogwarts. No matter how pure your blood may be on paper, it surely can't be up to the standards that I hope we would maintain at Hogwarts."

I was trying to analyze this bizarre statement when several people approached us. There were several Weasleys, Harry Potter, and Hermione Grainger. Malfoy's attention was diverted to the Weasleys. He dealt out a number of insults to them. I was disappointed to see that the Weasley twins weren't there. Hearing them trade insults with Malfoy would have been entertaining and possibly instructive.

Then something really bizarre happened. Malfoy senior pulled a book out of Ginny Weasley's book bag and commented on it. It was such an act of familiarity and effrontery that we were all frozen into inaction for a moment. That moment of frozen time disappeared, the book was back in Ginny's bag, but the mystery remained.. What in the world had that been about?

Then I noticed that there were a couple of adults who had been behind Ms. Grainger and that they now seemed shaken. I walked past the

Weasleys and talked to them. "May I introduce myself? I'm James Wendt, a professor at Hogwarts. Are you related to Ms. Grainger?"

The man said, "Yes, sir. We're Hermione's parents. I'm Greg and this is my wife Elizabeth. What do you teach?"

"English Lit."

"You're kidding." Elizabeth said.

"No, really. But the two of you seemed a bit disturbed a minute ago."

Greg looked around as though he didn't want to be overheard and said, "Well, frankly, yes. This whole idea of wizards who can do all sorts of unbelievable things is pretty scary when you consider what they could do to defenseless Muggles."

I had this irreverent idea of pulling out my Glock and commenting that that was why I cared the Glock around with me. But, of course, I didn't have it with me. I repressed that idea and instead said, "I understand what you're saying. You see, I'm a Squibb and .-.-."

Greg interrupted, "A what?"

"Oh, a Squibb, that is someone from a magical family who can't do magic."

Elizabeth commented, "That sounds an awful lot like a Muggle to me."

I smiled at the speed with which she'd picked up on that. "You're right. I might as well be a Muggle. But you really don't need to be afraid. The vast majority of wizards have no interest in harming Muggles. I'll grant you that there is the rare exception." And I nodded my head back toward where Malfoy was going on and on about the Weasleys. "But, there are people like that among Muggles too. They enjoy hurting people."

Greg seemed anxious to change the topic. He asked when his daughter would be required to take one of my classes.

"Well, under the current plan, that would be her 4th year. I'm trying to get the program built up and she is just in an unlucky year that I don't get around to for a while."

Elizabeth commented that Hermione would be disappointed to wait that long.

"Oh, I understand that she's quite the student and I'm looking forward to having someone like her in class. Unfortunately, I've not had that privilege yet. Most of my students are like the Weasley twins. Has she told you about them?"

"The only Weasley we've heard about is Ron. He doesn't seem to be very interested in studies but he seems like a nice young man." Elizabeth said. "As a matter of fact, I think that Hermione perhaps fancies him a bit."

"Well, I have no idea about that. I hardly know any of the 2nd years."

"You surely know Harry Potter."

"Oh, I've spoken to him a few times. He seems to be a decent kid. I'd like to see him overcome a prejudice that he has against a teacher or two, but he's basically a modest, hard-working fellow."

"Hermione does speak highly of him, especially after that awful adventure that she, Potter and Ron Weasley had in the spring." Elizabeth shuddered, apparently at the memory of the story.

"Yes. I know a good bit about it. Really tragic in a lot of ways." I looked around to see if Minerva had shown up. She hadn't, so I decided to go looking for her. "Well, I've got to get going. I hope Hermione has a good year."

They thanked me for stopping to talk with them and we parted company.

I hoped to find Minerva out of the pesky line. She wasn't. She was still in line with a book to be signed. She was close to the front of the line. I sidled up to her and got grumpy stares from the witches behind her. I looked back and said, "Don't worry. I don't have a book to be signed."

To Minerva, I said, "Why are you wasting time on this troll."

She stared at me askance and I could feel the eyes of the witches behind me drilling into me. She said, "Oh, he's not that bad. He's a good writer."

We worked our way to the head of the line. Lockhart took Minerva's book, opened it, and prepared to sign it. He asked, "How would you like me to sign it?"

Minerva seemed a bit flustered but said, "Oh, just 'To Minerva'."

He wrote with a flourish, "To my Dear Minerva, Love, Gildy." He asked Minerva, "Are you the same Minerva who's the assistant Headmistress of Hogwarts?"

She almost simpered, "Oh, yes."

He went on, "Good." And he added in a softer, almost conspiratorial tone, "Would you join me after the signing for lunch. I'd like to talk to you about something."

She stared at him for a moment, eyes wide, and finally said, "Well, yes. When should we meet you?"

He asked, "We?"

"Oh, yes. I'm sorry, I should have introduced my fellow professor at Hogwarts, James Wendt." I frowned at him.

"Well, the book signing is over at 1PM. Just meet me back here at Flourish and Blots."

We got out of line and I asked Minerva, "What do you suppose that he wants?"

She didn't say anything. We left the bookstore and we strolled down the street. I asked her about something that had been bothering me most of the morning. "Minerva, I met Lucius Malfoy this morning."

"Really, did he have anything interesting to say?"

"It wasn't what he said; it was what he did that was interesting. While we were talking, the Weasley family was walking nearby. He went over to them and started talking with them."

Minerva said, "You're right about that. That was strange! He actually struck up a conversation with them."

"That isn't the half of it. He actually started poking around in Ginny Weasley's book bag, pulled out a book, and started commenting on its second-hand nature."

"I admit it's bizarre, but what's the significance?"

"That's just it. It's been rattling around in the back of my brain. I've been trying to figure out what would possess him to do such a thing. He obviously doesn't like the Weasleys, so why associate with them at all? And rummaging in a young girl's bag? He should get sent away to someplace unpleasant—like Azkaban—for that. In the Muggle world that could get you sent up as a child molester. He must have had a reason, but for the life of me, I can't figure out what it might be."

"We can't always expect rationality from crazy people or Deatheaters but he surely had a reason—even if it was not normal. And you don't have a theory?"

"Nope."

Minerva asked, "I suppose that's not all?"

"Well, there was one other thing that struck me as strange. It doesn't have anything to do with Malfoy though. Malfoy said that Mr. Weasley had written some laws about Muggle artifacts. Could that be true?"

"Probably. So?"

"Well, most democracies that I'm familiar with have a legislature to write laws—you know—Parliament, Congress. Weasley wasn't elected to anything, was he?"

She laughed, "But even your American democracy has bureaucracies that write laws. They're doing it all the time."

"Well, if you're talking about regulations written to implement laws passed by Congress, I suppose you're technically correct. But some bureaucrat in the EPA deciding that the smokestack limit on Arsenic is 2 parts per billion rather than 1 is a world of difference from a bureaucrat coming up with a law out of whole cloth.

"And it doesn't bother you that Weasley is writing criminal laws —you know, the ones where you can go to jail if you break them."

"Weasley, no. Does it bother you that Weasley is writing laws?"

"Well, not necessarily Weasley, but it bothers me that someone who wasn't elected would be writing laws."

We both chewed on that for a while. Eventually it became time for us to go back to Flourish & Blots to find Lockhart. He was waiting for us outside. He suggested a Muggle French restaurant. It wasn't far from Diagon Alley, so we walked, thank goodness. It seemed to be the real thing with waiters who spoke flawless English rather than cheesy French accents. I only ordered a croissant with Lobster mayonnaise. Lockhart ordered something off-menu that he concocted with the waiter.

He was simperingly sweet with Minerva. I was trying to figure out what he was up to, but Minerva seemed to be taking it all in at face value. Finally he got down to the bottom line.

"My dear lady, since we are going to be working together, I thought that we should get to know each other better—much better."

Minerva politely rejoined, "But Gilderoy, if you've got a concern, you should let us know what it is."

He was about to answer when our waiter showed up. Gilderoy ordered a bottle of wine for all three of us. My undergraduate French was just good enough to catch the main points—such as his ordering a bottle of wine—Coine Perdue 1985. I was good with numbers, so I caught the year pretty easily. The waiter seemed impressed. After the waiter left, he continued with what he was about to say, "Look here, Minerva, I've heard rumors that the Defense Against the Dark Arts post is cursed. What do you know about that?" He kept glancing around as though he expected someone to be standing nearby to overhear us.

Minerva leaned forward and said conspiratorially, "That's a good question. To the best of my knowledge, no one has either claimed that it was or claimed to have cursed it." She hesitated, 'But, as long as I've taught at Hogwarts, I can't remember any teacher lasting more than a year in that post. Now, hardly anyone dies—as Professor Quirrell did, but .-.-." She let the sentence die away.

"But what?" Lockhart seemed to be a bit disturbed.

"But no one has left the post completely whole."

"What the deuce to do you mean by 'whole'?"

"Oh, just that they all seem to have little accidents—you know, a lost digit or toe, maybe an extra scar."

Lockhart turned introspective and said, "Hmmmm." At that point, our waiter brought our salads and the wine. Each of us tried a bit of the wine before commencing with the salads. I usually don't like red's but this was exceptional. I could see from the others' expressions that they were enjoying the wine as well.

I commented, "Well, this meal is worth the trouble if only for the wine. Interesting name. Almost always wines are named for the chateau that produces them, but 'Lost Corner'—strange name."

Lockhart smirked and said, "I know all the best restaurants on the continent and I found this wine in one in Provence. Ever since, I've been looking for restaurants that have it wherever I travel. You know, Minerva, we could pop over to Le Havre this evening before the term starts and I could show you a really interesting little café."

This was going too far. I thought desperately to come up with a scheme to prevent such a travesty from happening.

11

Lockhart brought us back to his main topic, "So, what do you two think? Is there anything to it?"

I leaned back and thought. Maybe I could scare him away. "Well, let's think about it. In the two years that I've taught at Hogwarts, there have been two people who have had serious injuries. Both of them were Defense against the Dark Arts professors. One of the two died. What do you think the chances of that are?" I hesitated but not long enough to let either of them answer. "I'll tell you. With total staff almost 100, that's about one chance in a hundred. In two consecutive years, it's one chance in 10,000."

Minerva snorted and said, "Come on. Teaching DADA is a lot more dangerous than working in the kitchen. That's not so strange."

"Well, there's an easy way to find out. Are there other schools of wizarding and witchcraft around the continent?"

Minerva said, "Sure. There's Beaux Batons in France, Durmstrang (which is who knows where), there's the Italian school Bacchetta del Destino, and Verruga Cerdo in Spain and a couple of others that I can't remember."

I went on, "Well, Lockhart, just send 'em an owl. Ask them how much turnover they've got in the D.A.D.A. position in the last 25 years. Do they have lots of injuries?" An idea occurred to me. I asked Minerva, "What about Hogwarts? Has anyone got in touch with us asking how often there's been turnover in our post?"

Minerva looked at me quizzically, 'As far as I know, nobody's inquired. Why?"

"Well, there you are. That's pretty significant. Nobody else is interested in lots of injuries in the Defense Against the Dark Arts post. What does that tell you?"

Lockhart stared at me—hard. "Do you think?" Minerva kicked me under the table and scowled at me.

She said, "You know what I am thinking? You're the very man for this post. With all your experience in defeating dark magic, you're the very one to end the curse."

Lockhart drawled, "Well, sure. I suppose.-.-. " and trailed off.

I had another idea, "Listen. This is perfect. You know, Lockhart, there's probably a book in this, don't you think?"

Lockhart turned canny. "Sure. You know you're right. This would make a perfect next book."

I thought to myself and could barely restrain myself from saying, "Sure, I can see the title now, *Whoring at Hogwarts*." But I only smiled.

Lockhart said, "What do you think, Wendt? Would you like to pick up a few pointers on dealing with the dark arts? We could work together on it."

I sighed an exaggerated sigh, "Oh, I'm afraid not. You see, I'm a Squibb. I couldn't do anything if I wanted to."

Lockhart grimaced and turned to Minerva, "What about you Minerva. It'd be a great opportunity to pick up some practical experience that you could use in class."

Minerva smiled a crocodile smile and said ever so sweetly, "I've been at Hogwarts more years than I like to admit but I've not yet come up with any idea about whether there even is a curse, let alone figure out what it is and how to remove it."

By this time the main course had arrived, and we ate for a while in silence. Whne finished lunch, I was ready to get back home, but I sure wasn't going to leave Minerva alone with Lockhart. We sat around drinking coffee and tea for what seemed to be an interminable time. Minerva seemed to be drinking in all the attention. Finally she announced that she had to get back home and finish packing before going back to Hogwarts. I quickly asked her for a "lift'" to my home.

"Do you mean that you'd like me to disapparate you there? I thought you kind of had the motto, when in Rome do as the Romans do and insist on traveling by Muggle means when in London."

I had to smile and say, "Oh, no. Disapparation would be just fine, thanks. You know how much I love it."

Lockhart stared at me for a moment and asked, "Are you sure. You know, I don't know anyone who really likes disapparation. There are certainly people, mostly juveniles, who pretend to like it because it marks effective transition to adulthood, but they get their fill of it pretty quickly."

"Yeah, I've heard that the same is true of Muggles when they get a license to operate an auto. They love driving for a while, and then they eventually tire of it when people start mooching rides off them all the time."

Lockhart asked, "How do you happen to know so much about Muggles?"

I began, "Oh, you know. Being a.-.-."

Lockhart interrupted there, apparently wanting to change the subject. He said, "Well, if the two of you are heading off, I'll be on my way too. See you at school."

When we arrived at my rooming house, I asked Minerva about getting to the platform 9 3/4 in a couple of days. She invited me to finish packing right now so we could go to her sister's right away. Then, we could leave from there together for King's Cross to catch the Hogwart's express. I had to suggest a one day postponement so that I could pack and settle up with my landlord.

She scoffed at that, "Come on, you can pack all your belongings in a large duffle and since you don't bother to fold your clothes, you can be packed in ten minutes. You can settle up on what you owe on your rent on the tell-phone and send him money through the mail"

I disagreed about the way I pack and said that I didn't want to be seen as sneaking out without having paid. We finally agreed that bright and early the next day, I'd be ready to be picked up. We'd spend a couple of pleasant days and nights before the train left for Hogwarts.

We did have a VERY pleasant time. Minerva and I were among the first to board the Express. She felt that it was incumbent on her to patrol the cars to keep order. I felt that it was incumbent on me to stay out of the way, so I stayed in the Teacher's Car. It was a beautiful day, bright, almost cloudless. We got into the countryside, and I gazed out over the beautiful rolling hills as we rolled north. It always seemed, well, sad to me somehow riding on this train, whether it was the beginning or end of term.

Just then, I was jarred from my thoughts by a voice, "A brass knut for your thoughts." I looked up and saw Minerva sitting across from me. She was smiling.

"Oh, I'm afraid you'd be cheated if you paid that much for them."

"No, really, what were you thinking about."

"Well, you'll probably not believe it, but I was having some sad thoughts. I don't know what it's all about, but I have always found beginnings and endings sad. And somehow, looking out across the fields this fine summer day, it seems especially sad. Have you ever seen the movie, *Breakfast at Tiffany's*?"

Minerva shook her head "No But you've told me about it."

"I'll tell you again. The Express reminds me of that movie. The lead female character in that movie declares that when she has breakfast at Tiffany's (a high-end jewelry store), she figures nothing bad can happen, because it's Tiffany's. I sort of feel that way about the Express. Nothing bad can happen on it, but once we arrive at Hogwarts or London, bad things can and do happen. So, I cherish every minute of this trip. I actually get to the point of hoping it won't end."

Minerva didn't say anything in reply and we watched the countryside flow by in silence. Finally. Minerva broke the silence by standing up and saying, "Well, I've got to go do rounds. See you in a little bit."

I had my lesson planning folder out and was half-way trying to plan my new class. This time I heard the door to the compartment open and I was surprised to see Lockhart come in along with Minerva. I stared at him for a minute as he found a seat on the opposite side of the car. He seemed to be completely oblivious to my existence or the fact that I was staring at him. Minerva sat next to me and was reading the *Prophet*. I couldn't restrain my curiosity further, so I walked over to his table and said hello and asked him, "Professor Lockhart, do you mind satisfying my curiosity?"

He looked up with a start from what he was doing—apparently writing a letter. "Oh, sorry. I didn't notice you. What did you say?"

'I'm curious about something. I know that I'm on this train because I'm a Squibb and can't disapparate myself to Hogwarts. I know that Minerva's on this train because she's part of the administration at Hogwarts and is here representing the school to make sure that nothing untoward happens to the students." I added to myself, "AND she's here to be with me." But I said," What I don't understand is why you're on this train."

15

Lockhart blinked once, rotated his head anti-clockwise a few degrees, and seemed to be pondering the question as though he were trying to understand why anyone would ask a question with such an obvious answer. He said, "Well, my dear boy, surely you see that I need to make sure all the students realize how lucky they are to have me as their professor. And, of course, I signed books and souvenirs as I toured the train."

He went on, "But what I don't understand is why a particular someone isn't on this train."

That caught Minerva's attention. She looked up and attended his next comment. "Harry Potter is nowhere to be seen on the train."

Minerva definitely was interested now. She asked, "What do you mean exactly?"

"I mean that I made a point of seeing every student and Potter was not among them."

Minerva got up from her seat and came over, "Are you sure? How can you be sure that he wasn't in the loo?"

"Unless he was in the girl's loo, I'm sure. I visited the boy's myself while I was touring the cars.'

"What about Hermione and Ron Weasley?"

"Who?"

Minerva dismissed him with a wave of her hand, "Oh never mind." She looked off to the side and wore an expression of intense concentration on her face. Then she said, "We've got to check to make sure that Potter isn't somewhere on the train before leaving. Come along Lockhart and Wendt. I'll check the ladies' loos just in case. You never know with Potter."

We left the Teacher's Car and worked our way back through the train, one car at a time, I visited the men's loos and Minerva visited the ladies'. We reached the car where Hermione was. Minerva asked her, "Ms. Grainger, have you seen Potter on the trip yet?"

Her eyes opened wider than usual and said, "No, Professor, and I've been trying to find them."

I asked, "Them?"

"Yes, I've not seen either Ron Weasley," she said with a bit of a blush, "or Harry at all today."

"Not even on Platform 9 3/4?"

16

She thought a moment and said, "No. The last time I saw either of them was when I was at Flourish & Blots a couple of days ago. You remember, Professor Wendt, we were all there that morning?"

'Yes, I do remember. What about the other Weasleys? Have you seen them?"

"I think that the twins and Percy are in the next car back. I saw them when I was looking for Harry."

I nodded and said to Minerva and Lockhart, "Let's keep going. When we find the other Weasleys, we can find out what's going on— maybe."

In the Hufflepuff car, there was a wizard chess game going on. I stopped to watch some of the game.

"Mr. Diggory, you seem to have a substantial advantage. Have you always played?"

He looked up at me, "Oh, Professor Wendt. No, I just got interested last term after Weasley defeated Professor McGonagall's chess game." I didn't recognize his opponent at first but when he looked up, I kicked myself. With the red hair, I should have recognized one of the Weasley twins.

"I didn't recognize you Mr. Weasley. You're quite a chess player, yourself, are you? Are you just leading Diggory down the primrose path to some subtle trap?"

"Blimey professor, Diggory's beating the pants off me. Don't you believe that he's not been playing all his life."

Diggory took on a shocked look, "Don't you believe him. The first game I played was on August 12th."

"Well," I said, "you certainly look like you've been playing all your life. You've got Weasley here boxed in so he can hardly move. It looks like you're playing the Ruiz Lopez defense."

"Never heard of the gentleman, Professor."

"Hmmm. Would you consider playing in a serious tournament?" I was beginning to think that he could get an official rating and I could become the chess team coach. There was some resentment among the teachers that I didn't have any extra-curricular assignments. They all require magic. That exempted me from them, but it didn't exempt me from the unpleasant implication that I was somehow shirking duty. Being the Chess Team Advisor would get me out of that fix.

"Well, it depends. I'd have to fit it in with my school work."

"I was thinking on holiday."

"Would it be a wizard chess tournament?"

"No, I was thinking Muggle. They have the most serious chess players."

"I'll talk with my dad about it."

"Thanks. I'll see if I can talk with him too."

Minerva was humoring me, but now she gave my arm a squeeze so I decided that we really should move along. "Have a good term, Diggory. You too, Mr. Weasley."

We continued our search. The next car did have the other Weasley twin. He could contribute nothing. Fred (or maybe it was George) said, "Did wittle Ron get lost going through the barrier at Kings Cross?"

Minerva was getting worried by this time. She was really short with him, "If you know anything, you'd better start talking right now. I'll make you regret it if you aren't straight with us. AND then, I'll turn you over to your mom."

That sobered him up immediately, "OK. OK. We've not seen the two of them since we went through the barrier this morning. They were going to be the last two through and you know how much of a madhouse it is on platform 9 3/4 at start of term—what with kids who haven't seen each other for the summer getting together and first years sniveling. Georgie and I both just supposed that they'd got on another car. We don't exactly babysit them."

Minerva was obviously disturbed. We continued our search in cold silence. We eventually saw Percy, but he couldn't contribute more. Minerva was silent until we got back to the Teacher's Car. It was now getting on to late afternoon and we were all silent for a while. Finally Minerva said, "OK. I've got to inform Dumbledore. I'm going to send an owl. The two of you, keep walking the cars. Let's just hope that Weasley and Potter have been under Potter's invisibility cloak all this time as a joke."

I was startled into speech. "Potter has an invisibility cloak?"

"Yes. No one's supposed to know it, but I think that the trio knows it and probably other people. If Potter has driven us crazy for worry all this time by hiding under that, he'll be spending so much time in detention with me that he'll know me better than you do, Wendt."

"God, let's hope not."

The rest of the trip was spent in nervous pacing through the cars. Minerva was especially nervous. I happened to be in a car that was mostly Slytherin's when Malfoy made a comment under his breath. I had no idea what he said and Minerva was even further from him than I but she recognized his voice. She marched over to him past me so quickly that I didn't realize what had happened, at first. She snapped out, "Mr. Malfoy. See me in my office tomorrow night for detention at 7PM. And never let me hear another comment like that."

Malfoy was genuinely surprised and looked about to say something but held back when he saw Minerva's face. When she turned to go back to patrol, I got a glimpse of it. All I could think of was the Medusa and how lucky I was not to be the target of that expression.

We arrived at Hogwarts and Minerva greeted the first years as usual. She spoke to Dumbledore who was waiting on the train platform when we arrived. I later learned that it was the only time that Dumbledore had greeted the Express in his time as Headmaster of Hogwarts. They exchanged a few words that I didn't hear and he immediately took Lockhart and me with him back to the castle. He asked us as we walked, "What can you tell me about this regrettable incident?"

Lockhart immediately said, "This is obviously a case of dark magic. If only I'd been present when the boys disappeared, I'd have captured the foul creature responsible."

Dumbledore frowned and said, "Well, I think you actually were present Gilderoy." Then he turned tom me, "Mr. Wendt, I can usually depend on you for some useful information. What did you observe?"

"Sadly, nothing more than Professor Lockhart. Minerva and I arrived early at the platform. I think I was the first passenger on the train. I don't think that any students had arrived when I boarded. I didn't see a student until the three of us went looking for Potter and Weasley. Potter's friends had not seen him at all except for the Weasleys who brought him to the train. He and Ron were apparently the last to go through the barrier. But no one actually saw him on the platform. I suspect that something prevented them going through the barrier. Has anyone checked with the Weasleys' parents to see if they were found on the Muggle side of the platform at King's Cross?"

"I sent an owl to the parents, but we haven't heard back yet."

I scratched my right ear and asked, "Surely, you'd have heard from them already if the boys were just on the Muggle side of the barrier?"

"I'm afraid that you're right. I think they were either kidnapped or tried to find their way here on their own. But I can't imagine how they'd do that or why they'd not just wait for help.

"I've got to get into the banquet shortly. You two might as well come along. I can't think of anything useful for you to do."

Lockhart nodded and we proceeded to the banquet. Dumbledore introduced Lockhart at the banquet. Dumbledore was his usual imperturbable self, presiding at the banquet. It was obvious that the girls were thrilled that Lockhart was to be one of their teachers. There was wild applause from the distaff side when he was introduced and not just from students. Most of the female professors seemed to be equally smitten. Even Sinistra seemed to be paying more attention to him than me—a definite improvement. Late in the banquet there was a small disturbance. I nudged Lockhart who seemed to be paying about as much attention to Sinistra as she was to him. "Lockhart, look out there at the Gryffindor table. Isn't that Potter and Weasley making a very late appearance?"

"Yes. I think you're right, by Jove. He looks somewhat banged up." And he did indeed.

After the banquet, I intercepted Dumbledore. "What happened to Potter?"

Dumbledore grumbled under his breath. All I could pick up was something that sounded like, "Why's it always Potter?" Then he said audibly, "Apparently, the barrier refused to let either Weasley or Potter through and the two numbskulls decided that rather than wait for the Weasleys to return through the barrier that they'd 'borrow' the family car to 'drive' to Hogwarts."

"Drive? Surely they couldn't have gotten here that quickly by driving?"

"Oh, it's a flying car. They crashed it into the 'Whomping Willow'. Now Snape's angry about that. Excuse me. I've got to get an owl off to the Weasleys so that they know what's happened to their son."

As Snape strode off and I tried to keep pace, I asked, "But surely the barrier didn't just arbitrarily decide to not let them through?" He outdistanced me and was obviously not interested in questions like that. Later that night, I asked Minerva if she'd ever heard of the barrier failing like that. She hadn't and she wasn't particularly interested in investigating the mystery.

"They're here and OK. What more do you want?"

"Look, when things happen that I can't explain and nobody else can, it worries the hell out of me and I almost can never let them go."

She smiled and laughed and said, "I'll bet that I can make you let go of that." She demonstrated. I had to admit that she could certainly hold my attention when she wanted to.

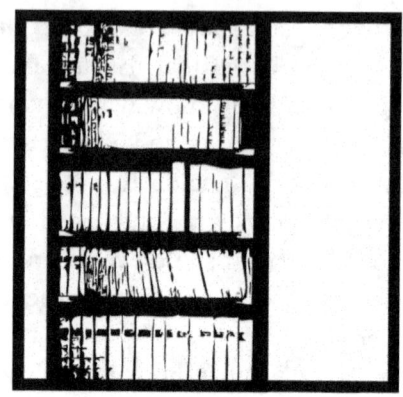

Halloween

By the end of the first week of school, both Minerva and I were completely drained. We met in my office and I got out my bottle of Dewar's whiskey. I'd kept it in the bottom right drawer of my desk locked securely ever since the beginning of my 2nd year. I'd never felt that there was an occasion—either good or bad—that warranted it until now. When Minerva had arrived about 8:30, I'd immediately unlocked the drawer, pulled it out, and lifted it so that she could see what it was. She just nodded. I'd poured each of us a couple of fingers in shot glasses. We both dropped onto the sofa and sipped the stuff. The astringent burn was comforting in a way that some soft, smooth drink could never have been under the circumstances.

We both just sat allowing the fire to burn out the tiredness and pain of the week. She set down her glass and turned toward me, snuggling under my right arm. "God, after a week like this, I'm glad I can come here."

"I am too" was all that I could manage. She closed her eyes for a few minutes, and I put my arms around her. When she opened them, she suddenly sat bolt upright.

She said, "Well, I've got some lesson planning to do." She put her arm on my shoulder and leaned toward me in a familiar gesture that I knew would end in a kiss. It did. She got up and walked to the door.

When she reached it, I said, "Thanks for coming down."

She smiled and seemed to be closer to her normal self, "Believe me, the pleasure was mine."

$\triangledown$

The next couple of days were uneventful. Other than the announcement that Dumbledore made at dinner one evening that the normal Halloween ball was going to happen as scheduled. He stood at his podium and it seemed like there was nothing more normal in the world than having the Ball.

He concluded, "The Ball is a costume Ball. Costumes are optional, being recommended but not required. I should add that there has been a recent tradition of a certain nameless professor doing inventive costumes. We hope that he won't disappoint us."

I said to myself that this year, if he were waiting for me to come up with some crazy idea of disguising myself, he would have a long wait indeed. Moments after that, I felt someone sit beside me. I tried to pretend that I hadn't heard her, but she would not be denied. She punched me in the ribs and said, "Well, we can't let Dumbledore down, now can we?"

"We most certainly can let Dumbledore down. Sinistra, I swore off costumes last year. And I'm not breaking my word."

I refused to look directly at her, but talked across the table toward the students. She said, "You haven't heard my idea for this year. It's a perfectly safe one."

"No."

"Come up to my office. This is too good an idea to chance anyone hearing it."

"No. No."

"I promise you that if you don't like it, I'll never again suggest a Halloween disguise to you."

"No. No. No." Then I thought about it a second. "Do you really mean it? You'll never come to me again with one of your hare-brained schemes if I don't like this one?"

"Of course."

I thought a moment. Here was my chance. Sinistra had always been straight with me. If she would never again come to me with one of these crazy ideas, maybe it would be worth the risk. "OK. But, you've got to promise me that you won't back out of your promise."

"If you don't do this one with me, I'll never ask you again. Witches' Honor!"

I tried to see if I could detect any dishonesty in her voice. She seemed to be in earnest. "OK. You have a deal. When do you reveal this crazy idea?"

"Right now, in my office. Let's go."

I said a little prayer, "Don't let this be a good idea!" and got up to accompany her.

We arrived at her office, and she offered me a drink. I declined with thanks. She sat down on the sofa and patted the spot beside her. I dragged a chair over next to the couch and sat down on it, saying, "I think I'll just sit here. Get on with it."

She pouted a little pout and said, "Well, if you're going to be that way about it, I'll tell you."

"Please do."

She turned business-like as she laid out her proposal, "I was thinking about what kind of a disguise would appeal to you."

She hesitated and I said, "Go ahead. What was your idea?"

"Well, I thought, wouldn't you like to understand Minerva a whole lot better than you do now?"

I spoke a hesitant agreement, "I suppose so."

"Well, what if you could get inside her skin, so to speak. Really understand what she felt. Wouldn't that be good for you—and her?" Sinistra added quickly.

What was the trick here, I wondered to myself. I gave very hesitant agreement.

"Then, I've got just the disguise for you." She stood up for dramatic emphasis and said, "What if you went to the Halloween Ball disguised as Minerva?"

"What are you.-.-. talking .-.-. . about?" Each of the words were spoken more slowly. "Wait a minute. You're not thinking of .-.-. " I didn't dare say what I had in mind.

Sinistra nodded triumphantly, "Yes, I am thinking of it. It'd be perfect. You could literally be inside her body. Part of her. All you'd have to do is get a lock of her hair. That can't be hard for you."

"You're talking about using Polyjuice potion to disguise me as Minerva."

24

Sinistra looked at me appraisingly and said, "You're half-smart when you put your mind to it."

"It's perfect," she enthused. "Not only do you get to see what it's like being her, but you get an idea of what kind of a life women in general have."

I laughed out loud. I couldn't help admiring her determination and intelligence. She was going on, "She'll be sooo impressed when she finds out what you've done."

"She'll laugh her head off at me."

"She'll admire your daring."

"I'll think it over and let you know my decision in a day or two." I got up walked to the door and didn't turn around as I left.

The next couple of days I did think it over. I tried to come up with all the reasons that it was an awful idea. Unfortunately, I couldn't think of any. It seemed like it was a way to get close to Minerva in a way that was completely unique. I finally admitted to Sinistra that it was a good idea and that I would do it. She was thrilled, which didn't encourage me much. Anything that she found so exciting had to have a catch that I just wasn't seeing. But I couldn't think of what it was.

Finally, Halloween arrived. Minerva was suspicious of Sinistra and asked me several times if I'd agreed to one of her crazy ideas. I said (quite truthfully) that I was not co-operating with any crazy ideas. She was doubtful but let it pass.

Sinistra had suggested that we meet at the library. No one would be there on a party night. When I arrived, I found that she was already there and had a pair of bundles in her hands. She quickly handed me one of them and explained that she was going to have a disguise of her own. She held out her hand to me.

"Well, what do you want?"

"You surely haven't forgotten what we need to make this disguise work."

I thought a second and then remembered. I'd taken a lock of Minerva's hair from my sofa a couple of nights ago and had put it in a small glass vial that I'd gotten from Snape. I handed it over and Sinistra practically danced with glee.

She put it in a small cup that sizzled when it went in. She handed it to me and watched avidly as I forced it down. It was never easy drinking that stuff. She then handed me a mirror and said, "You'll find it a lot easier to dress with this."

I looked around and decided that I'd better change out of sight of Sinistra, so I went to an aisle of bookshelves some distance away. Sinistra called out, "Spoil sport."

I sneered and quickly started taking off my clothes as I found myself shrinking. I propped the mirror on a bookshelf and watched the transformation which was really astounding. My hair grew much longer and I shrunk.

I unwrapped the bundle and found a set of dress robes, a slip, a bra, a pair of stockings, a pair of high heel shoes that I thought I could never fit my feet into, but amazingly, I had no problem putting them on. There was also a lipstick, a compact, a jeweled comb, a brush and a few other sundries.

As I dressed, I kept finding that my long hair was getting in the way. I had to brush it out of my eyes way every time I leant over. I could hear Sinistra dressing nearby and wondered why she was having as much trouble as I. I asked her, "Hey, Sinistra, this long hair is a real pain if you don't have it up or in a pony tail or something. I can see why Minerva always wears it in a bun."

"Don't worry. I'll help you put it up when we're done dressing."

"Somehow, I thought that it'd be, well, "up" when I transformed. Minerva almost always wears it up."

There was some exasperation in her voice, "How, do you think it stays up, by magic?"

"Well, it's a reasonable guess. Don't you do everything by magic?"

"No. Her hair stays up because she uses hair pins."

"And this hose—it's such a pain putting it on."

"Don't tell me that you've put a run in it!"

"I.-.-. uh.-.-. no," I added silently, "I hope."

26

She asked, "Aren't you done yet?"

"Well, no! This is the first time that I've tried putting on a slip and hose and a bra. What did you expect?"

"I'm dressed."

"Yeh, but you're just putting clothes on that you're used to."

"No more than you." I thought about that for a second. Was she cross-dressing or whatever as well? If so, whom was she impersonating?

"OK. OK. I'm just putting on the heels right now. But I'll need help with makeup as well as hair."

"Come out and let's see what you look like."

I hesitantly stepped out. I couldn't remember having felt so naked when I'd used Polyjuice potion before. This time, even though I was wearing full dress robes and everything, I felt like I was completely exposed. It didn't help that I'd never worn shoes with high heels. I wobbled out. Sinistra lit her wand as I came fully into the open and whistled. I was too shocked to say anything. What I saw in her wand light was not Sinistra or some other woman that Sinistra was impersonating, but me! That is, not me—Minerva—but me, me. Professor James Wendt.

I finally got my voice, but it kept breaking because I was overwhelmed by two emotions—one was anger about her impersonating me and the other was a flood of joy at seeing the person apparently with my body. I/Minerva.had a strong physical attraction for him. I hadn't expected that at all, but as I thought about it, I realized that my previous impersonations—Snape and myself—were both men and neither had strong sexual desire for anyone that Sinistra was impersonating. Snape hadn't had any feeling for Sinistra nor did I. The first thing I said was, "This is about the stupidest idea that I've ever had the poor judgment to go along with. I must look like a.-.-. a.-.-. tramp." Where that word had come from, I had no idea.

Sinistra or whoever, was just smiling a broad silly smile at me. She said, "You are gorgeous."

"Oh, just can it."

She assumed a more business-like attitude, "Just, let me help you with your hair and your makeup, and you'll feel a lot better about yourself." She took my arm and pulled me over to a chair that she'd apparently been sitting on. She set me down on it, facing her mirror.

"Now, let's start with the hair. You've really got your hair tangled. It's too bad that I don't have some conditioner, but we'll just have to do with a comb and brush."

She stood behind me and pulled my hair back over my shoulders. The feel of her manipulating my hair was, well, pretty sensual. As she brushed my hair, even with tangles getting caught in the brush, it was even more so. I watched the results of her brushing my hair in the mirror and I kept finding my eyes wandering up to her/my face. I never had a notion how attractive it was—at least, seen through Minerva's eyes. She/he noticed and smiled at me. Shit, my—er, Minerva's—heart skipped a beat at that. I'd have to watch that.

At one point, she said, "Ok, bend over."

"What!"

"Just bend over. I can't brush all your hair properly if I can't get at the nape of your neck."

"Oh, OK." I bent forward and she pushed on my back to push me all the way forward. My heart leaped in my breast as she did that and her brushing those back hairs was unbelievably sensual. Each brush stroke was seductively luxurious. After what seemed to be only a few strokes of the brush, she pulled me back up—another thrilling move. She quickly brushed my hair back and started to twist it into something that I recognized as my usual bun. She slipped a few hairpins into the hairdo and was finished. Then she said, "Turn your chair around so that I can do your makeup."

I was still stunned from her handling my hair and it took a moment to concentrate on the present.

"Did you hear me?"

"Sure. Sorry. I almost thought you were talking to someone else."

I turned my chair around. He took me by the shoulders and twisted me a little to get me where he wanted me. Then he took my chin and tilted it up a bit. I was looking into his face. He took my compact and started to apply a little powder. He commented to himself as he worked. My skin was incredibly sensitive to the applicator. It felt like a caress, each time he applied it. His middle finger and index finger gently touched my eyelids and closed them. He applied eye-shadow and then eye-liner and then mascara.

He commanded me to open my eyes. I complied and found that I was looking directly into his black lustrous eyes.

Finally, he picked up my lipstick and tilted my head back a bit further. He said, "Open your mouth slightly." Then he applied the lightest coat on my lips. He laid the lipstick down and seemed to be studying my face and then his eyes returned to mine. My lips were still parted and our lips met in a liquid, stunning kiss. It went on and on. When he finally broke it, I came to myself a bit. "What in the world!"

He/she seemed surprised too. He took a deep breathe of air. "You seemed to be so very kissable at that moment."

"Well, maybe I was, but it's this stupid body. I didn't mean that."

He said, "It felt like you meant it. Anyway, I've ruined your lipstick. Come back here and I'll fix it."

"You will not." I was incensed. "You just want another chance to steal a kiss."

"Believe me, that kiss was not stolen—at least by me." And he put his arms around me and drew me quickly to him and we kissed again. It never occurred to me to break the kiss. His tongue licked my lips with fire and I lost all sense of time or self or anything. My arms surprisingly had encircled his waist and one of his hands came off my back and had somehow reached the buttons of my blouse and had begun unbuttoning them. My hand came up and was ready to rip the remaining buttons off. He took my hand and held it. He broke the kiss after a moment and said, "You still haven't let me fix your lipstick."

I pulled him closer and kissed him. A thought drifted into me, seemingly from nowhere. "Forget about the party. If you play it right, you could wake up tomorrow in his bed, wrapped around him." I had no desire whatever to break the kiss. But he did.

I said, "Well, just forget about the lipstick. If I let this go on much longer, we'll not get to the party at all. . I'm just fine. Let's just get to the party."

We collected our clothes and various accessories and headed down toward the Great Hall. We stopped at both our offices. I insisted that Sinistra wait outside as I tossed my clothes into my office. We were walking at arms length. When we were getting close, she said, "Come on, we're on a date. You have to take my arm."

I looked over at him trying to figure out if I could trust my body not to do something stupid. I decided that it was either take his arm or call the night a bust. So, I sidled over toward him and reached out my arm for him to take. He smiled and did so. We entered the hall--no one paid particular attention. He immediately pulled me to him and we joined the dance that was in progress. I couldn't help myself. I clung to him with my cheek pressed to his. He whispered the sweetest words I'd ever heard into my delicate ear, but I couldn't ever remember what any of them were.

I glanced about the room to see if Minerva were here yet. I didn't see her. But I did see Dumbledore coming over to me. He said, 'Professor Wendt," we both looked up expectantly at him, 'it's good to see you. I see you have your habitual date. "

He reached out, took my left hand in his right and raised it toward his lips. He only bent slightly, and his nose barely touched it. "Ah, Minerva, you're looking particularly lovely tonight."

Knowing the problems that people frequently have with voice when using Polyjuice potion, I merely smiled pleasantly and nodded.

He said, "Discreet as ever. I hope you'll enjoy the night. May I have a dance or two before the evening is out."

Sinistra seemed to have the voice control thing in hand, she said, in a voice that even I would have sworn was mine, "I'm not sure that I'll give up even a single dance tonight."

"Don't be greedy." Dumbledore smiled and walked off. Just then the band struck up a slow romantic dance and Sinistra swung me around into his arms as though I were as light as a feather. Before I realized it had happened, we started dancing.

I said, "I don't remember you asking me for this dance."

"Would you prefer Dumbledore?"

"Oh, can it. How did you do my voice? That was really good."

Sinistra smiled wickedly, "Haven't you noticed that women's voices are more distinctive than men's and more modulated depending on emotion, etc?"

"I suppose, though I never thought about it."

"Of course you didn't think about it, you're a man. Men don't have to use subtle means to influence others—mainly men. But, women

30

do. Every woman controls her voice, chooses a 'voice' that she'll always use."

"Really."

"Yes, really. And that sort of control is available to everyone— including men, if you ever practiced it. Now that you've got Minerva's vocal gear, you could do a presentable version of Minerva's voice if you practiced."

"I think that I'll try. Listen." And I started trying to carry on a conversation in Minerva's voice. The first couple of tries, I thought that Sinistra was going to suffocate from laughter but by the end of the next dance I had a reasonable version of Minerva's voice. If I only kept to short, infrequent sentences, I thought I might be able to pull it off.

That was good because after the next dance, Dumbledore came over and claimed a dance. I looked at Sinistra, who nodded and added, "But just one, Minny." I shot her a frown at that nickname that I knew would infuriate the real Minerva if she ever heard it.

Dumbledore was an amazingly good dancer. For someone who was reputedly in his 100's, he cut quite a waltz. I kept my comments as brief as I could manage and looked for signs that Dumbledore had tumbled to my deception.

He asked, "I hope Sinistra's fascination with Wendt hasn't been too hard on your relationship."

I tried for a short reply that would pre-empt further discussion. I tried, "Relationship challenges that don't outright kill a relationship, only strengthen it."

Dumbledore smiled and said, "I suppose that's true. But I've got an idea that you may be entering a time of 'Relationship Challenge' that will test the truth of that maxim."

I wondered if he knew something more than he was letting on, but I said nothing in response. We ended the dance without further conversation. However, as the dance ended, Dumbledore said, "I'm sure that you've had enough tedious time with an old man. You'd much rather spend your time with your gentleman. Oh, and you really must take better care of your throat, I think you must be coming down with a cold or something." With that he winked at me and strode off. I thought that he must have penetrated my disguise—probably by my voice.

31

I found Sinistra. She was talking with Snape and the real Minerva. As I approached, Snape broke out into soft applause, "I see you have pulled off a stunning coup."

I said, in my best Minerva voice, "Oh, I can't imagine what you're thinking of."

The real Minerva stared at me and said, sotto voce, "We really have to talk after the party. I simply must know who does your hair." I tried to make my smile seem unforced.

Snape said, "Well, the band's starting again. I want to dance with my date. But which is she?" He pretended to be studying the two of us with intense concentration. Suddenly, he took me by the hand and said, 'This is she."

As he dragged me out onto the floor, I felt like kicking his shins, but I kept with the disguise and tried to make my voice as Minerva-ish as I could, "Oh, I think you have the wrong one."

Snape's voice turned serious and he said, "Oh, I've got the right one. I have to admit that you have a knack for getting into trouble. You might come in just behind the Potter gang and the Weasley's if anyone were keeping score. Just what is the point of this particular charade?"

I said, "You know Snape, somehow trouble just seems to follow some of us around like a bloodhound. No matter where we go, there he is. Anyway, this little disguise was not my idea. My accomplice, Sinistra had the idea."

Snape seemed to consider that for a moment, 'Really?"

"Oh, yes."

"I had no idea that she was so inventive. Perhaps I should spend more time with her."

I breathed a sigh of relief and said, "Believe me, there wouldn't be anybody happier than I if you did that."

By this time, the dance was ending. so I quickly separated myself from Snape and returned to my alter ego. She had been dancing with the other Minerva. That would have been a conversation to have heard.

Just then, Hagrid came up to the four of us and exclaimed, "Blimey, I didn't have any idea that you had a twin, Minerva."

Both of us answered, "Oh, Hagrid, one of us is false."

His mouth gaped for a few seconds and then he said, "Of course, Professor Wendt, I knew all along." He was speaking directly to me.

I answered, "Why do you think the counterfeit is I?"

He drawled, "Oh, Minerva, you are so particular about your appearance and here you've got your lipstick mussed—like you'd kissed .-.-." He hesitated, thought a moment and said, "I should not have said that, I should not have said that." He turned a couple of shades of red and backed away, mumbling something about having to see to some bowtruckles.

The real Minerva turned to me and hissed, "I really have to find out who your hairdresser is." This time my smile was frozen in something more like a grimace and I wished that I had the knack of backing away like Haggard.

Snape saved me for the moment by taking the real Minerva by the hand and smiling as he said, "Come Minerva, let's get some punch and leave the lovers to their own devices."

When they left, Sinistra laughed and said, "Did you see the expression on Minerva's face?"

"It's not the expression on Minerva's face that bothers me. It's what my face is going to look like the next time we're together."

"Oh, don't be such a sissy."

We danced most of the rest of the night and managed to avoid Snape and Minerva, although I think Sinistra was not particularly trying to avoid them.

We left the party a little early so that we wouldn't change back to our normal selves before we departed. So, we came to my office. Sinistra asked, "Can't I come in for just a few minutes. I hear that you have a special bottle of something that you pull out for very special occasions."

"Where did you hear that?"

"I'm not at liberty to divulge my sources."

"Well, I've had as much excitement as I want for quite a long time. So, just move along and peddle your papers elsewhere."

She was beginning to show breast so I advised her to get moving. She wasn't excited about moving along, but perhaps the fact that I was already growing taller and my hair was growing shorter killed the desire to see more of me at that moment. As she left for her office,

33

her parting shot was, "I've still got some Polyjuice potion. We could have quite a little party starting where we left off in the library, but we wouldn't want to be interrupted—we could use my office."

I locked the door. I'd never done that before, but it seemed doubly advisable now. I didn't want a crazed Sinistra breaking into my office/room.

I don't know why I got the gun out of my purse, made sure it was loaded and put it under the 2nd pillow on my bed. I'd never done that before. I made doubly sure that there was not a bullet in the chamber and that the safety was on. I made sure it was pointing at the other side of the bed. I also made sure that I could reach under the pillow quickly and draw it quickly before I went to sleep.

The Scalded Cat

The next morning, I arrived late for breakfast. There were hardly any students or teachers left in the Great Hall.

Sinistra was still there. She sidled over to join me. I groaned and asked hopelessly. "What now?"

She stared at me and asked, "Haven't you heard yet? I'd supposed that Minerva would have run to your office after all the commotion last night with the news."

I was grumpier than ever, 'No, she didn't. And it's none of your business if she did." Then I added, "What caused all the commotion last night—other than us?"

"On my way back to my boudoir, I noticed that there seemed to be a commotion going on the 3rd floor. Percy Weasley ran into me— literally. Seeing that I was all right, he sprinted off. I took off after him. As I went, I wondered if I should go find my date of the night, but I discarded the idea."

I was pleased to hear that she hadn't involved me in any further adventures of the night.

She went on, "When we reached the 2nd floor, the noise had declined considerably. By the time we reached the 3rd, floor there was a large crowd assembled. We slowed down a little as we got close to it. When we arrived at the back of the crowd, I could hear Dumbledore saying something about curing Mrs. Norris. I wondered to myself what in the world could possibly have happened. The crowd started dispersing while Weasley and I worked our way toward the center of it.

"When we got there, we found a cat suspended in air and as stiff as a board. I wouldn't have identified the cat as Mrs. Norris, if I hadn't heard Dumbledore say so. But, knowing that it was Mrs. Norris, it was easy to identify her. Filch was standing under her bawling like a baby. Everyone seemed to have somewhere else to be except Dumbledore who seemed to be levitating the cat away and Madame Pomfrey who seemed to be as concerned about the cat as she was about any person. Weasley was herding Gryffindors back to their tower.

"Since all the commotion was over, I went back to my office and bed." She smiled a sly smile at that point. Then, she got up and announced that she had a class to conduct and waltzed out of the Great Hall.

I decided that I should find Filch and see how he was bearing up. I knew that he cared more about that darn cat than anyone at school.

I went over to Filch's office and found him muttering under his breath. I asked him, "How about coming down to my office." He looked up at me for a moment as though he didn't recognize me. Then he did.

"Oh, Wendt. It's awful what that Potter kid did. Did you see Mrs. Norris?"

'No, but I heard about Mrs. Norris. Come on down to my office."

He seemed to be in shock. I took him by the arm and dragged him away. We went down the flights of stairs slowly and he seemed to need my support. I found my office door and got him through it and into my sole armchair. I pulled out a couple of glasses from my desk drawer along with a bottle of real fire whiskey. I poured a stiff shot for him and a small one for me. I pressed it into his hands and clinked my glass with his. He put the rim to his lips and took a little sip from it. Since he seemed to be in command of the glass, I sat and sipped at mine. He took another, larger sip and looked up at me, as though he didn't realize that I was in the room until just then.

"That Potter kid is a murderer. He killed Mrs. Norris."

"What happened?"

"I and Mrs. Norris were patrolling the halls. Mrs. Norris was ahead of me around a corner. I heard a screech from her that was awful. I ran around the corner as fast as I could and found the damn Potter kid standing there with his wand out and Mrs. Norris suspended in air, dead as a doornail. I'll kill that bloody Potter."

"Are you sure that it's not someone else?"

"Who else could it be? He was right there. There isn't any worse kid in the school!"

I looked at him for a long time and asked, "Is he even worse than the Weasley twins?"

"What!" Filch seemed to only then realize that I'd said something. He took another swig of fire whiskey and said, "Well, the Weasleys are in a class of their own."

"Right! Potter's nothing to them."

"Damn right!" Then he seemed to think about that for a minute.

I went on, "I don't think even the Weasleys would actually do anything to seriously harm even an animal, do you?"

Filch chewed on that for a minute and said, "I don't think they would, but it's hard to be sure. They do some amazing things to fellow students."

"But to an animal?"

"Oh, I suppose not." He finished off the fire whiskey, looked at the glass and realized that it was empty, "Do you suppose that you've got some more of this? Not bad. Not like mine, of course, but not bad."

"Sure." I reached into my drawer and pulled out my bottle and poured him a small shot and added a little to my glass. He took a good swig and smiled. I said, "I think that Dumbledore said that they would cure Mrs. Norris."

"Are you sure?" The tears were forming in Filch's eyes again.

I said, "Sure. Let's go down to your office." I got up and we slowly navigated to his office. I opened the door and got him inside and seated behind his desk. I patted his shoulder and said, "Try to get some sleep. I'll say 'Hi' to you tomorrow."

▽

After a few days, I found a note in my mailbox in my office. It was from Dumbledore. There was to be a teacher's meeting the day after tomorrow in the Teacher's Lounge. When I arrived, I found Dumbledore at a podium that he'd brought from the Great Hall. He took a look around the room to make sure that everyone was there and said, "Fellow teachers, there have been rumors of a return of Slytherin's monster. The last time that it was active here at Hogwarts was thirty years ago when Hagrid was a student here. I was an assistant professor. Valdemort," At this name everyone groaned, "was a student here.

"It was believed that Hagrid had released it."

There was an immediate raising of a half-dozen hands. Dumbledore recognized Charity Burbage. "Didn't Hagrid actually release the monster?"

Dumbledore looked her directly in the eye and said, "I do not believe it. I've know Hagrid ever since that incident. I'm convinced that he has never been a violent person, nor is he now. Nor does he have any animus against Muggles or Muggle-born wizards and witches."

No one raised any objections, so Dumbledore went on, "Why has it happened now. That I can't understand. This will not be the last attack unless we figure out the reason that they are happening now. We need volunteers to do research to find out what there is in common between now and thirty years ago. Do I have volunteers?"

He looked around the room. No one raised a hand. So, he said, "In that case, there's a simple way to handle this. Ms. McGonagall, Mr. Wendt, meet me in my office in 15 minutes." And with that he left. We stared at each other, and Minerva asked, "What did we do to deserve that?"

I looked around. Everybody left the room amazingly quickly, perhaps fearing that Dumbledore might deputize one or two of them to help us if they were still in the room. Snape strolled by, apparently not afraid of being deputized and said as he passed us. "I suppose the rest of us should be thankful for the two of you. We're safe from the really thankless tasks as long as you're around."

I pretended to not have heard him and replied to Minerva, "I suppose the little adventure with Quirell convinced him that we would be good at tracking down troublemakers."

Minerva made a face at me and said, "Well, I suppose we'd better head up to Dumbledore's office and find out the worst." We made our way up to his office. The current password was "lemon meringue pie". All professors got an owl with the password whenever it changed.

The previous password was "pralines". We entered his office. He was standing over what looked like a bird bath. It was filled with a fluid that was too viscous to be ordinary water.

As we entered he said, 'Ah, good. I'm glad that you didn't dawdle coming. I've just taken a quick look in the pensive to remind myself of what happened the last time there was an attack here that was attributed to the monster of Slytherin. Do you care to see?"

I said, "Maybe later. But for now, just what do you want us to do?"

"I thought I made that abundantly clear. You two are to figure out who or what did the attack and apprehend him/her/it."

"You wouldn't have a hint about how we would do that, would you?"

Dumbledore looked exasperated. He looked from Minerva to me and back to her again, "Minerva, you have some influence with this Muggle. Surely you can 'encourage' him to apply his creativity to this problem."

I couldn't tell if Minerva was about to laugh or throw something at Dumbledore. Finally she said, "It's amazing that you think that he can accomplish something when none of us have been able to."

"That's just the thing," he said. "I think that he might be able to do something precisely because he is a Muggle. I've exhausted everything that I can think of to solve our problem. I've tried all the magic that you and I and Snape could think of. We're stuck. Muggles have to live without magic. They can solve problems that we could solve ourselves with the aid of magic. But their solutions have to come without magic. We're just not used to solving problems without magic."

I was getting disgusted, "Look. Some problems just aren't soluble with or without magic. Do you have any suggestions or are we completely up to our own devices?"

Dumbledore shrugged and I looked at Minerva. She smiled and I couldn't help smiling myself. "OK, OK," I said. "Let's brainstorm. Maybe Dumbledore will have an idea. OK. . ." I stopped talking and began to think—really think without depending on a magical *Deus ex Machina* from Dumbledore. "What do we know about the Slytherin monster?"

Minerva spoke, "Well, not much. There really are only legends from the early days of Hogwarts. The official source for Hogwarts history—*Hogwarts, a History*, doesn't have much to say about the monster. There is an entry about the recent death of a student, Myrtle, about 30 years ago that Haggrid was blamed for. At the time, it was thought that the monster was a great Arachumanchula. But I personally doubt that it is the monster. These deaths almost certainly aren't being caused by it. I can't believe that it could get back into the castle. It was very young and small when it left the castle."

I nodded, still in thought. "OK. So, we don't even know if there is a monster. To start with, let's do the obvious things. Like curfew. Nobody but professors walk the hall after dusk or before dawn. We run a watch for several hours after curfew. Pairs, patrolling together.

"Another thing. What kind of monster can petrify?"

Dumbledore said, "Only, wizards, witches, house elves, as far as I know."

Minerva asked, "House elves can—without a wand."

"Oh, yes. They can do quite powerful magic without wands." Dumbledore agreed.

I asked, "What about the possibility of one of the staff—oh, going wacko and petrifying the cat. Did anyone hate Mrs. Norris?"

Minerva looked at me and shook her head disapprovingly, "No one on the staff would petrify anyone."

"Well, then. What about our resident 'GhostBuster'"

In unison, Dumbledore and Minerva exclaimed, "What?"

"Oh, it's a reference to a Muggle movie. I was thinking about Professor Lockhart. He claims to be a genius at getting rid of monsters."

Dumbledore shook his head. "I've talked with him. He may be a genius, but he's not willing to do any actual work."

"Great! Minerva, let's take the first watch."

"Us?" She said. "What are you talking about? You don't have any way to defend yourself from. . ." She stopped and a smile came over her face. "Oh, no you don't. You're not thinking of that Lock thing of yours?"

"I'm coming along, and you can't stop me."

"We'll see about that."

Dumbledore seemed to be bemused by the scene of the two of us bickering. Finally, he chuckled and said, "Why don't the two of you go play elsewhere."

That brought us to the recollection that we were in Dumbledore's office, We (or at least I) stood up sheepishly, and we left his office. Actually, I'd only been in his office a couple of times and I found the portrait-covered walls and collection of strange instruments oddly peaceful. I had no idea which of the instruments were functional and useful and which were merely historical curiosities.

The next night at supper Dumbledore announced the curfew restrictions and that there would be teachers patrolling to both protect the school and to find those defying the curfew. Minerva had given in to the idea of my coming along. I had armed myself with my Glock. It was in an inner pocket of my robe.

We met at the Great Hall and started systematically prowling the halls. We were quickly out of the lighted area. I pulled the Glock out of my inner pocket and Minerva said, "I knew you'd bring that thing along!"

"You bet. It could save our lives."

"Or get us killed."

"Look," I showed her the safety of the Glock, "As long as this is where it is, the Glock can't fire. And then, I don't have a bullet in the chamber, so it can't go off. finally," I flourished the gun and went on, "the clip doesn't have any bullets in it."

Minerva shook her head as if trying to shake a fly away. "What's a clip?"

"A clip, my dear is the device that holds the bullets. If you have more than one clip—as I do—you can quickly reload a gun. Let me demonstrate." I released the clip. It dropped out of the handle of the Glock, I caught it neatly, turned it upside down over my hand, and watched a stream of bullets come out of the clip.

Minerva sniffed, "Well, I've heard that more people are shot by unloaded guns than by loaded ones."

I stared at my hand. Where had the bullets come from? I knew perfectly well that I'd put the empty clip in the gun just before starting this adventure. From then on, I'd check at least three times. "Are you sure you didn't .-.-. uh .-.-. magic them into the clip?" I stared at her hard and long. She was the picture of innocence. She just shrugged her shoulders.

"OK". I put the now empty clip back in my Glock and slipped the bullets into my inner pocket along with the other clip. "OK. Let's go on."

"And you're going to keep your gun out?"

"I think that we can all agree it's empty now."

She didn't make any comment but simply walked on. As we got deeper into the castle, it got to be darker and darker and more and more quiet. As dark-adapted as our eyes became, we could barely make out the walls of the passages and the forms of each other. I finally reached the point where I couldn't stand the silence, broken only by our steps on the hard flagstones. So, I started a conversation, "Do you have any theory of what the monster is?"

I couldn't see Minerva, but I could read the clipped anger and something else in her tone even though she was barely audible. "Shhh! Quiet! We're trying to take the monster by surprise, not the other way round."

I whispered back as quietly as I could, "OK. I'm going to be walking with my back to you to cover our rears."

In spite of herself, she laughed, heaving convulsively but quietly, "Hold that thought until we're done."

We kept walking through the mostly dark passages. Occasionally we would encounter pools of light coming from lighted rooms in the distance. At one of these brief respites we heard something. We had been walking in utter silence so long that we both were alarmed. I whispered into Minerva's ear, "Which way?"

She took my hand and pointed with it up an intersecting passage. We walked that direction as quietly as we could. The noises became clearer and more discernable as we continued. I was mostly watching our rear as we proceeded, with an occasional glance above us. At one point, it became clear that the sounds were coming from a room. The door of the room was closed, but we could hear sounds that struck me as being something like a struggle. The passage was lighter there. I signaled Minerva to stop. I signaled to her that I would go in first. At first, she shook her head, "No", but she saw that I was determined so she shrugged. I reached into my pocket, pulled out a clip that I made sure was loaded and exchanged clips with the truly empty one in my Glock.

Minerva had her wand out, pointed at the door from the opposite side of the passage. I had the Glock grasped firmly in both hands, readying myself for the assault. Minerva had her wand in one hand and had raised her left hand clenched in a fist. She waved that hand down and then up once, raising one finger. She repeated the gesture, raising a second finger.

She hesitated a moment as if readying herself for the final burst of effort. She motioned the third time, raising a third finger. When it reached the apex of it's movement, the door flung inward. I ran across the threshold in a crouch and swung around, my arms fully extended trying to ensure that if I pulled the trigger, the target would not be missed. My eyes adjusted to the new environment of the interior of the room and I saw it. It was sinuous and seemed to be coiled upon itself. I flicked the safety. At that moment Minerva entered the room and lit her wand.

My eyes took a few seconds to adjust. I was shocked to see a couple of teens rolling on the floor, arms wrapped around each other and mouths locked together. The dissonance with what I was afraid that I was going to see was so complete that I stared for a moment. When the significance sank in, I lowered my gun and flipped the safety on.

Both of us simultaneously exclaimed, "Shit!"

Minerva recovered more quickly than I did. She addressed the two youth, saying, "Well, well. It's Mr. Stark of Slytherin, I believe. And," as the girl uncoiled herself and became more visible, "Miss Watson of Ravenclaw."

The boy regained his composure first and quickly said, "Please, Professor McGonagall, don't tell anyone that we were here together."

Minerva looked from one to the other and said, "The two of you are guilty of breaking curfew. You're both up for detention. AND, you'll have to join us in the Head's office tomorrow right after breakfast to determine what it will be."

Miss Watson recovered at that and begged that we not tell her parents. "They'd not let me out of the house all summer holiday. Please!"

I could see Minerva's face relax a hair at that but she said, "You'll have to wait for tomorrow to learn what your punishments will be."

Stark picked up on the plural "punishments" immediately and protested that this was the first time that he'd been out of line and it wasn't fair.

Minerva said, "For now, get to your dorms. Professor Wendt will accompany you, Mr. Stark. And I'll come with you Miss Watson."

She turned to me and said, "I'll meet you afterwards in the Great Hall so we can continue our patrol."

I took Stark off into the dungeons. I was not particularly pleased at getting that assignment, but it was what it was. I watched him enter the Slytherin dormitory and as he entered, Snape came out. He stopped for a moment and spoke to Stark. "Meet me in my office tomorrow, Stark. I was wondering what you were up to."

He turned his attention to me as the door closed. "Well, Wendt, did you have an entertaining evening, catching young lovers?"

"How did you know that he was out with his girl friend?"

Snape broke into a quick, but rare, smile. "Anyone who had seen him and the comely Miss Watson together in class couldn't doubt that they were romantically entwined. Stark isn't Potter, after all. He doesn't enjoy breaking curfew just to irritate the staff."

"Well, I've got to get back to duty or I'd hang around here to chat with you."

"Oh, I know very well why you're so anxious to get back to your partner in crime-breaking." He flashed the briefest smile again and said, "After all, there should be some compensation for the thankless duty of breaking up young romance."

He returned to Slytherin, and I headed back up to the Great Hall as quickly as I could. When I got there, Minerva was already waiting for me. I glanced around quickly and at my watch and said, "Look, our shift's almost over. We might as well finish it here, de-briefing."

Minerva clucked her tongue and said, "Taking off briefs?"

"No."

"I know, it's another of your Muggle expressions. What does it mean?"

"It means talking through the results of something you've done. Have we learned anything from this patrol?"

"Sure, Never, never, let you bring a gun along." As she spoke she became more heated, "You could have killed those two young people. If I hadn't lit my wand when I did, you'd have shot them, wouldn't you?"

I was a little surprised at her vehemence. "Look. If that had been the monster, we'd have been lucky that I'd had my gun along. And you had your wand out there. You could have done something rash too."

She got up and paced a minute. There was real strain in her voice, "You're right. I was readying my most powerful hex." She still paced and after a minute said, "It's so hard to keep control when you're expecting a monster that could petrify you in an instant."

I reached out to her and pulled her by her right hand to me and embraced her. I tried kissing her but found that she wasn't co-operating. In that moment I realized that the only times that we had been together was when required by Dumbledore. In all the excitement, I'd forgotten about the other events of Halloween night. I screwed up my courage and asked, "When do we patrol again?"

"Next week—about ten days."

I ventured, "We've got to do something fun before then."

She just turned away coldly and said over her shoulder, "I'll see you then."

Persimmon Tarts

The next day, at breakfast, Minerva came over to me as I approached the head table. She whispered in my ear, "I've spoken to Dumbledore. He'll see the four of us immediately after breakfast. Go out and hit Stark with the good news. I'll find Watson and do the same." Then she nuzzled my ear for a second and headed for the Ravenclaw table. It took me several minutes to find Stark at the Slytherin table.

When I did, I simply said, "Mr. Stark, you need to see me for a few minutes after breakfast. Come up to the head table." He seemed a bit more confident than he had the night before. I made my way back to my seat at the head table, beside Professor Lockhart.

He smiled broadly at me and said, "I see that you've been polishing the Headmistress's apple in your spare time."

I'm never in much of a mood for Lockhart at the best of times, and this was certainly not the best of times. So, I gritted my teeth and said, "Don't you have some Ghouls to Gad with?"

"Oh, oh. You're that serious are you?" and he clapped me on the back, "Well, for my galleons she's as good a catch as there is in this sea." He nodded his head, approving of his own bon mot.

Under my breath, I said, "In any sea, buddy." The always redeeming feature of meals at Hogwarts is that they can take your mind off of most of your problems. This breakfast was no exception. There were croissants as light and flaky as I've ever had—even when I went to Paris one time before I'd taken this job.

After breakfast Stark came up to the table and presented himself to me. We headed up to Dumbledore's office and found that Minerva and Watson had arrived first. As soon as we arrived, Minerva spoke the password, "Persimmon Tarts" and we were admitted. We climbed the stairs and walked into Dumbledore's office where he was seated behind his desk. He was apparently writing a note. He rose as we entered and asked us to take seats. There were two red leather chairs pulled up in front of his desk. There were two other chairs—both yellow on either side of the leather chairs.

"Well, Miss Watson and Mr. Stark, Do you realize that you've broken a very serious school rule—curfew?" He leaned back expectantly. For a moment neither of the young people said anything. Dumbledore seemed perfectly ready to wait until lunch if necessary to hear what they had to say. The silence lengthened and became almost brittle.

Finally, Watson said, "Headmaster, we thought that it would be a safe opportunity to get together. Lawrence and I never get to be together alone. We thought we could find real privacy." She blushed with that last word.

"Miss Watson, let me remind you that you were not just putting yourself in danger, but Mr. Stark here also. There really is some sort of creature prowling the castle. It's only a petrified cat this time, but the next time it could be a person or a couple," He looked significantly at Stark.

"Also, you could have been injured or even killed by a teacher who was nervous and mistook you for the monster. Right, Professor Wendt." He looked straight at me.

I was forced to admit, "Yes Professor Dumbledore. I came a lot closer than I like to admit to injuring these students seriously."

Dumbledore kept his eye on me and urged, "Or."

I could feel a few beads of sweat on my forehead, "Or," I went on, "even possibly killing one or the both of you." I looked at them.

Then Dumbledore quickly turned his attention back to the students, "What discipline should we apply to you?"

"A severe dressing down?" Stark ventured hopefully.

"I was thinking of something that you would be unlikely to forget for a very long time. Ms. Watson, what do you think would be appropriate?"

47

She gulped as his stare focused on her. She swallowed and wet her lips and said, "I suppose you'll have to tell our parents." And then she swallowed again, "But please don't tell anyone at school. I would just die if my Ravenclaw friends knew that I was seeing a Slytherin." She hastily looked over at Stark and quickly said, 'Oh, Tony, it's true. Ravenclaws think such awful things about Slytherin's. They don't know you like I do."

Stark said, "Well, I wouldn't want my Slytherin friends to know that I was seeing you—er—a Ravenclaw."

Dumbledore said, "Well, I think that we can avoid telling Ravenclaw or Slytherin students about this, but you're right. We have to tell your parents. And be sure that if there is a next time, we'll not spare anyone's feelings.

"Now, the both of you get on to class." With that he waved his wand and two notes materialized out of air and gently wafted down to his desk. "These hall passes should satisfy your teachers."

We started to get up and Dumbledore cleared his throat and said, "Professor McGonagall and Wendt, please remain for a few minutes."

I gulped and Minerva looked a little unnerved. Neither of us dared say anything, we just sat down again. We had thought that we'd get out of the office without further incident.

Dumbledore got up and began pacing beside his desk. I'd almost begun to think that he'd forgotten that we were present. Just when I'd thought that we were going to get out without incident, he sat on the edge of his desk and said, "The two of you realize that I've begun to wonder if we should not close the school until we get to the bottom of things." He looked exhausted. "As a matter of fact, I've begun to doubt my own abilities. I should have uncovered the monster by now. What do you think, Minerva?"

Minerva turned a fine shade of scarlet. She looked down into her lap like a student caught cheating on her OWLS. She seemed to set her resolve and said, "I think we're all lost if you've lost your abilities."

"And you, Wendt?"

"I think we're stuck. What can we do? Without students here, there'll be no reason for the monster to come out and make attacks. We've either got to find it with students here or close the school for

48

years. I don't say that we shouldn't do that—just that it may be the end of Hogwarts if we do."

Dumbledore set to pacing again. I was beginning to wonder if we'd ever leave his office, but he stopped and sat down again. He looked at Minerva and asked again, "What do you think?"

"I don't know. Nobody's been hurt yet—other than a cat. And we expect to bring Mrs. Norris out of petrifaction. Let's keep up the patrols and maybe we can prevent anything really bad from happening."

Dumbledore sighed and agreed. He dismissed us and we trudged back to the normal school day—which had just begun, even though Minerva and I were wrung out—as though we'd spent the day climbing the Matterhorn. When we reached the hallway outside the Great Hall, we had to part ways to go to our classes.

The next day, I had my usual classes. I didn't see Minerva at breakfast, but that wasn't unusual because she frequently was up much earlier than I and gone from the Great Hall before I arrived for breakfast. She wasn't there when I was for lunch or dinner either. That was really unusual. Everyone is normally required to be in the Great Hall at least for the announcements before dinner proper. That worried me a little. We weren't due to have a patrol for a couple of days, but I didn't want to have a set-to on the night that we were going patrolling. So I decided that if we didn't see each other by lunch tomorrow, I'd have to go find her before the next day.

I had lots of grading that night, so I got to bed kind of late. So, I barely got to the breakfast table in time to get a croissant off the tray at my table and have some fruit. I made a point of arriving early for lunch. My intention was to be sure to catch her if she showed up at all. I finished my lunch, but she'd not shown. It was only 5 minutes until the end of the lunch period that she breezed through, magically pulled a plate and a sandwich or two and some fruit from the head table, and breezed back out the way she'd come. I didn't notice her until she was almost out of the Great Hall.

I jumped up and ran after her. Doggone it, she's fast, I thought as I reached the door that she'd come in by—next to the dais. When I went through, I just saw her rounding the corner of the corridor. I really turned on my best speed, but by the time I got to the corner, she'd disappeared somewhere. There were several possibilities. So, I decided that I'd just have to use plan B.

Every teacher has to have published office hours.She has to be in her office during them and available to all students. I went to the main bulletin board and found that her published hours were Tue-Thurs from 2PM to 4PM. Tomorrow was Tuesday. If I hadn't found her by then, I'd drop in at the middle of her office hours tomorrow.

She showed up for dinner. Now that she was actually available, I didn't find it so easy to just get up in the middle of dinner and walk over to her seat by Dumbledore and start a conversation that was likely to be of a very personal nature. I spent a lot of time working up my courage. I'd decided to walk over when people started leaving the Great Hall. Unfortunately she was the first out. I knew better than to try following her. She'd got a head start, so that was that.

After supper, I tried her office, even going into the Gryffindor tower. I knew the password, and I viewed it as a good sign that she'd not had the Fat Lady change it.

I ran into Potter in Gryffindor but he had no idea where Minerva was. No one else did either. So, I decided to go back to my office and wait for office hours the next day.

When I arrived, I started to unlock the door and discovered that the door was not locked. I wasn't absolutely sure that I'd locked it the last time I was there, but I didn't exactly feel confident that I'd not locked it. I released the knob very slowly and stepped back a step. I pulled my purse out. My hands were shaking a little. So I was not having an easy time getting it open. When I finally did, I pulled the Glock out and checked the clip. It had bullets. I advanced a bullet into the cylinder. I paused to decide whether to leave the safety on or not. I decided "on". I took a deep breath. I counted to five to still my nerves. I reached for the knob and had to decide whether to try to enter quietly and hope that I wouldn't be noticed immediately or to kick the door open and hope for surprise.

I finally decided that surprise was the key. I had the Glock in my right hand. I turned the knob as slowly and as quietly as I could manage. I kicked the door open with my right foot and dived into the room, landing on the floor with the gun pointed up and my eyes scanning the room. I was close to my desk. I wouldn't have been able to see anyone sitting behind it if there were someone. But I didn't have to speculate, a head raised itself into my sight-line. It was Minerva.

I got up and said, "Damn you, I was ready to shoot. Why don't you just wait outside like every self-respecting caller until I got here?"

She laughed, "Did you forget that you gave me a key to your office?"

She was right. "Oh. Yeh. You're right. When you're right, you're right. I give up. OK." I made sure the safety was on. I softly put the Glock down on my desk in front her but pointed away from either of us. "Go ahead and shoot me."

"It's not like you don't deserve it!" She was mad. "What the bloody hell were you doing, going out on a date with that Sinistra. I suppose you snogged her too."

I dropped down in the red leather guest chair and was despairing at the chances of both being honest and not being shot at. I finally said, "Well, you might as well just go ahead and use that on me. Just make it a clean shot directly into my heart. I don't want to linger."

She didn't look any happier, "Why would I want to do that?"

"Because you're right—on both counts. I don't think there's any way of explaining what happened that I don't come off smelling like a rat."

Minerva sat down and picked up the gun—not a good sign. "Why don't you try me?"

"OK. Just don't shoot me until I've finished, if you let me start."

She just said, "We'll see. Get started."

"First, why I was on a date with Sinistra at all. She offered me something that I couldn't resist—an opportunity to get a real idea for how you feel. She claimed that I could really feel what you feel by using Polyjuice potion to, well, become you for a couple of hours. I couldn't resist that."

"OK. Maybe that makes a little sense. But what about the snogging?"

51

"Well, the one thing that she didn't tell me was that she was going to use Polyjuice potion to impersonate ME.

"I discovered that only after I'd transformed to you."

"So, you discovered how my hormones affect me when you're around?"

"Oh, yes, with a vengeance. When I'd finished my transformation, she had as well. But I had your long hair, which was a mess."

Minerva interrupted, "Which, of course, she offered to help you with. She put it up for you." She was nodding sagely.

"Yes. But before that she brushed it out."

"Very clever. You men have no idea of how luxurious and, well, exciting it is to have someone brush out your hair. Yes."

"By the time she was done brushing my hair and putting it up, I was very—uh—stimulated. And then she did my face. I had to sit there and practically stare into her eyes at close range as she did that."

Minerva shook her head. "I had no idea she was so devious. Yes, I suppose that we're all lucky that you didn't do anything more than snog her."

She went on, "I suppose that I've really got to do something to her—something to convince her she can't take advantage of a poor dumb man with impunity."

"Well, let's not carry that 'dumb man' too far. That kiss was enough—too much—for me. It didn't happen again and won't."

She was still holding my Glock and I was beginning to be afraid that she just might fire it accidentally. So, I reached out a hand and asked, "Are you about done with that?"

"I'm not sure. You really did a stupid thing going along with Sinistra even if she did take advantage of you."

"OK. OK. But let's not play with that Glock any more."

She smiled as if she had found some new toy to bedevil me with. "But you play with them all the time."

"I don't play with them, I learn to use them safely."

"Oh and just how do you do that? Do you have an instructor?"

"No, I practice with it."

'Like I said, you play with it." I reached across the desk with the palm of my hand up. She let a pouty frown cross her face and placed the

Glock in my hand like a recalcitrant kid handing over the darts that he'd been throwing at the rough bulls-eye drawn on the pristine wall of the living room.

"Tomorrow night is our turn to patrol again. We need to get a good night's sleep tonight."

Minerva pouted again, "And I was hoping for something more exciting tonight."

"Oh, we'll have plenty of excitement tomorrow night."

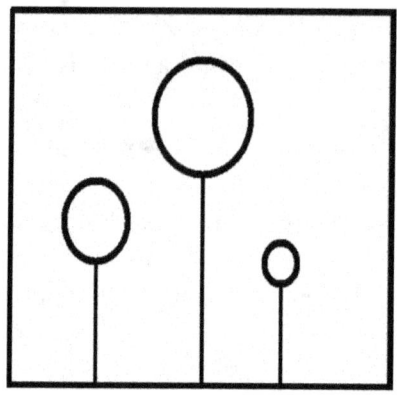

The Problem with Bludgers

There were no further incidents for a while. As a matter of fact, people became interested in things like Quidditch matches. And for the last couple of years, the hottest matchup at Hogwarts was the Slytherin/Gryffindor game. Both teams were always in contention for the school cup, so that game was usually the game that would decide championship. Both teams had individual match-ups that always guaranteed fiery action. There was Potter vs. Malfoy at Seeker. There was Wood vs. Flint at keeper. The Weasleys were always fun to watch regardless of who played against them.

I usually didn't attend school Quidditch matches regardless of what the matchup was—much to Minerva's consternation. She was an avid fan of Gryffindor and attended all of their games plus most of the others. Attendance wasn't required of teachers for any game, but most did. I always attended the Gryffindor/Slytherin games.

This one had all the features of a good Quidditch game. Plus, there was an additional feature that was completely unexpected. More on that later. There was the battle between seekers. Malfoy and Potter were going at each other tooth and nail in the air. They both seemed to have exceptionally fast brooms. They were almost blurs as they shot across the field of view. The Weasley twins were, as usual, having a wonderful time hitting bludgers at all the opposing players—especially chasers. And, of course, there was the play of the keepers for those who like good defense.

After the first few games that I'd seen, I'd decided that it was an insane game. The play of the chasers, keepers, and even, to an extent, the play of the beaters had all seemed pointless because the game seemed always to come down to the play of the seekers. The team whose seeker caught the snitch won and that was that. My question to myself was always, "Why wasn't Quidditch an individual sport with Seeker vs. Seeker—mano a mano?"

I finally came to an answer in my third year at Hogwarts. The thing was that, as important as the winner was, the game of Quidditch gave even the losing team and fans lots to cheer about. The people who like to see chasers against chasers could have their losing team win the chaser against chaser competition. The people who loved to see keepers save goals could triumph in that. Even the rare sadists who like to see beaters square off could have their day.

The one group that never seemed to win was, like in all other sports, the referees. No side ever thought they had a fair shake from the refs. It took a real masochist to be a ref. With the three dimensional game that Quidditch was and there being only one referee in the air, it was hopeless that the ref could catch all or even most infractions. The only sport with a more hopeless position for referees is soccer refs having to judge off-sides, frequently without the aid of sideline judges.

Anyway, this game featured a really strange added attraction. One of the bludgers seemed to have a mind of its own. It seemed to be determined to hit Potter—or maybe it was both seekers. It was hard to know. The blodger seemed to be invincibly determined to not just hit but actually crush them. Everyone seemed to realize that one of the bludgers was faulty, but of course, the referee, who seemed to be unaware of the mayhem that was about to ensue.

Any sensible referee in any sensible sport would immediately have called a halt to the game and dealt with the errant blodger, but nooooo. This referee went blithely on as though it were perfectly normal for a blodger flying at 200+ kilometers per hour, to perform right angle turns on a dime in the pursuit of the seekers.

Finally, Potter caught the snitch and ended the game, but the blodger just kept rampaging, seeking to crush him and eventually caught him on the arm before it was finally dispatched.

Then the second bizarre event happened. Professor Lockhart, attempting to give aid to Potter de-boned his arm. That sent him to the hospital wing. Lockhart himself seemed un-apologetic, but it was hard to tell with Lockhart what might be an apologetic attitude. He seemed to have them so rarely.

$$\triangledown$$

I think that everyone thought that we'd had as much excitement as you could have in any single day, but it turned out that we weren't quite there yet. We didn't know it, but there was one last amazing event of the day. I'd gone to bed a bit early because I was coming down with a cold. I hit the pillow and slept the sleep of the innocent until the morning. I got up and arrived at breakfast as late as I could while ensuring that some of the best that the Hogwarts house elves could do was still on the teacher's table.

I sat and noticed that there seemed to be more buzz in the air than was normal. I looked around the table trying to decide what to have for breakfast. There were fried and scrambled eggs, kippers and herring, various breads, cereals (of course) but nothing French. There was almost always something like croissants or beignet's or something. I was a bit distracted and didn't notice it when Minerva sat beside me. However, I soon discovered her presence because she started talking in a low voice.

"Isn't it awful?"

I glanced up and said, "It certainly is. There aren't any beignets left."

"No, no. I mean about Mr. Creavey."

I looked around suspiciously. "What do you mean about Mr. Creavey?"

She stared at me. "You haven't heard then?"

"No."

The monster has struck again. Colin Creavey is in the hospital wing. He's been paralyzed."

I thought for a moment. "Creavey. Is he the 3rd year who likes to turn rats into wine goblets?"

Minerva stared at me still, "No. He's a first year and he's always carrying a.-.-."

Then I remembered. "Oh, yes. He's always got a camera with him." Then a wonderful possibility hit me, "He didn't happen to get a shot of the monster?" I asked hopefully.

Minerva shook her head, "He did get a photo, but .-.-."

"But?!"

"But when the camera was opened to retrieve the film, it burnt up immediately."

I threw my unused fork down to the floor and nearly shouted, "I could just scream! Why don't we ever get any breaks?"

Minerva said nothing. What could she say?

As we continued to patrol, there was a disheartening certainty that seemed to be building that the patrols were pointless and that there would never be a resolution of the Slytherin Monster. I'd begun to wonder if there were not something altogether different going on.

One morning at breakfast, there was some sort of buzz of rumor circulating. I asked Hagrid who happened to be sitting nearby what was going on.

"Oh, Professor, you've not heard about Potter?" Hagrid asked disconsolately.

"No, I'm afraid not. What is it this time?"

"Well, he's a parsel-tongue."

This was a new word to me. I had a theory that it must be some magical term that only wizards knew. My confusion must have been evident because Hagrid looked around furtively and said, "Come down to my house after dinner, and I'll explain.

I started to object that right now would be just fine, but he seemed to anticipate me and just shook his head mutely. So, I finished my dinner as quickly as I could and made my way to his house immediately afterwards. I could have asked Minerva about it, but I just had gotten tired of displaying my ignorance to her time after time. This time I'd learn without her help.

The path down to Hagrid's house was usually abandoned. It leads nowhere other than the forest in which no one that I knew had any interest. Hagrid had few visitors so I was confident that I wouldn't interrupt anyone else.

I wasn't surprised then to find him alone when I arrived. His house is small, but he's managed a few comforts. The furniture is really sturdy if a bit uncomfortable. He invited me to sit at his kitchen table, which under different circumstances served as his desk and his parlor table. It was solid and didn't wobble in the slightest.

He offered tea and biscuits. I accepted his offer. I was pleasantly surprised when the tea was hot and strong and the biscuits were actually what one of my aunts made. She called them Springerlies. They are made with anise seeds for flavor and are as hard as rocks. Most people would consider that unpleasant, but I'd learned from my aunt that the way these were to be eaten was with hot tea or coffee. They were to be dunked into the drink and softened somewhat as they soaked. I loved my aunt's version. I even liked them when they were eaten un-dunked and hard as rocks.

Hagrid was delighted at my evident pleasure in eating them. After we'd each had a couple, he explained about parsel-tongue. "You see, Professor, and I'm surprised that you don't already know about it, but parsel-tongue is the language of Serpents."

"Really! Do serpents have many words?"

Hagrid scratched his beard and said, "I don't rightly know. I don't speak it myself. As a matter of fact, speaking it is something that can't be learned—only inherited-like."

My eyes widened in wonder. "Is that true?"

"Oh, yes. As a matter of fact, some people say that only descendants of Salazar Slytherin can speak it. I've never heard of anyone who spoke it other than people in Slyterhin house."

I chuckled, "I bet Snape speaks it."

But then he became sober, "I shouldn't say that. It's disrespectful of a professor."

"Why in the world would that be? Where I come from, the more languages that you speak, the higher regard people are held in."

Hagrid's mouth drew tightly closed and he seemed to be thinking through something. Then he spoke, "Well, that's usually true. I've heard

58

that Barty Crouch, the head of the department of international relations can speak hundreds, including the Goblin language, Gobbledy-Gook. But parsel-tongue is different." He hesitated and finally said, "Almost all really dark wizards spoke parsel-tongue."

I nodded and said, "And Potter speaks parsel-tongue and saying that someone is a parsel-tongue is sort of an insult."

"You have the right of it Professor." Hagrid seemed pained at every step of the discussion.

"And," I went on, "Because Potter speaks parsel-tongue, he's suspected of being a descendent of Slytherin."

Hagrid nodded again and pulled a gigantic handkerchief from his pocket. It would have made a tablecloth for a small card-table. He blew his nose, a sign of his disturbance at what I was saying. I began to feel truly repentant for following the trail of syllogisms of Potter's guilt so far. But I went on, "And because he's possibly related to Slytherin, people suspect him of sending the monster out for its attacks."

Hagrid nodded silently.

"Well, that seems to me to be only valid if you think that the monster is a snake." That idea expressed out loud brought me to a disturbing idea. "In a way it makes a lot of sense. Snakes are frequently venomous and some snake venoms cause paralysis.—even to the point of death." Having named the monster in the room, I was really sorry. But somehow that seemed to cheer Hagrid up a bit.

"Oh, no, Professor. That's a false trail. We know that it isn't a poison. Madame Pomfrey is sure it's not that."

"What about Snape? Does he agree?"

Hagrid nodded enthusiastically. "Yes. He tried tests for every poison that he knows." He paused for emphasis and continued, "He even tried the general cure for poisons."

This was interesting. There was a general cure for poisons? "What was that?"

"A bezor. It works with almost all poisons."

"But there could still be an unknown poison that neither Madame Pomfrey or Snape could detect?"

Hagrid shrugged, "Anything's possible."

It was getting late and dark outside, so I took my leave of Hagrid but not without asking if I could have a couple of his Springerles to take with me for later. "Oh, sure, Professor." He got up, went to his oven and took a sack which he filled with all the Springerles that he had.

"Oh, really, I wouldn't rob you of your last Springerles."

Hagrid sniffed back a little sob and said, "Oh, there aren't a lot of people who appreciate these. Sometimes I even think that Potter, Ron, and Hermione don't. I'm happy for you to have them." I couldn't refuse such a generous-hearted offer.

A few days later Minerva and I were preparing for our turn at guard-duty when there was a scream that echoed through the castle. We both ran from our offices. I ran with my Glock in hand and Minerva with her wand. We reached the source of the screaming and found several students gaping at a student, apparently paralyzed.

By this time, several teachers had arrived. Minerva organized the teachers, to take the students who had collected there to their houses for the night. Minerva levitated the student, Justin Finch-Fletchley. We started off for the hospital wing.

The Problem with Study Habits

The next night was boring. I was ecstatic. As a matter of fact, for a couple of weeks nothing happened with the Slytherin monster. Everyone had begun to feel safe. Dumbledore insisted on maintaining curfew and the patrols. The students were definitely getting bored with it and even the professors were starting to chafe under the strain of the late night tours of duty.

I had been having a hard time keeping up with my classes. But now with a lengthy period without adventures, I could spend quite a bit more time grading assignments and giving them. One of my classes consisted of first-years. We were reading one of my favorite authors, Mark Twain. I had been giving small writing assignments each class, and now I could give larger assignments.

As I graded them, I entered the grades in my book and noticed patterns. The good students tended to improve. The poor students tended to stay the same or get worse grades. But then there was an anomaly. I wanted to consult with a more experienced teacher than I was, so I checked Minerva's schedule and found a time that she had office hours. I knocked on the door and entered when she invited me.

She seemed surprised and expressed it quite freely, "Since when do you knock before entering?"

"When I'm here on official business and asking a favor."

"Well?"

As I took a seat across her desk from her, her already wide eyes got wider. "You ARE being serious if we can't snog a little before getting down to business."

"Right. This is about a student—a student who I think may be getting into some bad habits. This student started off in my class as quite a strong performer and has rather suddenly taken a turn for the worse."

"And you want advice from me?"

"Advice and, well, confirmation. I want to know if the student has been having recent problems in any of your classes as well."

"OK. Who is it?"

"I'd rather describe the behavior and see if you can name a student that it fits."

"Oh, we want to be mysterious, eh?"

"Well, I just want to be sure."

"Can you share what year this student is in?"

"I'd rather not."

She rolled her eyes and said, "OK. Let's get started with 20 questions."

"This student's performance began to fall off about 6 weeks ago."

Minerva said, "About the same time that we had the first attack. A lot of students were off for a couple of weeks after that."

"Yes, but then they improved as more time passed from the attack and life returned to normal. But this student's performance continued to worsen as time went on."

'Hmmm. And she has seemed distracted in class lately?"

"As a matter of fact, yes."

"The student is Ginny Weasley."

"You've noticed too?"

"She started my transfiguration class with quite a flair and then her performance has been falling off. She's still pretty good, but the last week or so, she's not been paying attention in class."

"I've been trying to decide how to approach her. She's obviously intelligent, and unlike most smart students, she started the semester off working hard. I don't know how to approach her with this problem."

"Well, you'd normally schedule a conference with the young lady and see if there's a problem that's affecting her performance."

"Would you mind being present?"

"No. But why do you need me? Moral support?"

"In a way. Where I come from, when you're dealing with a minor of the opposite sex, it's customary to have another teacher present —usually of the same sex as the student."

"Really? I've never heard of that kind of requirement. Do teachers in the States have a bad reputation?"

"No. It's just that there have been a couple of unfortunate cases that got a lot of publicity. Really, I agree that it's a good idea, though."

"Well," she smiled the first really warm smile of the interview, "you know my schedule. Whenever, I've got a free period, I'd be happy to chaperon you."

At the next class period, I handed Ms. Weasley an envelope with the request to meet Prof. McGonagal and me at Prof. McGonagal's office at 10AM the next day. She didn't open the note but just rushed out of the classroom.

▽

The next day, Minerva and I were in her office waiting at 10AM when Ms. Weasley arrived. She was quite punctual. When she entered the room, she was civil but cool. Minerva invited her to sit. She got the red leather chair. I was seated at a small table to her right. Minerva got straight to the point, "Ms. Weasley, we've invited you here to discuss your falling grades. Both Professor Wendt and I have noticed that you seem to be plummeting into a decline that we would very much like to arrest. Perhaps we could start with your interpretation of what's been happening with your grades."

Her reaction was not what either Minerva or I expected. She looked down at the floor and seemed to be evading our eyes. She didn't say anything. There was no defense, no explanations, no protestations of innocence. Instead, after a long delay, she said, "I don't know." She said it very softly and perhaps hopelessly.

Minerva and I were dumbfounded in our turn. We'd never had a student who didn't offer at least some excuse or even denial that there was a problem.

63

Minerva finally said, "What do you mean, dear, you don't know?"

Ginny looked up at her and seemed close to tears. She wrung her hands together and finally almost screamed in a strident tone of desperation, "I just don't KNOW!" She leaped up and ran out of the room. We were left to simply stare at each other.

I broke the silence, "What do you make of that?"

"That is a very disturbed young lady. I've never seen a student who looked just like that except once."

"Who was that, if you can tell me?"

"It was Hagrid on the day that he was expelled from Hogwarts." She suddenly got a faraway look and then returned to the here and now. She spoke the words slowly, "That's funny."

I shook my head sadly, "Yes, that's just about the funniest thing I've heard today."

She just frowned back at me. "Well, Hagrid was expelled because there was strong evidence that he was implicated in the death of a student due to the release of a monster, an arachnamanchula. Many thought it was the monster of Slytherin."

I was disgusted, "Well, it looks like that was crock."

"Oh, you mean that the current incidents seem to disconfirm that the monster of Slytherin was actually released by Hagrid."

"Well, YES! I can't believe that you went along with that phony idea."

"I admit that I didn't fight as hard against it as I should, but I was much younger then."

I thought a moment. "Curious that two people have that same sense of desperation just when the monster of Slytherin seems to be active."

"Do you think they're somehow related?"

"I can't think of a way that they could be."

"You didn't exactly answer my question."

"No, I didn't."

She stared at me. I stared back. Then I said, "Well, we can't just leave it there. What do we do next?"

Minerva just shook her head. Then she said, "We give her some time to think and see her again."

64

I got up and started to go. Minerva rose from her chair behind her desk and signaled to me to come to her. She said, "Haven't you forgotten something?"

I stared at her, uncomprehending. She saw my confusion and pointed a finger at her cheek. Finally, I woke up and took her in my arms and kissed her on the cheek and then full on her mouth. When we broke, I said, "You've never had a student like her have you?"

"No. I've had students who were rebellious. I've had the Weasley twins, who are in a whole class of their own. I've had students that I wished I could help do better but they just didn't seem to have the will to try. However, I've never had a student like her, who is smart, talented, but troubled in some way that I just don't understand."

She finally said, "Like I said, I've only had one student who had that desperate look. I've had other students like her in having the potential to be good or great, but were troubled. They usually came from broken homes or homes where the parents didn't care. You never get used to these failures but then you eventually accept that they happen sometimes. The first is hard.

"But Ginny may turn around. I've seen it happen. Not too often, but enough that you don't want to give up on her."

I decided to give Ginny a couple of days and see what happened. Eventually something did. It was at the end of a class. Ginny hung around and after all the other students had left came to my desk and asked, "Can I see you and professor McGonagall again?"

"Sure." I pulled out Minerva's schedule of office hours that I kept at my desk. "She's got office hours this afternoon at two. Let's try her then. I'll see her at lunch and make sure that she doesn't have an appointment."

Ginny asked, "Do you keep all the teacher's schedules in your desk?"

She caught me by surprise and I blurted out, "Well, no."

She smiled a knowingly. I grimaced a little in pain that one more student knew that Minerva and I were an "item". I knew it was inevitable that everyone in the school would know it, but I didn't have to be happy about it.

As we lunched together, I discovered that Minerva had the two o'clock hour free. I went directly to Minerva's office with her after lunch and worked on grading some papers as we waited for Ginny. She arrived punctually. We all took the chairs we had before. This time, though, Ginny spoke first. "Well, I don't know where to start."

Minerva looked at me and asked, "Would you like to get us started?"

I said that she was much better at this than I, so, she began. "Ms Weasley, we all know that your work in both Professor Wendt's class and mine is declining in quality. Why don't you just talk about how you feel about our classes?"

Ginny looked from one to the other of us. Her eyes returned to me, "Professor Wendt, it's not that I don't like your class. It's different from all the others. You don't have to have special talents for your class; you just have to read and think. But, I just can't seem to concentrate in class the way I could at first. I'm tired even though I seem to get lots of sleep. As a matter of fact, I sometimes wake up more tired than when I went to sleep."

Minerva asked, "Do you have disturbing dreams?"

She shook her head and said, "That's strange, I don't have any dreams and I don't remember waking up in the night.

"And there's something else. I have this strange feeling that I'm being watched. After a while it gets quite unnerving. I find it hard to concentrate when I study."

I asked, "Do you ever remember feeling like this before?"

She didn't, and neither Minerva nor I could elicit anything more definite about this "strange" feeling. I suggested that she see the Healer, Madame Pomfrey. She resisted the idea. That seemed to me to be worth following up on. I asked her, "Have you ever seen a healer before?"

"Yes, old Madame Smedici was a good Healer that our family has used for as long as any of us can remember."

Minerva asked, "Smedici?"

"Sure, that was what we called her—short for Smelly Medicine. It seemed like her cures were all bad-tasting medicine."

I agreed, "Yeh, the medico's never seem to have anything that tastes good."

Minerva smiled inwardly and then said, "Well, Madame Pomfrey is an excellent Healer. I'd trust her with my life."

That seemed to disturb her. She said, "Look, I feel fine. I don't need a healer."

Minerva was firm, "Well, I'm going to have to insist that you go to her."

"What If I won't?"

"Then I'll have no choice but to inform your mother that you're not co-operating at school."

Ginny's mouth fell open. "You wouldn't."

"Yes, I would."

Ginny had nothing further to say but "OK."

Minerva told her that she'd make an appointment and inform her by owl of when it was. And, she'd better show up or Mrs. Weasley would hear about it. Ginny seemed just on the verge of being surly as she left but didn't do anything that would get her in trouble. We discussed the situation, but even though we turned various ideas over, neither of us had any good ones. We were reluctant to contact Mrs. Weasley before we had removed the possibility that Ginny was ill with some obscure disease.

That evening, was our next shift to patrol the halls. We had the early shift —up to 1 AM. To break the monotony, I talked. "We haven't had another incident in weeks.. Do you think that it's over?"

She just stared at me. So, I went on, "You know, the last time that there was an incident with Slytherin's monster, there was only one incident."

She just sniffed and then added, "You know that it's not established that either incident involved Slytherin's monster, and the other ended after one death. Are we shooting for that?"

I had to admit that we weren't. Neither of us felt great about where we stood, but neither of us had any better way to proceed. We finished the early tour of duty at midnight, which would not have been really late for either of us, but we were both totally exhausted. The day's events and the tension of walking the halls constantly alert for danger, perhaps even death, had taken a toll. I just saw Minerva to the Griffyndor tower and she didn't even object that I was going back to my office in the dungeons alone.

The next couple of days were quiet and everyone in the castle had begun to hope that the end might have come. You could hear grumblings about continuing the night vigils more and more at the teacher's table in the Great Hall, in chance conversations in hallways and especially in the Teacher's Lounge. One afternoon I had gone there to get a cup of tea. While I was there, I overheard an argument. It involved Snape and Lockhart.

Snape rarely entered the teachers' lounge. As a matter of fact, I'm not sure that I'd ever seen him there except for teacher and staff meetings. But he was there today, and the talk between him and Lockhart was becoming strident. I moseyed over to the table where they were sitting and listened for a couple of minutes before speaking myself. Snape had been saying that he doubted very much that we'd seen the last of Slytherin's monster.

Lockhart responded in that laconic drawl that all men find irritating and many women seem to find fascinating, "Oooh, but now that I'm patrolling the halls, the monster will be well-advised to stay in its slimy lair."

Snape replied, "Then you think the monster has been reading the thrilling accounts of your victories over other monsters and evil-doers?"

"Don't be silly professor, Snape. Of course, the monster can't read, but I dare say that it's overheard people talking about them."

I couldn't resist baiting him, "How do you know that the monster speaks English."

"Oh, I don't, but my books have been published in 16 languages including Mandarin.

I couldn't resist letting a little sneer enter my voice, "Of course, a Chinese monster. Probably reads the 'Thoughts of Chairman .-.-," but I was interrupted before I finished my thought by a stare that would have frozen a dragon in its tracks. He finally said, "You know, I almost think that you're not taking this seriously."

I rejoined, "Oh, I take the monster very seriously." I left unsaid how seriously I took Lockhart.

Snape got up and commented that he'd had as much light entertainment as he could stand for the evening. As he was making the comment, there was a very clearly audible shriek that came from outside the Teacher's Lounge. We all jumped up and ran to the door.

Once outside, it was apparent that the continuing shriek was coming from higher up in the castle. We all ascended the stairs and I reached into my pocket to find the purse that contained my Glock. As we approached the sound, I decided against getting the gun out. In the presence of so many expert wizards and witches and even Lockhart it seemed superfluous.

We found a large crowd of students and teachers. The cause of the commotion was immediately apparent. Suspended about ten feet into the air was the immobile form of Nearly-Headless-Nick. The crowd was falling silent, apparently slowly realizing the enormity of a ghost being frozen into immobility. The Proctors got the students moving to their dormitories, and the teachers went along with them, leaving only a few of us still contemplating the really lifeless form of Nick.

Even Lockhart was silent. Those of us left just looked at each other in stunned silence. Lockhart seemed about to make a pronouncement, but Snape just gave him one of his patented disapproving stares and said, "Oh, just can it, Lockhart." With that we left to return to our quarters. On the way, I ran into Minerva and asked her if she'd heard about Nick.

"Oh, yes. It's all the talk among the portraits."

I asked, "What are you going to do about Nick?"

Minerva was very disturbed and snapped, "Nothing. And to anticipate your endless questions, I'm doing nothing because there's nothing I can do. There's very little magic that works with ghosts and I

69

don't know any way to move Nick." She took a breath and said, "And that really disturbs me. I haven't the slightest idea about what could freeze a ghost in his.-.-. his.-.-. " She trailed off.

Just then, Madame Pomfrey showed up. She was not in much better mood than Minerva, 'Well, we're developing quite a collection, aren't we?"

Both Minerva and I nodded and Pomfrey said, "Merlin's beard! How could a ghost be paralyzed? This is bad." And after a pause, "Really bad." Neither of us denied the truth of it.

I commented that this really put an end to the theory that the monster paralyzed its victims with poison. After a few minutes when none of us could think of anything else to say, Minerva and I left.

"Well, this burns it. What is Dumbledore going to do?" I asked.

'I don't know." She said, "But I'm going to find out if he doesn't tell us tomorrow." Her determination was a thing to behold. If you were standing in the way of it, it was scary. She then said, "Look, I don't want you walking around by yourself."

"Well, I'm all for that, but .-.-." I said.

"Yeah, but, if I go back to your place with you.-.-. . "

"Then you have to go home alone."

She brightened suddenly and said, "Come with me."

"Hey, I appreciate the thought and believe me I could use a good night's sleep in a warm bed next a warm body, but we can't do that, can we? I mean, the little tykes wouldn't uh understand."

"Oh, yeah. Sorry to disappoint, I wasn't thinking of our sharing. I was thinking of YOUR sharing with the male head of Gryffindor."

"Great." I looked around the now completely empty halls of Hogwarts. "That's the best offer that I've had all night."

We went back to Gryffindor where I learned the Gryffindor password as we got in—Ticonderoga. I asked Minerva about that. She said that she'd decided to study American History and that was a famous location in American history. I asked what the significance was.

"Oh, it was a fort that the Americans never succeeded in winning from us during the Revolt in America."

"Hmmmm. I guess that explains a lot." She just smiled at that comment.

That night I had a lengthy negotiation with Professor Jameson who was my roommate for the night. He wanted to offer me exclusive use of his bed. I insisted that I'd just sleep on the sofa in his room. He didn't give up—nor did I. We'd probably have been up all night if I hadn't compromised. I asked if there were a room with upper classmen that had an extra bed that I could use. He reluctantly agreed to allow me to stay in the room that Percy Weasley shared with a couple of 6th years. There were not just one but two spare beds. I picked one. Everyone else in the room was nervous about having a professor share their room but was hospitable. Percy loaned me his shaving kit in the morning.

Breakfast was a quiet affair. Everyone was speaking in whispers or just eating silently. Dumbledore joined the staff but had no comments. After I'd eaten, Minerva came over to my end of the table and quietly spoke so that no one else could hear. "Come on, we're paying the Headmaster a little visit."

We went to his office. Being the headmistress, Minerva not only knew the password to get into the outer office/waiting room, but she also knew the password to get into the inner sanctum. But we only went into the waiting room and sat there waiting for his arrival.

He arrived not much later than we did. He took one look at us, sighed, opened the inner office door, and signaled us to come in. "I hoped that I'd at least have one day before the arrival of the army of people questioning my judgment about the Slytherin Monster." He signed for us to take seats. Minerva took the red leather chair and I took one of the yellow chairs. He looked from one to the other of us and frowned again. "Well, go ahead."

Minerva looked at me and gave me that "you go first" little sideways nod. I gave her a dirty look in return. Dumbledore said, "Have the two of you invented a new language of facial gestures?"

I grimaced and said, "I guess I'm elected. Here's the deal. I'm not an expert on ghosts."

Dumbledore interrupted, "We have one in the castle, you know."

71

"I thought we had several."

Dumbledore laughed and said, 'Oh, you mean ghosts. I meant experts."

I snickered, "You mean Lockhart, I suppose."

Dumbledore smiled, and I went on, "As I was saying, we don't have a real expert on ghosts, but I'd pretty much bet that there isn't anyone who has ever heard of ghosts being petrified. Usually it works the other way."

I pressed my point forward, "Whatever this Slytherin Monster is, it's outside everyone's experience. Anything that can petrify a ghost is beyond anyone's ability to overcome. It's time to seriously consider packing it in and giving up. I know that would probably mean the end of Hogwarts—at least as a school.

Dumbledore looked from me to Minerva. She just nodded mutely. He said, "Well, I've been expecting you or someone to say that. I've been trying to decide if my reluctance to do that is just an old man's resistance to change, or if it's truly avoidable.

"This school has been around for almost a thousand years and I was foolishly hoping that I'd be around for its millenial anniversary in 1999. Perhaps that won't happen."

Minerva screwed up her face in a scowl, "But I thought the school had already had its anniversary!"

Dumbledore stared at her, "Do you remember the celebration?"

She seemed dumbfounded, "Well, no, but I thought it had happened before I came here. When I went to school here, I'm sure that Professor Bins said that Hogwarts was over a thousand years old."

"I'm sure he did, but that doesn't mean that he's right. You notice that he didn't give you a precise year. Rather, he just referred vaguely to its being over a thousand years old.

"There's a book that's been handed down from Headmaster to Headmaster since the founding of the school. Each Headmaster adds pages to it, chronicling the events and achievements of his or her stewardship. It includes the years that the Headmaster became Headmaster and left the Headmastership. Some entries barely fill a page, others extend to dozens. The first Headmaster's entries begin on September 7, 999—the first day of the first term at Hogwarts."

Minerva was downcast. "Then, we may miss the millennial by only a couple of years."

"It's beginning to look that way. But I don't want to give up and I don't think that we need to. So, far the attacks have happened at night. And there's only a fortnight until the end of term. We can hold out until then by strictly enforcing curfew. Of course, there'll be no Yule ball this year.

"I've been thinking about doing an all-out search for the creature during the holiday break. It'll be every wizard and witch on deck."

Minerva shook her head and said, "I don't have a lot of hope for success."

"I suppose that I don't either, but we're stuck—unless we just want to give up."

On that cheery note, we parted company. I had an idea as Minerva and I were headed back to classes. "Minerva, I've got an idea for a Christmas gift that you could give me. I'd like a subscription to the London *Times*."

She thought about it and agreed that she didn't mind getting me the subscription—but—nobody delivers the London *Times* to Hogwarts. I objected that the Daily *Prophet* was delivered every day. She just sneered and said that she'd see what she could do. Again, there was a "but". This time, the "but" was that she would have the right to read the front section first. I happily agreed to that stipulation.

I was surprised the next morning when my breakfast was interrupted by Minerva's walking behind my chair and dropping a copy of the *Times* of London into my lap about ten minutes before the end of breakfast. The front page had obviously been read or, at least, crumpled. That didn't matter in the least to me. I greedily thumbed through the various sections. I didn't stop to read anything; I just feasted my eyes on the various sections—the editorials, the book section, the headlines from the world of Muggles, the sports section. The breakfast had ended before I was finished with that cursory perusal, and I had to go to be in my office for my first office hours of the day.

That evening, I buttonholed Minerva after dinner and invited her to join me in the Teacher's Lounge to work the *Times* Crossword. We arrived to find there were one or two teachers sitting in armchairs pretending to read the *Prophet* with interest. I smugly displayed the front page of the *Times* on the table where Minerva and I sat while we worked the crossword together. It was a quiet pastime with occasional "ah, ha's" as one of us solved a clue and entered the word in the squares. It was a little slice of heaven as we worked happily and silently together, coordinating our entries and smiling secret smiles at the other's cleverness in solving a word. There was the occasional "accidental" bumped knee or briefly caressed hand. It was one of those rare, truly happy moments that we had that particular fall term at Hogwarts.

We both went to bed (each to our own) that night satisfied and secretly joyful.

The next night we had a tour of duty—after midnight this time. It was quiet and we both staggered into the Great Hall for Breakfast. Fortunately, it was Saturday. We both could catch a nap but we never missed breakfast in the Great Hall on Saturdays. The house elves outdid themselves on Saturdays. Also, Saturday morning was less formal and teachers could sit by preference not by seniority. So, Minerva and I always sat together on Saturdays.

I was digging into an egg soufflé that would have been admired in Paris when an object dropped onto Minerva's plate. It was the *Times*! I looked up and saw an owl flying away. I asked her who sent the owl. I was pretty sure it wasn't the Circulation Department at the *Times* of London. Her answer was, "Why, my sister, of course. You didn't figure that out."

"I didn't figure that out! Of course, I didn't figure that out. How did I know that there wasn't some wizard service that delivered the *Times* to wizards who had an insatiable appetite for a decent crossword if not The Crossword."

She looked up at me and said, "You're not getting the front page first."

"I'll take the sports page."

She handed over the section and I started reading. She kicked me in the shin and put the front page under my nose, "Look at this. Did you know that the President of the United States signed something called the Brady Gun Control Bill? What is that about? If you were in the States, would the Glock be illegal?"

"No, I don't know that. But look," I pointed out a paragraph in the article. "No, don't get your hopes up. That bill outlawed what are

74

known as assault weapons and requires that people get checked for sanity before they can get a gun."

Minerva smirked, "Then, you'd not be able to buy that Loc thingee on two grounds. You're crazy. It is an assault weapon if I ever saw one."

I shook my head and tsched her, "No. No. In the first place, that weapon is not an assault rifle. You would really be offended by a real assault rifle. They can shoot in a matter of tens of seconds as many as a hundred bullets. They're really designed for nothing other than killing people."

She broke in, "And THAT's not specifically designed to kill people?"

"It's issued to people stationed in Greenland to defend themselves against Polar bears."

Minerva rolled her eyes, "When's the last time that you saw a Polar bear around here."

I ignored that and went on, "Secondly, I'm not clinically insane and I'm not a criminal." I paused and went on, "So long as you ignore how I got the Glock to start with, which wasn't entirely legal."

"Yes, how DID you get that thing?"

"I'll let you know sometime."

I turned back to the sports page. There was the usual news about soccer and off-season cricket deals. As I turned the page a quarter column advert attracted my attention.

"The Tradewise Trafalgar Chess Tournament—December 23 through January 2" was the headline.

Tradewise Trafalgar

As I read the advert, an idea solidified. I nudged Minerva and said, "Would you mind looking at this." She leaned over my paper and said, "The score of the Manchester United game?"

"No, no, the advert at the corner of the page."

She made a face and asked, "The Tradewise Trafalgar Chess Tournament?"

"Yes."

Her eyes popped a little and she asked, "Do you plan on playing in the tournament?"

"No, I know someone who should."

She stared and asked, 'You don't mean that crazy Ron Weasley kid?"

"No, I mean a kid who can really play chess, a kid who mopped up the chess board with Fred Weasley." I stopped and thought. Or was it George? "Do you remember on the train? You know."

She paused in thought and then said, "You mean Cedric Diggory?"

"Of course."

"OK. Go talk to him. I think he's still having breakfast."

So, I did. I got up and scanned the hall. Diggory was at the Hufflepuff table with several other students. I suddenly realized how strange my question for him would sound surrounded by 5th years. So, I decided I'd ask him to my office where we could discuss the idea. I went over to the group of students and addressed him, "Mr. Diggory."

Everyone including Diggory immediately stood. He said, "Yes, Professor. uh. . . uh. . . "

"It's Wendt."

"Oh, yes. Professor Wendt, what can I do for you?"

I was about to ask him to come to my office, but the rest of the students quickly evaporated. I guess they figured it was bad Karma to be around when a teacher had sought out a student at one of the House tables. So, we were suddenly alone. I decided to talk to him there. "Mr. Diggory. You're an excellent chess player from what I saw on the train."

"Thank you sir, but I don't see what. . "

I interrupted him, "Mr. Diggory, there is a major 'open' chess tournament going on in London over the holidays. I want to suggest that you enter that tournament."

Diggory looked at me quizzically, "Do you really think that I'd be good enough to play in a tournament?"

'I'm sure you would. For one thing, it's an open. Anyone can enter. Besides that, the Weasleys are good chess players. You heard Dumbledore's opinion of Ron's chess skill at the final Feast last school year. You made short work of his older brother. You've got talent. And you're young and an athlete. Believe it or not, you have to be in pretty good physical shape to play in top level tournaments."

Diggory seemed bemused, "I. . . I never considered playing chess in a tournament. I only learned the game this year."

"Well, it's certainly up to you—and your parents. But think about it. If you'd like to give it a try, I can make the arrangements."

Diggory nodded and then left.

I didn't hear from him again until two days later. I was in my office grading the final papers of the term. There would be an exam later, but I gave it less weight in determining the final grade than I gave the final term paper. There was a knock at the door and I asked him to enter. It turned out to be Mr. Diggory, "Professor, do you have a few minutes to talk?"

Anything would be a relief from grading papers, so I was glad to say, "Of course. Come sit down and tell me what you're interested in."

He sat and seemed to be trying to figure out what he was going to say. He finally looked me in the eye and said, "I'd like to play in the chess tournament."

"Excellent. I was hoping you would, but first we've got to cover a couple of points. You may not be so interested after you've heard. If not, it's OK.

"First, the tournament starts on December 23 and ends on Jan. 3. Your holiday starts on the 18th and ends on the 9th. That uses up most of your holiday." Diggory just nodded.

"Second, it's not wizard chess. It's Muggle chess. You may be the only wizard in the tournament." Again, the nod.

"Finally, I'm not a chess expert. I think you're really good and ought to at least win a game or two in the tournament, but that doesn't guarantee anything. You may end up losing all your games."

He didn't nod this time. He seemed to be thinking. After a couple of minutes, he smiled and said, "That's OK. It's like any other game. At the beginning you don't do very well, but you learn."

"Fine. I'll still need to get your parents' approval, since you're a minor. I think that I ought to see them myself rather than depending on owl post to do that. We don't have a lot of time. Do you think that we could see them on Saturday?"

Diggory smiled and said, "Sure. But I hate to make them trek up here."

"Oh, I think I can arrange for you and me to go to your home without too much trouble. You just get hold of them and let them know to expect us after lunch on Saturday. I don't want to impose on them by arriving near lunch time."

He got up and started to leave, but he turned, "OK, Professor Wendt. When you know exactly when we'll arrive, let me know."

As soon as he left, I checked Minerva's schedule to find the earliest time that she'd be free to talk about our upcoming trip to the Diggory's. As it turned out, she was not very excited about a visit to the Diggory's. "Why would you think that I'd want to visit the Diggory's. The next week is first term exam week. I'm putting the finishing touches on exams and you should be too!"

78

"Oh, I've already graded all my real final exams. I'll have a little exam that will be 10% of the course grade, but they've already written their big term paper and I've graded them all."

"Well, bully for you. I jolly well haven't, and besides, I don't want to help you talk the Diggory's into sanctioning this adventure." She had raised the real issue. She didn't want to seem enthusiastic about this tournament when she wasn't.

"Look. I'll make it clear that this is my idea and you can argue against it as much as you want."

'Very generous of you."

"Yes, it is."

"But, in the end, I'll have to help you. How will you get Diggory from his home to the tournament each day? It'll be my won't it? Disapparating the both of you."

"Maybe Mr. Diggory will."

"Maybe a dragon will land out of the blue and fly you there. That's more likely than my doing it."

"Is there a difference?" You might have thought that comment would have gotten me transfigured into a frog or something, but I have the key to charming women or, at least one woman. I gave her a shy smile. She chuckled and said, "Funny, but I'm still not taking you to visit the Diggory's."

I had a couple of days to convince her, so we kissed. I returned to my office. I finished composing my final exams during the next couple of days. Sadly, Minerva and I didn't have much time to be together. Diggory dropped by to tell me that he'd gotten in touch with his dad, Amos, to approve our coming to visit. He'd given the OK. But I couldn't tell him a precise time to expect us. I just said, "I'll get in touch shortly." Diggory wasn't happy, but that was the best I could do.

On Friday morning at breakfast, I went over to Minerva's seat in the Great Hall and was going to beg her on my knees for her to take me, but before I arrived, Dumbledore rose and walked off. So, I had a change of plan. I walked around to the other side of the table and when I reached her, I sat in Dumbledore's chair.

"What in the world are you doing?!"

"I'm sitting. Why?"

"But that's Dumbledore's seat! Why are you sitting there?"

"He's not using it at the moment. Why not?"

She shook her head in exasperation. "It's about taking you to Diggory's, right."

"Could be."

'Oh, all right." The decision seemed to release some internal tension and her face relaxed. "Well, if you must sit here, take the seat on my left side."

"With pleasure." We talked about details of when to go, where to meet, etc.

I got in touch with Diggory and told him that we'd arrive at 1:30PM. He ran off to the owlery to send an owl to his parents about our plans.

The next day, we met at the Great Hall after lunch—according to plan. Minerva said we were going by flu network. So we walked over to the hearth in the Great Hall and submitted to the form of wizard travel that I probably hate the most. At least disapparation is clean—usually, but traveling by flu always involves soot and sometimes being in a hot uncomfortable confined space. The Great Hall floo is different, but at best, it just reaches the level of unpleasantness that disapparation has.

Diggory stepped in first and disappeared in a flare of green. Then, we stepped in. After a brief wave of sooty nausea, we found ourselves squeezed into a narrow dark enclosed space with a little light leaking in at chest height. We bent down and wriggled out.

We discovered Cedric waiting for us along with two adults who must have been parents. Minerva immediately greeted them by name—Amos and Reina. I introduced myself. Amos asked why we'd both come through the floo at the same time.

Minerva responded without missing a beat. "You know that Professor Wendt is a Squib?"

There was an uncomfortable moment as the adult Diggorys adjusted to that fact. They glanced at each other, trying to decide how to react. Finally, Amos said, "Yes, I think we must have read that in the Daily *Prophet* when you were hired. I'd just forgotten."

They were still avoiding my gaze, but I tried to set them at ease. "Don't be concerned on my behalf. I've been a Squib all my life and am quite used to it. The sad cases are the ones who are in denial trying to pretend that they're just not great at magic. But we're here to talk about an opportunity for Cedric that has come up."

Mrs. Diggory seemed to come to and asked, "Can I get you some tea or coffee. As a matter of fact, we could have an afternoon tea a little early if you liked."

I assured her that just a cup of tea would be wonderful, and Minerva echoed my sentiment. Reina practically ran to the kitchen and started a kettle a-boil. Meanwhile Amos had motioned us to a circle of chairs and a sofa in the living room. He took a seat on the sofa and was saving a seat for his wife. Minerva, Cedric and I took armchairs. Amos urged me to start saying that his wife would be in soon.

I looked around to see if there were any sign of Reina returning but there was none. I proceeded anyway, "I've noticed that your son is not only a good student and talented at sports, but he's a fine chess player."

Diggory sat a little straighter and said, "Well. .. well.-.-.of course, he IS my son. Are you here about his studies?"

Minerva put in quickly, "No. No. Nothing like that. He's doing very well in school. We're here because Professor Wendt would like Cedric to compete in a wizard's chess tournament over the holidays."

I added, "Yes. It's going to happen in London starting the 23rd and ending the 3rd of January. There would be games most days with breaks for Christmas and New Years eve. Of course, the last days would be for the winners of the tournament, so he might well not have to play much after Christmas."

Mr. Diggory looked from the one to the other of us, trying to understand why we'd care about this tournament. He asked, "I don't understand. Do people actually play wizard's chess in this grand way? I thought it was pretty much just a game for people on park benches and children."

I answered, "Actually there are quite a lot of people who take chess very seriously. This tournament even has fairly substantial prizes for the winners."

That peaked his interest. "Really. What do you mean by substantial?"

"Well, the top prize in the most serious group is well above 10,000 galleons."

At that his eyes bulged and he asked, "Are you saying that my son could win that much?"

"Well, he'd not be entered in that group. I think in his group the prize is more like 500 galleons. And, of course, he'd probably not win the tournament the first time he tried."

Amos Diggory looked at me sharply, "And why would you be thinking that he wouldn't win on the first go? He's smart and a great athlete." At this Cedric turned pink and started to say something.

I interrupted and said, "It would be almost unheard of for a player to win his first tournament, especially a major tournament like this one. Your son is an excellent player, but it's only the very top players in all History who have ever done that."

"What makes you think that he won't be one of those great players?"

"Well, I was actually wondering if, after all, it would be such a good idea for your son to enter this tournament." As I said that, I tried to keep as straight a face as I could.

Diggory's face screwed up. He seemed to have conflicting emotions playing over it rapidly. Then he said, "Yes, he's going to play in that tournament and he's going to give those other wizards the fight of their life."

Here was the sticking point. I knew that if I got past it, we'd be OK. "Well, there's one little thing that I should mention. Most of the people in the tournament will be Muggles. As a matter of fact, Cedric may well be the only wizard in the tournament."

Amos' eyebrows raised and he asked, "How in the world can a wizard chess tournament be played without wizards!"

"Well, it's really not a wizard chess tournament. It's an ordinary chess tournament. There are some special rules, but it's basically just chess."

Amos Digger's eyes widened, but he didn't say anything. Reina broke in to suggest that we stay to supper.

The main course was to be roast beef and Yorkshire pudding. During the course of the meal, we talked about school and Cedric's splendid performance so far this year. That allowed a transition back to talking about chess. The Diggorys were interested in the reason that a wizard would want to spend effort to get someone to compete at Muggle's chess. I knew that this question would arise sooner or later so I'd been working on an answer.

I started making my points by comparing chess to Quidditch. "Mr. Diggory, I know that you are a Quidditch fan. I saw a Chutley Cannons poster in your den when you showed us around the house. Although the two games are superficially different, there are more similarities than you may realize.

"Both sports require good athletic conditioning. In serious competition in chess, it's frequently the better physically prepared player who wins. The strain of intense training and the intense competition that requires players to concentrate strenuously for hours on end makes for frequent physical breakdowns. The .-.-."

But Amos interrupted me, "Now, don't you be telling me that chess is going to make anyone break a sweat."

I returned his gaze and said calmly. "Physical exertion makes you sweat, but chess at international competition levels brings competitors close to sweating blood." He finally broke our mutual gaze and played with his fork.

"Well, let's make a little deal. I'll let Cedric compete in this 'sport' but if it ever gets in the way of real sport, you're finished." He had been addressing me, but he turned and faced Cedric to be sure that his point was not lost on his son.

Cedric smiled broadly and said, "No, sir. I still love Quidditch and I'll be playing with my school team and training as hard as ever."

His dad nodded and added, "See that you do, laddie."

Then we went on to minor details. Minerva would pick me up and drop me off at Diggorys. She'd take us on to the hotel where the tournament was being held—the Northumberland Hotel, the Grand Ballroom. The first games would start at 2 PM. We'd drop by the Diggorys shortly after noon.

We told them that we didn't want them to provide us lunch. But they insisted, so we decided that we should arrive a little before noon then have a quick lunch and then we'd be off. Minerva would leave us at the hotel. I'd stick around and watch Cedric's games and give Minerva a call when we were ready to leave. We'd have dinner together then and drop Cedric off at home.

With that crisis passed, we finished our meal. Amos became quite the good host. He invited us to stay after the meal and look at the family album. Minerva and I were saved by Cedric's reluctance to have his baby pictures displayed to his teachers. He declared that he'd die of shame. Minerva and I assured the Diggorys that we'd love to see the baby album, but we really did have another commitment.

Minerva said, "Oh, yes. There's a department Christmas party that we can probably just make if we leave now. I wouldn't want to disappoint the Department Head." She did a really good job of keeping a straight face as she told that bold-faced lie.

Reina said, "We'll have a chance to look at them again if Cedric is good at wizard's chess. Don't you think?" She addressed the question to Minerva and me.

I immediately agreed and said, "If I know Cedric and his abilities, he'll be going to a number of tournaments before he graduates. We'll have another shot at those family albums."

Amos reluctantly let us go.

We left the Diggory's, and for once, I was happy to disapparate and get away as fast as we could. I took Minerva's hand without being asked and a moment later we ended up at her sister's house. I asked her, "I don't remember getting a Christmas party invitation to a department party. And what department would it be anyway?":

She had a smirk on her face and something of an arch look in her eyes. "Well, what department are you in, anyway?"

"The English Department and the Department Head is .-.-. "

Her smile broadened and she said, "Me. I would be terribly disappointed if we missed this party." And with that, she took me by the forearm and pulled me to her embrace which included a serious kiss that promised more.

When we broke, I only commented that I was certainly happy to get invited to this Department Christmas Party.

Back at Hogwarts, Christmas was coming. Most people were getting into a festive spirit and beginnng to ignore the curfew. The last tour of duty for Minerva and me was early morning. Nobody was around then, but in conversations with people who had earlier tours of duty, we learned that neither the students were respecting the curfew nor the professors enforcing it.

Both Minerva and I were unhappy about the situation, but nothing had happened. Even we were getting to the point of feeling that maybe it was all over. Our last tour of duty before the Christmas holiday was just the next-to-the-last night before the great exodus for the holiday. We spent a lot more time planning our vacation than we did being alert and sharp. Toward the end of the tour, we'd ended up holding hands as we walked and chatting amiably about our Christmas lists. She hinted that she had something very special in mind for me for Christmas. She dared me to guess what it was.

I spent most of the tour of duty wracking my brains to come up with good guesses. I didn't have any luck. I also spent a lot of time trying to come up with ideas that would make good gifts for her. What do you give a very accomplished witch? I'd spent a lot of time trying to come up with something but was stuck on the usual things—a new pointed hat. I briefly thought about a new broom, but she didn't like flying brooms and didn't even own one. Besides that, what if she decided that we should go on a ride on her new broom. Yuch! I can't imagine riding on a broom. That would be worse than wing-walking on a crop-duster airplane.

All this time that we'd been patrolling the corridors of Hogwarts I had very little attention for our duty. It's luck that we'd not run into the monster because I'd not have been able to do much, deep in thought as I was. As a matter of fact, I ran into a wall when the passage took a sharp turn.

It was dark and Minerva was jumpy. She had her wand up and shot a curse at the supposed thing that had knocked me down. Then she lit her wand and I realized that in the dark, I'd just not noticed the turn in the passage. I started laughing uproariously. She was as mad as a wet

85

hen. "What the bloody .-.-. were you doing running into that wall? Weren't you paying attention?"

I got a semblance of control and gasped, "Sorry. I was daydreaming or maybe it's night dreaming."

"Well, it's bloody lucky that you didn't have your gun in your hand. I don't know what would have happened if you had."

"Probably not the same thing that would have happened with your wand. I always pack with the safety on. Those wands don't have safeties, do they?"

"Pack?

We were both sort of miffed for a while, but by the end of our shift at 6AM, we literally kissed and made up. I asked if I could come up to Gryffindor and help invigorate her for the long day that was coming up.

She still had her arms around me, pinching my butt but said, "Now, we can't be setting a bad example for the little tykes especially with Christmas so close. "

I hadn't expected her to go along with my idea, but I always try.

I spent the day having a party in my various classes. The previous year, we'd read Dicken's "A Christmas Carol". The classes were all expecting that, so I decided that I'd do something different. We read Lewis Carol's "Through the Looking Glass". On these occasions I always allow everyone to have a chance to read, but anyone can opt out who wants to without prejudice.

When we got to the part about the Walrus and the Carpenter some people were offended by the way the oysters were treated. One young lady, a miss Clearwater was particularly incensed. She asked, "This is for children?"

'Yes."

"But that awful Walrus is so cruel—deceiving those poor oysters!"

I asked her, "Do you know anyone like that in the real world?"

"I'm sure I don't. No one could be like that in the real world, could they?"

'I'm afraid there are people like that. And, really, much worse. Surely, someone in the class can think of an example."

A boy in the back raised a hand. I recognized Mr. Longbottom. He said a single word, "Deatheaters."

"Yes. Good example. Can anyone else think of any others?"

There was general silence. "OK. Let's keep going."

We got to the point with the Jaberwocky. There were questions about what a Jaberwocky was. I said, of course, that it was a mythical creature. "Actually, it's not even a mythical creature. It's just a made-up creature for this story."

One young wizard wisely said, "No, I'm sure my Mum's talked about them. They're real creatures—sort of like Grindylow's." Another kid assured us that they were a variety of dragon. Then we'd hardly moved on when we hit the "Vorpal" blade.

There were all kinds of ideas about what that was. I assured them that it was a sword. That seemed to fit in pretty well with their ideas about swords. There were then questions about what kind of a sword had a "Vorpal" blade. Who would make such a sword?

I broke in at this point and assured them that it was made by Goblins. I pointed out that such famous blades as the sword of Gryffindor were made by Goblins. At least that put an end to this discussion. The rest of the class was equally contentious, but everyone had a good time debating things when a grade didn't hang in the balance.

Later that day over supper, there was a lot of jubilation. The Christmas holiday officially began after supper. It was never quite clear why that was. Everybody stayed the evening. Most students were to leave by train the next day—except for the lucky few whose parents came to pick them up. That was not the last meal at Hogwarts—there was still the breakfast the next morning, but somehow that didn't mark (in anyone's mind) the beginning of the holiday.

Nobody got much sleep that night or any eve before the Christmas holiday. One piece of good luck about leaving the Gryffindor tower was that I wasn't kept awake by the incessant tom-foolery that went on that night. At least in my own office, no one disturbed me. I didn't have an easy time getting to sleep either, but at least I did get some decent sleep that night. Most teachers in dorms had a miserable night.

Minerva was no exception. I was relatively chipper at breakfast. She dragged herself into the Great Hall just in time to hear Dumbledore's final words before the holidays. He wished everyone a safe and happy holiday and said that he expected everyone to be in especially good spirits on the start of the next term—especially teachers. This comment brought a groan from most of the bedraggled, motley bunch at the Head table. Dumbledore himself was in very good spirits. Of course, he'd not had to spend the night in the same tower with a gaggle of gangly teens intent on celebrating the end of term even if they couldn't do it legally.

He turned to leave the podium but then turned back and said, "Oh, one last thing. Would all teachers join me in the Teacher's Lounge immediately after breakfast? That includes all teachers, not excluding those taking the Express."

All teachers groaned again. We all finished breakfast as quickly as we could so that we could get this "one last thing" over as quickly as possible and head off for our well-earned holiday. Dumbledore was waiting for us as we arrived. He was impatient as we were, but he waited for the last stragglers to arrive. When we finally all had arrived, he made his announcement.

"We have been struggling under a threat of attack by Slytherin's monster all term, I intend to go on the offensive before the next term starts. All teachers are to report a week early."

There was a general upheaval as dozens of voices were raised in protest. Dumbledore silenced us with a look and went on, "We will systematically scour the castle and use our pooled magical skills to root out the lair of the monster. This goes for all teachers—except, of course —for Professor Wendt who can't help us magically."

I immediately protested, "It's not fair to the rest of the teachers or me to receive a 'Get Out of Jail Free' card for this effort. I'll be here along with the rest of the teachers and accept the same risks that they do. I'm sure Minerva won't object to my accompanying her on whatever duties she draws."

Snape sniffed and said, 'If we want to get any use out of either of them, we need to keep them separate. Otherwise, they might spend the week snogging."

There was some tittering but Dumbledore's stern look silenced that quickly. He said, "Mr. Wendt, if you truly want to be here, I won't prevent you. But it really isn't necessary.

"In any case, those of you who are riding the Express need to get moving so you don't hold it up. Anyone who has questions can remain. The rest are dismissed." Virtually everyone left swiftly lest some other idea occur to Dumbledore.

I went to my office and grabbed my duffle bag and headed up to the Gryffindor tower. I met Minerva on her way down. We exchanged a quick kiss and hurried off to the train station. When we got there, we found that most of the students had boarded and just a few stragglers were getting on board. I tossed Minerva's bag and mine into the baggage car and we hopped on board. The conductor was announcing the departure of the train as we went forward to the Teacher's Car. The cars seemed to segregate naturally into houses.

There was always a mixture of students in all cars, but you could usually tell which house dominated which car. Even if you didn't recognize any of the students, something about the tone of the conversation, the look of the students, and the fashionability of their dress gave clues to the house that dominated the car. I had no trouble recognizing the Ravenclaw car when we went through it. For one thing, most of the students were reading and the conversations were muted.

On the other hand, the Gryffindor car was boisterous and few were reading. Even Hermione Grainger was deep in conversation with the Dynamic Duo.

The Slytherin car was easy to tell as well. There was almost a palpable resentment that I felt as I went through it with Minerva. We were outsiders and we knew it instantly.

As we got to the Teacher's Car, we were deep in conversation about what we would do during the holiday. Minerva wanted me to spend the whole holiday with her at her sister's. I wanted to stay in London for a couple of days to do shopping (frankly without Minerva so I could come up with a true surprise for her).

We were bantering back and forth about that as we entered the Teacher's Car. Suddenly Minerva went silent and I wondered what had happened. When I scanned the car, I immediately understood. I commented, "Well, what would the world be without its little surprises?"

"Surprises indeed!" Minerva said because there was Sinistra sitting in an armchair in the middle of the car.

She smiled a sly cat-like smile and said, "I've not taken the Express for such a long time. I thought it would be fun to help out this time, chaperone the tykes and the young lovers."

She went on, "How are we going to break the time up into shifts to patrol the cars? I really wouldn't send a Squib out there alone with all those magical kiddies." The cat-like grin appeared again.

Minerva said, "Quite right. I volunteer to be Wendt's partner."

"Yes, you would. But what does Wendt say," she batted her eyelashes at me with the most innocent expression that I'd seen yet on her face.

It was a dangerous point—for me. The obvious thing to do would be to quickly choose Minerva, but I saw a danger in that course. If I did that too quickly, Minerva might just think that I really would like to spend the trip with Sinistra and the quick response was to mislead her. I decided that I should treat the offer lightly with humor. So, I said, "Well I seem to be in a seller's market. What am I offered for the privilege of accompanying me on the rounds?"

Minerva didn't take it quite the way I'd hoped. "I'll give you something you'll never forget", she said in a menacing voice.

Sinistra also said, "I'll give you something you'll never forget, either." But she said it in the smoothest, silkiest voice that I'd ever heard her use. It was long and languorously drawn out. There seemed to be all sorts of promise in it.

I smiled and, trying to keep things light, I said, "Oh, I'll take Minerva's unforgettable thing any day." I saw out of the corner of my eye that Minerva cracked a quick smile that came and went in an instant over her features, crinkling her eyes,

There was a definite chill in the air after my decision so I was happy that Minerva and I had to get started right away. We walked back through the cars. I recognized most of the students with whom we occasionally exchanged greetings.

When we reached the next car, the Slytherin car, I stopped to talk with Minerva. They seem to have a bunker mentality. Anyway, the "atmosphere" in this car was definitely non-friendly, but it actually worked to my advantage because no one wanted anything to do with us. So I could talk with Minerva without having anyone come up to me with questions or requests.

I had a dilemma. I could spend the holiday with Minerva. That would be wonderful, but then the trips to Diggory's wouldn't be so special. Minerva was pretty skeptical of that interpretation, but she took it stoically.

"You'll be lucky if I don't boycott you the entire holiday."

"Don't you know that absence makes the heart grow fond?"

"You'd better have a great Christmas present for me to just make that a sure thing."

The rest of the trip was uneventful. Minerva and I were the last ones standing on the platform of Track 9 ¾. I took her in my arms and gave her a kiss to remember. That kiss made me reconsider the decision to go it alone for the holiday. She could tell that. It just brought a smile to her face as she walked away.

The Feast of Stephen

The problem with gifts. Of course, there were always Muggle gifts for Minerva. You never knew what would appeal to her or, for that matter, any witch. One birthday, in desperation after having spent hours in various stores in Diagon Alley (such as Madame Malkin's, Flourish & Blots, and so forth), I'd been walking in a Muggle neighborhood and had seen a teacher's supply store. I went in and saw one of those corny coffee mugs. This one said, "My favorite teacher." This was followed by a large empty space. I asked the sales clerk about it. Apparently, they could have it personalized with a name. In real desperation, I had them print "Minerva" in the empty slot. It barely fit so they wanted me to shorten it to something like "Minny." I soundly refused and they relented.

My idea was that that cup would be my secondary gift and I'd find a "real" gift for the main gift. Well, I never found one that I thought she'd like. So, I had them wrap the cup in the store when I went to pick it up. They did a very fancy job of it. The clerk asked if I had a photo of the recipient.

"Sure," I'd said and I got out my purse and pulled out the photo that I always carried with me. It was taken at a photographer's in Diagon Alley. I'd insisted on her image not moving. I didn't tell the photographer why, but Minerva understood and didn't object. It had cost me more for the photographer to fix her motionless in the photo. He didn't understand why I wanted it and I sure wasn't going to tell him that I wanted a photo that I could show my Muggle friends that wouldn't freak them out. But, he did something subtle with it that I didn't notice at first. The background for the photo was a fake brick wall that had dappled sunlight playing over it—as though it were coming through leaves of a tree. Whenever I looked at it, I thought there was something funny about the picture. After a few viewings I realized what the problem was. If you looked at it for more than a minute, the dappled sunlight and shadow began shifting as though there were a gentle breeze blowing the leaves and making the pattern of light and shadow shift slowly.

Fortunately, it was a subtle effect and hard to notice, especially at a casual glance. The clerk looked at it and said, "There's something spooky about that picture."

I said, "Sure, she's hauntingly beautiful, don't you think."

She looked at it again and said, "No, that's not it. It just looks too realistic to be real. I could almost swear that I can see the wind blowing in that picture."

I just laughed and asked for the photo back. The clerk handed it back reluctantly and said, "Is that your mum?"

I'd faced that question or a variation on it nearly every time that I showed someone the photo. How seriously I answered depended on how I felt about the questioner. When I was feeling kindly disposed toward the questioner, I'd answer seriously. This time, I really was thankful for the nice job she'd done wrapping the gift, so I did answer seriously. This time I said, "No, we work together. I've been trying to get her to agree to marry me for a while now, but she's a stubborn and independent woman."

Her jaw dropped, "No, really. No kidding?"

"No kidding."

"But why? You could get practically any woman out there."

I smiled what I hoped was a sad smile, "That's the thing, isn't it? She's not 'just' practically any woman out there. I've never met another one like her."

"Well, coffee mugs are great, but have you tried a ring?"

"I have to admit that I haven't. I've tried a lot of different ways to ask her though."

"Well, think about a ring. A ring is worth a lot of heartfelt poetry."

Anyway, Minerva actually let a couple of tears drop when she opened the package and saw the mug. She was amazed that I could get her name put on it—and without magic. I rode that piece of luck as far as I could, but it wasn't worth a trip up the aisle apparently.

But you could only do that cup thing once. So, I was still stuck for a Christmas gift.

$$\triangledown$$

There were a few bed & breakfasts in the London area that I sometimes used when I was on my own. I started giving them calls and found one that I could stay at for the holidays. I took the underground to get within walking distance. The proprietor recognized me when I arrived and seemed to be glad to have me join them. The first couple of days, I mostly shopped for presents for family. Minerva, contrary to indications, found me, and on the third day, popped over (literally). She asked if I wanted some company going to Diagon Alley to do some Christmas shopping.

I acted surprised but quickly accepted her offer. I insisted on taking the underground to the vicinity of Diagon Alley. Minerva disliked the train as much as I did disapparating, but we both took turns going the way we didn't like. We both were good-natured about it. It gave us some time to talk before hitting the craziness of Diagon Alley at Christmas time. That was Monday.

We stopped off at Gringott's. I'd been there enough over the last couple of years that most of the goblins recognized me. They enjoyed playing little jokes on me like forcing me to prove my identity every time I dropped in. I had to dig my ID out of my purse. I handed over the polished wood card that had my picture on it and had a spell embedded. They enjoyed taking it and lazily going to the security wizard who scanned it with his wand. This made my name and picture appear on the polished wooden surface.

They were so busy at Christmas time though that they just waved me past the security checkpoint with a smile and a promise that the next time would be different. The trolleys that went down into the vaults of the bank were larger and carried several wizards and witches at a time

94

into the depths. I pulled out a thousand galleons and converted about half of it to pounds sterling. The goblin who did the conversion glanced at the number of galleons and instantly counted out the notes and pence.

My next stop was at Madame Malkin's. I thought I'd see if I could find a scarf that Minerva would like. As I enered her shop, she recognized me. Her first reaction was to smile, and then the smile was instantly replaced with a scowl. "I suppose that I can't talk you into a new suit of robes?"

I shook my head. She nodded and said, "Yes, yes. I know. You are immune to fashion. You Muggles wouldn't know what kind of robes were pretty if they came up and kissed you on the lips.

"I suppose that you are here looking for a Christmas present for someone special. Oh, don't bother trying to be subtle. I know that your Minerva.-.-." I had started to object to the characterization of Minerva as mine. "Yes, YOUR Minerva is in need of a new hat. She's been admiring this fur-lined silk party hat."

I looked at it. "May I examine it?"

"Of course."

I picked it up and had to admit that it was most beautiful. The sable fur lining was very plush and warm. The exterior had small jewels in constellations that I didn't recognize on the surface. "Yes. Yes. It is beautiful. I see why she wanted it." I gulped and asked, "How much?"

She named the number and I counted out the outrageous pile of galleons from my purse. She asked if I wanted it gift-wrapped. I was tempted to comment that for that number of galleons it should come gift-wrapped in gold leaf, but I just nodded. She gift wrapped it and put it in a shopping bag with a second smaller gift. I frowned when I saw it.

She smiled and said, "I put a little something extra in. It's a scarf that that special person will like. It'll go with the hat too."

I thanked Madame Malkin profusely and left the shop. Next I went on to Flourish and Blots to look for gifts for my family. Minerva and I met at the Leaky Cauldron for lunch. She had a large shopping bag; mine was not much smaller. We ended up having to wait a long time to be seated, so we talked about the upcoming tournament and when I would come to her sister's for the holidays. I also tried to bring up how beautiful she is as a topic. That topic resulted in some dispute. She thought she was rather plain and I tried to show her herself through my eyes. The time slipped away and we were suddenly seated. Tom himself took our order. He knew we'd stand him a pint of ale. He was right.

We finished our shopping together. There is an unspoken understanding between us—as with many couples—that shopping separately is normal and necessary for the really important gifts. We finished off buying gifts for our friends at Hogwarts and our relatives. I was still trying to figure out how we might break it to my parents that I had a girl friend or lady friend who was a little bit older than I. I had written them about a fellow teacher whose name was Minerva and whom I was currently "seeing". They had been cautiously encouraging. They begged that I bring her to America to meet them. I always answered that I would—but not until we were really serious. They also begged for a photo. I was afraid to send them a duplicate of the one that I had of Minerva. I was sure that they'd find the "spooky" features of the photo. I tried to have "muggle" copies of it made, but the camera shops that I tried to use could never make a decent copy. As a matter of fact they were such muddy copies that you couldn't make out any details. I told my parents that Minerva was very camera shy, so I couldn't get a photo of her.

That night at my B&B I couldn't get to sleep right away. I worried and worried at the question of how I would ever introduce Minerva to them. Could they accept her as my lover? Forget lover, could they accept her as my. . . my girlfriend? As a possible bride despite the age difference? As a witch? I finally fell asleep from exhaustion.

I took Minerva to a concert one night. In the day I went to the Northumberland Hotel and applied for Cedric to play in the tournament. They were somewhat reluctant, since he wasn't present and I wasn't a parent. However, I assured them that I was one of his instructors at an exclusive school. They accepted that rather naively. I wondered if magic was rubbing off on me—maybe the Imperious curse.

Bright and early on the 18th, Minerva showed up at the B&B and invited herself to breakfast. My hosts didn't object, so we had an excellent meal with them. Minerva told me that she'd approached the Diggorys and they wanted to have us over for dinner to discuss chess tournaments. We were invited the evening of the 19th. I was completely available, so we agreed to accept. I asked the obligatory question—what could I bring as a good guest.

Minerva had a ready answer because as a dutiful woman, she was always ready with the answers to social questions. Her answer was a bottle of elf-made wine that we could get at Diagon Alley today. Since I had done all my Christmas shopping and even gift wrapping, I felt that a little further adventure in Diagon Alley might be entertaining. At the very least, I could go and heckle all the last minute Christmas shoppers who were still trying to find gifts.

When Minerva heard that good idea she stared at me and said, "You're, of course, joking." It was a statement not a question. But I felt in a feisty mood that day, so I decided to see how far I could push her.

I answered, "No, seriously. Think about it. Every year, hundreds of shoppers descend on Diagon Alley a day or two before Christmas. No one among them has the slightest idea what they will buy for their good friends and relatives on their shopping list.

"If I point out the folly of their way and—now get this, even better—if they think that I'll be there next year to heckle them for their poor planning and judgment, they'll be a whole lot less likely to wait for the last minute next year. They'll start to get into the habit of planning ahead. Maybe it will extend to other areas of their lives besides Christmas. They might become more productive, better regulated citizens.

"I'd be doing a regular public service of inestimable value for the community. They should award me a metal or maybe even erect a statue honoring me."

She just stared and shook her head. "If I wanted comedy, I'd go find a troop of bears."

So on the morning of the 19th, we went to Diagon Alley via the Leaky Cauldron. Tom was fully in the spirits of the season—in every sense. We promised that we'd be back for lunch. We went directly to the Spirit of Conviviality shop, which features wines and spirits of all sorts. They had a fine selection of elf-made wines. We bought two bottles—a red and a white so that we would have all bases covered for the meal.

Over lunch we discussed our Christmas plans. Minerva invited me to spend the weekend starting after dinner with the Diggorys. That meant that I had to get presents from my room after dinner. Minerva dismissed problems with timing. We'd just disapparate to my room. Then I'd pac (including presents) and we'd disapparate to her sister's. She thought we'd all have a smashing time since her Aunt Beryl was going to stay for the entire weekend. We could do a proper Christmas celebration with the four of us. I had to admit that it sounded idyllic—if her sister was in good spirits.

We had the afternoon to while away. I suggested taking a walk in a Muggle shopping district, drop in a few stores at random, and window shop. As we walked, I had an inspiration. Why not go to a real Muggle Department store—like Harrod's? Minerva was a bit nervous about it, "That isn't like the awful department store over the Minstry of Magic, is it?"

"Oh, MInerva, it's a world of difference. Harrod's is bright and beautiful." Then I had an inspiration, "We can have high tea there. It's supposed to be one of the top ten teas in the country."

She was willing to give it a try. So, we took the tube to the Harrod's station. It was an interesting afternoon. Even Minerva found herself fascinated. The difference between the ultimate wizard shopping experience, Diagon Alley, and Harrod's was staggering. On one floor of Harrod's there were more unique shopping opportunities than Diagon alley offered together. She tried to stay non-committal, but it was just impossible for any woman to deny the attractions that Harrod's offered. They already had a bridal shop dedicated to June brides. I tried to steer us clear of there, but it was hopeless. After the bridal shop, we had high tea. By that time, I was beginning to regret my decision to take her there. Before we were finished, she insisted that I give her some Muggle money to buy a few things.

That necessitated handing her some cash and stepping back. We separated and agreed on a meeting time that would let us get to the Diggorys in time for dinner. That turned out to be the saving grace. I might never have gotten her out of there had it not been for that commitment.

After leaving Harrod's, we disapparated to the Leaky Cauldron where we'd left our bag with the wine. Then we were on to the

Diggory's. We arrived at 6:30 PM. It was pitch black. The Diggory's greeted us warmly.

Minerva pulled out the bottle of Elf-made red wine that we had brought and offered it to accompany the meal. Then we insisted that they accept the white wine as a little Christmas gift. That capped a very successful day.

Northumberland Hotel

We appeared at Cedric's home the next day, the first day of the tournament. His mother was busy cleaning the house for Christmas. Amos had to go into work. And so it was that Cedric, who wasn't licensed to apparate, found himself holding Minerva's left hand while I held her right hand. We appeared near the Northumberland hotel where the tournament was being held. We walked out of the alley and entered the hotel. It was relatively easy to find the event because it was located in the largest ballroom. At one end was a series of tables where players registered and got assigned to tables to play. On one of the two longer sides, were a series of tables with chess boards. At the opposite end of the room from the registration tables were the tables where officials had set up temporary office. In the middle were chairs for spectators. On the wall above the players were video terminals where game boards were displayed.

Cedric was surprised at the video screens. "Of course, newspapers and posters have moving pictures but I've never seen so many or so large—except, of course, at Hogwarts with the paintings. My game will be up on one of those?"

"Perhaps, but I think they're probably reserved mostly for the upper division of play. At your level, you'll not see many games displayed."

We found his table. The program told us that his opponent was to be a rated player with 1738 points. Cedric wanted to know if that was good. I responded that it was close to the top of the group at his level of play. I went on, "I have no idea what to expect because you're not rated. I know you're very good, but everyone at this tournament is probably very good. Just concentrate on the game and you'll do well. Good luck!"

Cedric hesitantly sat down at his table. A 20-something man approached the table and said, "So, that's the way it is?"

Cedric was puzzled and so was I. Cedric replied, "Excuse me?"

The other shook his head and said, "You're in my seat."

Cedric was still more puzzled, but I got it. "What do you mean?"

The young fellow had dark red hair and was as thin as a bean pole but he projected confidence and seemed to be as imposing as someone twice his heft. He said, "Look at your program. You're playing black, but you're sitting on the white side."

Cedric apologized and got up and circled the table and took his place on the black side. Minerva took me by the forearm and pulled me away. When we'd gotten out of earshot, she said, "Now, now, little mother, it's time for your chick to fly on his own."

I had had my fill of her humor. I simply sat at a chair in the front row of the spectator area without dignifying her comment with a response. She joined me and said, "Really, this game doesn't look to be getting off to a good start."

I reflected and said, "Oh, it's hard to tell. If that guy thinks Cedric is a real patzer and takes it easy, he may get a rude awakening."

Then the Tournament Director stepped to the center of the players' tables with a wireless microphone, tested it a couple of times, heard the squealing feedback, and after it was under control, spoke. "I want to welcome you all to the Tradewise Trafalgar Tournament. This contest is organized under FIDE rules and we expect strict adherence to them.

"We hope all contestants and visitors will enjoy the games. As you can see, we have an innovation this year." He pointed up at the video screens and said, "All of the games in the first division will be broadcast to these screens. We'll rotate through the boards so that everyone's position will be visible every couple of minutes. In the lower division, visitors are allowed to move freely but should in no way distract or annoy any player. Visitors who abuse their privilege will be asked to leave the tournament.

101

"Now, at my signal, the contestants will begin play. On my mark, ready, set, go." And dozens of clocks clicked into action.

I turned to Minerva and said, "Well, now the hard part starts for us."

We talked about the holidays, the monster of Slytherin, and what we would do for New Year's. Minerva wanted to go to a party. That was fine with me, but I didn't know of any parties. Finally, we could stand the suspense no longer. I got up and Minerva came with me to Cedric's table. A quick glance showed a confused board. I stood trying to count pieces. It was equally hard counting pieces off the board as on because there were lots that were off. Neither player had arranged them in a nice neat array to make it easier to figure who had more forces off the board.

Meanwhile Minerva was nudging me. I glanced up at her. She gave me a quizzical look. I returned an annoyed stare and resumed my count, having now lost my place. She nudged me again and I shook her off. I did eventually finish my count, took her by the elbow, and walked her away from the board.

She stared and whispered, "Well?"

"Cedric seems to be holding his own. He's slightly down in pieces. I think by a bishop vs two pawns But there's a lot more to chess than just count of pieces won and loss."

She interrupted, "I know. Different pieces have different strengths."

"Yes. I tried to take that into account, but there's a lot more than that. There's the strength of the position. Things like control of the center of the board. Then there's something called tempo. It's sort of a recognition of the fact that if you arrive first at a position, it can give you an advantage."

She was clearly getting impatient with the long story, "OK. OK. But overall, how's he doing?"

"I don't know, but he's not far behind, and frankly, he's doing better than I hoped for, I think."

"Let's go back and see what happens. I don't see how you can stand to sit down there and not know."

"Yeh. It's better to stand by the table and not know."

She gave me a queer look and dragged me back up. As the game wore on, it became clear that Cedric was happy to trade pieces evenly. It

102

seemed like he was always trying to force that kind of trade. After a while, Minerva pulled me away from the table and asked, "What's going on? Cedric doesn't seem like he's trying to win."

I agreed. "You're right. He's trying to force a draw. He's playing against a pretty strong player and has the disadvantage of playing black. He'd be happy to get a draw." Minerva frowned and I added, "And the other guy would be sad to get a draw." That seemed to mollify her a bit.

I opened the programme and inspected the various players in his group and their ratings. "I think this guy is the worst game he'll play in the first round. There's someone else rated a little higher, but Cedric will play him as white."

As we were talking, someone had come up behind us. I looked around and saw Cedric. I asked him, "Is it over?"

"Sure." He was moping a little. I feared the worst, but he went on, "I just got a draw. That guy is good!"

"Of course, he is. You're in the big times now—at least, the lower division of the big times. There aren't going to be any easy games from here on out."

We checked the time and place of his next game and left for home. We dropped Cedric off at his parent's. They wanted us to stay for some dinner. Amos demanded to know all about the game. I told him that Cedric could tell him about it a lot better than I could.

He nodded and asked, "Just tell me how he did."

I nodded too and said, "He did just fine. He drew his first game in serious play against a much older and more mature player. You should be proud of him. He gave as good as he got." Amos smiled and hit me a pretty good whack on my back.

"I told you he'd be great! I wish I could get away from work to see some of these games."

"If he makes it to the next round, they'll be after Christmas. Maybe you CAN attend then."

We said goodbye and were off.

Back for More

The next day at the tournament was very different. We were already registered. We knew our way around. The nervousness of the previous day was largely gone. Minerva and I stayed with Cedric for the start of his game. Cedric was playing white.

The quality of opponent was different too. This time, the rated opponent was in the high 1500's. It was a terrible temptation to congratulate Cedric on a win that hadn't happened yet. I bit my tongue as hard as I could to keep myself from expressing my relief. Minerva didn't have any such problem,

The opponent looked like an escapee from Cambridge. He was short, nonathletic, and wore glasses. His hair was dischevelled. Although he was wearing a sweater and I couldn't see his breast pocket, I'd swear that he had a pocket protector. I was beginning to feel sorry for the fellow and almost wanted to go sit down so that I didn't have to witness the slaughter.

Minerva wanted to stay, so we stayed. And as a matter of fact, the fellow put up quite a fight. He seemed to have studied openings thoroughly. The first dozen or so moves were made confidently and with not a lot of thought. He seemed to be holding his own against Cedric. As a matter of fact, there was a good more time off Cedric's clock than his. I began to feel just a little less sure about how this game was going to end.

Eventually, they got out of the explored openings and into the middle game. There, Cedric shone. He systematically picked his opponent's defenses apart and the end came quickly. There came a time when the young man sat studying the position for a full ten minutes. Then, he looked up from the board, nodded once—seemingly more to himself than to Cedric, set his king on its side, extended his hand to Cedric who shook it.

Then he stood and said, "That was really well-played. Good luck with the rest of the tournament. I hope you do well."

Cedric just nodded and said, "Thanks for playing. Good luck to you, too."

As soon as the Tournament Director came, they signed copies of the game record. Then the young fellow turned and walked off without another word.

The game had ended quickly, so we did a little walking tour of Trafalgar Square and nearby streets. We found a coffee shop (not Starbucks) and had tea.

Cedric started the conversation, "You know, winning in a tournament is different than I thought it would be.

"I thought there would be this celebration—something like Quidditch with your teammates shouting and high-fiving and a big party. But that's not the way it is at all. You just feel this relief that it's over and you've got a victory and on to the next game.

"Don't get me wrong. It's sure a lot better to win than even to draw, like yesterday, but one on one games are different."

Minerva looked about to say something, but Cedric pushed on, "Oh, I'm not complaining about you or my parents. It's clear that you're overjoyed when I win, but you just don't have that shared experience of winning, like you do on team sports. It's all out there and it's all on you and when you win you're alone. Even worse, when you lose you're alone."

I changed the subject to Christmas and what we all were going to do to celebrate. Cedric's family always got together with his mom's side of the family. There were lots of cousins. When they were younger, there was usually some kind of game like four-on-four quidditch or four-on-three quidditch. Now, that everyone was getting older, there was still quidditch, but there were also board games—like Parchesi and Brooms and Carpets.

I had never heard of the last game and asked about it. Cedric was surprised. He thought everyone had played Brooms and Carpets. "See, the idea is that you start at the bottom of the board and you roll the dice. You move forward toward the end of the game. The course is laid out on the board like climbing a hill. The 'road' winds back and forth up the hill. When you land on a broom, you zoom up the hill and get much closer to the end, but when you land on a flying carpet, you zoom down lower on the hill."

I almost remarked on how similar it was to a Muggle game called Shoots and Ladders, but bit my tongue just in time. We'd wasted enough time that we could have been using to take Cedric home. Reluctantly, Minerva agreed.

The next day, the last day before Christmas, we returned and watched Cedric demolish a player who was rated somewhere in the 1600's who was playing white. It was so easy that we were done really early and I decided that we could do a little real sightseeing. I proposed going to the National Portrait Gallery next to Trafalgar Square. It took a little persuading on my part to get Cedric to agree. His argument was, "Look, I've seen all the historic portraits that I ever need to see at Hogwarts. All the common areas are stuffed with them!"

I, of course, pointed out how much better quality the art was in the Gallery than at Hogwarts. That got me the evil eye from Minerva, but I held my ground. I said, "There's even a portrait of the three most famous witches in history."

Cedric asked, "You mean Rowena Ravenclaw, Helga Hufflepuff and." Here he paused, looked slyly toward Minerva and added, "Minerva McGonagal?"

"No, I mean, well," I had to think fast. Then I remembered my Greek mythology, "I mean Clotho (also known for spinning the thread of the lives of mortals), Lachesis (also known for measuring that thread), and Atropos (also known for cutting the thread)."

"You mean that Atropos is another name for Death?" Cedric thought a moment and said, "A portrait of Death—that would be something to see. And Death is a woman?"

Minerva looked warningly at me and said, "Don't you dare go there."

But, I couldn't help re-joining with a quote, "You know, 'Hell hath no fury as a woman scorned.'"

So, we agreed to visit the museum. I think that we all enjoyed it. We even looked up the portrait that we'd discussed. Cedric expressed disappointment that he couldn't ask them questions—especially Death.

To that remark I misquoted C.S. Lewis, "It a bad thing to know either too much or too little about Death."

Minerva said, "Well, it's certain that we'll meet HER sooner or later and then we'll know as much as we want. And no one knows how soon that meeting will come."

Cedric laughed and said, "Yes, all three of us could run into one of Hagrid's dragons and be burned to a crisp next term." That comment put an end to conversation for a good while.

We finished our tour after a couple of hours, which is probably as much as a person can stand of concentrated art at a sitting (or in our case, a standing). We dropped Cedric off at home and parted company until after Christmas.

▽

Christmas was a quiet time at Minerva's sister's home. Somehow Maggie was visiting their aunt Beryl, who was supposedly not well. Minerva said that she had something that sounded like "splatter goit'. So, Maggie had volunteered to go nurse her. It was very contagious, so no one else should go. It all sounded very fishy to me but I decided not to make a fuss. I would have to impugn Maggie's or maybe Minerva's honesty or maybe the honesty of both.

So, we found ourselves living in Maggie's house all by ourselves for a few days around Christmas. It was a bizarre experience. I thought we'd be alone, but this was REALLY alone. Even on vacation, the hotel would be full of vacationers and you just had to walk outside your room to see them every day. When we'd been together before, it was at Hogwarts during a time that students were mostly away and staff still mostly there. There were house elves. When I'd stayed in this house before, there'd always been Maggie.

It was strange in other ways. At other times, it seemed like we had to steal time to be alone. But now, it was different. We didn't have to "steal" time. It was all there. It was all ours and we could do as we liked.

107

It turned out that what we liked was reading. We both had brought books that we'd been reading at school and in the evenings. We'd read. We also would talk. But when we really had nothing to say, we could be silent together without being bothered.

We did the things that you normally do—wash dishes, do a little laundry even, and cook meals together. I could make anything with a decent recipe. If the recipe said a pinch of this or season to taste, I was lost. But if it had lots of big T's and little t's and 375 degrees for an hour and a half, I could make it. I guess that I'll never be a chef, but I don't need to be. The way meals usually worked out was that I took nice mechanical chores like making salad or browning onions and Minerva organized and took the more complex things.

We went for a couple of walks in the neighborhood. We didn't run into too many people. It was cold and snowy. Most people wanted to stay indoors. We always had a fire in the fireplace. We had a little fight about that. Maggie and Minerva used a spell to keep the fire stoked, but I liked doing the stoking by hand. We finally resolved the dispute by agreeing that I'd keep the fire going during the times we were up and around the house and she'd set it on auto-pilot the rest of the time.

This idyll of domestic joy was interrupted by the fiery spasms of sex, but it wasn't a continuous orgy. When we returned to the tournament, our time together returned to something like "normal". I could never use our quiet pleasure later as proof that we'd be good as a married couple. As a matter of fact, she never let me talk about it at all. If I tried, she'd put two fingers to my lips and just smile into my eyes. It was as though her memories were too precious as they were to take a risk of them being changed by interpretation.

The first day back at the tournament was interesting. Everyone was refreshed and there was almost a feeling of good will among the contestants and their supporters. That didn't last very long, of course. As a matter of fact, for Cedric, it ended only a few moves into the next game.

His opponent was a middle-aged man with thinning and graying hair that you might have mistaken for a banker. He was beginning to put on some weight, but he seemed to have been working hard to keep himself fit. The muscles of his arms were clearly accustomed to lifting something heavier than a briefcase and he moved with an assured gait that had something to do with running.

After a few hesitant moves, he got into the swing of his game. Each move was delivered with such force that I was afraid that he'd knock the nearby pieces off the board. He had white and he appeared to be determined to squeeze every bit of advantage that he could out of that. His force of will for a moment made me wonder how well Cedric would end up doing against him.

It didn't help that Cedric's manner was laid back to the point of being laconic. As a matter of fact, I began to suspect that he was having fun with his opponent, deliberately taking the opposite stance that he did in everything. Whether that was true or not, I never learned. But there was no doubt about the relentless way that he demolished the banker's attack and, shortly after that, the defense. The banker refused to surrender until he'd forced Cedric to announce mate.

Finally, only at that point, did the banker extend his hand and apparently squeeze with all he was worth when Cedric took it. Cedric was very athletic himself and only held his grip firmly. The muscles bulged in a hand that had long practice in directing a heavy broom whichever way they wanted. Cedric didn't make it painful for the banker but merely would not be the first to release. The banker almost flung Cedric's hand away and didn't say a word before or after signing the score card.

The next couple of days were pretty much repeats of the previous games. Cedric won except for one draw when he was playing white. He had done well enough to move on to the next phase of the tournament—a single loss knockout round.

That evening, we'd invited the Diggorys out to dinner to celebrate. We went to the Leaky Cauldron. It was a pleasant evening if not a particularly memorable one. Amos was not surprised at his son's early successes. If anything, he was surprised that he didn't win every game. We called it an early evening because the next day was the beginning of the next round.

Before closing out the evening, though, I wanted to set the stage for the next round. "You all are familiar with this sort of tournament. The Quidditch playoffs are all like this. One loss and you're out. But you may not be quite ready for the level of competition. Each of the other players has won his group. This will be a really difficult part of the tournament for Cedric."

Amos frowned with disapproval, "What are you talking about? Ced's brilliant. He'll blow through these games just like he did the last."

Cedric was obviously embarrassed by his father's boasting. He tried to signal his father to lay low with the commentary but to no avail.

Amos went on, "And talk about jinxing someone! Tell them, they'll probably lose right away?"

Reina was unhappy too but the shared suffering that everyone except Amos was going through at least caused us all to have sympathy for each other. Minerva and I left as soon as we politely could.

The next morning when we picked up Cedric, his father had the day off from work, and the whole family went with us to the tournament. The number of boards was much smaller. There were only 16 tables. It wasn't hard finding Cedric's table. The opponent was already there. There were a couple of pages hastily printed and stapled into a program showing the match-ups and the tournament brackets. Cedric was matched against a strong player who had won all of his games.

I gave Cedric my last word of encouragement. "I know that you can beat this guy. But he's a strong player. In this situation, I suggest that if you don't get an early lead and you see an opportunity to draw it, go ahead and do it. You can come back playing white and have a good shot at him."

His opponent was silent. He just nodded when Cedric sat. They inspected their board, the clocks, the surroundings. Cedric held out his hand and started to say, "Good Luck." But the other interrupted him with a shake of the head. He shook Cedric's hand and then released it.

The game started with us all determined to be there for every move. The opening seemed to be going normally. We watched as the game proceeded fairly quickly with nothing unusual happening. Then, things suddenly went south. Cedric lost in quick succession a pawn, a bishop and a knight. In return, he got a bishop. From there on, it was a constant battle just to stay even. I could see that Cedric was trying to get a draw, but it didn't look good."

We kept watching, but it was hard. Cedric made a good fight of it. In the end, he was just overwhelmed. He resigned after he fell another knight behind. He congratulated his opponent, who simply shook his hand and nodded to him.

We all felt pretty dejected. We just went silently to have dinner at the Leaky Cauldron. No one was really interested in talking. Even Amos didn't have much to say. But as we were about to part company, he asked, "When's the next tournament?"

I admitted that I hadn't tried looking up what was available in the future. He just shook his head and said, "We Diggorys don't give up that easily. We'll be back again and we'll be ready next time."

I smiled a sad smile and said, "Well, you'd better check with Cedric just to make sure that he wants to play in another tournament."

Cedric looked back and forth between the two of us before he asked his dad, "Do you really want me to try again?"

"You bet I do, Ced."

"Then, Professor, we'll be back for another go. And if you've got any ideas about how to get better, I'm all in."

I had to admire their determination. "You bet. There are lots of books about chess. The first thing to do is start studying openings. We'll talk about it when you get back to school. But for now, enjoy the rest of your holiday."

Monster of the Waterway

Minerva and I spent the next couple of days in a continuation of the idyll that we had been living at her sister's house. One day we actually went to see their aunt. It seemed that the spatter goit was real. She was well on her way to getting over it, but she was still contagious, so we couldn't stay long. Minerva offered to take over nursing duties, but Maggie said "no". She maintained that the fewer people exposed the better. So, we returned home. The last day before returning to Hogwarts early, we had one of our rare real fights.

I, figuring that this little interlude proved that we could live together as man and wife successfully, had asked her to marry me. Minerva lost her temper. She was so mad that she was incapable of speaking. When she finally did, she said, "NO." in a way that was not possible to mistake.

She went on, "Look, you think that just because we play house for a day or two and don't drive each other up the wall that we can live together for a lifetime!" She ended the conversation in a way that left no doubt that it was over permanently. I just stared at her. What in the world had caused that explosion?

I just stood there staring at her and wishing I could think of something—anything—that would be a good response to that statement. The key was the emotions behind the words. She sounded angry. But why was she angry? Was there something that scared her? I had no idea.

We spent the rest of the night pretty quietly. I found myself trying to avoid starting another conversation that might turn into a shouting match.

The next day, we had a normal breakfast. We both were going out of our way to be pleasant, and there was no mention of yesterday's one-sided "discussion". We talked about the start of term, the search for the monster, and what the house-elves would have prepared for dinner the first day.

We had come to London via the Hogwarts express, but we were going back early so it would be via floo. I was trying so hard to be pleasant that I didn't even complain. We packed and disapparated to the Ministry of Magic. From there, we took one of the dozens of floo's to the Great Hall of Hogwarts. We found that there were already several teachers who had arrived. It was almost lunch time, and those who were there were seated around the Huffelpuff table waiting for the house elves to deliver lunch.

Shortly after we arrived, Dumbledore entered the room and took a seat at the table. He was smiling and had a good word to say to everyone. Shortly after he arrived, Professor Snape joined us. Snape gazed around serenely observing everyone. His gaze stopped at Minerva and me.

"Have a good holiday?" He was smirking and seemed to have an insight into what had been going on with us. I was darned if I was going to admit that he might have some idea what was going on. I decided to play it cool.

I looked up at him and said, "We had a very pleasant holiday. Minerva and I spent a lot of time with Cedric Diggory and his family. He's quite a chess player. He was in a prestigious tournament in London over the holiday."

Snape nodded and asked, "Is he better at chess than he is at Quidditch?"

Minerva smiled and said, "He might just be. Professor Wendt and I had a wonderful time." Her attention left him and focused up toward the dais where we normally had meals. "Actually, it was the most wonderful time that I've ever had." she said softly.

113

Snape seemed to sense that there was something more personal going on. He turned toward Professor Lockhart and asked him something.

Dumbledore spoke more loudly saying, "I want to say a word of grace". He looked up toward the ceiling that was currently showing a clear blue unbroken sky and said, "Kindness."

Then he looked around and said, just as platters of food appeared around us, "Tuck in."

We gratefully did. Toward the end of the meal, Dumbledore sat back and commented to no one in particular, "Well, it's always good to have a Hogwarts meal under your belt."

Then he spoke to everyone, "We resume searching for the Slyterin Monster today. I've prepared a schedule so that we can systematically search the entire castle. It's posted in the Teacher's Lounge. Please begin at two o'clock this afternoon. We'll meet at the Teacher's Lounge and go off to our assignments from there. If anyone has any suggestions, I'm more than ready to hear them."

He looked around from face to face. Finally, he said, "Anyone? Anyone? Well, then, see you at the Teacher's Lounge."

Minerva and I knew that we'd be assigned together, so we met at my office after unpacking. We thought about and brainstormed strategies for finding the Monster, but we were as clueless as anyone. Finally, the beginning of an idea occurred to me. "Minerva, how does the monster get around?"

"Do you mean, 'Does it crawl or walk or run or gallop?'"

"Not exactly. But how does it get.-.-. ." I was interrupted by Professor Snape who stuck his head in the door of my office and said, "Well, I hate to interrupt this pleasant little tryst, but it's time to go off to work, Hi Ho, Hi Ho."

The interruption broke my chain of thought, but I was determined to start it up again after the day's search was over. At the Teacher's Lounge, we found that the entry password had been changed. However, Snape knew the new password—Calliope.

Inside there was a sheet posted that had pairings and assignments. Snape and Sinistra had the dungeons on the east side of the castle. Minerva and I had the men's and women's bathrooms throughout the castle. I commented, "What a drudge. What kind of monster would hide in a bathroom?"

Minerva laughed and said that there was at least one strange resident of one of the girl's bathrooms. I thought a moment and said, "You mean 'Moaning Myrtle?'"

"Yes, have you met her?"

"Well, I don't get into the girls bathrooms that often. I've never had the privilege."

"This may be the day."

We visited all the bathrooms. the boys bathrooms, I entered the boys bathrooms first to make sure that no one was using it and then Minerva joined me and vice versa. She used some sort of spell like "Revellio Monstrum". Nothing happened in any bathroom. We didn't even see Myrtle.

When we got back to the Teacher's Lounge, we discovered that no one had had any luck. By this time, I was pretty much thinking that we would never have any. However, we found a note pinned to the bulletin board in the Teacher's Lounge addressed to the two of us in Dumbledore's inimitable hand. It read, "Please join me in this lounge tonight after dinner."

I commented to Minerva, "Another fine mess for us." She only nodded and pinched me on the bum. Well, it was the first sign of affection that we'd had in a couple of days for which I was happy.

After dinner, Minerva and I went directly to the Teacher's Lounge. We arrived before Dumbledore and since we had a little time, Minerva asked me, "What were you beginning to ask me this afternoon?"

I stood and began pacing. That usually helped me think. "Well, it just occurred to me that we don't know how the monster gets around."

"Yea. And we don't know what it eats, we don't know what color it is, and we don't know what it does for fun—other than paralyzing its victims."

"No. This is important. Those other things are just incidental." Just then Dumbledore entered the room.

He looked around, seeming to want to make sure no one else was there. Then he addressed us, "Well, we're going to do some brainstorming. No idea is too stupid. Every idea is worth exploring. What are your ideas?" Neither of us spoke. He said, "Don't be shy. Surely you must have an idea Mr. Wendt?"

I frowned in concentration. "Well, it's not an idea. It's a question."

Minerva broke in, "He wants to know how the monster gets around."

Dumbledore just continued to stare at me as I composed my thoughts. "Well, I was thinking that this was an important question. Let me break it down into several questions—does the monster Disapparate?"

Minerva waved her hand and said, "OOh. OOh. I can answer that. Nothing can disapparate in Hogwarts."

Dumbledore cautiously agreed, "As far as I know, no one can."

I went on, "What about floo powder? Does the monster get around by floo powder?"

"Now you're being ridiculous." I could tell that Minerva was beginning to lose her patience. Her eyes were showing a tendency to roll up.

I was undeterred, though, "Then how does the monster get around without any of us noticing it? Is it invisible?"

That jogged them into thought. Dumbledore considered a few minutes and said, "Invisibility is hard. Even the best wizards can only produce a temporary moderately effective version of it." He mused for a minute. "It's interesting. The only really effective invisibility cloak that I've actually seen, no pun intended—even though legends are full of invisibility cloaks—is in this castle right now."

Minerva and I stared at each other and Minerva asked our question, "Where?"

"Oh, it belongs to Harry Potter."

Then a terrible, ironic thought occurred to me and I blurted it out, "But that makes perfect sense, doesn't it?"

Dumbledore looked at me suspiciously and said, "This is no time to keep your thoughts to yourself."

116

"Well, it all fits nicely together. Harry Potter summon's Slytherin's monster." With those words both Minerva and Dumbledore started objecting so loudly and in such conflict that I couldn't make out what either of them said. When they finally cooled off I went on, "No, think about it. Potter speaks parsel-tongue, right." There was grudging agreement.

"Parsel-tongue was Slytherin's language, right?"

Dumbledore said, "Not exactly, but go on."

"Well, Potter summons the monster in parsel-tongue, gives it its instructions, and puts it under the cloak. It goes and does its dirty deed and then returns to Potter, who removes the cloak and dispatches it home. It all fits neatly."

Minerva said, "You don't really believe that. You think that Harry Potter cold-bloodedly has been sending a monster out to attack people?"

I sighed and said, "No, I suppose not. I don't know him very well, but I don't really believe that. You might as well believe it was one of the Weasleys like the twins or .. or .. that 1st year girl. What's her name?"

Minerva supplied, "Ginny."

Dumbledore said, "Let's get back to planet Earth, Mr. Wendt."

"Well, you said to think outside the box."

He looked puzzled and I answered his implied question, "Oh, it's a Muggle term. It means without limits."

We all sat there for a few minutes reflecting. I broke the joint reverie, "OK, let's stay on planet Earth. How could you get around the castle without being seen?"

Minerva said, "Secret passages through the walls?"

Dumbledore pulled at his beard and said, "Yes, I know of a couple of secret passages that Hogwarts has. They go outside the castle. One of them ends in the Whomping Willow."

I jumped on that, "So, the monster could be coming in through that, attack, and leave the same way."

"Oh, I don't think so," Minerva answered, "The Whomping Willow doesn't have that name for no reason. It would be very dangerous for anything to try entering or leaving the castle that way."

I wouldn't give up, "But there wouldn't be a secret passage if it weren't possible to get around the willow."

Dumbledore broke in here, "The passage was built long ago—possibly when the original castle was constructed. Nearly all castles from that era had secret passages to allow the owners to escape in times of trouble, shall we say.

"Much later, the willow was planted to prevent pranksters like Harry's father from using that route of egress."

"But there may be other secret passages that no one knows about—except the monster."

Dumbledore agreed, "Yes, there are secrets of Hogwarts that even I don't understand. There's at least one hidden room. " He paused.

Minerva and I said together, "Well?"

"It's a little embarrassing. It was late one night and I was in a third or fourth floor corridor, far from a W.C. when I needed rather badly to find one. I was thinking of piss pots at the time. It's kind of hard not to, you know. Anyway, suddenly a door appeared in an otherwise blank wall. In my desperation, I went in. Not terribly wise, you know, entering a magic room that you know nothing about. Anyway, it was crammed wall to wall with piss pots. I made use of one."

"So, the monster could just be hiding in a hidden room and moving about the castle by secret passages?" I suggested.

"Yes, I think so."

In some way that suggested another idea to me. "Maybe the monster isn't what we think—a huge thing like a troll. Maybe it's so small that nobody notices it—a rat or a mouse or even a spider. Maybe it attacks people by injecting them with a powerful venom?"

Minerva dismissed that idea, "Well, Madame Pomfrey has tested for every known poison and even unknown ones. They weren't poisoned."

I wouldn't give up, "Well, how can you be sure that an unknown poison would be detected by her tests?"

Minerva just frowned at me exasperatedly. But Dumbledore was dismissive, "Have you forgotten Nick, the ghost? But, you know the first case long ago seems to have been something like that."

Minerva agreed, "Yes, poor Hagrid. He was stripped of the right to do magic because of that incident and only a student too. He'd found an arachnamanchula egg, raised it, and it attacked a girl."

Dumbledore nodded and said, "And it's ironic that the only testimony against him was Tom Riddle's."

My mouth dropped open involuntarily, "You're telling me that a minor was found guilty and punished because of the testimony of one person. What kind of criminal justice system do you have?"

Dumbledore said, "I was an instructor at the time. Haggrid admitted that he'd raised the creature and protected it."

I got up and paced. I blurted out, "But, he was only a minor. Even in Muggle justice, a minor isn't punished for a crime after he becomes an adult. Why, even the record of the crime is removed from his record. What kind of insane justice system do wizards have?"

Dumbledore was silent but Minerva showed a little of her temper, "Don't tell me that Muggle justice never sends the wrong person to prison or even the gallows? If you had magic, you could probably prove that lots of innocent people were really innocent!"

Dumbledore said something softly that neither Minerva nor I heard in our ranting's. She asked, "What did you say?"

He spoke up a little, and I noticed some glistening in his eye, "That it was Riddle who accused Hagrid is the real injustice."

Minerva nodded and sat. I asked, "What's the deal with Riddle. Why did that make it so awful?"

Dumbledore had a little trouble getting the words around the choking in his throat. Minerva patted his hand as he said, "You know Riddle by another name. He's 'He Who Must Not Be Named'."

That struck me dumb. I finally managed, "And you mean to tell me that Hagrid was accused by the most powerful dark wizard of the age —maybe of all time—and in all the years since there hasn't been an appeal or a pardon?"

Minerva hung her head now and just muttered, "No."

That seemed to put an end to constructive thought for the night, so we said goodnight and went to our beds.

Honeydukes

The next morning at breakfast Dumbledore announced that there were new search assignments and that we would all meet at the Teacher's Lounge at 9 AM to continue. We all arrived more or less on time. This time the list that was posted on the bulletin board was much like before, but it was much shorter. There were only about a dozen names on it—and I wasn't one of them. I immediately asked Minerva if she knew what was going on. She had no idea, but I stuck around.

Shortly after nine, Dumbledore showed up and there was a tumult of questions. They boiled down to two—from Minerva and me. Why wasn't I on the list. From the rest, why weren't there more teachers on the list? Dumbledore let the questions flow for a while in all their variety but then cleared his throat and silence fell. "You no doubt are surprised at how few searchers there are today. We came up with something new to search for, and there aren't many qualified to search. We're looking for secret passages—into the castle or from one part of it to another. Finding those take special talents that I think only those on the list have."

There was a little quiet grumbling, but I objected opening, 'I thought it was agreed that although I don't have magic powers, I could participate in the search?" Dumbledore sighed and shook his head.

"Mr. Wendt, you are the most persistent person at looking for danger that I know. Do you really insist on coming along?"

Snape spoke up, "Of course, he does. True love never is to be thwarted."

Dumbledore mumbled something about assigning Snape and me to work together, but he only added me onto the list as an assistant to Minerva. Dumbledore's instructions were, "Each team will search the area that it's assigned to for secret passages. If you find one, send your patronus to me in the great hall to tell me where it is. Then, with my permission, you may explore it. However, I may want to come to accompany you. Is that clear?"

Everyone was satisfied that the instructions were clear. So,we headed off to our assigned areas. Minerva and I were assigned the environs near the Defense Against the Dark Arts classroom to start with. We made our way there and started with the DADA classroom itself. Minerva and I went in and found our old buddy Lockhart in his quarters that were attached to the classroom. He hadn't been assigned to anything in the Secret Passage search. I was sorely tempted to ask him about it, but Minerva explained what we were doing in his classroom.

Lockhart drawled, "Secret Passage is it. Dumbledore should have mentioned that he was looking for secret passages. In the book, *Voyages with Vampires*, I tell how I found a secret passage into Dracula's castle that let me catch a number of vampires during the daytime and vanquish them."

I was sorely tempted to ask him to check his classroom for secret passages, but Minerva just thanked him and went ahead with her spell for revealing secret passages. There didn't appear to be any. We moved on to the classroom. We covered every wall, the floor, even the ceiling looking for passages. Nothing showed up.

Then we worked our way down the stairs. There were no passages apparent on the stairs—even though we stopped at every step to use Minerva's Revelium spell. We eventually reached the statue of the one-eyed witch at the base of the stairs. There Minerva's wand lit and illumined a patch of the floor behind the witch. Minerva fairly purred and said, "Now we have something. The only problem is how we get the passage to open."

She began using a variety of spells, including "Alohomora" when she began to get desperate. She finally stopped trying spells at random and tried to think of something logical. After a number of minutes of watching her pace, I asked her if maybe we ought to consult Dumbledore.

She turned sharply on me and said, "If there is a way in, I'll find it." She continued to pace and every now and then would mutter something under her breath. When nothing happened, she kicked the statue.

I decided that I'd suggest something to her. She was losing her temper but asked, "What is it?" with amazing forbearance.

I said, "Well, in a book I once read, the way to open a door was just to say, 'friend'—in the appropriate language."

She shrugged and said, "Amicus." Nothing happened. She paced some more and shrugged again. "I suppose, I will call on Dumbledore." She then sent her patronus, a cat, off. In a moment, she was looking off in the distance and said, "Professor, we've found a secret passage at the statue of the one-eyed witch, but I've tried everything I could think of to open it. No luck."

She fell silent and after a minute said, "I've tried all those and none of them worked." There was more silence and then after several minutes, she said, "I'll try it. Sounds reasonable. That's why it probably won't work." Then she pointed her wand at the witch and said, "Descendium." To my surprise, the witch slid back and stairs appeared in the floor underneath.

"Professor, that worked, and we're going in, unless you'd like to accompany us."

There was silence, and she said, "OK. We'll go and report back to you in a half-hour or less." With that she lit her wand and started down the stairs. I took her by the arm and stopped her.

I said, "I'm going down first. Just a minute, while I get my Glock out."

She grimaced and said, "Do you really have to put us in more risk than we already are?"

I just shook my head and said, "Wait." She did. I quickly retrieved the Glock from my purse. I loaded a magazine and checked to make sure the safety was on. Then, I walked forward to the stairs and asked for light. She cast a beam ahead with her wand and we began the descent. It was only six or seven feet. It took us to a flat, stone floor. When we had cleared the entrance, the witch statue returned to its original spot, and we proceeded slowly down the passageway. It led us on for about thirty meters where we reached the end of the stone floor, which became a rough-hewn dirt floor. We kept walking and eventually reached a door that turned out to be locked. We looked at each other and I whispered, "Try to unlock it. If it unlocks, I'm going in first. I'm going to be crouching to give you a clear shot if there's something waiting for us on the other side. If you can't stun it, I'll try to take it out with the Glock. OK?"

Minerva shook her head no, but said, "I suppose that's the best we can do. I'm going to do the 'Alohomora' at the count of five. You open it and we're in for it." Then she began the count, "One, Two, Three.-.-."

I steadied the Glock with both hands and then prepared to use my left hand to open the door.

"Four.-.-. Five. . " She used the spell and the door lock clicked. I swung the door open. Minerva had decreased the brightness of her wand light so that we could only barely make out the outlines of what was behind the door. I found that I'd started sweating. Drops were flowing down my forehead and into my left eye. I wiped them with my free hand and found that my mouth was suddenly parched. I wiped my hand on my jeans and took hold of the Glock with both hands.

I whispered to MInerva, "I can't see anything except what looks like packing crates. How about making it a little brighter?" She did and then I could clearly see the crates.

No markings were visible on the crates. I crawled forward keeping my head below the level of the top of the boxes. Something touched my left shoulder. I almost jumped out of my clothes, but I heard Minerva's whisper, "On the count of three, let's stick our heads up."

I nodded. She could feel the nod through my shoulder. She counted up to three, and we lifted our heads. I brought the Glock above the line of the packing crates. I could see more crates with labels that I couldn't read. I pointed silently toward my chest, then to the packing crate, toward her chest, and finally at the floor at her feet. She shook her head. I gave up and we both got up and walked around the crates that we were behind.

When we got close enough to the other crates to read, I gasped. It said, "Bernie Botts Every Flavor Beans."

Minerva burst out laughing—so hard that she couldn't catch her breath. As a result, she hardly could be heard. She gasped, "Do you.-.-.

ho ho.-.-. Do you know?" Then the laughing fit got worse and she couldn't say anything for almost a minute. Eventually, she calmed down enough to manage to squeak out, "Do you know where we are?"

In the meantime, I'd been looking at the labels. Another one said, "Chocolate Cauldrons". There was one that said, "Acid Pops." Then it hit me ,and I had a laughing fit of my own. I managed to force out, "We're in the basement.-.-. of .-.-. of.-.-." Another fit hit me, and I finally spit out, "HoneyDukes!" Minerva nodded vigorously and continued laughing.

Just then, we heard footsteps going down a staircase. I grabbed Minerva, we ran around behind the original packing cases, and hid. We heard voices. One said, "Virginia, I could have sworn I heard voices down here."

Another voice said, "See, there's nobody down here." Just then a light went on and we knelt further down. It went on. "As long as we're down, we might as well bring up a case of Bott's Beans. We're running low." We heard one of them use Wingardium Leviousa to lift the crate, and the stairs creaked again with the added weight on the way up to the store.

Then, we snuck back through the door to the secret passage, locked the door behind us, and strolled back to the castle. I commented, "I don't suppose that any monsters have been forcing their way into Honeydukes, through the passage and into Hogwarts."

Minerva squeezed my arm and agreed. By the time we got back, it was past time for lunch. We went up to the Great Hall. Apparently, no one else had missed lunch. We found Dumbledore waiting for us. We reported our discovery. Dumbledore sighed. "I think you're right. Nothing is stealing in through Honeydukes. However, it is good to know that when my sweet tooth gets the better of me, there's a way to satisfy it at any hour."

Minerva and I grimaced. Dumbledore had saved us a couple of sandwiches and some pumpkin juice. We ate and went back to our duty post and continued searching, but we didn't find anything else worth reporting.

That was the case for everyone else. There was one other secret passage discovered, but it was another dead end. We kept up the search until the students returned but with no good results.

Azkaban

After the students returned, we had another lull of activity on the part of the Monster. But it was broken This time, a Ravenclaw and a Gryffindor were the victims. They were Penelope Clearwater and Hermione Grainger. I heard the news in the Teacher's Lounge while I was checking my box for mail. Sinistra had come in and made the announcement.

After the hubbub had died down, she came over and took my arm, "I'm really glad that you aren't Muggle-born. I'd hate to find your body outside your office."

I barked a little laugh, "Right. Much better to find it in the main entrance."

She punched my shoulder, "You know what I mean."

"Yes, but what makes you think that not being Muggle-born is a get-out-of-paralysis-free card."

She looked at me quizzically, "What kind of card?"

"Oh, just a bad joke. I mean, how can you be sure that anyone is safe? Was Nick Muggle-born?"

She mulled that over. "I suppose that we could check with Professor Bins and see if he were."

"I'd just rather that we find and destroy the monster or shut down the school." That left her too shocked to say anything further.

At lunch that day, Professor Flitwick stopped at my place at table and handed me a note. It was in a blank envelope, but as soon as I opened it and saw the neat, flowing hand of Professor Dumbledore, I knew we were in for it. I looked over to where Minerva was sitting and saw that she also had a note. Mine read, "Prof. Wendt, Would you be so kind as to drop by my office immediately after lunch? You needn't consult with Professor McGonagall. I have also invited her. Yours, D."

I felt sure that Dumbledore had another scheme for smoking out the monster. Maybe it involved tying a beautiful sacrifice to a rock in the courtyard and waiting for the monster to arrive. I glanced over at Minerva again, and she gave me a little nod. I hurried to finish lunch and casually walked toward her. She got up and, being closer to the exit, preceded me. I caught her up a few paces outside the door.

I looked over to her and said, "Here's another fine mess we've gotten into."

She asked where the expression came from. I explained, "It was a common phrase in a series of early movies. There were a pair of bumbling characters—one tall and thin (Stan) and the other short and stocky (Oliver). Stan was always getting the pair into trouble, and Oliver's comment was usually the one I just used. It's a bit of a misquote. The actual phrase was 'Here's another fine mess you've gotten us into.'"

By this time, we'd reached the stone gargoyle. Minerva had it. She said, "Lemon Meringue Pie." The gargoyle got out of our way, and we stepped onto the revolving staircase.

When we entered his office, Dumbledore motioned us to chairs. He commented, "Have seats." I chose a red leather one and Minerva a yellow..

He steepled his fingers in front of him and gazed into them as though the answer to some problem was to be found there. After a moment, he said, "I have some bad news for you. I suppose there's no putting off telling you—as much as I would like to."

I sighed and said, "I'd rather guessed something of the sort. Go ahead."

"Well, the board of governors of the school have decided that they don't want to take a risk that Slytherin's monster will claim another victim. As you may know, a young student was killed many years ago. The death was attributed to Slytherin's monster."

Minerva interrupted, "So, of course, they've decided to close Hogwarts? Right?"

Dumbledore's face became really dour, and he said, "Wrong. In a way, it's worse. They're going to arrest Haggrid and send him to Azkaban."

I interrupted, "Wait a minute. I seem to remember a conversation about this very topic not too long ago."

"Oh, Mr. Wendt, there's nothing more that I can do about this. I hate it more than you do."

Dumbledore suddenly became business-like. He said simply and without further signs of disturbance, "The Minister of Magic has authorized Haggrid's arrest on suspicion of causing the paralysis of Colin Creavey and the loosing of the Monster of Slytherin. I have to accompany the Minister to see to the sacking and help with the arrest of Hagrid."

I stood and paced the floor. When I reached the boiling point I asked, "And you invited us here to share that cheery news because you're a sadist who likes to see people suffer when their friends are unjustly accused of heinous crimes?"

"No, I just was hoping that you might have a trick up your sleeve that you've been saving for a rainy day. And this day is a torrential downpour."

I stopped pacing and just stared at him for a while. Then I said, "I guess we could help him escape to America. Although, I don't know that he'd be in any better shape there than here."

Minerva said, "Anything would be better than Azkaban." I'd not heard the name, so I filed it away for later reference.

I had another idea. "Dumbledore, there must be somebody behind this. It sort of sounds like a vendetta against Haggrid. Boards of Directors rarely interfere with business without a very good reason."

"Oh," Dumbledore said, "I thought you would know. It was Lucius Malfoy who is on the Board and is a generous donor to Hoggwarts. He also has influence with the Ministry."

I snorted, "Maybe we should send him to Azkaban."

Dumbledore rose and said, "Well, I've got to prepare Haggrid for this ordeal. I don't suppose that either of you would like to come along."

I quickly pointed out that I had classes all afternoon and Minerva's schedule was almost as bad. We left together but had to part immediately for our classes. That evening, Hagrid was not at supper. Minerva and I sat together at the teacher's table picking at our food and not really feeling very competent at anything. We'd look up at each other, hopeful that the other had an idea. But there was no hope in either pair of eyes. I asked, "Well, what can we do?"

Minerva sighed and said, "Well, sooner or later, Hagrid's case will come up and he'll have a trial and we can testify as.-.-. "

"Yes, I know. As character witnesses. But that's not going to happen."

Minerva looked a bit puzzled and asked, "OK. You've got me. Why isn't it going to happen?"

"Because long before it comes to trial, the monster is going to strike again. It will be patently obvious that Hagrid's not responsible and even keeping him in jail as a preventative measure is preposterous."

Minerva said, "You badly overestimate the intelligence of the Wizengemott. But, I suppose you're right that eventually, when Hogwarts is closed because of continued attacks, it will occur to someone that it might be a good idea to quietly let him go." She paused thoughtfully and added, "I hope."

The next day at breakfast, Dumbledore made an announcement. He was sorry to report that the Gamekeeper, Hagrid, had been required to leave the castle by the Auror office to assist in the investigation of the attacks on students and others at Hogwarts. He hoped that the gamekeeper would be able to return soon and that we should all soldier on.

I turned to Minerva and said, "It looks bad."

She could only say, "Right."

"I suppose that we could visit him."

She made a face—not a very pleasant one—and said, "I suppose that we should. I'll get hold of the Ministry to arrange for a visit."

I didn't hear much more about it for several days, but one day, there was a knock on my office door. Minerva entered never waited to actually be invited it.. She took the red leather chair and leaned forward on my desk. "It's bizarre. They won't let us visit."

I don't think I caught her complete sentence and had to ask her to repeat herself. Then I tried to puzzle out what she meant. "Do you mean that someone won't let us visit each other?"

She stared at me with an exasperated expression on her face, "What have we been talking about?"

I thought back. I don't think there had been a conversation today between us besides this one. "I don't know. I didn't think we'd been talking about anything."

She shook her head as though she were dealing with a particularly slow student. "Hagrid, of course."

Then I got it. "You mean that the Ministry won't let us visit Hagrid?"

"Of course. Who else could I have been talking about?"

I thought about saying, "Anyone in the world." but decided that discretion was the better part of valor and shut up. Then I asked, "Why in the world not? Do they think that we'll sneak in a hacksaw baked into a cake?"

She stared at me, "What good would a hacksaw do?"

I dismissed it, "None. It's just an old Muggle joke."

"You Muggles do joke about the strangest things."

Minerva leaned back and turned contemplative, "I don't know." She drawled out. "They seem to have turned unusually suspicious of Dumbledore and all of Hogwarts for that matter, lately. Maybe they do think that we'd try to.-.-. uh .-.-. You Muggles have such colorful expressions for things. What would you call breaking someone out of prison?"

I laughed, "Springing him."

She smiled, "Yes. They seem to be afraid that we'd try to 'Spring Him.' Or at least that Dumbledore would want us to."

"So, we've just got to wait for the trial?"

"Yes."

"Do you know who Hagrid's lawyer is?"

She stared at me, confused again, "What do you mean, lawyer?"

Now it was my turn to be confused, "Don't all accused people get to have a lawyer, uh attorney, barrister, you know—someone expert in the law to represent the accused before the court?"

She shook her head, "I've never heard of that before. Magic courts and law are based on the idea that all you need is the truth on your side."

I growled and said, "Sometimes the truth needs a hand." Then I added, "Or even a fist."

"Well, that's not true in Ministry courts."

That was the last that we heard about the case for a while.

Easter

One day, I saw an advert in the sports section of the *Times* for an Easter chess tournament. It was to be in Bath. I tracked down Cedric at lunch and asked if he were interested in a tournament opportunity over Easter. He said that he'd check with his parents about it and get back to me. In the meantime, I sent a letter to the Director of the tournament, asking for application forms, etc. I had Minerva owl-post it for me. She was curious about the addressee. "Oh, it's obvious. There's a tournament coming up over the Easter holiday. I'm asking for an application in case Cedric's parents approve of his attending."

"That's interesting. We could turn that into a little outing, couldn't we?"

"Well, I suppose that if you consider disapparating to and from the tournament each day, an outing, I suppose so."

"I was thinking more of staying on site. By the way, just what is the 'site'?" She was massaging my shoulders as she asked.

"Bath."

"Later, but for now, where is the tournament?"

She asked it with a roguish grin, so I just went on as though she knew, "That's an interesting idea, but there's the question of what Cedric would do."

"Oh, Cedric! He could stay at home, and we'd pick him up each day."

I grimaced with the thought of four disapparations each day, "And drop him off at night?"

"Well, of course." She seemed to think better of it. "Maybe we can get his parents to come along and make it their holiday."

I agreed to that. Then we could each have our own room and Cedric wouldn't have to be in a room by himself. Minerva had added, "And I wouldn't have to have a room by myself."

But, of course, that was getting the cart a bit ahead of the cart because we didn't know if anyone would agree to anything. The answer to that came a few days later at breakfast. A large barn owl dropped a large envelope into my bowl of yogurt and granola. I sometimes thought the Department of Muggle correspondence took care to instruct owls to do that to me. Minerva noted that delivery and walked by me on the way out of the Great Hall. "Well it looks like you've got some interesting mail. Get Cedric to meet us at your office tonight after dinner."

I agreed, and early that evening we were all in my office. I'd offered, and we all had a glass of pumpkin juice. I opened my right upper drawer and withdrew the envelope that had plopped into my yogurt (less the yogurt). I'd opened it and knew that it was from the Tournament Director. I handed it to Cedric, "I know this is addressed to me, but it's really for you."

He took it and pulled the inner envelope out. He then produced his wand from an inner pocket of his robes and ran it along the edge of the envelope, slitting it open. There was a fairly thick sheath of papers that came out. Cedric looked at the top one, which was evidently a normal letter. Minerva asked if he minded reading it aloud, so he began,

"Mr. James Wendt, PO Box .-.-. etc.-.-. .

Dear Sir,

We are pleased to inform you that the deadline for applying for the Easter Junior Tournament has not passed. You are quite welcome to apply on behalf of Mr. Diggory. As a matter of fact, considering his excellent showing in the Tradwise Trafalgar, we would be happy to stretch a point to get him in.

Please find attached a tournament application. The normal deadline is Saturday, March 12. Please fill out the form and return it to us postmarked before midnight the 12th and there will be no problem getting him into the upper division of the tournament.

Yours, Peter Osbourne, Tournee Director, Bath Junior Easter Tournament

P.S. It would make it ever so much easier if we could communicate by telephone in the future"

I sniffed, "Ever so much easier for you perhaps, but it's not that easy to communicate by telephone here."

Minerva had taken the application, which consisted of two single-spaced pages of questions. She clucked her tongue and sighed, "I'm afraid that we can't complete this application."

Both Cedric and I stared at her. He asked why not.

She put the first page of the form down on the desk and said, "Question #7. We can't answer that question." The question in question was "name and address of the school currently being attended." She went on, "That would break the code of Wizard secrecy."

I picked the page up and scrutinized it for a few minutes. "No. No. That isn't a required question. Look at the asterisked questions. They are required questions. #7 is just an optional question."

Minerva took the sheet back, stared at it, and mumbled to herself, "Why do they put the question in if they don't care if you answer it?"

I smiled and explained, "Youth tournaments like to hand out little Bio sheets with a paragraph or two about each player. This is just fluff."

Minerva stared, still exasperated, "At Hogwarts," said with emphasis, "we only ask questions on applications that we want answered."

I'd picked up the other sheet to see if there were any other deal-breakers. I scanned through them and didn't find anything. The applicant had to be under the age of 18 as of Easter day, had to either be a member of the United Kingdom Junior Chess Association or willing to join. And then I found an interesting instruction, "Applicants must attach a check or money order for the entry fee AND a copy of the original birth certificate of the applicant."

Minerva said, "No other problems on this page. How about yours?"

"There's nothing bad—provided that we can get a copy of your birth certificate, Cedric."

He stared blankly, "My birth what?"

"Birth Certificate. When all," and I hesitated a minute. I didn't know if wizards used birth certificates. "Well, all Muggles get a birth certificate at their birth. To be honest, I don't know if English wizards get birth certificates." I looked to Minerva for help.

She nodded absently, as she started filling in the first page of the application, "Sure they do. Do you know where you were born, Cedric?"

He scratched his head and thought, "I think at St. Mongos."

Minerva nodded, "Then, you certainly have a birth certificate. If your parents don't have a copy, there's surely one on file at the Ministry. But why does he need to prove that he was born. I'd think that would be self-obvious."

I sniggered at her little joke, "That's obvious, but how old he is, is not quite so obvious. They want to be sure that he isn't over-age."

Minerva looked at him. "Yes, I suppose he could be mistaken for a young adult."

"It's not just that. Even if he didn't look that old, it would be unfair to not ask for birth certificates and then at the last minute ask for one from kids who looked like they might be older."

She grudgingly agreed.

"Well, Cedric, as you can see, the professor is busy filling out your application for you. Have you heard from your parents yet?"

He didn't say anything, but pulled a rolled-up parchment out of his robes and handed it to me. I unrolled it and read it aloud, "Ced, your dad and I are thrilled to hear that you've got another chance to play in a tournament. Of course, you have our permission. Please write with details as soon as you know them. Love A & R. P.S. Ced, you be sure to hold up the honor of the Diggorys, Hufflepuff and Hogwarts! Dad."

"Well, that seems pretty clear. Please write your parents and have them send a copy of your birth certificate if they've got one. We should get this in the mail by Saturday."

Minerva quickly added, "If there's any problem with the entry fee, let Professor Wendt know. There are Hogwarts funds that we could use." I stared at her but didn't say anything. I'd not heard about any slush funds for Muggle tournaments and the like. But then, I wasn't either Headmaster or assistant.

Cedric left, and Minerva pinched my nose playfully, "Well, it looks like we've got a trip coming up."

▽

The next evening, at supper, a lone owl flew over the Hufflepuff table and dropped something. After the meal, Cedric came up and announced that his parents didn't have a copy of his birth certificate. Apparently, they weren't used much in the wizarding community.

"Don't worry, Cedric. The professor and I will find out how to get a copy."

We talked it over and Minerva suggested that we go to the Ministry on Saturday morning. It turned out that the offices have Saturday morning hours. We could get a copy. We'd have to have a parent along to request the copy—or at least, it'd be easier if we had one along. She'd send an owl to the Diggory's to see if one of Cedric's parents would be available to help Saturday. We got Cedric to sign the incomplete application.

On Friday, we got an owl from Cedric's mom, saying that Amos was going to a big Quidditch match with work buddies on Saturday, but she'd be happy to come along with us to get Cedric's birth certificate. It all seemed straightforward. We just had to meet Reina at the Ministry on Saturday morning, get a copy of the certificate, finish the application, including her signature as parent, find a Muggle post office to get it mailed and postmarked. We'd probably have time to have lunch at the Cauldron.

Saturday morning started off well with a scrumptious patented Hogwarts breakfast. We were to meet Reina at the Ministry at 9 AM, so we had lots of time. We went by floo from Minerva's office and found Reina waiting for us in the atrium. We consulted the receptionist, who directed us to the Department of Vital Statistics. The ministry was open, but we found a line of people already waiting. There was a ticket dispenser and a sign over it that said, "Take a number."

"Minerva, this number is written in runes." She glanced at it and said, "Of course,"

"Well?"

Minerva returned my question with interest, "Well what?"

"What's the number?"

Reina piped up, "That's two thousand four hundred and seven."

Minerva pointed at the message board that read, "Now serving number.-.-. " In runes, of course. She said, "Now serving two thousand three hundred ninety nine."

I commented, "That doesn't sound too bad." And, it wasn't—the line moved fairly quickly. When we reached the end and told the clerk what we wanted, he handed us a form and said, "Fill this out and get in that line." He pointed, of course, to another clerk who had another ticket dispenser beside her. This time, the line was a bit longer.

At least, we had plenty of time to fill out the form. It was after 10:30 when we finally came to the end of the line and the clerk looked at our form, glanced at us, and asked for identification from Reina. She pulled out her wand and handed it to the clerk, who said a spell inaudibly and then handed it back to Reina. She used the wand like a pen to write on a piece of parchment. She had simply signed her name.

I asked Minerva, "So what did that prove?"

Minerva harumphed, "Don't you do any reading?"

"For the purposes of argument, let's just suppose that my answer is 'no'"

She rolled her eyes and said in her professorial tones, "The signatorum verum spell insures that the person writing with a wand which has been spoken over can only sign her own name with it."

"Good." Meanwhile the clerk had gone to a gigantic credenza, thumbed through it, and pulled out a piece of parchment. She placed it on the desk in front of her and with a flick of the wand a copy was created, which she handed to Reina and called the next number.

I asked to look at it. My face fell when I saw it. Superficially, it looked pretty much like any birth certificate that you've ever seen, but there was one key difference. There was a seal, which was not only raised, but which alternatively showed an official looking seal and a picture of Minister Fudge. "Minerva, why is Fudge's face appearing on the seal?"

Reina said, "Oh, that's easy. It's a security thing. Real birth certificates have the image of the current Minister on them."

"I suppose when there's a change of Minister, the old Minister stays on the seal?"

Reina laughed gaily, "Oh, no. It always shows the current Minister."

Minerva's face now matched mine, "I suppose that's going to be a problem, isn't it?"

Reina was looking confused, but I said, "Well, it depends. The application just said a copy of the birth certificate. It didn't say one with a raised seal. I think we could make a copy of it, and it'd be OK. The copy wouldn't have the Minister, I hope."

Reina asked, "But, surely not. Every copy would have the Minister's face on it, or it wouldn't be a real copy."

Minerva nodded, "Every Magical copy would, but Professor Wendt is referring to a Muggle copy, I think."

I agreed. And then I thought for a moment while the ladies waited. "This might not be so bad. We have to go to a post office anyway. They'll have a copy machine—Muggle—that should work with this." But as I said the words, I wondered, "Would it?"

Reina just shook her head in confusion, "But we could go into Flourish & Blots and have a copy made."

Minerva was beginning to appreciate how hard this always was for me, "No, I'm afraid not. Wendt's right. We need a Muggle copy machine." She turned to me and said, "Well, we need to get some money changed to Muggle pounds, don't we. We'd better head to Diagon Alley."

We all agreed. Then, we used the Floo Network to go from the Ministry to the Cauldron. As we entered, I waved at Tom and said, "We'll be back for lunch." I added to myself, "I hope."

There was a line at Gringotts as well. Why in the world a dozen people wanted to change galleons to pounds, I will never understand, but there they were. We got in line. Both Reina and I changed money. By now it was almost noon.

Reina smiled as we left Gringotts, "Oh, good. It's time for lunch. I always like lunching at the Leaky Cauldron."

I grimaced again, "I'm afraid that we're running short of time. I don't know how late Muggle Post Offices are open, but I'm pretty sure

137

that they don't go late into the afternoon." Minerva wasn't looking any happier than I was. She agreed.

We left Diagon Alley, and I realized that I didn't know where the nearest post office was. We wandered a bit before finding a shop where someone could direct us to a post office. Even disapparating there, we arrived only ten minutes before it was to close. At least there was a copy machine. Of course, I didn't have anything smaller than a pound note, so I had to stand in line to get it changed. Then, armed with coins to feed the machine, we started experimenting.

The first copy was brilliant, crisp, and clear. It had a picture of Minister Fudge's face that would have pleased his mom. I decided to keep trying. Maybe I was unlucky, and his face just happened to be up when the copier ran. While we kept trying, I almost ran out of coins. But after getting a couple of smudged transition copies, a clean one came through.

Minerva sighed, "At last. Let's go."

"No, I want to make a copy of this copy. We may need it later." I made the extra copy, which was pretty decent. Then we went back to get in line to buy a money order and mail the application. Before we reached the end of the line, they cut off the line. I asked one of the postal workers if there were a station that stayed open later. He just pointed at a sign on the door as he ushered us out. It said, "For later mail pickup, go to .-.-. "

I didn't recognize the address, but we disapparated there and discovered that it wasn't open either. We went to the address on its door. No luck. Then, we were on to the next address, which turned out to be the main post office of London. It was open 24 hours a day and had at least one clerk on duty at all times. We got in line, bought a money order, put the letter together, got in line again to get it mailed and make sure that it was postmarked before midnight

By the time that we'd finished all that, we realized that it was practically time for dinner, so we returned to the Cauldron. Tom greeted us, "I thought you were coming for lunch?"

Minerva replied, "Let's just call it a late tea."

We went to a table and seated ourselves. We were all ravenous, so it would have seemed good if it had been old shoe leather, but it wasn't.

As we ate, I raised THE question, "Mrs. Diggory, would you and Amos be interested in attending the tournament?" Even before I finished asking the question, I realized that the question meant something very different for wizards than Muggles. She was answering something about her plans to attend several of Cedric's games.

Even while I was trying to compose a question that asked what I really wanted to know, Minerva had come to the rescue, "What Professor Wendt really means is that he and I are considering going to the tournament as a sort of vacation, actually staying there at a wizarding inn and perhaps even." Here she hesitated with a bit of distaste at the idea and went on, "walking to the tournament. Perhaps you and Amos might want to do the same."

Reina cocked her head to one side. She seemed to consider it from some other angle, as though it were a completely unheard of idea. "Well, that's interesting. We didn't think of it, but it might be interesting to do some sightseeing there. I've never visited before. I'll ask Amos what he thinks and get back to you."

When we got back to Hogwarts, we went up to my office and Minerva asked me what I'd do if they decided not to attend. That was a real problem for me. I didn't fancy disapparating back and forth for maybe as many as nine days. "Well, I was really thinking that I wanted to stay on site and not have to disapparate four times a day" She seemed ready to object, but I quickly added, "I know. We did that at the last tournament, but this is different. It's fairly likely to be a week or even eight or nine days in a row, if Cedric makes it to the finals. I just don't know if I can take that much disapparation."

She gazed at me speculatively, "Then your idea is that you and Cedric would stay together in a room for the tournament. You know he is almost sixteen. He could very well stay in his own room."

"Well, maybe in a wizard inn, but in a Muggle hotel? I don't think I'd trust him alone with all the ways to screw things up that electricity and phones and so forth offer."

Minerva seemed miffed, "What about a wizard inn?"

"Well, it would certainly not be very close to the tournament site, so I'd still have to disapparate back and forth. We might as well be disapparating back and forth from Hoggwarts."

"You are the most exasperating man I know. You are just determined to be there without me!"

I could only shrug, "Maybe the Diggory's will come."

Minerva just shrugged her head in a kind of left-right manner that made me think of Indian students that I'd gone to school with who'd used that peculiar rocking motion as their nod of assent. "Oh, maybe."

"But if not," I could tell her dander was rising, "I am definitely not coming. So how are you going to get there?"

I leaned back in my chair and thought about it. "Well, I suppose .-.-." I offered her something to drink to give me time to think. She accepted, and I poured us each an inch of Dewars. Back in my chair leaning back, I answered her. "Here's what we'll do. First, Cedric and I will go to the Cauldron by floo powder. He can do that and he can bring me along.

"Next, after we get there .-.-.

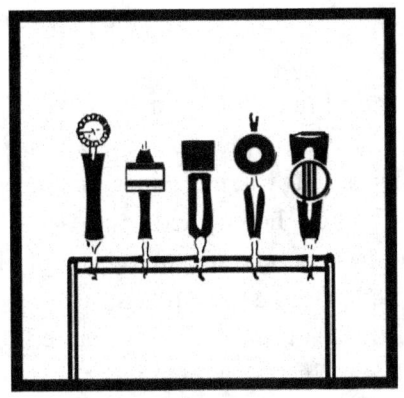

Bath

After we arrived at the Cauldron, Cedric and I went to the bar where I ordered two butter beers from Tom and a third for him. He passed the time with us talking about our plans for the Easter holiday. Cedric talked about going to the tournament.

Tom asked, "I didn't know there was a Quidditch tournament on this week."

Cedric explained that it was a chess tournament in Bath. Tom was interested, "Wizard's chess, eh? Never played it myself. it takes real brains for that."

I bragged on Cedric a little. "Cedric is the best wizard's chess player in Hogwarts in living memory. I'm sure that he'll do well, but we've got to get on our way."

Tom waved, "Young Cedric, you do Hogwarts proud, there."

As we left the inn, Cedric asked a very reasonable question, "You can't disapparate and I can't. We're not going by floo. Just how are we getting there?"

"Easy. By train."

Cedric smiled, knowingly, "You mean like the Hogwarts express?"

"Well, yes. It's Muggle trains, but they're just like the Express. You might not be able to tell the difference if I hadn't told you. We'll use at least two, maybe three. The first thing that we have to do is find a Muggle Underground station."

Cedric seemed surprised, "The Muggles have underground stations?"

"Yep. We'll find one shortly, and then you'll see." We walked along Oxford street and shortly found the Euston Road station. Cedric thought I was kidding about it being underground but when we walked down the stairs to the station, he laughed.

We bought passes, and he marveled at the way the tickets worked. He commented, 'It's just like magic."

"I guess I'll let it pass." We boarded a train headed for Paddington station. We arrived there and went up to the train station. We bought a couple of tickets for Bath and caught the next train, which left shortly after 11 AM. We arrived at the station in Bath just before 1 PM. We were both getting hungry, but I didn't want to wander around outside the station looking for a restaurant, so we ate in the train station. That was a mistake. After we left, we found that there were a half dozen little restaurants in the area.

We found a cabbie and got a recommendation for somewhere to stay—the White Hart. It happened to be close to the tournament—within walking distance. We settled in and had a little time to kill before the Opening Banquet of the tournament. It and the awards ceremony were the only meals included in registration. I had to pay extra because I wasn't a registered player.

The meal turned out to be the normal rubber chicken and cold mashed spuds that you find at tournaments, but we had the compensation of getting to hear a boring address by the Tournament Director on the procedures or the tournament.

The highlights were that the first round of the tournament was a round-robin with 6 games guaranteed. There would be one each morning and one each afternoon Sunday thru Tuesday. There was a day off, Wednesday, when players could tour Bath. The lucky few who survived to the next round had two or three games each day, depending on how the players faired. In the knockout round, each pair of opponents played two games, one as white and one as black. If they were tied, they would play a third decisive game, with the lucky player to get to play white chosen at random. The first two games were, as before, morning and afternoon. If the third were necessary, it would be played at night. Sixteen players started the knockout round on Thursday, and each day cut the number in half until Sunday afternoon (hopefully) there was one winner left. There had been a few occasions in history when the third game Sunday evening was required to settle the winner.

Games used standard FIDE rules and the third game, when necessary, was a speed game played with 40 moves each half hour. Officials handed out schedules of play and checked player IDs. Various other minor points were covered and we were all wished a pleasant night's rest and sent off.

▽

The next day, we got up early and did a light jog before breakfast and the first game. The hall where we played was rather disappointing compared with the Tradewise tournament. There were folding chairs and tables. No video screens. Game results were posted on a bulletin board.

The first game Cedric had was against a kid who might not have been in his teens. He seemed to play a standard opening, but I didn't know enough about openings to be sure. He moved quickly and confidently and seemed to be doing pretty well. Then, when he slowed down, his game seemed to fall apart. Cedric, who'd been burning a fair amount off his clock during the start of the game, demolished his opponent then. There weren't many more than a dozen moves from that point until the end. The kid, who had chewed gum throughout, removed the gum, wadded it up, and threw it into a trash can nearby. Then he came back, glanced at the board, set his king on its side, and extended his hand. The only thing he said through the whole game was, "Good game." He signaled to the Tournament Director who came over and recorded the result. It went up on the big board and that was it for the first morning.

We went out and had lunch. We did a little post-mortem. There wasn't much to discuss. Cedric just said, "He had a memorized game that he played, hoping that I'd make a mistake. When I didn't, he sort of gave up."

The next game or two went similarly. There really wasn't much competition, but the game after than was different. This game, the opponent was tall, thin and gangly. He pushed Cedric very deep into the opening game, Cedric made a mistake or two, and was down both a piece and time. His opponent seemed to reach the end of his opening game, and then there was a long slogged out middle game. They reached the forty move limit and they were allowed to take a break.

I made sure Cedric stayed hydrated. In the resumption, the game moved amazingly quickly. Cedric quickly built a material advantage and his opponent gave up. Cedric asked us if we minded his family joined us for dinner. Neither of us did.

He introduced us to his parents who were not even in the hall. They were waiting in a coffee shop nearby. They were the Ripleys—Joan and Leonard. I suggested eating at our inn. They agreed.

I explained that I was Cedric's chess club advisor at school.

Joan wanted to know where the school was located. I laughed, "I'm afraid it's pretty remote. It's located in the far north of Scotland. The nearest town is a little place called Hoggsmead."

Their son, Tony, asked the name of the school. Cedric gave the name, and we all had a good laugh at the name. Then, the question that I'd been fearing happened. Leonard asked what Cedric liked to do when he wasn't playing chess. Cedric smiled shyly, "Oh, you know, sports." I breathed a sigh of relief temporarily. The inevitable follow-up question came.

I jumped in, "Oh, Cedric plays a little of everything—pickup football, basketball, rugby. He's not great at any of them, right?" I was getting worried now.

Tony reacted to the football, "Oh, I'm a footballer. What position do you like to play."

I blanched but Cedric immediately said, "Oh, I'll play any position. What do you play?"

Tony was excited, "I'm a goalie."

"No, really? I think goalie is the hardest position to play. It's so depressing. Everyone blames you if you lose. If you win, it's the offense that gets the glory."

Tony laughed, "You can say that again, but if you win, you know that it was you who won—most of the time. And if you lose, well, everyone feels the loss. What's your favorite position in Rugby?"

I strove valiantly to keep the subject matter to academics. I interrupted and said, "I'm not that interested in sports, but I love the subject that I teach, English Literature. Tony do you have a favorite author?" It was weak, but I had to turn the subject elsewhere.

Then I had an epiphany. I started talking about myself. "You know, I'm from the States. I'm from the state of Ohio. Have you heard of it?"

Joan said, "No, I can't say that I have, but I was wondering about.-.-."

I never discovered what she was wondering about because I jumped in as if she had shown the greatest interest in Ohio, "We like to say that Ohio is round on the ends and high in the middle. Get it? Round on the ends—the O's and HI in the middle."

Leonard said dryly, "Very funny, I'm sure, but I was wondering if .-.-."

I broke in, "Have you ever been to the States?"

Joan answered, "Well, no, though we'd like to have done."

"Oh, you've got to come over sometime. There are so many things to see and do. You can take a steamboat down the Father of Waters, the Mississippi. There's great theatre in New York. There are the museums of the Smithsonian in Washington DC." I went on and on through dinner and by the time we were through with the meal, I'm convinced that they must have thought that I was the world champion bore. But I got us through the meal without any really bad slip up with magic.

Cedric laughed as we went up to our room, "You were so funny. I could hardly keep from laughing. I thought you were going to have a heart attack when I almost mentioned Quidditch."

"You're right, I did. From now on, no dinners with other contestants. We keep ourselves to ourselves."

"You're being too pessimistic. Nothing's going to happen if something slips out."

"Just remember the motto, 'Youth should be seen and not heard.'"

Cedric assured me that that would be his password.

That night, I slept the sleep of the dead, I was that exhausted by that dinner.

That was the only close game of the prelims. The rest were as easy as pie. With a day off, we took a tour of the Roman baths that the city is named for and then we went to lunch at our hotel. And while we were there, Cedric's parents showed up.

Amos was unhappy. "Why haven't you sent an owl. We had no idea how things were going! I had the devil of a time finding you two."

Reina tried to smooth things over, "Now, now. It's hard when there's so much excitement to think of the people back home."

Cedric explained, "I don't know where we could find a wizard post office. I'd have sent an owl the first day, but we're in the middle of nowhere here."

Amos was somewhat satisfied, but he was still not very happy. We all had lunch and talked about how the tournament had gone.

After he learned that Cedric had a perfect record, Amos' chest swelled with genuine happiness, "Well, I'm not surprised. What's next?"

We talked about the knockout round and explained that the first game would be in the morning tomorrow. The Diggorys decided to stay the night and watch the first game in the morning before returning home. Amos was so sure that his son would reach the semi-finals that he declared that he would return again on the weekend.

That night, he and Reina stayed at the White Hart, but the room was really too small for three, so Cedric stayed the night again in our room. The next morning, we broke training and had a real "English" breakfast at the Hart and then proceeded to the tournament.

Cedric's next opponent was a nervous, twitchy sort. He had a handkerchief that he kept wiping his brow with, removing imaginary sweat. As a chess player, he was pretty decent. He didn't have the masterful command of openings, but he seemed, like Cedric, to have a natural talent for Chess. The opening went slowly with both sides thinking out their moves with some care.

Eventually, the opponet wiped his forehead more and more frequently. He eventually made a tragic blunder that resulted in mate in six. As soon as he removed his hand from the fateful piece, he took hold of it again as though to change his mind. But it was too late. He played on for two more moves, hoping that Cedric didn't see the blunder, but Cedric would not miss such a misstep. Cedric's opponent stood, apologized, and resigned.

Of course, Amos was overjoyed and was on the verge of being a bad father of the winner. Reina forestalled that by kicked him in the shin at the critical moment, and shut him up before he said something that even he would have regretted like, "Well, Ced, all too easy, isn't it?"

We had lunch at the Hart again, and the Diggorys left with a promise to return on the weekend. I just hoped that we would be here to see them again. After lunch his opponent, having to play black, resigned immediately. So, we had the afternoon free.

We had a quick post-mortem.

"Cedric, the Directors of these tournaments usually seed the players in the final round so that the players that they think are strong play the weak players in the early rounds. That way, the strong players play each other at the end rather than the beginning. I think they've seeded you high, and the games are going to get progressively harder as you go."

"Where do you think they've seeded me?"

"Certainly in the top four, probably in the top two."

He nodded and thought a moment, "Then they expect me to be in the final?"

"It kind of looks that way. Don't get a swelled head."

"No, sir."

The next day started with Cedric playing white and winning easily. The afternoon game seemed to be going easily with Cedric having a nice advantage in material building. Then suddenly before I even realized it was happening, the game was ended with a loss.

We'd dropped post-mortem analysis for most of the games because the games had been so easy. This one we analyzed. Cedric explained what happened, "It was a trap. He offered me a piece, but when I took it, I made myself vulnerable to discovered check. I was way ahead and just got greedy."

"Well, the next game will be a blitz game. You have to be ready for speed. You'll have 45 seconds per move, but you'd better use less

147

than that on the early moves." I thought a moment and added, "Well, maybe not a lot less."

Cedric just frowned, "Thanks."

We went off to dinner. The weather was actually pleasant for April Fools Day, and we found a restaurant that had outdoor seating. We were about half-way through dinner when a owl flew over us and dropped an envelope in Cedric's salad. He opened it quickly. "It's from dad. They're coming down here tonight as soon as they've had dinner. They'll meet us at the White Hart about 7 PM."

"Great. We've got to be at the tournament to start the game at seven. Well, let's get to the Hart and leave a message for them."

We had to take a cab from the Hart to get to the tournament in time for the game. I'd written a quick note for them, telling them to come to the tournament hall quickly so they might catch the final game of the day.

We arrived just in time for Cedric to get seated. The Tournament Director came to their table and explained that he'd flip a coin. He'd let it fall to the floor and the side that was up would decide who would play white. He asked who wanted to call. Neither boy spoke up at first, but Cedric said, "I don't want to call it."

The other lad nodded and said, "Tails."

The Director flipped the coin. It struck on edge and rolled around and finally fell under their table. The Tournament Director knelt down and said, "It's heads. Does anyone want to examine it before I pick it up?"

No one did. He retrieved it and started the game. The other boy played even more quickly than the beginning of either game before. After they'd played ten moves each, Cedric had almost ten minutes off of his clock and his opponent had less than five off. It was beginning to look like Cedric would be out of the tournament before his parents arrived.

Then, play slowed for both. Then something happened. Cedric moved quickly, and the other's play slowed. The last five moves took only seconds each for Cedric and the other took his time. I don't know what his opponent was hoping for. In the last several moves, it was clear to even me that Cedric was going to promote a pawn and that would be the end. But the kid stayed doggedly in there until Cedric announced "Mate" with forty seconds left on his clock.

I hadn't noticed, but sometime during the game, Cedric's parents had arrived and stood behind me watching over my shoulder. Amos started a whoop but choked it in mid-whoop. The Director gave Amos a sour look and came to make the result official.

We all went back to the Hart, had drinks, and discussed the day and the rest of the weekend. I had a question for him immediately when we arrived, "Cedric, you must have had a forced mate several moves before you announced. Why didn't you announce?"

Cedric turned a shade of magenta, "Well, frankly, I was scared. If you announce like that, then you have to state the moves that you're going to make up to mate. Then, if the other player wants, he can require you to actually play those out regardless what he does in response. I just didn't want to take the chance." Then he added, "And then too, it just seemed to be too conceited to make that kind of announcement. If the other guy wanted to resign, that would have been fine, but I wanted to leave the decision with him."

Reina smiled, "Always the gentleman. That's our Ced."

I agreed, and we talked about the weekend. I had to admit to them that I'd planned everything pretty well—except how we'd get back to Hogwarts.

Cedric asked, "Can't we just go backward, the way we came?"

"Maybe, but if we're at the award dinner late, we'll not get back to London until really late. I don't know how late the Cauldron stays open on Sunday night. And even if they are open, we'd not get back to the castle until well after curfew."

Amos said, "Don't you worry about that. We'll disapparate you directly back to Hoggsmead afterwards."

That plan was settled.

The next day, we were up bright and early, as usual. The games went smoothly. There was not a scare like on Friday. Cedric won as white and drew as black. I was convinced that he could have won fairly handily, but he said afterward that he didn't want to take any chances. So, when he had a chance, he got the other fellow into a perpetual check and it was over quickly.

The next game on Easter morning had Cedric playing white. It was a hard fought game. His opponent, a strapping seventeen-year old had the opening game locked down. He had a definite advantage in position when they entered the mid-game. It went straight through the first 40 moves and then was resumed. After another 40, the Tournament Director suggested a draw and the players agreed. It was already afternoon. We went to lunch. We had been given only an hour before the next game would begin.

At lunch, I reminded Cedric, "This guy has the openings all memorized. He'll have white and will choose the opening. You can bet you'll be in trouble by the mid-game. You'll have to play really well to win. A draw will do you no good. With his knowledge of openings, he'll have an advantage in the third blitz game. By the time you get to your part of the game, he'll run you out of time."

"Have you got a big idea then?" Cedric was as testy as I'd ever seen him.

"I guess blitz-krieg."

Everyone else said, "What?"

"Oh. It's a German word. It was invented in World War II. The Germans had this technique for fighting battles that was designed to keep them from getting bogged down.

"You see, in the First World War, the Germans got stalled and the war went on for years with neither side getting anywhere. Both sides dug in, and both sides had terrible losses when they tried to attack the other. The Germans finally got exhausted and gave up.

"They swore to themselves that that would never happen again. So they invented a new style of war that they called blitz-krieg. That means 'lightning war'. Attacks were extremely fast ferocious attacks, using airplanes and mechanized cavalry. It worked pretty well."

Cedric asked, "Then you mean that I should play blitz chess?"

"No. You attack fiercely, taking chances that you ordinarily wouldn't. It's a long shot, but I think it may be your only hope."

Amos was not happy with the discussion, but he didn't have anything to add.

The final game started off pretty much to form, but something strange happened in the mid-game. Both sides attacked fiercely. "The chess board was chaotic, disorganized," I thought to myself. Then, I thought, "What do I know?"

I was watching the chaos swirl around and the other player picked up his King as though to move it. He held it in his hand a few seconds and placed it down on its side. At first, I didn't realize what had happened. People see what they expect to see. I'd expected to see him place it on an adjacent empty square. That was what I saw. I thought perhaps he'd dropped it and just hadn't righted it yet. But no. He extended his right hand toward Cedric who promptly grasped it.

I suddenly realized that someone was hitting my back and I turned to protest when I realized that it was Amos. Then I noticed the applause and Amos's shouts. I smiled and shook his hand. The Tournament Director silenced the crowd and reminded everyone of the awards ceremony dinner. He repeated that it would start as scheduled at six.

We agreed to go to the bar in the hotel. Eventually we were able to order a round of ale and found a table in the corner. Amos was talking intensely with his son. Reina thanked me for helping Cedric win the tournament.

"Oh, believe me. I had nothing to do with Cedric's victory. I gave him very little advice, and the ONLY good advice I gave him was not to get cocky."

She laughed and patted my hand, "Oh, I think you had more to do with it than that." Cedric had apparently been listening and agreed. Then she had another thought, "Where's Minerva? I thought the two of you were—well—close?"

I didn't say anything. She went on, "You'd think that she'd show up for at least a few games and certainly for the final."

I remained silent. She shook her head. "When I was at Hogwarts she had a reputation for being stubborn. I hope it's a little spat that the two of you resolve quickly."

I still held my silence.

After the one drink, we decided to go the meeting room where the dinner was nearly set up. We picked a table near the head table and sat. Presently, the salad was brought out and we ate. When the main

151

course was being served, the Tournament Director got up, took the temporary podium on the head table, and made some announcements. He thanked sponsors of the tournament and the volunteers who did not go nameless.

By the time the desert arrived, he had reached the point that everyone had been longing and longing would arrive. He said, "Now, for the highlight of the night—the presentation of medals to the winners." He picked up the bronze medal and announced the winner. "I want to stress that any of these young gentlemen could have won the gold. They all had sterling records in reaching the semi-finals."

The Tournament Director presented the medal and the young man simply said thanks. His parents stood behind him, looking supportive. Then the Director announced the silver medal winner. In the mean time, I looked around to see if I could see the fourth-place player. I'd not paid a lot of attention to him during the semi's, but I had wanted to at least recognize him if we had to face him. I found him sitting with his parents at a table toward the back of the hall. I got up to go over to him.

Cedric asked, "Where are you going?"

His mom added, "Aren't you going to go up with us when the gold medal is presented?"

I shook my head, "No. This is all Cedric's time and yours as well. I'd be a fifth wheel."

Amos squinted trying to figure out the reference, but Reina took my arm and tugged gently, "Really, you should be up there with Ced and us."

I simply shook my head and pulled free gently. Just then, Cedric was announced, and the three got up and walked the short distance to the podium. Meanwhile, I walked briskly back to the table with the fourth-place player. There wasn't anyone else at that table other than his parents. I introduced myself as a chess advisor for a school chess club. They introduced themselves: the player, Todd Stearns and his parents, Millie and Rob."

"Do you mind if I join you for a few minutes?" When they didn't say anything, I sat and addressed Todd, "Mr. Stearns. I wanted to congratulate you on reaching the semi's." I extended my hand to shake it.

He took my hand..I said, "I think that you might well have been up there had you drawn Cedric's opponent in the semi's."

He thanked me and his parents added theirs. "Were you Mr. Diggory's chess adviser?"

I laughed, "Oh, yes. But he's well past my chess playing ability. Like most teachers, I have to volunteer to be adviser for a school club. I was the only one who was willing to take the chess club. That's all."

They all laughed as well. I went on, "I hope that you all have a good spring, and who knows? We may meet again at one of these things —though I doubt it."

Mr. Stearns asked, "Why do you say that?"

"Well, I think Cedric will mostly be playing in open tournaments from now on. He already played in one of the 'bigs', and I think he'll want to keep playing them. But we may run into you folks at one of those." I rose to leave.

Meanwhile the Tournament Director had presented the gold medal and congratulated Cedric. He was now talking about next year's tournament—application deadlines and so forth. I rejoined the Diggorys..Amos was more than ready to leave. Really, we all were. So, we went to the front desk of the hotel and claimed our bags that they had kindly been keeping for us. We went outside and found a secluded spot.

Cedric took his mom's hand, and I took his dad's. I was reminded about how happy I was to not have to disapparate nearly 40 times in the last week or so. We landed in front of the Three Broomsticks. Amos declared that he and his wife were going in for a drink. Did we want to join them? It was already nearly 8 PM. We declined with thanks and headed for the castle. We arrived just at the stroke of eight and I accompanied Cedric to the Hufflepuff house to avoid his getting detention from Filch or someone. I politely stood back so as not to hear the password and the door swung open.

He walked in and turned to beckon me to join him. I silently shook my head, but he signaled all the more fiercely. Then Grubbily-Planck stuck her head out and said, "You come in right now professor. You deserve a little of Cedric's glory." I decided it would be better just to accede and followed her in.

There was a group of students in the common room cheering and applauding. Grubbily-Planck silenced them and asked Cedric to say something. He examined the floor for a moment and said, "It's good to win. But whether you win or lose, it's better to have friends to celebrate with you or buck you up, right Professor?"

He was clearly indicating me, so I stepped up next to him. I shrugged and said, "Cedric, you've got the right of it. I absolutely couldn't say it better. Congratulations." There was more applause. Then, the crowd broke up into little groups, and I slipped out the door.

I found my way to my office. I noticed the door was unlocked. I reached into my duffel bag for my purse and then thought better of it. I decided that I knew the person waiting for me in the office. So I simply picked up the duffel, swung the door open and said, "Good evening Professor McGonagall."

She was smiling, "You were expecting me, then?"

"You can't teach an old dog new tricks."

Minerva laughed and said, "I'll ignore the implication and just .-.-." She leaped up and demonstrated what she would do.

When we broke for air, she said, "Congratulations! I hear that young Cedric took the golden ring."

"Actually, it was a golden medal, but yes, he won the whole shooting match."

She slapped my rear end and declared, "I don't know that I'll ever forgive you for not taking me along."

"Well, it wasn't exactly my idea, you know. You could have come—even if it were only to see a couple of games."

She grimaced her disapproval. Then she said that she had to prepare for the resumption of classes and headed for the door. At the door she turned and said, "I hope that you've learned something from this little fiasco."

I just smiled sweetly and said, "I hope so, too."

Evacuation

I was headed for Minerva's office when the hubbub started. I was walking up the stairs toward Gryffindor tower when there was a flow of people down the stairs. At the head of them was Minerva. I waited for them and joined her on the way down. "What's up?"

She ran down the stairs and talked as she did. "Ginny Weasley was carried off by the monster. A couple of witnesses saw her being carried off by a snake-like creature."

"Where did this happen?"

"In the lower level. But no one saw where they went."

Everyone seemed to have assembled in the main entrance. Dumbledore was there. When we all arrived, he announced, "There's been an abduction. Ms. Ginny Weasley has been kidnapped. We can no longer allow students to remain at Hogwarts. Everyone is to return to their house and pack immediately. As soon as everyone is packed, the House Heads and Prefects will accompany the houses to the Hogwarts Express Station. The Express is being sent up here as quickly as possible. With a little luck, it will be here before midnight.

"Everyone's parents will be sent owls informing them to arrive at the station and pick up their students in the morning. We're estimating that the Express will arrive at King's Cross at approximately 10 AM. Now, Prefects and House Heads, accompany your students to your Houses to pack. We'll assemble here and then all will walk to the station as soon as everyone is present. Now, let's go, let's go, let's go."

Since I didn't have a house that I was assigned to, I asked Minerva what I should do. "Go, up with the Hufflepuffs. Keep them moving. I want them out first, if possible."

"Good, I'm on my way."

I found Professor Grubbily-Plank at the head of the procession of Hufflepuffs and reported for duty. I asked her, "What do you want to do?"

She seemed stumped by that, but an idea occurred to me, "I'll go to the back and make sure there aren't any stragglers."

She nodded and said, "Good. Get on it."

I worked my way back. As I went, I shouted, "Hufflepuff Prefects, where are you?" A girl and a boy raised their hands. "What are your names?"

The girl's was Stanton and the boy's was Burbidge.

"OK. Stanton, stay in the middle of the line. Make sure everyone keeps moving. Burbidge, come with me. We're going to the back to make sure there aren't any stragglers."

He and I trotted to the back of the line. Everyone was pretty anxious to get away, so we didn't have to do much urging. Burbidge asked me, "Do you think the Weasley girl is dead?"

"I doubt it."

Burbidge asked, "Why? Surely that monster must have killed her by now." One of the students ahead of us looked over her shoulder and said, "Sure. Why else grab her?"

"No. She'd have been dead already if it were just murder. I don't know what it's up to, but it's not murder—at least not immediately."

"What's going to happen to her then?"

"I don't know. But I know this. After you guys are safely off, we're going back in to rescue her."

Burbidge looked at me quizzically, "You're going back in?"

"Yeh, so?"

"But, you're a Squibb. What can a Squibb do?"

"I'm not going to tell you, but I'm not completely helpless just because I'm a Squibb."

We reached the entrance to Hufflepuff house. Everyone trooped through into the dorm and Burbidge and I were last. People were milling around in the common room. I stood on an end table. "Listen up

156

everyone. Everyone needs to go to their rooms right now. Pack one suitcase. Just clothes and wand. You'll be down here in 15 minutes. Bring nothing that you can't carry yourself without magic. Now, move."

People started moving but not quickly enough for me. "If you aren't packed in 15 minutes, you're leaving without anything."

People moved faster. Even Burbidge ran up to his room. In ten minutes people started showing up with suitcases.

Grubbily-Plank was down with her suitcase and was lining up the students, youngest first. I said to her, "You lead the way again and Stanton, Burbidge and I'll take up positions as before."

She asked if I really wanted to be in the rear. I answered, "Yes. Don't worry about me. Let's just get going."

She led the way out the entrance while Burbidge and I waited for the rest of the students to file out. As we waited, I got out my purse and pulled my Glock. I thought for a minute about whether to leave the safety on or not. I finally decided that "safety on" was the best policy. We started out the door ourselves when one of the kids up the line apparently slipped and fell. He moaned and then tried to get up. Immediately he slipped down to the floor again. I shouted for Grubbily-Plank to stop. Everyone did pretty quickly. Burbidge and I reached the kid. He had fallen into the false step that shows up just when it's the most inconvenient. I helped the kid up and asked him, "Can you walk?" He shook his head, apparently trying to hold back pain. I looked around for someone who could help him walk. Burbidge might be a 6th year but he had a small frame and I didn't think that he could serve as a support for him very far. Then I saw him. He looked like he must be a 7th year even though he was among the 4th years. I shouted over to him, "You. Yes, you in the red robes. What's your name?"

He answered, "Diggory, Cedric Diggory. What can I do, professor Wendt?" Of course, in the dim light, I didn't recognize him.

"Come over here. Can you give this young man a hand walking to the train?"

He was over by us in two strides. He lifted the fellow like he was a twig. He smiled and asked the kid, "Does that hurt?"

The kid shook his head but still didn't say anything.

157

I said, "OK. Let's go. Burbidge, take the suitcase. AND EVERYONE, watch this step. I don't want to have another sprained ankle."

We got going again. Burbidge now had two suitcases and he was having a hard time, but he was bearing up well. I said, "Burbidge, I'll take one of those suitcases, but I want to have both hands free until we get out of the castle. Then I'll take it."

He huffed and puffed as we went down the stairs. "What's that in your hand, some kind of strange wand?"

"I guess you could say so."

"But I thought you were a Squibb. No offense meant." He added quickly.

"None taken. Yes, I am. But this wand doesn't require magic."

I could see his eyes widen even in the dim light in the castle. "Really, how does that work? Could a Muggle use it?"

"I don't have time to explain and yes, a Muggle could use it."

"Wow!"

"Right. Keep moving."

We had reached the bottom of the last flight of stairs. Diggory was holding up pretty well with the kid he was helping and Burbidge was doing OK with the extra suitcase. I was keeping my eyes open trying to look every direction at once. When we got to the bottom of the stairs, we ground to a halt. It wasn't clear what the problem was. I didn't like it, but I didn't really want to move to the front and leave Burbidge in the back by himself.

After a couple of minutes, I decided that I had to chance it. I told Burbidge to keep his eyes open and shout out if he heard or saw anything unusual. Then I worked my way forward.

When I got close to the front, I saw what the problem was. There was another house trying to evacuate at the same time. Everyone was stuck. When I reached Grubbily-Plank, I found her in a heated discussion with Snape. "But look here, Severus, we've got to keep our houses together so that we know if we've missed someone. One of us has to wait for the other to go first."

Snape smiled and said, "That would be Slytherin."

Grubbily-Plank looked mad and as though she weren't ready to give up. I reached them and said, "Look, we don't have time to argue.

158

We've got to get everyone out. You go first Snape. Don't doddle. The Hufflepuff house will be happy to let the brave Slytherin's go first." Snape looked ready to snarl, but he got his house moving.

Grubbily-Plank laughed as soon as they were well on their way. "I don't think I've ever heard anyone tell Snape off like that."

"Well, there's always a first time. I just want him out of the way so we can get going. I'm on my way to the back. Let's just get out of here."

I reached the back, and Burbidge asked what the problem was. I said, "We need a traffic cop."

He was confused by the reference. But we were moving again, and he had to pay attention to the two suitcases. Shortly the head of our line reached the main entrance and started out. Burbidge said, "At last. You can take one of the suitcases."

"Not until we all get out the main gate." Burbidge groaned. But this close to being out, I sure wasn't going to put my gun away to carry a suitcase until I was sure we were completely out. We eventually walked through the main gate. As soon as we were a hundred paces out, I turned, put the gun back in my purse, and took one of the suitcases from Burbidge.

After a short while, it started to get light ahead. In a few minutes, I realized what was happening. Everyone was lighting their wands and holding it high in the air. The amount of light was tremendous. The entire area was well lit. I could see that the Ravenclaws were behind us. I wondered where the Gryffindors were, but we had to keep moving. I couldn't leave my spot in the parade to find out what had happened to Minerva. We eventually reached the train station. I told Burbidge to make sure people didn't wander off. I headed on up the line and reached Grubbily-Plank. She had apparently just talked to Dumbledore, who wanted each house to stay together and take a headcount to make sure that nobody was lost.

Grubbily-Plank gave me permission to leave the Hufflepuffs because I really didn't know her students and I couldn't help in the headcount. "You go find Minerva. I'm sure that you'd much rather be with her than here."

"Thanks. I'll see you when the Express arrives."

159

I discovered that the Gryffindors had been the final house to leave the castle. Minerva was at the head of her house's line and was just starting to take a count as I arrived. "Oh, there you are Wendt. You know the house pretty well. Help Percy Weasley and Crowley with the count." I started working my way back the line, counting years. They were all grouped together by year, and it seemed that everyone was there among the 1ˢᵗ years. Apparently, Weasley and Pam Crowley were working their way from the back. We met at the 2ⁿᵈ years. We all looked over the 2ⁿᵈ years and we all agreed. "Where the hell is Ron, and Potter!"

That brought the other two Weasleys out from further in the back. Fred said, "I haven't seen Ron since we reached the Fat Lady's portrait."

"Me, either." Chimed in George.

▽

We had to go back to Minerva and report that Ron, and Harry were missing. Just then Dumbledore showed up and asked for our count. Minerva reported that Ron and Harry were missing. He glanced up heavenward and exclaimed, "Why is it always those two?"

"Well, now we have three kids to go back for." I commented.

Dumbledore agreed and said, "I can't order anyone to go back with me."

I said immediately, "I'm going back." Minerva said, "Me too!".

Dumbledore disagreed, "Minerva, both of us can't go, since we're the heads of the school. I outrank you. You're going to have to stay and represent the school when the Express arrives and when any parents do, though I've insisted that they not show up. They'd just be a nuisance and a hazard to the student body."

She had her dander up, but she didn't really have anything she could say in disagreement, so she said, "Well, Wendt can't go. He doesn't have magic."

Dumbledore agreed, "Sorry, Professor Wendt. You really can't come."

I disagreed, "Look, I want to go and there's no reason that I shouldn't. I have my own 'magic'. I pulled out my purse.

I started to open it but Dumbledore said, "You don't have to get that thing out in front of the students. OK, you can come."

Minerva was now really angry. "You're not going to let him go with you!"

"Oh, I'm afraid I am." She turned to me and said in her frustration, "If you get yourself killed, I'll never talk to you again." It occurred to me that it wasn't as impossible a threat as it seemed.

I put my arms around her, and we kissed. We broke and I said, "I'll see you."

"God damn it, you'd better see me." She was holding back tears.

We started off back to the castle. I had my Glock out, still safety on. Dumbledore said, "I'm glad you have that with you."

"Me too."

"Do you have any idea what Slytherin's monster is?" I asked hopefully.

"Not the slightest."

"Me, either." We walked along for a few more minutes and I asked, 'What's your plan?"

"Don't have one."

"I was afraid you'd say that." And we went on in utter silence. Dumbledore had his wand lit dimly—just enough to let me see roots and rocks just before I tripped on them. As we approached the main gates of the castle, Dumbledore lifted his wand, and the gates swung back on their hinges. We went on to the main entrance to the castle, and the doors opened of their own accord. The interior was utterly dark. As we crossed the threshold, I put a bullet in the chamber and flicked the safety off. The sounds seemed to echo. We stood in the doorway a minute allowing our eyes to adjust to the dark.

As we did that, Dumbledore commented, "It's funny what sounds are comforting, and what aren't. Take the sound of you readying your weapon. It is music to my ears. There's no sound with a wand being raised, but that metallic, mechanical klunk is strangely reassuring."

"Yeah. I was thinking exactly the same thing."

Just then there was a scream from somewhere higher up in the castle. Dumbledore, said softly, "Follow me. That came from the 3rd floor, I believe."

With that he bounded off toward the main stairs. I followed him as quickly as I could, but he was making better time up the stairs than I could! He rounded a bend in the stairs, and I lost sight of him for a few seconds. He was heading straight up toward the 3rd floor. I lost sight of him again when he reached the 3rd floor, but I saw which hall he entered. I followed him as quickly as I could.

When I got into the hall, I could see a light in the distance and what looked like several people huddled on the floor. As we approached, it became clear who they were. I saw Potter and Ron Weasley standing over a girl. It was Ginny Weasley, of course, though I could not see her clearly yet. Also Lockhart was seated on the floor, staring around the hall like a tourist without the slightest concern in the world.

Dumbledore reached them and looked quickly over the tableau. He said, "I'll take her to the hospital wing. Wendt, help Ron walk there. And, Wendt, make sure that Lockhart doesn't do any more damage." Dumbledore strode off, levitating Ms. Weasley. He left us far behind. I helped Ron hobble along, and I questioned him as we went. "Ron, what happened? How did you find Ginny?"

He gazed at me and said, "That Lockhart was going to run off without even trying to find Ginny. We forced him to come with us. He tried to escape and was going to wipe our memories clean."

At this point Lockhart interrupted, "This is an amazing place isn't it? Look! The pictures move!"

I looked over at him. He wore a look of wonder at every turn in the passageway. I commented, "I suppose it backfired. But why did he try to do it at all? He didn't strike me as the vicious type."

"Yeh. He used my wand, and it really hasn't been working right since we crashed into the Whomping Willow.

"But why did he try to wipe your memories?"

"He was a big fake, you know? He never did any of the things that he wrote about. He wrote about other wizard's adventures and never had any of his own. He was afraid that we'd expose him if he didn't.-.-. uh..-.-."

"I get the picture, but what happened to your sister? And how did you rescue her from the monster? And where is the monster now?"

"I wish I knew the answers to those questions. All I know is that Harry killed the monster and rescued my sister and somehow He Who Must Not be Named was involved and well, you'll have to talk with Harry about all that."

I was about to ask Harry about those questions when we arrived at the hospital wing. Madame Pomfrey took charge of Lockhart. Dumbledore insisted that he and Ron spend the night in the hospital wing and that Harry be allowed to get a good night's sleep. He sent me off to bring everybody back to the castle.

"But what do I say when everyone asks me what happened and why is it safe to be back in the castle?"

Dumbledore said, "Oh, isn't it obvious Wendt? The monster is dead. All the students in the hospital wing are going to be all right. What more does anybody need to know for now?"

I admitted that I didn't know, and I trudged out of the castle and off to the train station. By the time I got there it was almost midnight. The Express hadn't arrived yet. I got the Heads of Houses together for a quick conference. They all wanted to know the same things I did, but I could only repeat Dumbledore's explanation (such as it was) and instructions. They got all the students going back to the castle. Minerva pulled me aside and insisted that I tell her the real story.

"Look, I opened the bag completely. I didn't reserve anything."

She was clearly exasperated and showed it in the snappy reply, "But you were there. What did you see? You must have found Potter and the Weasleys. What did they say?"

"Yes, we found them all—and Lockhart, the stinker. He tried to sneak out without looking for Ms. Weasley. The boys found him and forced him to go along to help find her. You're not going to believe this, but he actually tried to use a memory charm on them to wipe their memories. At least, that's what Ron Weasley claims, but it backfired. That's for sure; I saw him. He seems to have no recollection of anything. Somehow Potter killed the Monster, and somehow Valdemort was involved."

"Well that's the most confused jumble of crazy things that I've ever heard. What good was it telling me that?"

"Well, you insisted. That's everything I know."

We walked for a while in silence, and suddenly Minerva exclaimed something under her breath and looked over at me. "We forgot about the Express. Someone has to meet it and tell them that we don't need them. Be a good fellow, go back, and wait for them. Invite them to stay at the castle overnight. If they come, bring them up to Gryffindor tower and let them in. You can put them up in one of the vacant rooms on the boys' side. "

I stared at her and groaned. She said, 'Oh, don't be such a wuss. They ought to be along any minute. And you can stay in Gryffindor tower too." Her expression softened, and she added, "I'll make it worth your while."

"OK. OK. But you'd better."

'Believe me, I will."

I arrived at the train station for the third time that night and waited until the train arrived at 1 AM. There were two people who got off the train—the engineer and the conductor. I explained the situation and they were hopping mad.

"Bloody monster! Why couldn't it have got itself killed 8 hours earlier?"

I said, "Well, there is a bright side to this. You're welcome to stay for the night at the castle AND stay for breakfast. It's really worth it. Hogwarts has great meals. Breakfast is wonderful."

The conductor was a little mollified. The engineer was still pretty unhappy. We walked mostly in silence to the castle. I told them that they'd share a dorm room in the Gryffindor Tower. They'd both been to Hogwarts, but neither had been in Gryffindor. The engineer was feeling a little better at the idea of seeing the interior of Gryffindor.

We got to the Fat Lady's portrait about 2 AM. We had to wake her up. I gave her the password, and grumbling, she opened the door.

The conductor asked why I'd let them hear the password. I answered, "It's easy. The password gets changed every couple of weeks. You're not going to be back before it's changed. And I trust you guys."

We walked up to the boy's dorm, and I checked the roster to find an empty room. We went there, and I invited them to make themselves at home, telling them that breakfast was over at 9 AM, and they'd better not be late. I left them still not entirely happy, but progressively becoming more content with the situation.

164

I went down to the Common Room, and as I entered, said, "Hello, Minerva." She wasn't visible, but almost immediately, a tabby walked out from behind an armchair and transmuted to a beautiful lady —Minerva. She walked up to me and put her arms around my shoulders and kissed me. We went up to her room.

As we entered, I asked her, "I suppose that I'll have to get up early before any of the kids do.

The next day I slept in—it was Saturday. Of course, sleeping in meant until 6:30 AM. I dressed and found my way down to my room. I showered, changed, and went to the Great Hall. I was just about the only person there. Minerva joined me. We talked about what had happened. Hardly anyone knew much about the events of the previous evening. I was hoping that Dumbledore would meet with the teachers and fill us in on details. Minerva played "footsie" with me discreetly as we ate. I teased her, "You know, one of these days Snape is going to catch us at this and that will be it for our careers."

Minerva laughed and kicked me discreetly in the shin.

Dumbledore announced a teacher's meeting in the Teacher's Lounge after breakfast. Minerva and I left early and found a small sofa on which we sat. We talked tête-à-tête about the end of term and what we'd do in the break. We'd almost forgotten about the events of the previous night when the rest of the teachers started filtering in. Minerva put her right arm around my shoulder and leaned back. Dumbledore entered the room.

He stood before the fireplace and paced for a moment before speaking. "It's hard to begin one of these talks. Even with some very good news, the bad news is still bitter."

He sighed and began. "The good news is very good news. First, Ms. Weasley, who was the latest victim of Slytherin's monster has been found and rescued. She's in the hospital wing right now and is expected to recover completely within a couple of days.

"Second, Slytherin's monster has been slain. It was Harry Potter who did it, and Hogwarts will be always grateful for this courageous act.

"Third, the mandrakes that Professor Grubbily-Sprout has been growing are very near maturity. It will be possible shortly to resuscitate Ms. Grainger, Mr. Creevy, Mr Finch-Fletchley, and Mr. Filch's cat." He hesitated for breath and added, "Oh, yes, and Sir Nicholas as well.

"The sad news is that Professor Lockhart was injured by a landslide in the tunnel where Slytherin's monster lived. He was struck on the head and is now suffering from amnesia, which we all hope is of short duration. Questions?"

Snape raised his hand, "Professor, you keep referring to the monster as Slytherin's monster. Would you please explain why it's Slytherin's monster?"

It was one of the few times that I'd seen Dumbledore exasperated. He said, "Oh, Severus, you know perfectly well that there've been legends and stories going back to the time of Slytherin himself that there was such a thing.

"Furthermore—and more important, there have actually been recent attacks on Muggle-born."

Snape smiled and said, "But isn't Ms. Weasley the child of two magical parents?"

This is the closest that I've ever seen Dumbledore come to true anger. He didn't say a word for what seemed like five minutes, but probably was less than a minute. He took a long deep breath and seemed to be struggling to restrain himself. Finally he said, "Professor Snape, you know perfectly well that there are reasons that Ms. Weasley was attacked that had nothing to do with being Muggle-born.

"Please, let's stick with the main points. Are there other questions?"

Sinistra stood, 'What exactly was the monster, whomever it belonged to?"

Dumbledore seemed relieved to have a definite, non-controversial question to answer. "Well, Professor Sinistra, it was a basilisk."

She replied, almost as if speaking to herself, "Of course. Basilisks kill all who look upon their eyes."

Dumbledore said, "Yes. Rather like the Greek legend of Medusa. However, fortunately, no one of the current victims saw the basilisk directly. They all saw her reflected—in a pool of water or through a camera lens or with a mirror—again, like Perseus. Mr. Potter was lucky. Faulks, the phoenix, clawed out the serpent's eyes, which allowed him to slay the creature with the sword of Gryffindor."

Snape laughed a short, bitter bark and asked, "And just how did he get that?"

"It was delivered by Faulks in the sorting hat."

Snape shook his head again and said, "It's amazing what he gets away with!"

I couldn't resist standing myself and said to Snape, "Severus, you'd think that you were hoping that he'd been killed by the basilisk."

He turned sharply to look at me and then slowly turned back, "It's just that he has more luck than any person deserves, and he gets away with all the pranks under the heavens."

That seemed to end everyone's appetite for more so there weren't any more questions. Everyone found something very interesting at their feet to look at. Dumbledore dismissed us, and we slowly filtered out. Dumbledore remained while Minerva and I were among the last to leave. He commented, "I'm glad that at least the two of you enjoyed something this morning."

Surprised, I looked up at him. Minerva didn't give the slightest sign that he'd said anything unusual. Dumbledore went on, "I know perfectly well that the two of you didn't spend the night alone. Don't be so coy. Be seeing you." He left us alone in the room.

Minerva put her arms around my shoulders and kissed me seriously.

The rest of the term was blessedly back to the tedium of writing exams and then grading them. I still had times when the funny letter grades of Hogwarts sent me into fits of hysterics or insanity. Minerva had taken to writing and grading exams in my office with me. We had completely different subjects, but we were constantly appealing to each other for help in grading.

At one point while I was grading, I broke out into gales of laughter. Minerva raised her eyebrows at me and asked, "OK. What have the numbskulls done this time? Did they mistake Mowgli for Macbeth? Or maybe Tom Jones for Tom Sawyer?"

I was laughing far too hard to answer. As a matter of fact, I'd reached the point where I couldn't breathe and didn't have enough air in my lungs to make an audible laugh. I was walking or more like staggering around the office slapping my thighs, trying to regain control of myself. When I finally did, I rasped out, "No. No. The paper I was grading was really quite good. I had just marked it with an 'E'.

"Then I realized that I hadn't marked a single correction on the paper and I started wondering how I could mark a perfect paper with an 'E'. Then," and I started laughing again, but quickly controlled myself, "And then, I remember that in Muggle grades, an 'E' is a terrible grade. That struck my funny bone just right and I couldn't control myself."

"So, are you going to give the paper an 'O'?"

"No. Even though there's no flaw in it, there just isn't anything extraordinary about it either. There's no special insight or nice turns of a phrase or even humor."

"Sounds like it was written by Snape."

'Oh, Snape's got humor. It's just extremely dry humor."

"You mean like the Atacama desert?"

"Yeh."

The last day of the term, I was in a funk as usual. There was only the long train ride to look forward to. Minerva had selflessly (of course) volunteered again to ride back to town on the train (coincidentally, I was the only other teacher on the train) rather than disapparate back. She truly selflessly spent most of the trip patrolling the train to make sure nothing really bad happened. She would drop by for about 15 minutes every hour. Sometimes, I'd accompany her. If I didn't, I'd drop my writing project and we'd talk or talk and neck or just neck.

The time was golden and long enough that I actually could lose myself in writing and enjoy the occasional interruptions. In one of them we were talking about what we'd do after we arrived. I said that I'd gotten my old attic room from my old landlord. She was a little bothered by that, "I suppose Miss Blonde Art Student still lives there."

"Actually, she doesn't. My landlord told me that the term after I'd returned to school, she'd finally graduated, had found a job in a graphic design firm, and had moved into the city."

"Well, I hope so. I'll come along."

"What? Come along? Don't you trust me?"

"It's not exactly that. Although it's true that I definitely don't trust the blonde. But what I was really thinking about is that every time you leave Hogwarts for Summer holiday, you nearly get yourself killed. I was thinking that it might be a good idea for me to be along."

"Oh, come on. What can possibly happen this time?"

"I don't care what possibly can happen. I just know it's not going to happen. So, just get used to it." She sniffed and that was apparently that. There was no way that I could prevent her from coming along, so I might as well enjoy it.

The trip to London via Hogwart's Express was its usual amalgam of pleasure—getting to sit in the Teacher's Car and read or talk or .-.-. with Minerva—and pain—having to patrol the other cars making sure that nobody was thrown off the train or choking on a weird flavor of Bernie Botts Every Flavor Beans. For example in my first year, a 3rd year girl had gotten a vomit-flavored bean. She was very succeptible to suggestion and was gagging and vomiting herself almost the whole trip. She'd eventually ended up in the Teacher's Car or at least the lavatory of the Teacher's Car for most of the trip. Then I didn't have a refuge to retreat to throughout the whole time.

The ride was uneventful this time. After a couple of hours of writing, I enjoyed the view. It was early summer, and the English countryside was beautiful. I got a magazine from my bag and did some reading. But as we neared London, I began to get that feeling of specialness that all long trips excite in me as they ebb away. We pulled into the King's Cross Station, and I began to wonder if something would happen on the way out of the station. Of course, this time Minerva would be along.

We left the train among the hubbub of the students and parents reuniting. Minerva had to hang around until all kids and parents had been accounted for. There were two pairs of parents that arrived late. I didn't recognize the one set but the other set I would never mistake for anyone else. It was the Malfoy's. They profusely apologized to Draco for being late. He took it stoically.

They never thought of apologizing to Minerva and me—not that I cared much. Minerva was quietly dignified. Finally we were the last

169

two people on the platform. Even the conductor and engineer had left. "Well, finally, we can get going. Minerva, would you like a bite?"

"I thought you'd never ask. Sure. How about the Cauldron?"

"Fine by me."

We disapparated to the Cauldron. I was so hungry that I didn't even complain about disapparating. Tom, the Barman, was there. I sometimes wonder if he ever leaves the bar. Anyway, we were seated in a cozy corner and had ordered. She leaned across the table slightly and asked, "What REALLY are your plans for the summer?" At the same time, she nudged my calf under the table.

"Well," I shrugged, "I'll hole up in my apartment, write, read, go for walks in the park. Occasionally I"ll go to a play or concert—I hope with you. Nothing special. What about you."

"I was thinking shorter term—like tonight." And she ran her toe up my calf.

"Well, now that you mention it, it occurs to me that I've never spent the night at the Cauldron. Have you?"

"A few times—when I had business in Diagon Alley a couple of days in a row."

"Really? But if you can disapparate here instantly, what is the advantage of spending the night here?"

"Well, you know, a special night."

"Oh, oh. Of course. Are the rooms nice?"

"Actually, they are. Most have a four poster bed," her toe inscribed an arc down my calf, "Some even have a canopy."

"I see. Bed's a big deal for you."

Her eyes looked demurely down. "You might say so."

"Well, then I'd like to find out what the beds of the Cauldron are like. A guided tour, you might say."

She smiled, not demurely at all, and we had a pleasant supper. Tom was happy to sell us a room for the night, and I discovered that Minerva was right about the beds. Not only were they picturesque but they were also very comfortable—provided good support for tossing and turning and tumbling.

The next morning we had a continental breakfast at the Cauldron and Minerva consented to take the Tube to the neighborhood of my apartment. My landlord had my apartment ready and gave me a little lecture about guests in the rooms. I suppose because Minerva was along. I dropped my duffle in my apartment and we went out to the street. We took a leisurely walk up toward our favorite alley. We stood at its mouth and wondered just how long we could stand there without attracting attention. We talked about little inconsequentials and I finally said, "Minerva. It's time to go, I suppose."

"Yes, you're right." And with that—no more ado—just a hug and quick squeeze of my ass—she was gone.

"Cheese and Rice," I said aloud to no one.

What I did on my Summer Vacation

I had given in to my Mom and Dad's desire to see me and meet Minerva. I invited them to come for a visit during the summer holiday. After a trans-Atlantic telephone call or two, we agreed that they would come the week after Wimbledon. They'd come for a week, and they would really, yes really, get to meet Minerva.

I'd taken the attic room from my old landlord again. It was nice having a nearly sure inexpensive room in London for summer holiday. Of course, the reason it was sure was that nobody else would live in that drafty, ill-lit, low-ceilinged, small attic apartment. Of course, Mom and Dad couldn't stay with me, as much as they insisted that they wanted to.

In the meantime while I waited, though, it was good to be able to read the *Times*, do some writing, and occasionally see Minerva. It was the only time that I could make trans-Atlantic calls to my parents—other than Christmas. And that's how the trouble began. In my first call home of the summer, my Mom and to a lesser extent my Dad pressed me to let them come over for a visit. They were particularly interested in meeting Minerva. I tried to put them off, but Mom was determined that if she didn't actually get to meet this shadowy Minerva, she wouldn't believe that she existed.

So, one day after an outing with Minerva to the Serpentine, I found myself asking her if she minded meeting my parents. She surprised me. "That would be great!"

Then she added, "We'll finally see the end of your silly infatuation with me once you have to actually admit to another person that your 'girl' (she pronounced it "gerl") friend hasn't seen the sunny side of 40 in a number years."

That made my halting decision into a firm determination. I would show her whether I was a true lover or not. When I said as much, she laughed. It wasn't a mean laugh, just the laugh of someone who loves you and wants you to give up your fantasies.

So, the next time that I talked with my parents, I called their bluff (I didn't think they would really come—they hardly traveled outside their county, let alone across an ocean). But they proved the validity of the old lawyers' dictum that you should never ask a question when you're not sure what the answer might be. In this case, the answer was an emphatic "Yes, When?"

That knocked me back on my heels. I thought furiously trying to come up with delaying tactics. I decided that I could reasonably suggest that they come after the big European events and thus get better air fares. The big events all happened about the same time—the running of the bulls in Pamplona, Bastille day, Wimbledon—that would put us in mid-July. It would give me some time to prepare for the onslaught of my parents. Who knew? Maybe a miracle would happen before then, and they wouldn't be able to come. Maybe the value of the dollar would plunge. Maybe my Dad's consulting business would have an emergency. Maybe terrorists would hijack an airplane and go to Cuba. Maybe Minerva and I would elope and make the trip moot.

So, I suggested mid July, which they bought. My mom hates spending money, and the suggestion of bargain fares later in the summer sold her on the idea. The rest of the month of June, I was reminded almost daily of the up-coming trip. My mom wrote daily letters asking what the weather would be like, could we see Buckingham Palace; could we go to see a play at Stratford-upon-Avon? What was Minerva's favorite color? What was her family like? If nothing else, the stream of questions gave me lots of topics for conversation with Minerva. They weren't always happy talks.

For example, when asked about her favorite color, her reaction was, "You don't know my favorite color!"

"I think so, but I just want to be dead sure." Bad choice of words.

"You'll be dead all right, if you're not sure." This was followed by a pregnant pause. I pretended that I didn't realize that she wanted me to provide that favorite color. That gave me a minute to come up with an answer. I furiously thought about the colors that she usually wore. All I could think of was Gryffindor scarlet. She said one word that many a student has dreaded in her classes, "Well?"

I tried to say the color nonchalantly, "Scarlet." I added quickly at her scowl, "Gryffindor scarlet.'

She hesitated and said, "I suppose that I can't fault that, but for future reference, it's Lavender."

Counting myself lucky to be able to walk away with my head, I avoided the danger that many a student has fallen into when lucking out in such situations—being cocky. I said absolutely nothing and let her provide the next topic of conversation. I was rewarded by a change in topic to the question of what kind of food my family liked. That answer was easy. They liked anything provided that it was meat and potatoes and the meat had better be beef—and none of your fancy, shmancy beef bourguignon or shish-kebob.

Minerva laughed and asked, "You mean they don't like haggis?"

I just made a face, and we passed on to more pleasant topics. The topic that I'd been avoiding so far was just how much we would reveal to my parents about her. One evening over dinner at the Leaky Cauldron I raised the topic.

Her comment was, "Well, surely you're going to tell them everything." I winced at that, but she went on, "Oh, come on, you're not going to be like that mom of Finegan who never told her fiancé that she was a witch until after the wedding?"

I asked, "How did she manage that? It would be a lot easier for us to do that."

She just frowned that incredulous frown that said, "I can't believe that you're even considering that."

My answer was, "There's a lot of cultural shock built into this situation. I think that we ought to take the shocks one at a time. First, give them a couple of days to get used to England. Second, give them a couple of days to get used to my having a gerl (I poked a little fun at Minerva's accent) friend who's a bit older than I am."

Minerva snorted, "A bit older than you? A bit older than you! I could be your mother!"

"No you couldn't. Since when do 14-year old girls have babies?"

"Since every day! Sometimes I wonder if you have any sense at all." Her smile belied her words. There was a twinkle in her eyes, and we both broke into laughter. She recovered first and said, "OK. I don't mind going slow, provided that they know everything before they leave."

An idea occurred to me. I screwed my face into a grimace, "Wait a minute! Isn't there some sort of rule about not revealing that you're a witch to Muggles?"

She shook an index finger at me, "Nice try, but the rule is against doing magic before Muggles—not admitting to being a witch."

"Seems like a distinction without a difference to me. How can you do one without the other?"

Minerva didn't have a ready answer but just sat staring into my eyes—an occupation that I wouldn't interrupt for anything.

Finally, I broke the silence. "Yes, yes. They'll have to know everything. I just wish that I didn't have to be in the room to tell them—especially my mom. Just promise me that they don't have to meet any other wizards or witches before they leave."

She thought that over a minute. "Well, I guess that my sister would be a bit much to take along with everything else. We can save her for another time."

I breathed a sigh of relief—silently.

After that, I suggested that my parents come July 17 and return on the 25th. These dates were safely after all the big events in Europe and well before I would have to start preparing for the new school term. My plan was to spend the first three days touring the country. I didn't dare do that with Minerva along. It would be far too likely that she'd insist on joining us by disapparation or, God forbid, even suggest that we all disapparate somewhere. I had visions of one of my parents being splynched. No, far better to tour the countryside on our own.

Then, the next three days would be getting acquainted with Minerva. We'd just tour places in London, travel by underground, tour buses and cabs. There were far more things to see than we could in three days. Minerva would enjoy them too.

The last three days were the real problem for me. I'd have to introduce my parents to the inner witch. I really didn't have a good idea about how to do that. I'd never had to do anything so dangerous before. Despite watching reruns of the TV series "Bewitched" as a kid, I really didn't think that it had much of anything to say to me about people learning about witches. I ran through lots of different scenarios and they all ended badly. The closest that I could come to something that seemed doable was having Minerva start doing little magic things and thus force my parents to confront her with being magical. The only problem that I saw in that was that my parents might think they were going crazy. So, I stopped thinking about it, hoping that my subconscious would come up with a brilliant idea if I only slept on it for a few days.

When we reached July, I did my usual call home on July 4th. My parents were ecstatic about getting to come to England, meet all my friends and co-workers, and of course, see all the sights. I had to put a brake on that sort of talk. They were never going to meet my co-workers, except Minerva, until they understood about wizards and witches. Also, of course, I had few friends outside of Hogwarts. Most of them were wizards. So, I emphasized how they would meet a few very close friends (I didn't specify just how few) and that we'd mostly do sight-seeing—a good way to spend time on a first visit to England. Their next visit would be one where we would concentrate on friends and lovers (I didn't use the word).

They seemed satisfied with that program, but I suspected that my mom would not be satisfied with meeting one or two very good friends. I decided that I would burn that bridge when we came to it.

For the first two-thirds of the visit, I had a long list of things to do. They included visiting the Cotswolds, the city of Bath, the White Cliffs, Stratford-upon-Avon, Cambridge. They could pick from those sites for our first phase of the visit. Then, the sights of London were so numerous that I decided that I'd just let my parents pick without guidance from me. I was sure that they'd have plenty of ideas without any help from me. Then there was the dark last third of the visit. I was afraid to speculate what would happen then.

So, as the days seemed to fly by as we approached the fateful ides of July, I couldn't help remembering that July was named for Julius Caesar and that he met his fate during the Ides of another month.

Heathrow

The seventeenth of July arrived, and I took the "Tube" to Heathrow bright and early. My parents' flight was to arrive at 10:15, but I wanted to be there a full hour in advance just in case. So, I was there well before their flight touched down. I was waiting at their gate where I was greeted by a tight hug from my Mom and a brief hug from my Dad with a brisk handshake. I was ready to take them to their B&B by "Tube", but they insisted on taking a cab and I couldn't entirely blame them. My Mom had packed two steamer trunks. My dad had a carry-on and a suit bag. Dragging around the steamer trunks on the "Tube" would be a hassle.

I'd reserved a room for them the previous day, so their room was ready immediately. They didn't have to wait around for the room to be ready. I'd learned that lesson when I first moved to London. I suggested that they take a nap for as long as they could. Then we'd go out for a little light sight-seeing and return early to help them get accustomed to the time difference. My Mom was against the idea, but when she saw the bed, she changed her mind. I left and promised them that I'd be back by 2 PM. I'd be waiting in the lobby whenever they wanted to come down and join me.

I went out, bought a *Times*, and worked my way through it in the lobby. They didn't need to know that I'd done that. As a matter of fact, when they did show up around 3, I was still puzzling out the last few words in the *Times* crossword.

My Mom asked if I'd been waiting for them there the whole time. I could honestly tell them that I'd not. In truth, I'd left the B&B for a light lunch. I was careful to leave for a late lunch so that if my Mom asked how long I'd been waiting, I could honestly say that it had been about an hour. Strictly true, but not entirely honest.

We found a tour bus and took an excursion, sitting in the open top deck of the bus. Fortunately, the weather was clement and we enjoyed the late sunset after stopping at a pub for dinner. They didn't drink, but they liked the idea of eating in an authentic English pub. The food was decent. I had ale with it. Of course, my Mom was worried about this bad habit that I'd picked up since I'd come to England, but that was the only difficult part of the day. We made an early evening of it, and I returned to my garret. One of the highlights of the evening was my presenting them with a cell phone. It was a pay as you go one. When the visit was over, they could take it home, where it couldn't be used as a souvenir.

The next day, they'd gotten a decent night's sleep and were quite ready to pick their own places to visit. I did insist on locations outside London. They picked the White Cliffs of Dover. I suggested that we rent a car for a couple of days and not return to London until we were going to do sight-seeing here. Then we'd just stay for the rest of the visit. My Dad thought that we might do another day trip or two out of London toward the end of the visit. I agreed that that was a possibility but said to myself that at that point there was the possibility that I would be disowned as a son and written out of the will.

I rented the car, which was not really easy because I didn't have a credit card. That bothered my Mom. Dad, who took nearly everything in his stride, declared that it took gumption to buck the trend to buy things on credit and that he was proud of my good judgment. Of course, it hadn't anything to do with judgment—just that nobody in the wizarding world accepted credit cards. He said that I could rent the car in his name and use his credit card. However, he'd let me pick up the cost of the rental. I actually never did repay him.

The weather was nice as we left the city behind and worked our way to the southeast. We arrived in the early afternoon and found a little hotel that seemed pleasant on the outside and actually was inside as well. After settling in, we strolled on the beach and saw the famous cliffs. My mom thought it was the most wonderful place in the world.

The Escapee

The last day before the world ended had arrived. At least that's the way I thought about it. Tomorrow Minerva and I were going to break the news to Mom and Dad. That would be going over the edge of the world. "Here there be dragons" (literally). I was determined to enjoy the last free day. My Dad and I both were interested in art, so we talked Mom into go to the National Portrait Gallery. We arrived there in the morning, and Minerva joined us in time for lunch. After lunch we continued touring the galleries, but I knew that Mom's energy was flagging. Even Dad was showing some signs of listlessness. Minerva, of course was going strong. We agreed to take a river cruise of the Thames. We took the cruise from Westminster, which was nearby. We took a cab anyway. Even Minerva seemed to enjoy it. I think that she had never taken a cruise before. We ended up at the Tower Pier.

After the cruise, we were close enough to dinner time that we looked for a place to eat. We ended up at the Gourmet Burger Kitchen. Minerva had her doubts, but two Midwestern Americans would not be denied a hamburger after days of dining on fish and chips and Chinese and even Indian cuisine. They got what they deserved. You don't go to London hoping for the ultimate hamburger paradise. We didn't find it. The hamburgers were decent—just not like home.

We had a good time though, reviling the food. My Mom got Minerva to promise to visit the States and be treated to a "real" gourmet hamburger. It actually turned out to be a pleasant meal. None of us were anxious to leave. My Mom insisted that we had to relinquish the table so that the poor server could make some money. This brought about a lively discussion of the difference between Europe and the United States.

My dad started it by declaring that he would reward the wait staff with a royal tip that would more than compensate them for the time that we enjoyed the table. My Mom wouldn't have any of it. Then Minerva entered the fray. She said, "Mrs. Wendt, the way that restaurants work in Europe is that the tips are quite small. Most of the waiter's income comes from his salary—not tips as I suppose it must be in the States. So, they really don't care how long you sit at a table. It makes very little difference to their income. And, of course, if Mr. Wendt, were to give them a good tip, they'd be especially happy that he sat at their table, regardless how long he stayed."

My Mom wouldn't give up, "Well, I worked as a waitress when I was coming up at college and let me assure you that waitresses care how long you sit at a table. And please call me Roberta."

Minerva was not a woman to be gainsaid, "Well, then," she paused as she forced the name out, "Roberta, let me assure you that I've known a fair number of waitresses myself, and they actually expect you to have a leisurely meal. That's the purpose of dining out—to enjoy the company of your friends and relatives."

Mom was still not entirely happy, but even she was having such a good time that she allowed herself to be convinced. By the time that we finished, it was becoming twilight. We walked about a bit and then took the Tube back to the vicinity of Charring Cross. We'd decided to spend the night at the Charring Cross Hotel. We were walking from the Tube station when my Mom said, out of the blue, "Don't you think it's turned cool."

My Dad, always the rational one, said, "Well, the sun is down and it does cool off."

Mom shivered noticeably and said, "No, this is more than that. I'm freezing."

I felt a little cool myself and even, well, depressed. What was going on? I looked over at Minerva who'd stopped walking and seemed to be very watchful. What was she wary of? I asked her, "What's going on, Minerva. You sense something."

All she would do was to shush me while she turned slowly about scanning the surroundings.

"Minerva, you're scaring me. What is it?"

Dad and Mom were staring at us, mouths agape. I was glad that they hadn't said anything because I knew that something serious was afoot. I stepped close to her and whispered to her, "Shouldn't we get moving?"

She nodded and said in a voice tight with tension that I rarely heard her use, "Come on, we should get indoors."

My dad was the first to speak, "What is this all about? Is there some sort of gang activity in this neighborhood?"

MInerva didn't answer but said, "Let's just drop into a pub if we see one. Otherwise, we'll go straight to the hotel."

The sense of an oppressive weight grew. We all slowed our pace, but Minerva urged us on.

Then suddenly, she pulled her wand from her handbag. That was it. I reached into my pocket to pull out my purse. But before I could get it out, she'd whirled and pointed her wand down an empty street. A white vapor shot out of her wand. It quickly resolved itself into a cat that shot down the empty street. Suddenly the sense of oppression lifted, and we all wondered what we had been so worried about.

Minerva turned to me and said softly, "We'd better get indoors quickly. They may be back."

My mom had caught that and asked, "Who might be back? I didn't see anyone."

Minerva relaxed and said under her voice so that only I could hear, "Of course, you silly Muggle, you can't see them."

We noticed a cheery-looking bar across the street and immediately crossed to it. We went in and found a table in a quiet corner and I offered to get drinks. Minerva immediately asked for a fire whiskey and then corrected to "just pick something strong." My mom asked for a gin and tonic. I'd never known her to drink anything but wine, but this seemed to be an unusual occasion. Dad asked for a glass of coke, and I decided on Dewars if they had it.

When I returned everyone was as silent as the grave. I distributed drinks and broke the silence, "OK. Minerva and I were going to hold this off until tomorrow, but I think now's the time for some honest discussion."

My mom sobbed and said, 'Don't tell me that you two are getting married."

Minerva sniffed and Dad frowned at Mom, but I had to start one of the harder conversations that I'd ever had. "Mom, no, we're not engaged. Though, I really wish I were announcing that.

"It's really in a way more serious."

Mom gasped and Dad asked, "You don't mean that Minerva's pregnant?"

This was really getting to be harder every minute. "No, she's not pregnant. Boy, I don't quite know how to start this, but here goes." I looked from one to the other of my parents, wishing I could think of some gentle way to start this conversation.

"Here's the deal. Minerva has an unusual talent. She has what I guess you'd call real magic ability. I guess you might say that she's a witch."

With that statement, an amazing change came over my Mom's demeanor. She stopped sobbing, and she actually smiled. My Dad's face screwed itself into a scowl. Minerva beamed, and she kicked me under the table.

The most amazing reaction was Mom's. So I asked her, "What is going on with you? Don't you think I'm crazy or something?"

Mom just kept smiling and said, "Oh, but Jimmy, that explains so much. Of course, Minerva's a witch. How else could a middle-aged, frumpy, boring woman attract such devotion from a handsome, brilliant, youth like my dear Jimmy?" She turned to Minerva and said, "No offense intended."

Minerva just said, "Of course. None taken."

"And that trick that she did with her wand—how else could she do that without magic? But don't you worry honey. We'll find a way to release you from her spell."

Well, that was a revolting development! "Look, Mom, if you think I'm bewitched or something, you're wrong. Believe me, I know a little about magic and enchantments and all that. If Minerva had used a love potion on me, I'd have been really, well, goofy. I wouldn't be able to have a conversation like this, talking about the possibility of being enchanted."

I turned to Minerva and said, "I mean, you're enchanting, you just haven't used magic to be enchanting."

She had a big smile on her face at my discomfiture. I did something that I rarely did, I kicked her under the table.

Dad had been glaring at all of us, "Look, I've seen better magic tricks in Vegas. Come on, Minerva. You're not a real witch."

I turned to Dad and suggested, "Suppose she could do a little magic right here that would be impossible for you to explain?"

He just hummed and didn't say anything, so I told Minerva, "Would you be willing to do Leviouso?"

She thought a moment and said, "I suppose so. On your dad?"

"Yes, but let me prepare him." I turned again to Dad, "OK. Minerva will do a little trick involving you. Nothing that will hurt you, but just be ready for a surprise."

Dad warily said, "OK. Will I have warning?"

"Sure. Go ahead, Minerva."

She pulled her wand from her handbag and pointed it at Dad and said very clearly, "Windgardium Levioso." With that nothing very evident happened, but Dad seemed to lift slightly. The table must have caught him before he went very far up. From the bar, it must have seemed that he was getting ready to stand.

He said, "OK. OK. You've proved your point."

Minerva silently let him down.

He went on, "OK. So, what was that all about outside with the smoky cat?"

I agreed, "Yeh, what was that all about?"

Minerva looked around to be sure that no one was within hearing range. "There were some creatures called 'Dementors' about. I was chasing a couple away with my Patronus."

Dad asked, 'Dementors? Patronus? What are they?"

"Dementors are magical creatures. They normally guard Azkaban."

Dad turned to me, "Do you know anything about these things."

"Well, let me explain a little. I think that one Muggle explaining to another would be the best way, Minerva. When I get stuck, you'll have to help out."

She just nodded. I went on, "You see, Mom, Dad, there are a lot of different magical creatures. Some of them are known to Muggles, and some aren't."

Mom interrupted, "What are these 'Muggles'?"

I went on, "'Muggles' are the wizarding word for non-magical humans. Everyone in our whole family are Muggles, of course.

"But to go on, there are many magical creatures that all Muggles know about—elves, goblins, dragons, ghosts, werewolves, vampires. But often, they're pretty different from what Muggles think they are.

"For example, elves. What do you think of when you hear the word, Mom?"

She was surprised to be asked a question. She fumbled a moment and then said, "Well, I suppose the cute little pixies like 'Tinkerbell'."

"And you Dad?"

He scratched his chin and said, "I suppose I think of the tall, slender, fierce, brilliant elves that Tolkien writes about."

"Yes, well the reality is different from either. Elves are roughly the size that we think of dwarves being. They are neither cute nor usually are they fierce. They are normally called 'house elves' by wizards and witches because they are rather like the slaves of the ante-bellum South of the States. They are almost always owned by a family or 'house'. Like the black slaves, their offspring belong to the family that their parents belonged to."

Mom was disturbed by this, "Do you mean that slavery is still practiced in England!"

Minerva said, 'For house elves, yes. I'm not proud of it and I don't own any. But I don't know how to put it to an end either."

"There were lots of well-meaning people in our South who felt just that way." I suggested.

"Well, it's barbarous!" When Mom had her dander up, it was pretty fierce.

I could see that Minerva was not happy about being called barbarous, but for once, she was at a loss for sharp words.

I quickly cut in, by going on to other magical creatures, "Goblins are much more civilized that the idea that Muggles have of them. They run the banking institutions of the wizarding world."

Dad chuckled, "Well, there's one example of the world being the same all the way around."

Minerva made a puzzled face at me, and I quickly explained, "Banks don't have a very good reputation in the world of Muggles either." And then I went on, "Werewolves are pretty much as Muggles know them, except that there's a treatment for werewolfism—not a cure. Then, there are vampires."

Dad interrupted here, "Don't tell me that there are Count Dracula's running around."

"Not quite. I don't know much about vampires. It's not 'catching' but they do crave blood.

"Dragons are pretty much the same too."

Dad had had as much as he could stand, "Look. Dragons are big, they fly, they breathe fire. How is it possible that they could exist and no. . uh.-.-. Muggle has ever noticed them?"

Minerva asked me, "You saw Hagrid's dragon, didn't you?"

"Hagrid had a dragon!" I asked incredulously, "How is that I didn't hear about that?"

"Well, it was strictly speaking illegal, and Professor Dumbledore wanted to keep him out of trouble. So it was pretty much a secret. Still, you are pretty close to Hagrid. I thought he might have shown his precious Norbert to you."

"Norbert? He gave it a name? Of course, he did." Then I turned to Mom and Dad and explained, "Hagrid is the groundskeeper at the school. He's the biggest man I've ever seen—in every way, height, girth, weight, and heart. He's got a heart as big as the world. I don't think he ever met a creature that he didn't like."

Minerva re-entered the conversation, "Dragons are kept on remote reservations—mostly. How do you think that you know about Dragons if some Muggle hadn't noticed them?"

Dad wasn't happy, but that just meant that he was trying to figure out how it all fit together. I went on, "Now ghosts are another matter altogether. I know some. They seem to be pretty much as Muggles understand them, but they're also different. Minerva, can you explain them better?"

Minerva was thoughtful. Finally, she said, "We really don't know. They seem to be shadows of the real person and yet they can think and talk. It's very strange. There are ghosts whom I almost consider friends."

My Dad asked, "Are all ghosts good-natured then?"

"No, they are as they were in life. Some are kind and generous. Some are fierce. Some are even jolly."

"But surely the world would be bursting at the seams if all the dead left ghosts behind?"

"No, only some do and really very few. I don't know why they remain."

My Mom asked, diffidently, "Will they tell of the afterlife?"

Minerva shook her head, "They know nothing of that."

I added, 'Yea, ghosts are amazingly un-curious. They could go anywhere—literally—and see and hear anything. But all they do is hang around one place and I'll be damned if I can puzzle out that they do anything for fun.

"But now we come to the limits of my knowledge. I don't know anything about these Demumblers. You'll have to take over from here, Minerva."

She cleared her throat and began in her best professorial tone, "DEMENTORS is the word, and it comes from the Latin roots, Mens—mind, and DE—without. Dementors are creatures that are invisible to Muggles. That's just as well, because they are rather hideous. They seem to be wearing cloaks with hoods. But most people think that is merely an illusion that the mind invents to hide the true form—whatever it may be.

"They're called Dementors because they live on real people's emotions—the good ones. They somehow suck them out and whatever is left leaves the victim depressed and hopeless. Sometimes they are greedy and remove every last bit of the soul. The body is left an empty husk. It's alive, but bereft of spirit."

My Dad almost leaped from his seat and asked urgently, "They don't react to stimuli, do they?"

Minerva was surprised at the outburst but quickly regained composure and said, "No. They don't react to anything. They don't have souls."

I'd rarely seen my Dad so excited. He said, "Look, we, uh Muggles, know about that condition. We call it catatonia. The victim seems to be lifeless, but they breath and can be fed and survive."

Minerva said, "OK. So, Muggles maybe are attacked by Dementors."

Dad said, "But you don't have a cure for it, do you?"

Minerva agreed, "No. Like I said, they don't have souls."

"No. No. They do. They just are so depressed, so hopeless that they can't act, but we DO have a cure that frequently works."

Minerva stared at him, speechless. He went on, "It's shock therapy. Sometimes doctors use electric shocks, sometimes chemical shocks. But they usually succeed in reviving their 'spirits' and then more conventional therapy can be used to bring them closer to normal."

This brought Minerva to her senses. "Electric shocks! You Muggles are crazy! How could you do such things to people? I like to think that I'm broad-minded and open to different cultures, but this is absolutely crazy!"

"No, if you want to help such people, you have to do things like that."

Minerva was dumbfounded, but I jogged her back onto the route with a swift kick to the shins. I was beginning to see the attractions of that. Then she went on, somewhat shaken, "Well, thank God, there have been very few victims of Dementors for a very long time. The Ministry of Magic worked out a bargain with them. We would provide them with a pool of people—criminals—from whom they could suck all the happiness. Thus, the Dementors would stay at the locations where the criminals are housed and not completely Dement them. The closest one of these prisons is in the North Sea. It's called Azkaban Prison."

Dad was still fired up. When he heard this he said, "And you accuse Muggles of barbarous practices. We would never condemn even serious criminals to such indignities."

Minerva was losing her temper, "Well, you Muggles have never had to deal with magical criminals. Imagine someone with magical powers that can't be completely removed by taking their wands from them. You couldn't keep the worst in the prisons. Before the use of Dementors, there were constant escapes. But ever since Dementors were made the guards at Azkaban, there hasn't been a single escape and that's been for over a hundred years."

I added, "And believe me, Dad, the worst of these magical criminals are .-.-. are .-.-. well, they're indescribable."

Dad was still not done, "Then what were those Dementors that you sent away doing here? It's not exactly the middle of the North Sea!"

That made Minerva pause, "I don't know. I've never heard of that happening. There should be something in the '*Prophet*' tomorrow morning."

I supplied, "The '*Prophet*' is the main Magical newspaper."

Minerva went on, "And if there isn't, I'll go to the Ministry and find out what is going on."

The night had worn on a long while and we were all feeling tired. So I suggested that we get Mom and Dad to their hotel. No one objected, so I paid up, and we left the pub.

We accompanied Mom and Dad to their hotel. Somehow we all felt better being in the large busy lobby. As we left, my Mom asked how I was going to get home. She quickly added Minerva to the question. I said, "It's not a problem. Minerva will drop me off. We'll be perfectly safe. How that will happen is a question for another get-together."

She seemed a little relieved at that but not entirely. I assured her of my safety even more vehemently, and she finally seemed to accept that.

As we left the hotel, Minerva said, "Let's go back to that pub. I want to talk with you a little more." I smiled at the idea. We arrived and resumed at our old table. I took her hand and was perfectly happy to just be in her presence.

She let go of my hand and said, "Look. I'm impressed by how forceful and reasonable you were about not being ensorcelled. You're right. If you'd been under the influence of a love potion, you'd have been unbearably goofy about it."

I wasn't sure where this was going, but I was pretty sure that I wouldn't like the endpoint. So I asked, "Are you about to admit something?"

She looked down and my heart fell. What was she going to say? She went on, "Have you ever heard of the Imperious Curse?"

That threw me for a loop. I just shook my head. "No, I've not. Does it have anything to do with sugar?"

That forced a laugh and smile out of her. "No. And it's Imperial sugar—not Imperious.

"The Imperious curse is something that Valdemort used during the great war. He could force people to do what he wanted them to and they weren't 'goofy'. They were damn hard to tell from ordinary people. That was the real thing that made fighting him so hard. He could have almost anyone as a willing ally—no matter how much they'd opposed him before."

"Spooky. But what has that got to do with us?"

"Well, if your Mum knew about it, she might think I'd put you under the Imperious curse. It's happened you know. Wizards and witches have used the Imperious curse to gain willing lovers or even spouses. For years no one has suspected that they were under the curse. It's certainly illegal and can get you a life sentence in Azkaban, but that doesn't keep it from happening."

I laughed and tried to make it not sound nervous, "But, you haven't done that to me." I couldn't help adding, "Have you? I mean I'd know it wouldn't I if I were under the Imperious curse, wouldn't I?"

She hesitated and then said, "I don't know. The people whom Valdemort put under that curse never talked about it or even how they were put under the curse. I sometimes wonder if being under the curse doesn't induce amnesia."

I said to myself, "Like being under anesthesia." Minerva heard and asked what I'd said.

"Oh, I was just commenting to myself that being under the Imperious curse must be like being under anesthesia. You don't remember what happened—frequently even from the time that you're apparently aware and can talk to people. That's another spooky thing."

She said, "This anesthesia. Is it something those 'doctors' of yours do?"

"Yes. Usually during operations."

Her face turned greenish and she said, "How you Muggles allow yourselves to suffer those things I never have been able to understand."

190

"Well, believe me, it's not like you have a choice. Usually."

"But, I surely wouldn't be able to think about it if I were under the Imperious Curse. I mean I wouldn't be able to wonder if I were under the Imperious curse, right?"

She bit her lip and said, "Oh, I don't know." with some tension and, perhaps, desperation in her voice.

"But what are we talking about? Even if I don't know if I'm under the Imperious curse, you surely know whether you put me under the curse. You know that you don't have to worry about that. And the very fact that we're having this discussion shows me that I'm not under the curse. You wouldn't be talking to me about it if you had done that to me. Anyway, you're the most law-abiding person I know. You'd just not do it to anyone—at least not for a trivial purpose like having a boyfriend."

She still looked worried. "That's just it. You're right. I haven't. BUT how do I know that someone else hasn't?"

I shook my head to clear it. This was the craziest conversation that I'd ever had. Well, maybe not the craziest, but way up there. "Look, Minerva, who in the world would have a motive to put me under an Imperious curse to fall in love with you. It's crazy. Not even that Sinistra would do something like that. Now, I can just see her putting me under an Imperious curse to fall in love with her—but you? It's just plain daft."

She looked a little relieved but said, "BUT your mother has a point. Why would a young handsome intelligent man fall in love with a plain, old spinster like me?"

"Is that's what's bothering you? Well, you know perfectly well, the answer to that. You're not any of those things—not even a spinster. You have reason to know," and here I bumped her thigh very gently, "that I enjoy every microsecond that I spend with you—more than any moment that I'm away from you."

She forced a laugh and said, "Oh, that's fine while I'm young and beautiful but what about when I'm old and really plain, and you're still young and vital?"

I shrugged and said, "You know that in the Victorian era and before, it was normal for people with 20 years and more difference in their ages to marry. We're way closer than that."

She relaxed some and answered, "But those were men who were twenty years older than their wives. The wives were economically dependent on their husbands. That's the glue that held them together."

"Same with us. You're the successful headmistress of an exclusive public school. I'm just an inexperienced teacher." She laughed at that.

Then I added, "Oh, in some marriages that was true, but I think that there were lots of marriages where love ruled and when the elder died and left a widow, that widow, despite being still fairly young, rich and comely remained faithful to her departed husband."

For the first time, she took my hand and said, "I don't want that for you."

"Oh, you needn't worry about that. I'll still be rich, handsome, and I'll have the young widows lined up like trolls at supper time."

She squeezed my hand really hard and said, "No, you won't. I'll come back and scare them all away."

I laughed through the pain. We finished our drink and true to her word, she dropped me off at my garret and went on to her sister's—as far as I knew.

The next morning, Minerva showed up in my garret at 7AM. She lit her wand and nearly scared me to death. "What the heck are you doing here? Haven't you ever heard of knocking! I was afraid that a Dementor was in the house."

She switched on the electric light and sat on the edge of my bed. That would ordinarily be cause for celebration, but she had a copy of the "*Prophet*" in hand. She unfolded it to the front page and plopped it into my lap. The entire front page was plastered with articles about one event. I asked, "Who is this Sirius Black, and how did he escape from Azkaban? You were just telling us last night that it was the perfect prison. Nobody escapes from it."

"Well, I was wrong! But the question is: do we tell your parents?"

"Of course, they're adults and intelligent. They can make up their own minds quite adequately."

"I'm worried. Anyone who can escape from Azkaban is very dangerous, perhaps as dangerous as Valdemort himself."

"Who was this Sirius Black anyway?"

Minerva swung her eyes around the room as though she thought he might be listening as we spoke. She turned her attention back to me and said, "Sirius Black was one of Valdemort's chief lieutenants, perhaps the very closest associate. He had us all fooled. He was one of James Potter's closest friends. It was he who betrayed the Potters to Valdemort.

"In his last act of terror before he was captured, he killed several dozen Muggles and one wizard, Peter Pettigrew. To use one of your phrases, he vaporized them. The only remains were one finger of Pettigrew. It was passed off to Muggles as a, what do you call it? Gas miner explosion?"

I corrected her to "Gas Main." She went on, "He was another of James' closest circle of friends. No one would have believed he was capable of such depravity."

I asked, "And he's loose on the public, now?"

"I'm afraid so. The Ministry is claiming that he'll be captured quickly, but I can't believe it."

"Well, I'll get dressed and we can go have breakfast with the parents. What do you think we should recommend to them? He's only one man after all."

"But most of the Dementors of Azkaban are loose looking for him and you don't want to cross them."

"We'll just have to be honest with the parents and let them make up their minds about what they do."

Agreed to that, we also agreed that it was early to go find them. So we made love and then forced ourselves out of bed to shower quickly so that we wouldn't be late to find my parents. I'd hoped to take the Tube there, but I was forced to admit that we'd ought to disapparate there. I didn't even complain about it.

So, we found ourselves walking up the stairs to the main level of the hotel and I started looking for a house phone. I finally found it and was just getting the operator on the line when Minerva poked my shoulder and said, "You don't need to do that. They're here."

They were walking away from the bank of elevators. We joined them, and they suggested trying the hotel coffee shop. We found a table in a distant corner (much to my Mom's displeasure) but were quickly served. Once my parents had coffee. Minerva and I had tea, Mom declared that there must be a problem. Otherwise, why did we sit far from all other guests?

Minerva immediately came to the point. She gave them a somewhat more detailed description of what had happened to cause the streets of London to be crawling with Dementors. My Dad immediately picked up on the bigger question, "Why does this Valdemort keep popping up in this story? Who is he?"

Apparently Minerva wanted me to explain it to him because she fell silent. So, I took a go at it. "Well, imagine the magical equivalent of Adolf Hitler. Then think of the Storm Troopers. They're the DeathEaters. Valdemort was born prior to World War II. He went to the school I teach at in the '50's. Then he became a more or less ordinary wizard for a while—several years. He went to ground and disappeared for a while.

"What he was actually doing was building up a band of followers who would eventually become his DeathEaters. Then in the 70's, he went public, and a great war began."

My Dad interrupted, "How is it that we Muggles know nothing of this 'great war'?"

"Well, wizards like to keep themselves secret. And they've got some pretty powerful tools for doing that. We can talk about those another time. The important thing is that he'd have won if he hadn't tried to kill Harry Potter. He was only a baby at the time, but somehow Valdemort couldn't kill him. Valdemort was, well, turned into a disembodied spirit by the encounter. This was in 1982, I think. Anyway, he was put out of commission, but he's still around and has even been observed a time or two."

Dad asked, "So, it's dangerous on the streets of London because of this Black Escapee and all the Dementors running around looking for him?"

Minerva said, "Well, dangerous may be too strong a word. Don't forget that there are over 5 million people in London. The chances of running into any of them by accident is pretty slight."

"But, they won't be looking among Muggles. They'll be looking among magical people, right?" My dad has a way of drilling into a point that he wants to make, and this was one of those times.

Minerva signed, "And I'm magical, so they will be attracted to me. Yes, I suppose that's reasonable. Maybe I should let you people finish your tour without me."

My Mom surprised me. She said, "No, we should leave and take Jimmy with us." She looked around and didn't find any approving faces. "It wouldn't necessarily be forever. Just until the summer vacation is over. Surely, this Serial Black will be caught by then."

I disagreed, "No, Mom, if there's danger to Minerva, I'm staying. And if there isn't any danger, there's no reason to leave. Besides that, this guy has escaped from a maximum security prison. It's the equivalent of escaping from Alcatraz in the US. It's just impossible. If he escaped, then he's a very tough cookie who will not be caught easily and maybe not at all."

Minerva added, "He's as dangerous as they get. His whole family were supporters of you-know, uh, that is Valdemort. Half of them were in Azkaban, and the rest should have been."

Trying to break the tension, Dad noted the similarity in name between Alcatraz and Azkaban. Nobody laughed. Mom just stared at him. Then there was a silent period where the two just communed silently. Somehow they communicated in some subliminal way or something because they always ended these sessions agreed about what to do.

Dad just sighed and said, "I guess your Mom and I will be leaving for home as soon as we can. I'll go call the airlines and get us on the earliest flight that I can. Should it be two or three tickets?"

I just shook my head. He got up, suggested that we stay here, enjoy the end of breakfast and think about some last little outing before the afternoon or evening flight that he'd surely be able to book. He left and I said, "Coward" under my breath. Of course, no one said anything. No one had any ideas. We all just waited for Dad's return.

He got back after about 40 minutes and announced that he had tickets on a flight leaving at 4PM from Heathrow. It was the earliest that he could get but not the shortest. It arrived in Lisbon after a two hour flight. There was a two hour lay-over there and then an eight hour flight to New York. It arrived at 11PM. They'd stay overnight there and fly on to Port Columbus the next morning—early.

While our tea and coffee got cold and no one expressed a thought, I had an idea. "Nobody else has any suggestions, so, I have an idea. But since we're all in such a glum mood, I'm not going to tell you what it is. There is this thing that they do here, 'Mystery Tours'. People sign up for a day trip or sometimes a couple of days' trip without knowing what is on the itinerary. This will be my Mystery Tour."

Dad never missed an opportunity for humor. He commented, "I suppose that you could call it a Magical Mystery Tour."

Mom groaned as did Minerva. It was one of the few things that they could share. Dad asked if we could get it completed in time to make the flight with time to spare. I assured him that it would be easy. So, he said, "In that case, I'll keep the room for another day. We'll be checking out very, very early—as a matter of fact the previous day, but that's OK. We'll go up to our room and pack, so that we'll be ready to leave as soon as we get back."

They did that. They came down after about a half-hour and we left the hotel. Mom wanted to take a cab, but I insisted on the Tube. She didn't like it a lot, but I urged them along saying, "All aboard for the Mystery Tour!" Minerva, at least, smiled and was getting into the spirit.

We arrived at the Knightsbridge station and got out. Nobody except me had an idea where we were. We got to the surface and crossed Carriage drive. We entered the park and Minerva nodded after we'd gone a short distance. Dad started trying to guess where we were. He eventually named Hyde Park, and I agreed. I led the tour on the route to the spot that I wanted. Minerva commented that we were going along the large pond called the Serpentine. I agreed. She didn't seem to know where we were headed. Maybe she had never known why it was special to me.

Finally, we reached an old deserted boat house. Dad caught on first. He asked, "Is this some place that's special to you? Something happened here, didn't it?"

I answered, "Right. This is where Professor Dumbledore met me for the first time for THE interview."

Dad commented, "Strange place for a job interview."

"Professor Dumbledore is a man who does things for a good reason. It's hard to figure out what that reason is a lot of the time." Minerva nodded her silent agreement.

Mom asked what that interview was like. I described it, "Well, I believed in the idea of arriving early for interviews. So I got here quite early, but sat about where we are now, waiting for the Professor to make an appearance on the path to the boat house. He never did. Finally, when I had only a couple of minutes until the interview, I decided that I had to be there on time even if he weren't. I found Professor Dumbledore waiting for me." Here Minerva smiled.

I went on, "Minerva, you may smile if you like because that doesn't surprise you at all, but it rather disconcerted me."

Dad wondered if maybe he hadn't ridden a boat to the boathouse or come very early. I just shook my head. "There are telltale signs if you've been in a boat. You usually can't keep yourself completely dry as he was. Also, I was there a half-hour early. I can't believe he was there earlier.

"Anyway, we went out on a boat supplied by a boatman at the boathouse that was suddenly in much better repair than it had been before or is now—and with boats that hadn't been there before!

"That bothered me. But the interview, which started very well, began to really disturb me. Dumbledore started with completely normal questions about background and interests, but when he heard that I had an interest in Science Fiction, he veered off into questions about Fantasy. They quickly became questions about wizards and witches. I gradually began to see that these weren't hypothetical questions about fiction but real questions about me and how I would manage in a world with real magic.

"That really bothered me. I began to worry that if I didn't 'pass' this interview something awful might happen to me—like losing part of my memory or worse. I was beginning to think that there was no clean escape. However, the interview finally ended, and I left the Serpentine thinking that I was lucky to get away intact. I was fairly sure that I didn't want a second interview."

Dad asked the obvious question, which you could always count on him to do, "So, then how did you get hired? Or maybe the question is why did you accept?"

"There was a second interview. It was with the Assistant Head—Minerva. I didn't realize it at the time, but even at that first meeting I think I started to fall in love with her."

Minerva inserted here, "We hit it off extremely well. Our philosophy of teaching and, well, our philosophy of life seemed to be perfectly matched."

I was nodding and added, "Meeting Minerva made all the difference. After meeting her, I didn't care if there were ghosts in the castle or that the students could use magic that I couldn't defend myself from or that there was a poltergeist who threw water balloons on the premises. I didn't fully realize it at the time, but all that was important was that I would be working with Minerva." With that I gave Minerva a hug. She turned and kissed me. That was something that I'd not yet done with my parents present. Mom sobbed and Dad was clearly uncomfortable, but we all got through that moment. Then we went on to lunch at one of the restaurants on the Serpentine.

Afterwards, we rushed back to the hotel, picked up the luggage, and my parents splurged in an unusual way. They hired a cab for the ride all the way out to Heathrow.

The British Chess Championship

I spent the next few days relaxing with the *Times*, working the crossword, doing some lesson planning for the next term, and walking in Hyde Park. One day when I was in a remote part of the park, a snowy owl flew up to me and landed at my feet. It lifted one leg. So, I was not surprised to see a parchment tied around it. I untied it and read,

"Professor Wendt, I'm bored to tears. Do you suppose that you could find me a nice tough tournament? Yours, C. D."

I wrote my answer on the bottom half of the parchment, "C. D., I'll do some research and see what I can find."

I went to the British Museum that afternoon and in the Periodical section found a recent copy of the British Chess Magazine. It listed tournaments, including the British Chess Championship. It was scheduled to begin at the end of July—just enough time to make an application. I got the details, including the phone number of the registrar for the tournament.

I called the number, which turned out to be in an office that was manned only one or two half-days a week, but it did have an answering machine. I left my cell number. When the Director eventually got back to me, it was after 9PM, but I was anxious to talk with him, so I was not too disturbed by the hour.

He explained that it was technically a week too late to register. In turn, I explained that I wanted to register one of the rising stars of British Chess, Cedric Diggory.

That name seemed to mean nothing to him. He hung up. I was trying to decide whether or not to tell Cedric of his bad luck to have missed getting in on the premier chess tournament of Britain by only a couple of days. I reasoned that he had never known that it was a possibility, so why even mention it. The next day, I was still in a stew over whether to write Cedric a note when a strange thing happened.

I received another phone call from the Director. This time, his tone was different. Rather than a bored indifference to my plea, his tone was almost one of excitement. He asked, "Was the young man—he was a young man, yes."

"Oh, yes."

"Was his name Cedric Diggory?"

"Yes. It is."

"Oh." There was a pause. "And was he the finalist in the U-1800 group in the T-cubed?"

I was confused by the term, "Excuse me."

"Oh, you, know, T-cubed—TTT—the Trafalgar Tradewise Tournament."

I was the one to pause, now. How did he know about that? I wondered. The Director sensed my uncertainty. He added, "And he was the winner of the Junior 4NCL Weekend Division 1?"

I asked, "At Bath?"

"Yes."

"Well, yes." I was beginning to wonder if this was such a good idea.

"Of course, we'd be honored to have him at the tournament. I thought there was something familiar about his name. I did a little checking and do you know," he paused for effect, "he's the mystery wunderkind of British chess. He's only played in two tournaments— unless he's been playing under a pseudonym. He's not been playing under a false identity, has he?" There was a little nervousness now.

I laughed, "No, he's not been playing under false pretenses."

"Well, this is so much like Bobby Fischer; it's just amazing. He shows up out of nowhere and plays in two tournaments in three months and walks away with almost 2000 master points. Who is he? Where's he from? Who's been training him? He could be on the cover of the British Chess Magazine. OF COURSE WE WANT HIM IN THE TOURNAMENT. Which division will he play in?"

I hesitated. I wasn't hoping for such an enthusiastic welcome. So, I asked, "How much is the entry fee?"

The voice on the other end of the phone line laughed, "How much? We'll give him a scholarship."

"OK. Then which group would you start him in?"

"ME? "

"You're his trainer, aren't you? What do you want for him? Build up points carefully? Stretch him further? Stretch him till he breaks?"

There was a thought. But I had to be honest. "Well, I'm not his trainer. He strictly speaking doesn't have one. I'll be honest. I don't have an idea where he should be playing. You're probably the best chess expert that I know. I honestly want advice. What group would you place him in?"

There was another pause at the other end. Then the voice slowly began speaking, "Well. I guess I have to ask you a few questions. Is that OK?"

"Yes."

"Then, how long has he been playing?"

"A little over a year."

There was a sort of whistling sound but not a whistle. "Oh, God, this IS like Fischer. How many tournaments?" He quickly added, "Really. REALLY."

"Two."

Slowly he said, "You.-.-. are.-.-. lying."

"No, sir."

There was another pause and he asked, "How stable is he?"

"Stable, what do you mean, 'stable'?"

"I mean, does he have a large range of emotions? Does he have lots of highs and lows? Does he have any neurotic habits? Does he obsess over his losses? Does he study them for hours looking for the right move that would have turned the loss to a draw or even a win?"

"I don't think so. No, wait." I just remembered the last tournament. "I remember that once after a loss, on our way back home, he smacked his forehead with his hand and said, 'If only I'd not taken the King's bishop pawn.'"

He commented, "That's not neurotic. It's not even strange. How is he at school?"

Finally, he'd reached a subject that I knew something about, "He's a great student. I've only had him in a couple of classes, but he writes a literate parchment and has a.-.-. "

The voice interrupted me, "Did you say, 'parchment'?"

"Oh, I, uh.-.-." I decided that I should just be casual. "Did I say 'parchment?'"

"Yes."

"I guess, I meant paper. Hmmm."

"Well, anyway, if you think that he's very stable—and it sounds like you do—then I'd suggest going for it all. He'll get his rear end kicked by Sarpinsky, but he'll learn a lot more in a few days than he could in the next best dozen tournaments. If he can stand being humbled a couple of times, he could be on a fast track to getting to the International Master level."

I thought a minute. Cedric was as level-headed a youth as I ever knew. He had half a dozen strengths that most people would give a bucket of galleons each to have. He was brilliant. He was a gifted wizard. He was hard-working. He was an athlete. He was a nice guy. I decided that he could handle the pressure.

"OK. Let's go for the gold ring or is it the First Circle of Hell."

The voice laughed for the first time, "The latter. It starts July 28. Please show up at 11 AM, so that Mr. Diggory can fill out the forms." He had other details for me, but there wasn't anything in the same ballpark with our getting into the tournament in the top group.

▽

I got Minerva to take me to the Diggory's. Amos and his wife were pleasant. Amos pulled me aside and asked me if his son was going to be in another Wizard's chess tournament.

202

I suggested that we include Cedric in the conversation and, as a matter of fact everyone. Minerva and Reina joined us and I addressed Cedric, "Mr. Diggory, there's a tournament that I found that wants you to enter."

Diggory's eyes bugged out. Then he smiled. Amos Diggory did more than smile. He insisted that Cedric play in the tournament. The only person who seemed reluctant was Minerva. She thought that it was too much too soon. I had sympathy with that view but she hadn't talked with Stephenson, the Director of the tournament. As a matter of fact she tried assiduously to talk us out of this tournament. All through the lunch— watercress sandwiches and tomato soup—she tried every tack that she could think of. Cedric was too young; he would be facing hardened adults; he'd lose his humility if he won: etc. Nobody was moved—except me. I'd begun to wonder if I hadn't been pushing Cedric too hard.

Finally, she accepted the inevitable. She surprised me by agreeing to disapparate us to the tournament and back each day. Later, when we were alone, she admitted that she was secretly hoping that he'd end up going to the tournament. She was arguing from her head that told her that he shouldn't be in the tournament. I had to admit that I had started following my emotions. They were imagining me being the discoverer of the next Bobby Fischer.

She stared at me and asked, "You're joking, right? Who's Bobby Fischer?"

I stared at her a moment. Minerva was extremely smart and pretty knowledgeable about things Muggle. However, she always caught me by surprise with her ignorance of something that I thought everyone in the world knew. "Bobby Fischer was the greatest American chess player of all history. He won the world championship once. There are people who think that he may have been the greatest player of all time when he was at his prime."

She just sniffed, "Oh."

Of course, later she admitted that she just didn't want to feel like she was responsible for his decision to play. She didn't want him to play to please us or his parents, but to please himself. Satisfied that he really wanted it for himself, she would happily help us get there and back.

So it was that on Thursday morning, July 28, at 10:30 AM the three of us appeared suddenly in an alley outside the Legacy Hotel in Hensley in Arden. We walked in cold, but the staff was very helpful in finding the tourney Director. He was a short, thin man who was trying to go bald, but definitely not there yet. He was nonchalant until I introduced Cedric. Then he was effusive about Cedric being in the tournament.

He'd already filled out a form with everything he knew about Cedric—which was substantial because of his previous tournament appearances. Really, the only thing that was left was for Cedric to date it and sign it. He assured us that no entry fee was necessary. Cedric was impressed. The assistant Director, Tom Bolyard, escorted us to the ballroom where the tournament was to happen. There was a lunch for the players. We arrived and Bolyard apologized that only players were free, but we could eat for 30 pounds per person. I got out my purse and we were sitting with Cedric at a table for six. We were among the first to arrive and a tall thin, brown-haired man who was in his late 30's sat down beside us. He had a brochure that he was browsing as he sat. After a minute, he looked up and asked, "Do you mind if I join you?"

I smiled and extended a hand. I introduced myself, Minerva and Cedric. He asked, "Let me guess. You're Cedric's older brother, and you're his mum?"

Minerva said, "No. I'm a teacher at his school, as is Professor Wendt. We're here because he's a minor, and we want to be sure that he doesn't get into a lot of trouble."

He answered, "Good idea, my name is Robert and I'm a player."

Just then, he turned to Cedric and asked, "Nimzo-Indian or Sicilian?"

Cedric just stared at him, but we were all interrupted by the Tournament Director, who tapped his water glass with a spoon to get our attention. There was a small portable podium at his table and a microphone. He introduced himself and laid out the ground rules for the tournament. It was pretty standard, but there were details about when games started, how long the clocks would be set for and so forth that he covered. I glanced at our brochure and found it all to be a repeat of what was in there. However, we all listened fairly politely.

After he'd finished, Robert returned to Cedric and said, "Well?" as though there had been no time elapse since his original question.

Cedric asked, "Well, what?"

"Which defense do you prefer?"

Cedric nodded and said, "I really don't have a preference. I guess I just improvise based on what's happening at the moment."

"Hmmmmmmm." Robert seemed to think on that a moment and asked, 'And you've got how many Master Points?"

Cedric looked over at me. I suppose he was concerned about whether he should give out that information. I just shrugged. So, he just said, "1985."

Robert nodded and said, "Interesting."

He went on, "I've been looking at your schedule of games. You've got a couple of easy one—people with fewer points than you, 1825 and 1898. But you've also got a couple of games with serious people. The toughest is probably Jason Born. He's got 2120 Master Points AND you get to play black against him. He's a really tough customer. If you're going to advance to the next round, you have to at least draw him. Good luck.

"Then the other one you have to play is this Nance. He's got 2048 Master Points. You get to play white against him, which would ordinarily be an advantage. But this Nance really likes to play black. He's really a better player controlling the black pieces. He likes the Sicilian defense, but every now and then, he'll deviate from it fairly early. That's probably your main chance—if he decides to deviate early, because he figures that you're weak.

I was suspicious of all this detailed information and asked him how he'd gotten it. "Oh, he's been in a lot of tournaments that I have, and I've had a lot of opportunities to observe him. Of course, it doesn't hurt that my last name is Nance."

Cedric's mouth dropped, "You're the guy I have to play.' Here he consulted his own brochure and went on, "Last."

"Well, last in this round. But maybe you'll advance and get to play another game. There is a wild card position, so you could theoretically finish 2nd and still advance." He chuckled and said, "Good luck. I genuinely mean that. I wish all my opponents good luck—and sometimes they get it."

Cedric reached across the table and shook hands with Nance. He also wished him good luck. I thought that it was truly a genuine wish. I didn't know so much about Nance's wish.

After the lunch, which was decent if scanty, the lunch tables were cleared quickly, and the tablecloths were replaced by chess boards and clocks. The tables were labeled so that players could find their opponents. Each player was given his scorecard for the game, and the play began.

I consulted the program and found that Cedric's first opponent was a Stuart Jeffries. He turned out to be a man with graying hair and a thin ascetic appearance. He was wearing a conservative grey suit and, according to the program, had 1898 Master Points. He had drawn white and promptly started with P-K4. He punched his clock, and the game was off.

I watched for several moves—until Cedric had apparently strayed off the beaten path of "book" defenses. Up till that point, Jeffries had responded crisply with precise unhurried moves. Then he stared at the board and unconsciously rested his chin on the palm of his right hand. That was usually the point at which I left Cedric. There's nothing more frustrating than watching a game that you don't really understand but have an emotional investment in. I moved on to find the table where our lunch-mate was playing.

He was playing white, and the program said that he was playing the other "weak" player in Cedric's group. This game was still in the opening stage. Both sides seemed to be following a standard opening. I watched this game until it got out of the opening stage and was in the mid-game. Nance was technically behind in material, having lost a pawn and knight against a bishop, but, he seemed to have a good position—if I were any judge of positions. I hardly need tell you that I'm not much of a judge of positional chess.

I glanced around to see where Minerva was. She was still watching Cedric. She caught my eye and signaled me to join her. I wondered what could possibly have happened so soon. When I arrived at his table, I immediately saw what had excited her. He was up a bishop, and his opponent seemed to be effectively immobilized with little leeway

206

for motion. I desperately wanted to know how he'd gotten his opponent in such a position, but I didn't dare do anything to break his concentration. So I just watched.

It was probably more frustrating than if he had been losing. I wanted to shout for joy or urge him on, but I knew I'd be ejected if I did anything like that. So, all I could do was watch and pray for the match to end quickly so that we could celebrate. I just stared and bit my lip.

Minerva was hardly less affected. She squeezed my arm so tightly that I thought that I'd turn blue below the elbow of that arm. The game seemed to go on forever, but after only a few more moves, separated by long pauses on the part of Jeffries, he picked up his king. Then he sedately, almost regally laid it on its side, stopped the clock, and recorded his last move on his scorecard. He extended a hand to Cedric who took it silently.

They both signaled the Tournament Director, who came over and officially recorded the score. He then congratulated Cedric and announced that he (and by implication, Minerva and I) were free until the evening session. We walked outside, and I clapped Cedric on the back. Minerva gave him a little kiss on the cheek, and he turned as red as a radish.

We tried to figure out what to do for the next several hours. Of course, we'd have some dinner before the next game, but that still left a couple of hours. So, we could think of nothing better than walking the neighborhood. We were all wearing comfortable clothing, so we made it a rather brisk walk with Cedric threatening good-naturedly to walk us into the ground. He didn't know Minerva as I did, so I was looking forward to the contest. I'm a pretty fair walker myself. I enjoyed the exercise. I have to admit that the two of them probably were not pushing as hard as they could. We'd built up a sweat after the hour of Olympic-style walking. Minerva dropped Cedric off at home to change and get a bite to eat. We went back to my apartment where I picked up some clothes. We headed to Minerva's sister's home and showered there and changed. I took Minerva out for an early dinner at an Indian restaurant that we liked.

We picked up Cedric and arrived back at the tournament with about ten minutes to spare. We found the board where Cedric was to play his next game. We discovered that the next opponent was the top-rated player in Cedric's group—and Cedric was going to have to play Black. I gave him one piece of advice—"Play a good game."

Against my normal plan, I decided to stay through the entire game. The game started much as they all did with Cedric—a few moves that proceeded quickly and then the diversion from the normal path. Both sides felt their way along slowly at first. After about a dozen moves on both sides, I discovered that Minerva was pulling on my shirt sleeve. I almost gasped and looked up from the board to see her signaling me to come with her.

When we got out into the lobby I said, "What happened? You're usually the one to want to stick with Cedric through thick and thin."

She shook her head and said, "I just wanted your opinion about how things were going for him."

I thought a moment and shook my head. "This is way beyond my pay grade. I haven't the slightest idea how things are going.

"You see there are three ways of analyzing chess games. The easiest and usually least accurate in serious chess is strength of material on both sides. Right at the moment, it's pretty close to dead even. The difference is a bishop against a knight. Cedric is down in that exchange. But that means pretty much nothing at this level of play.

"Next is positional strength. Who controls the middle? Is one side's potential moves more constrained than the others'. Honestly, I don't know how to evaluate who's ahead at this point positionally.

"Then there's time."

Minerva interrupted, "You mean how much time's left on each player's clocks."

"Exactly. There too Cedric is behind. They're both using about the same amount of time per move right now, but early on Cedric fell behind and he's not making up much time.

"Finally, there's the hardest to evaluate—tempo."

"I thought you said three ways?"

I was irritated at her. I just said, "Can it and let me get on."

She smiled mischievously and nodded. "Didn't we just talk about that?"

"No. Tempo is really hard to explain. It has to do with getting into a reactive mode versus being on the offensive."

"That doesn't seem so hard to understand."

"Right, but evaluating who's got that advantage is hard to know except in really obvious cases."

She asked, "Then who's ahead in this game?"

I just shook my head and said, "I told you this was way beyond my pay grade."

Minerva didn't say anything more nor did I, but neither of us seemed anxious to get back into the game room to see what was happening. Finally, I took her arm and said, "Let's go." We walked back toward the room and Minerva stopped.

"Oh, let's take a little walk. I just can't bear to go back in and see how bad things are."

I nodded, and we walked outside and strolled around the grounds of the resort for about a half-hour. By this time we both couldn't stand not knowing what was happening, so we went back in. We walked up behind Cedric, and I held off looking at the board as long as I could.

What I saw almost made me gasp, but fortunately I held it back. Cedric was down several pieces, but it was strange. Both players seemed to be very nonchalant about it. As I watched they quickly executed a series of repetitive moves, and then I understood. They both reached across the board simultaneously to shake the other's hand and both wrote down the same thing on their score cards. It was a draw. They called the Tournament Director over and went through the usual post-game routine. Minerva grabbed my arm and practically goose-stepped me out of the room.

When we were out of earshot, she threw my arm down and asked, "What the hell was that about? I thought Cedric was dead, but neither of them seemed disturbed or overjoyed."

"That was a draw."

"How in the world could it be? Cedric was sooo far down in pieces."

"Well, one way of forcing a draw is to force your opponent to repeat the same moves over and over again. I didn't see enough of the board to really get how the repeated moves were forced but he must have sacrificed some pieces to get into a position where he could do that. Usually, the force is repeated checks where there's only one escape which allows the opponent on the next move to put you in check again.

We can look at the score card and figure out how it happened or just ask Cedric." I'd noticed Cedric come up.

I shook his hands and congratulated him enthusiastically. He was not overjoyed but seemed not to be disappointed either. He said, "Oh, I thought I had him there just before you came in, but he found an escape. I was lucky to force him into a draw."

"Well, Cedric, getting a draw from one of the top players in the tournament when you're playing black is not shabby."

He looked down at his feet briefly, then raised his eyes and thanked me. Minerva was less enthusiastic, but she seemed happy too. We disapparated him back to his parent's house.

There he was greeted enthusiastically. His dad was anxious to hear how he'd done.

"Oh, Dad, I won one game and tied another."

His dad's face started to show a frown, but he quickly corrected to a smile and said, "Well done. We'll have to work on that tie," and gave him a stiff shot to the shoulder, "but well done." They asked us to stay for something to eat, but Minerva assured them that we had something waiting for us at her sister's home.

After the door was shut behind us I asked, "We do? What are we looking for?"

She just smiled, and I finally got it. "Oh, yeah. Yeah, we do have something good waiting for us at home."

The next day, there was only one game. It was against the other weaker player. Cedric played black, but I only stayed for a few moves before leaving—as usual. I walked among a few of the tables but couldn't concentrate on any of the games. I went out and laughed at the idea of how I couldn't stand the tension of watching a chess game. What the heck was that? I couldn't stand the wait for each move. I walked back and forth in the garden area. Maybe I couldn't stand not seeing the game as well.

Eventually, I couldn't stand the suspense. I went in and found Cedric's board. As I approached, Minerva smiled at me. Despite the fact that it was extremely easy to understand her smiling at my appearance, I thought there must be another reason for her obvious happiness. When I arrived, I saw that Cedric was well ahead. Even I could see that he was crushing his opponent. While I watched, the opponent grabbed his King and threw it down to the table. He got up and walked off. The Director came over and completed his scorecard for him. He apologized for the player. Then he signed Cedric's card and we were done for the day. "I'm sorry. This happens every now and then." He hesitated and laughed, "You did pretty much destroy him, you know."

On the way home, we talked about the next day's game. "You're going to play our old buddy Nance. He's got more Master points. He has to play black, but he likes playing black."

Cedric smiled. "I can take him. He's too confident."

I had to laugh. "He's too confident, eh?"

Cedric looked down at his feet and nodded. "Yup."

After dropping him off at home, Minerva asked, "Is tomorrow the last day for the tournament?"

"I don't know. I hope not."

Minerva blinked, and there may have been a tear that was being blinked away. "What does he have to do to go on?"

I didn't want to have to say it, but I did. "He has to win. The best he can do now is to tie for first place in his division. I don't know how they'll pick if there's a tie. Both he and Bolt would have 4 wins and one draw.

"But even if Bolt carries on as champion of the division, there's a good chance that Cedric would advance as the wild card player."

Neither of us got a lot of sleep that night. The next morning, we were both bleary-eyed and short-tempered. We went to Cedric's home and found the whole family in high spirits. Cedric had had a good night's sleep and had a spring to his step that I couldn't understand. We tried to bear up and be of good spirits.

We arrived at the tournament and found Nance to be in good spirits too. They joked about fighting for the right to play black. We went to the table, and the two sat. They shook hands. The game started and Minerva and I watched the game helplessly. The clocks wound their merciless minutes and seconds.away. After nearly three hours, Cedric was clearly ahead in all ways, but his clock had very little time left on it. He had two minutes and ten moves left.

Minerva kept turning to me. All I could do was shake my head in the negative. There was at least a half hour on Nance's clock. He took his time on the moves. He should. His position was bad, but all he had to do was stretch out Cedric's time for two minutes and it would all be over.

Cedric didn't hesitate over any move. He faultlessly pressed the attack home. On the seventh move, it was mate. There were 12 seconds left on his clock.

Nance gave his hand to Cedric. He said, "Well, Cedric, I thought I'd run you out of time. Well, done."

"To tell you the truth, I had no idea how much time was left on the clock."

"Everyone else did." Minerva said ruefully.

We went to have an ice cream in Diagon Alley after the game. Before we left, though, the Tournament Director approached Cedric and announced, "You've won the wild card spot, Mr. Diggory. Please return next Thursday for the next round of play."

"Thank you sir. Do you know who my opponent will be?"

"Not, yet, there are a couple of games still going that could affect the pairings for the knockout round."

We left and found our way to the entrance to The Leaky Cauldron. We entered and Tom greeted us, including Cedric, "It's young Mr. Diggory isn't it?"

Cedric smiled the smile he had for everyone, "Yes, sir, it is."

"What are you doing here so long before beginning of next term?"

Cedric was dumbfounded, his shyness overcoming his happiness. I said, "Oh, we're just going through to Diagon Alley to have an ice cream at Florian's."

Tom made a face and said, "Then you'll not be stopping for a pint afterwards."

Minerva confirmed that, and we went on through to Diagon Alley. Afterwards, we went straight to Cedric's home and left him. His dad was so confident that he'd win that he just shook Cedric's hand and congratulated him.

Minerva wanted to celebrate a bit more, so we went back to the Leaky Cauldron and had dinner. It was a cool evening and there was a roaring fire in the fireplace. It was a cozy evening. Minerva was exhausted by the tension of the day, so begged off doing anything further after she dropped me at my rooming house.

The next couple of days, I worked on lesson plans for the new term and decided that I'd done as much as I could until school actually started. *The Times* had a brief article about the qualifying round of the tournament and mentioned that a young lad had made it to the knockout round by turning in a surprising win in the final game after running into time trouble. It had the pairings for the first round of games.

Cedric was to be paired with a Master named Fenton. He had 2214 points. It was starting tough, and I was sure it would only get tougher as the games went on—if they did for Cedric. We arrived early and found the table where Cedric would be playing. Fenton hadn't shown up yet, but someone else had.

Nance was there. After we all said hello and discussed the weather—cool and cloudy, Nance walked over beside me and said, "There's some time before the games start. Why don't you and I take a little walk?"

I had not the slightest idea what he had in mind, but I decided it couldn't hurt. As we left the hall, I asked him, "What brings you here?"

"Oh, I'm curious to see how your student does. He's an anomaly you know."

"In what way?"

"Well, he doesn't know openings. And yet, he plays very well. I'm surprised that you haven't instructed him better."

"Ho. Ho. You don't think that I've been teaching him. When I first discovered that he had a knack for chess, he was already far better than I was—or, for that matter—anyone I know."

"Do you mean that he's self-taught?"

"I'm afraid so."

Nance had stopped walking and turned to stare at me. "You really don't know anything about chess?"

"Well, I know the rules of the game."

He nodded slowly. "That explains a lot. Well, let me tell you a few things."

I nodded assent and said, "Go ahead, I'm all ears."

We had reached the entrance to the resort and he opened the door for me. We walked out, and he scratched his chin. Then he started what sounded like a lecture before a class, "The student who wants to reach the level of Master, not to mention higher levels, needs to have a firm grasp on the major openings and the defenses of them.

"A really brilliant talent—like your friend—can reach the level he has on pure talent and fortitude, but if he wants to go further, he really should study openings. Every Master will trounce him until he has good command of the opening game. And he can only gain that by studying openings seriously. A good start—mind you, only a start—is the book, MCO—Modern Chess Openings.

"I'd advise you to find out if he wants to play seriously. If he does then get him that book and start him studying that the way he would study the hardest subject you teach."

I nodded and said, "Well, you know what they say about horses?"

"You can lead them to the pool, but you can't get them to swim?"

"I'll talk to him about it, and we'll see what happens. Thanks for the advice."

"Good. Well, let's go back in and see how badly this Master beats him."

We went in and watched the game—the three of us.

The game went a little differently than any of us thought. Cedric was playing black. The game started to form: fast, confident play from the opponent and slow play from Cedric, but something happened that nobody expected. Nance whispered to me, "Your student has forced him off a standard opening early. This is usually bad for the one who leaves the standard opening."

But it didn't go badly. There were long pauses from both players. The game went on and on. The material disappeared and the clocks ran and nobody had an advantage. They ran out of moves. The Tournament Director came by and let them take a break before restarting for the next forty. They did and the game resumed. The material disappeared and finally, something happened that I never had seen. The material reduced to a King and knight vs. a King—a certain draw. The next game would be in the afternoon.

Nance expressed his surprise. "Your student did well. I was sure that he'd be run into the ground by Sarpinski. What do you know? I've got to see the next game against him."

That afternoon, the next game started, and Nance was actually excited. As white, Cedric played with more confidence than I'd seen before. The game proceeded quickly, and I found that Cedric was moving forward, picking up material and position. He finished Sarpinski off without breaking a sweat.

Nance smiled at the end and said, "I've just got one word for you —Openings. IF he studies, mind you, he'll be unbeatable."

Minerva and I took Cedric home. Amos was overjoyed, of course. I warned everyone about overconfidence.

When we'd left, Minerva asked me about Cedric's chances. "I don't know. He did really well against Sarpinski. Who knows?"

The next day, we did find out. Nance had apparently seen enough. I didn't see him again at the tournament. We arrived at the table for the next game and watched the next opponent arrive. He was a young man with short hair. He exuded confidence. We watched the next game with bated breath. Cedric had white. The game started out unremarkably. Both played through the opening quickly. Then the game proceeded from good to bad to worse for Cedric. I had not the slightest idea what he might be doing wrong, but the play just kept going wrong. Cedric would make what seemed like a nice play and gained on an exchange of pieces, but then he found that he'd put himself in a terrible position. From that point the game dissolved and Cedric had resigned.

We had lunch at the hotel. There was that uncomfortable silence when there is an elephant in the room and it's so large that it crowds out all conversation and even all breath. Finally, Minerva acknowledged the elephant. "Cedric, what do you think will happen in the next game?"

He smiled wanly, "I'll get whipped." We all laughed, and that opened the floodgates. We talked about the next school year, guessed about who would be the new Defense Against the Dark Arts Professor, and predicted the next winner of the House Cup.

We returned to the hall. His opponent sat at their table and shortly the game began. Playing black, Cedric put up a valiant fight, but it was ended quickly. The Tournament Director congratulated Cedric on having a good tournament, and it was all over for us.

About a month later, I called Cedric into my office and handed an envelope over to him. But before he could open it, I said, "Cedric, before you open that. I'd like to have a talk with you."

"Sure professor. It looks like this is a letter from the British Championship Tournament."

"You're right. I expect that it has the final results from the tournament—including your current Master Points standing. I expect that you have a rating of Master. Before you confirm that, I'd like to discuss your future.

"Our friend Nance had a little talk with me before your first game in the final round. He said that if you wanted to stay at the rating of Master—notice, he said 'stay' not 'improve' your rating—you would have to study chess openings. That brings me to the 2nd thing that I have for you." I handed him a heavy package that I'd wrapped in plain white gift paper.

"Can I open this now?"

"Certainly." He tore the wrappings off excitedly and stared at the book that I'd given him. "It's the MCO, *Modern Chess Openings*. He suggested that you study it cover to cover and memorize a good bit of it —just to hold your current position.

"Now, I wouldn't suggest that you do that unless you really want to pursue chess seriously." Cedric was just opening his mouth to say something but I interrupted, "Don't decide too quickly. You should take your time thinking about this.

"I think that you could have an amazing career in chess if you really wanted to. Above the rating level of Master is Grand Master. I think that if you wanted to work hard on chess, you'd read this book and several more. You'd spend hours every day playing and studying chess openings. You'd read other books. Then, you could reach that level within a few years. I even think that you could reach the level of International Grand Master well before you're halfway through your 20's."

I paused for emphasis, standing and walking away from my desk to forestall any comment from him, "I even think that World Champion could be in your reach by the time you reach the age of 30."

His mouth was gaping open. I went on, "But, to do that you'd have to make chess your career. You'd have to spend 10, 12 hours a day, seven days a week studying and playing chess. You'd have to give up the idea of starting a family, even of having close friends until after you'd reached your goal—whatever it might be."

His mouth closed, "Well, why did you give me this?" He pointed at the book now resting on my desk.

"I think that you have this potential, and you should know about it and choose intelligently.

"I don't think you have to choose your life course this minute. I'd advise you to take the book, try reading it. We'll go to some more tournaments. You're already at a level where it's hard to find challenging tournaments that can fit in your school schedule. We can find a couple a year. You'll play in tournaments where you'll breeze through easily—not because you've improved a lot but because you're very strong right now.

"Just spend time and try to figure out how much you really like chess. You don't have to make a decision right away or even by the time you graduate.

"I wouldn't have bought you that book if I didn't think that you were both smart and pretty mature. I trust your judgment to come up with the right choices."

He picked up the book and held it gingerly, "Professor, you make this book sound a little bit like a book of dark magic."

I had to smile at that, "Well, in a way it is. But I think that there's very little purely dark magic—or white magic either, for the matter of that. Instead, almost all magic is without color. It can either be turned into black magic or white magic depending on how it's used.

That's what that book is, really, a book of colorless magic. It's your choice how you use it."

With that Cedric got up and walked to the door, opened it and turned. "Well, I'll see you around, professor." Then he had an afterthought, "Oh, I never thanked you for this," he held up the book, "and I never opened the letter."

"Go on. I'm pretty sure I know what the letter says. And, you're very welcome to the book. Whether you pitch it in the fire or read it cover to cover, don't think that you'll offend me by your choice. The only thing that would offend me would be if you didn't use your brains in making that choice. Good luck."

He closed the door behind him and headed down the hall. I thought about our conversation. I had no idea that I'd have a very similar conversation with another Hogwarts student a few years down the road, but for the moment, I had papers to grade.

Chocolate

The night before the Hogwarts Express left for school, Minerva and I had decided to celebrate the last day of freedom before being incarcerated. Like a school boy on Sunday night, we decided to live large or at least at-large. So, we went to Diagon Alley and strolled the streets and the shops and then had dinner at the Leaky Cauldron. We sat at our favorite table near the hearth and felt like life was good—at least for this night. We'd reserved a room and were on our way up when I passed a table that had a lone wizard sitting, sipping coffee.

He was reading a book. There was a picture of the author on the cover. I thought that he seemed familiar, so I stopped and asked him if he minded if I glanced at his book. He handed it over. The book was *A Brief History of Time*. "Where did you find that book?"

He looked up at me quizzically and said, "Why at Flourish and Blots, of course."

I hit my forehead with my fist. "How can that be? I was just there a couple of weeks ago and it wasn't on the shelves. Did you just buy it?"

He innocently said, "No, it was about a month ago."

I stared at him incredulously trying to think how I could have missed that book. I decided there was only one way, "What section did you find it in?"

The man was nonchalant as he answered, "Why, the Muggle Fiction section, of course. I enjoy reading some light fiction. I think the last thing I read was something called, uh, *Cosmos*, by somebody, uh, uh, was it Sovern or Sanderson, something like that?"

I nodded dully. Yes, fiction. I suppose that's it. I answered him absently, "Sagan."

"What?"

"The name you're looking for is Sagan—Carl Sagan."

"Oh, yeh. Could have been."

"Was."

I joined Minerva and walked up the stairs with her. As we went, I noticed a poster—a "wanted" poster. I stopped and looked at the fierce-looking face that seemed to stare out of the poster and even seemed to be screaming at the on-lookers. I asked Minerva, "So that's the famous DeathEater?'

"Yes, Sirius Black. One of the coldest-blooded killers of all the DeathEaters. With him around, I'd not blame you for carrying that infernal Grock of yours."

"That's Glock."

"Whatever."

We enjoyed the rest of the evening and "slept in" because the Express didn't leave until almost noon. We went down and found Tom, the barman. He nodded at us and asked if we wanted anything to drink. Minerva just said, "Only breakfast."

"You mean brunch don't you?"

"Whatever, Tom. Poached eggs and toast for me."

I thought about it and asked for eggs sunny-side up and toast. We sat at the bar and talked to Tom. He was always a good source of gossip. This morning he was talking about what had happened to Harry Potter—well, actually to his aunt who had somehow gotten blown up like a giant balloon and floated away on the wind. She'd eventually been found, deflated and her memory had been obliviated. Apparently, Harry had somehow done it, which was pretty amazing, given that he didn't have his wand at the time.

"You're kidding, right, Tom?"

He shook his head and said, "I heard the Minister himself, who ate here in one of the private rooms with Harry Potter last night, say so. He stayed the night."

I asked Tom, "What in the world had his Aunt done that justified blowing her up?"

"Oh, I don't know. Maybe, making him wash the dishes after dinner?"

Minerva said, "Don't be facetious. He isn't a vindictive young man."

I asked, "That sounds like a serious charge. If true, I'm not surprised that the Minister might be involved, so what happened this morning?"

Minerva said, "Well, technically, it breaks the underage wizardry law."

I asked, 'What do you mean underage wizardry? Every day at Hogwarts and even, occasionally, on the Hogwarts Express, underage wizards and witches are doing magic."

"Yes, magic at school or even on the train, which is considered an extension of school, is permitted. It's just away from school that underage wizardry isn't permitted—for just such reasons. It's too dangerous not to be under adult supervision."

"Right. I'd say, even under adult supervision, it's pretty darn dangerous. So, what's the age limit of underage wizardry."

Minerva answered, "It's the age of majority."

"Eighteen?"

"No, no. That's Muggle majority. Wizarding majority is 17."

"Then, seventh years can do wizardry anywhere?"

"Right. Usually seventh years are seventeen."

"Underage Wizardry sounds like a serious offence."

"Well, it depends on the age, don't you know." Tom interjected.

Minerva carried on, "Yes, before a young person is old enough to go to Hogwarts, it's practically impossible for them not to do underage wizardry without their realizing it. And, it's normally not detected because the kids are with their parents and relatives, at least some of whom are wizards or witches.

"But when they start at a school like Hogwarts, it's different. They're old enough to understand that it's wrong. Up through 3rd or 4th year, no one really pays much attention to underage wizardry unless something really serious happens."

"Blowing up your aunt strikes me as fairly serious." I couldn't believe that Potter hadn't gotten some sort of reprimand.

"Oh, those sorts of things happen. What is it that you Muggles say, 'No harm, no foil?'" Tom was grinning broadly as he said it.

"Something like that."

Minerva added, "Anyway, it's really 5th and 6th years that people pay attention to. They're old enough to really understand the consequences, and they should have fair reasoning skills and self-control by then."

"Well, Minerva, this puts a whole new light on visiting the Weasley's. I think I'll save up those visits and do them during term, while all the kids are at Hogwarts."

Tom shrugged and said, "Potter left for the station with the Weasleys just before you got up."

I was surprised, "You mean they stayed the night here too?"

"Certainly."

"It was a busy night for you."

"The night before the beginning of the term at Hogwarts always is."

We finished our breakfast and disapparated to King's Cross station or, at least, an alley outside King's Cross. We made the harrowing trip through the barrier between tracks 9 and 10 that led onto track 9 ¾. Minerva thought it was nothing to walk through, but I had nightmares of being disconnected from Minerva half-way through and finding myself imbedded in a brick wall. Several successful crossings allowed me to make the adventure with an apparent air of unconcern, but in truth I was internally sweating bullets. I always thought of the time I'd stood on the high diving board as a kid, unable to force myself to take the plunge into the pool for what seemed like hours. I'd gone back from time to time and done it a few more times. I'd seemed calm and collected, but I never had done it without my guts churning.

That obstacle surmounted again, I went on with Minerva to the train and took up my post in the Teacher's Car. It was, for me, a special sort of place, as always. It seemingly was suspended half-way between conventional Muggle reality and the magic world of wizards and witches. While you were on the Express, especially in the Teacher's Car, you might easily think that you were in a normal train crossing the vast wastes of Scotland. That was, of course, until a student turned his nose into a pig snout and the jinx had to be reversed.

Minerva and I took a couple of rounds of the train. For once everyone seemed to be on reasonably good behavior. That was so much true, that Minerva took a round without me. She insisted that I keep my comfy seat in the Teacher's Car, and she told me that she'd be back in a few minutes.

I was busy reading *The Times*. It would be a whole term before I'd be able to read it at leisure again. After a while, I noticed that the temperature in the car seemed to be a bit cool. I looked up and discovered that the windows of the car were glazed over with ice. What the hell was happening? We had passed into Scotland, which is generally cooler than England, but I'd never seen anything like this in early September. Suddenly, the train halted and nearly threw me to the floor. I staggered for a moment, regained my balance and went to the door that connected to the next car. I was going to find Minerva or the conductor.

The lights went out and I fumbled in the dark to find the handle for the door to the next car. I considered getting the Glock out, but decided to wait until there was some definite sign of menace. The next car was the Slytherin Car. I found that it was preternaturally quiet. As I entered, I felt it definitely get cooler and felt an oppressive sadness. That was it. I pulled out my Glock and asked the car in general, "Anyone hurt here?"

There was no answer. That was truly ominous for a normally cocky and boisterous bunch of kids. I told them to stay where they were and told them that I was going to find out what had happened. A voice that I recognized as Malfoy's said, "Like we'd want to go with you?" I was relieved that things weren't too bad here.

I fought an ever increasing reluctance to move on. I decided that was a good sign that I was getting close to whatever the trouble was. The next car had mostly Hufflepuffs who were as silent as the Slytherin's. I went on to the next car which had compartments. Suddenly out of one there was a silvery cloud that shot out and came down the aisle toward

223

me. I felt a rush of panic and fear, and then it was gone. For a moment I thought it was caused by the silvery cloud, but it had disappeared before it had passed me. I didn't have time to ponder over that. I headed on toward the next car but stopped at the compartment that had emitted the cloud.

There was now light coming out of it. I looked in and found that the light was coming from a wand that was held by a strange adult. Besides him there were the Three,—Weasley, Grainger, and Potter. Weasley and Grainger were ashen-faced, but Potter looked even worse. He was lying on the floor and the stranger was kneeling over him. He looked up and said, "I think Potter's going to be OK." Then he caught a glimpse of my Glock, which I immediately put in my pocket.

I said, "Good. I'm going to find Professor McGonagall."

The stranger nodded, and I left to look for Minerva. I proceeded back through the cars. The next several had mixed groups of kids from all four houses. Toward the end, I found MInerva. When I'd almost reached her, the lights came back on and the train lurched into motion. I barely caught myself before falling. When I reached her, I drew her aside out of earshot of any of the students and asked, "What the hell happened?"

"It was Dementors. Didn't you see—oh, of course, Muggles can't see them."

"I suppose they were looking for Black."

She nodded but seemed troubled by something. I went on, "We'd better take a survey and see if anyone else is hurt besides Potter."

Minerva's head lifted immediately, "Is Potter hurt?"

"Well, he looked like he was unconscious when I was at his compartment, but there's someone there whom I don't know. He seemed to be looking after Potter. The other two of the Trio seemed to be not a whole lot better."

"Let's not waste any more time here. Take me to him."

We went back to the Gryffindor car, but I insisted on checking on students in the cars in between. No one seems to have been harmed permanently. When we got to Potter's compartment, we found him up and eating a chocolate bar.

Minerva apparently knew the stranger, "Good evening Professor Lupin. Let me introduce another Hogwarts Professor—Professor

Wendt." We shook hands, and since everything seemed under control, Minerva and I proceeded to the Teacher's Car. We were quite close to Hogwarts now and the train had begun slowing.

We arrived at the station and helped students off the train and into the horseless carriages with their luggage. When the last had left, I started toward one of the few remaining carriages. Minerva cleared her throat and said, "I'm apparating to the castle grounds. Are you joining me? Or are you riding by yourself in that carriage, hmmm?"

I grimaced and weighed the options. The self-propelled carriage was just a little spooky for me to ride in alone. I mentally flipped a coin and held out my hand to Minerva, who took it with a smile. I was so disoriented when we arrived that I lost my balance and ended up on the ground. She gave me a hand up, which I took. I felt like pulling her down so she'd know what it felt like falling to the ground.

She urged me along, "I've got to be at the castle to welcome the first years. Hurry!"

We arrived at the main entrance, and she immediately sent me off on an errand. "Go find Dumbledore and let him know what's happened on the train. If he's not in the Great Hall, he'll probably be in his office. The inner password's 'Lemon Meringue Pie'." Only heads of houses got to know the password for that inner office, so I considered myself part of an elite group. But I'd rather have stayed with Minerva. She just shooed me off.

Dumbledore wasn't at the Great Hall but I found him in his office. He was surprised that it was I who showed up. I explained that Minerva wanted him to know about the attack on the train right away, and she was tied up with the first years.

"Of course. What was your impression of the 'attack'?"

"Well, I understand the Dementors hanging around where Potter is because of the presumption that Black would want to finish the job that his boss muffed. What I don't understand is why they apparently attacked Potter. No one else was so affected. One of them actually entered the compartment where Potter was. That was something that none of them had done in any other compartment. Surely they could tell that Black wasn't there."

Dumbledore, who had risen, apparently to go leave for the Feast, sat again. His expression black, he stared at a wall of portraits and after a while said, 'I don't know. I wish I did. And you don't have an idea?"

"Are you kidding? I didn't even know that Dementors existed until this summer."

Dumbledore shrugged and said, "Let's go down to the feast. There's no point in missing a good feed just because we're dumbfounded."

We left the office, and Dumbledore took off at a near-run. As he went, he called back at me over his shoulder, "Did you meet Professor Lupin?"

"Yes, I did. He was in Potter's car."

"Good."

We arrived at the Great Hall. It was beginning to fill with students, and most of the teachers were there. I took my place near one end of the table. Professor Charity Burbage sat next to me closer to the end of the table. Then Lupin showed up and took the end seat—his patrimony as the professor with least seniority. I got up and asked Charity to change places with me.

"But, you're in your proper seat. I don't want to break protocol."

I said, "That's all right. I want to talk with Professor Lupin." She acceded to my request, so I got to sit next to Lupin.

"Welcome, Professor Lupin. I hope you'll excuse my curiosity, but I'd like to know if you're aware of the apparent curse on the Chair of Defense Against the Dark Arts?"

Lupin stared at me a moment and answered, "You are extremely honest. Yes, I do know about the curse."

"And yet, you accepted the post."

'I'll be as honest as you. Frankly, I needed a post, and Professor Dumbledore was good enough to offer me this one." Then he looked down at his plate and began eating, but I would not be prevented from continuing.

"I know that you've seen some hard times recently. The well-worn condition of your trunk testifies to that."

He barked a short laugh and cracked a smile, "Yes, I'll give you the condition of my trunk."

I went on, "But, that certainly doesn't explain why you were in a student car sitting in the same compartment as Potter. I've got a feeling that it's not by luck that you happened to be there when trouble struck Potter."

He just continued eating, so I added, "and I think that you may have been doing Dumbledore more of a favor than he was doing you."

Lupin looked up from his meal and said, "Let's just leave it that we both did the other a favor. Hmmm?"

"OK, for now." After that Lupin asked me about my post. I told him about being the English Literature Teacher. He chuckled at that and commented that Dumbledore had had that particular bee up his bonnet for quite some time. He asked why Dumbledore had hired a Squibb to teach English Literature.

"Well, he couldn't find a wizard or witch to do it. I was the next best thing." We talked about my personal history—Ohio and Stanford and London. Lupin was very shy about talking about his history. He seemed like a decent sort, but there had to be something in his history that explained his apparent recent poverty. He was clearly a good teacher. Dumbledore wouldn't have put him in Defense if he weren't a good teacher. Then I remembered Lockhart. Well, everyone has their lapses, but I decided not to press Lupin any further.

Just before the end of the Beginning of Term Feast, Dumbledore announced that he wanted to see the staff in the Teacher's Lounge immediately after students were in their dorms. There was a general groan at the teacher's table, which Dumbledore conveniently pretended not to hear. Lupin wondered if this were normal.

"Well, I wonder. The first year that I was here it didn't happen, and then in the 2nd year, it happened. The staff was surprised, and it's been happening ever since."

"Any idea what it's about?"

"It's always been about externalities, as the economists say."

"You mean like Dementors on the grounds?"

"Yeh, that's the kind of thing I mean."

Neither of us had any responsibility for getting Das Kinder off to bed, so we decided that we might as well go directly to the Teacher's Lounge—especially since Lupin had never been there. We were not the only ones with the thought. When we arrived, a good quarter of the staff,

227

at least, had already taken all the good spots on sofas and comfortable arm chairs. We pulled a couple of hard-backed chairs out from tables, and at least were able to get good locations for hearing Dumbledore.

Over the next half-hour, the rest of the staff ambled in. Minerva was one of the last since she was in charge of Gryffindor. I had saved her a hard chair next to me, which she gladly took. Dumbledore came in shortly after she did. Then, he took his normal place at these fireside chats, beside the fire in the large hearth. He paced up and down a couple of times, surveying the staff, making sure everyone was here or who-knows-what.

Then he began, "As I announced at the feast tonight, we have some not-entirely-welcome guests this term—The Dementors of Azkaban prison. Nominally, they are here to protect us and capture the escaped prisoner, Sirius Black.

"In reality, they don't care in the least for our safety. They only want to capture Black. And, as a matter of fact, if they had to harm any of us—students or teachers—to capture Black, they wouldn't hesitate to do it for a second.

"Consequently, there are several things that we need to do to protect ourselves:

1. Stay out of the Dementor's way. I'll talk more about that later.

2. If you have any hint of where Black is or, indeed, of anything out of the ordinary, contact the house heads or me immediately.

3. Be prepared to use a Patronus charm to protect yourselves and any students who happen to be in harm's way."

I raised my hand and Dumbledore, lifted his and said, "Please hold your questions for a few minutes. I'll try to answer the most frequently asked questions, and then I'll throw the floor open for your questions.

"I realize that there are a couple of people on the staff who can't create a Patronus charm or even see Dementors because they are Squibbs. For them, I suggest—no, I insist—that you remain on the castle grounds. No trips to Hogsmeade until Black is captured.

"Also, remember that almost every student is in as much danger as you are. Only advanced Newt students can produce a Patronus, and those are usually pretty sad affairs that couldn't hold off a Boghart let alone a Dementor.

"Which brings me to my next point. I need to find out how many teachers can produce a potent, reliable Patronus. Don't be shy. Just raise your wands." About a dozen went up. There were the usual strong wizards and witches—Snape, Minerva, Flitwck. But there was also a surprise—Professor Sinistra. She was a good witch, but she was constantly trying to prove herself. Dumbledore went on, "All right, now a harder question. Everyone who couldn't produce a Patronus to save your life (and it might just come to that) should raise your hands. Again, don't be shy. It's terribly important for the welfare of all our students that every teacher knows how to produce a patronus.'

There were about ten slow hands raised. There were about another 15 who weren't in either group. Dumbledore said, "All right. We're going to pair up to teach the Patronus spell. Males with males; females with females. You're all assigned to work together one hour every other day until you all can produce a working Patronus."

There was a noticeable sigh of relief. I don't know who was doing the sighing but it was palpable. Dumbledore said, "Oh, one more thing."

The sigh stopped. Dumbledore went on, "And all you who didn't raise your hands will report to me in my office to demonstrate your Patronuses." It was as if the air were let out of the room. "So, let's get to it. All the ones who can do Patronuses on the right side of the room. Those who can't in the center and the rest on the left side of the room. Right and center pair up. Left side, I'll start making appoints with you tomorrow."

With that a few on the left side of the room migrated to the center of the room. And one went to the right side of the room. Of course, Filch and I were in the center. No one moved to pair with us, of course. After a moment, Filch said, "Care to join me for a spot of something?'

Since I knew what the "something" was if it were in Filch's office, I suggested, "Why don't we go up to my office." Filch was somewhat dumbfounded but agreed.

229

We reached my office and when I opened the door, I found Professor McGonagall waiting. I said, "Minerva, " and I was stuck for something to say next.

She picked up the slack. "I see that you've already invited a drinking buddy up to your place."

My mind raced trying to find an acceptable way out of this mess. Minerva again beat me to the punch, "Oh, never mind. I'll see you tomorrow."

Filch commented, "Well, you handled that well." and he took a seat in my red leather chair. "Well, we're burning moonlight, Professor. Are we going to do some drinking or not."

I sat behind my desk, and opened up my lower right drawer where I kept my Dewar's. I was still trying to think of a way to deal with the situation that I'd just muffed. Filch asked what I was waiting for. I answered, "I've got two bottles in here—one that's already open and one that's not. I was just trying to choose."

"Don't be daft, boy. The choice is obvious. We'll finish both off. It doesn't matter which you pick." And I could see the pleasure in his eyes. I shrugged and pulled out the already opened bottle and a couple of glasses and poured. Before I picked mine up, Filch had tossed off the glass at one go and held the glass out for a refill. As I poured, he smacked his lips. Well he should. That was much better whiskey than he ever had in his drawer.

Filch commented, "Not bad. Not a match for mine, but not bad."

As I took a sip of mine, I thought, "Not bad! Not bad! He should be so lucky as to get invited up to share some of my Dewars." I took a second drag on the smoky burning elixir. "Oh well, I guess I've just got to grin and bear this cross." I said to myself.

Somehow the evening passed, and I hadn't drunk more than two stiff shots. I'd lost count of how many Filch had had, but he was able to navigate himself down to his office, and he'd had a good time. At least one of us had. He'd loosened up and told stories of the real troublemakers the school had had over the years. One story in particular fascinated me. It seemed that there was a little gang who had made a curious map. The map showed the interior of Hogwarts and the immediate grounds—no big feat. But the amazing thing about it was that it also showed the location of every person on the grounds—along with their names. It had disappeared recently. He suspected everyone, but especially the Weasleys.

He told me about kids sneaking off to Hogsmeade when they were on restriction. There were some secret passages out of the castle. Filch had made it his life's goal to find and close them all. I wished him luck. I didn't tell him about the one that Minerva and I had found during last school year.

The next morning, I woke up with what I thought might be a hangover, but I decided it must only be a reaction to the first day of term and the thought of having to face a classroom full of students.

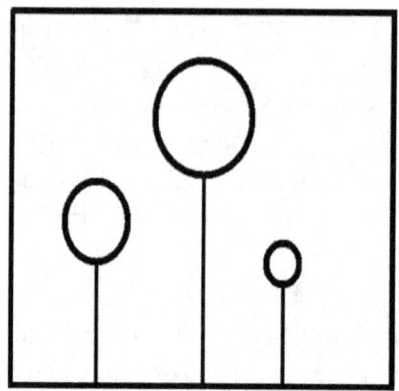

Dallying with Dementors

The next couple of weeks passed without significant incident. The weather had turned terrible lately. You couldn't go for a walk without being rained on. And it felt like it was only a few degrees from being snow. The Quidditch teams still practiced despite the terrible weather. I was so glad that I wasn't a Quidditch player that it almost made me feel comfortable to see the teams drag out into the weather and then come in dripping wet.

Minerva and I were having breakfast one Saturday. She asked me, "Do you have waterproof robes?"

I squinted at her with one eye and asked, "And why would I want waterproof robes?"

"You mean to tell me that you don't know what's happening today?"

"I mean to tell you that I don't want to know—if it means that I have to go out in that stuff."

She gave me one of her penetrating gazes that seemed to give her visibility directly into my heart. "Today is the first Quidditch match of the season."

I stared up through the transparent ceiling at the storm clouds roiling overhead. There was lightning. I said, "Look up there! There's lightning!"

She glanced up and said, "It looks like."

"It looks like? It looks like! You don't mean to tell me that people play Quidditch in this kind of weather?"

"Sure, why not. You Americans play that game you call 'football' in this kind of weather."

"In the first place, even the Pro's don't play when there's lightning, and any organizer of youth athletics would be lynched if he let kids play outdoors in the lightning.

Warming up to the subject, I added, "When I was at Ohio State, they wouldn't let you swim in an indoor pool if there were a bad storm going. You didn't even have to have lightning."

"I never thought you Americans were such namby-pamby's."

I didn't pay attention to the flippant comment but insisted that we go up to see Dumbledore to get the game postponed. Minerva shook her head, but we ran up to Dumbledore's office anyway. When we arrived, we found him just putting on rain-proof robes.

"Well, two of my favorite people. What can I do for you?" He was wearing his usual smile.

I found myself a little reluctant to start off. "Come, come, I know you have something that you want to talk about."

"Yes, I came to suggest to you that the weather is too dangerous for a Quidditch game. Lightning is extremely dangerous—even if you're standing on the ground, but for people in the air .-.-." I let my voice trail off.

But Dumbledore simply said, "But even you Muggles are often in the air during storms, thunder storms."

I laughed and said, "True enough, but airplanes are different. They have protection that wizards and witches on brooms don't have."

"Oh, really. What is that?"

"The laws of physics. Electricity can't penetrate conductors like metals—the metal skin of an airplane. Broom riders don't have that."

Regardless of my arguments Dumbledore would not relent. We, all three, went down to the Quidditch pitch. The entire game, for me, was one of constant fear and anticipation of disaster. The game was played in a pelting, cold rain. The skies were shivered by bursts of lightning and the crack of thunder. The air was dark enough that no one, including the student announcer could see the action to announce it. Quaffles were indistinct gray blobs in a dark grey background. Bludgers flew unheeded. There would have been a half-dozen serious injuries except that the beaters couldn't see where to hit the bludgers when they could find them —which wasn't often.

I leaned over to Minerva so that she could hear me in the din of thunder. I shouted, "How can anyone see the snitch in this weather?"

"I don't know."

"Well, how can the game end if the seekers can't see the snitch?"

"Is that all you care about—the game ending."

Sometimes she is so infuriating. "Yes, I want it to end before somebody gets killed."

Minerva shook her head and shouted back, "Nobody's going to get killed." We looked back at the game. I didn't see either seeker.

I asked Minerva where they were. Her response was, "Oh, they've probably just flown up into the clouds going after the snitch— see, one of them will catch it—I hope Potter, and then the game will be over before you know it."

Just then a body fell through the clouds. Minerva's mouth fell open. Dumbledore leaped up to his feet and pointed his wand at the body. He said in a calm voice, "Arresto Momentum." The body slowed but didn't stop until it hit the ground. I leaped up and said that I'd go get Madame Pomfry. Minerva joined me. We ran up to the castle and found Madame Pomfrey in her office. We explained what had happened. She sighed and said, 'Why is it always me?"

Just then, Dumbledore and Snape arrived with Potter suspended in midair between them. He was unconscious and they deposited him on a bed. Minerva and I got out of the way but waited outside the hospital wing for someone to come out. Snape was the first. He was striding away, but we hailed him down.

I asked, "Well?"

He turned and pretended ignorance. "Well?"

Minerva beat me to the question, 'Well, how is Potter?"

"Oh, Potter. He'll be fine. He only has some cracked ribs and a broken tibia. Madame Pomfrey has given him a dose of skele-grow. He'll be back in classes Monday or Tuesday."

I asked if he knew when visitors would be allowed to Potter. Snape said that sometime tomorrow he'd be able to have visitors. Dumbledore came out and found the three of us talking. He looked at me and asked if I were going to gloat about how correct I'd been.

'Oh, no, Professor. I'm not vindictive. It's luck. We all had bad luck—especially Potter."

Dumbledore looked over at Snape and said, "I wonder. I really wonder."

The next morning I dropped by the Hospital Wing just after breakfast. Madame Pomfrey allowed me to go in and have a look, but wouldn't let me wake him if he were sleeping. She had given him something to help him sleep because of the pain of the skele-grow regimen. I went into the ward. He was the only one there. He appeared to be asleep, but I went up to the bed just be sure. He showed no sign of being awake or awakening. So, I left.

In the afternoon, I went back to see if he were awake. He was sitting up and having a treat that a well-wisher had left—a box of chocolate frogs. As I approached he looked up and said hello. I wished him a good afternoon and asked how he was doing.

He answered that he was doing fine. I asked when he would be discharged.

"Oh, Madame Pomfrey says that she'll check my bones this evening and if everything is OK, she'll let me go tonight—in time to catch dinner."

"Good. I've got a question or two if you've got a few minutes and don't mind talking about the.-.-. uh.-.-. accident."

"Sure. What do you want to know?"

"Well, how did the accident happen?"

Potter looked up and answered, "I was chasing the snitch and it went up high into the clouds. Suddenly I was surrounded by what seemed to be dozens of Dementors. I tried to avoid them, but they seemed to be everywhere. I'm afraid I fainted and fell from my broom. I don't remember anything after that until I woke up here in the hospital wing."

"Do you have any idea why the Dementors were so interested in you? I mean I thought that they were looking for Sirius Black. You certainly don't look much like him—believe me, I've seen his poster."

"You've got me Professor. I have no idea why they paid attention to me."

I wished him well and left for the library. I'd asked the librarian if the subscription to *Scientific American* that I'd talked her into making had arrived by now.

That evening at dinner, I saw that Potter had been released. He was sitting among the Gryffindors. I managed to get a seat next to Minerva after the meal was almost over and a number of teachers had left the table. I asked her, "Doesn't it seem strange to you, how much the Dementors are interested in Potter?

"First, they stop the train, and the only car they spend any time in is Potter's. Then there's this Quidditch match. They practically swarm around him."

"How do you know that they 'practically swarmed around him'?" She looked at me quizzically.

"Well," I shrugged, 'nothing magical, I just asked him what happened."

Minerva looked at me even more quizzically. "Do you really think they are somehow interested in him?"

"Well, judge for yourself. But I think we should talk to Dumbledore about it."

She looked down at her feet for a moment and said, 'If there's anything more that happens I'll go with you, but not until." It seemed to me that she was being obtuse about it. It was pretty darn clear that the Dementors were spending a lot more time with Potter than they were with Black—even assuming he was somewhere in the area.

We turned to other topics. And for quite a while it seemed like everything was fine. There were no further incidents.

Halloween

One evening I was reading in my office when there was a knock on the door. I called out "Come."

The door opened and in came Professor Sinistra. I couldn't help sighing, "Well, what do you want?"

"You know what time of year this is."

I interrupted her. "I know what you want and I'm not having any of it."

I tried to make my voice sound like hers and said, "Oh, I have this wonderful idea. You can go to the Halloween Ball disguised as a troll. All we have to do is catch one and take a hair. Oooo, Oooo another good idea. Let's try for something easier—maybe a goblin."

"That last is not a bad idea. A goblin would be easy." She actually pretended to take me seriously.

"No. No. No! I'm not going disguised as anything."

"I could go disguised as you and do some really embarrassing things."

"No good. You've already done that. Old hat."

"Oh, come on. We've always had good fun at the party. Don't be a stick in the mud."

"You've," I emphasized the word, "always had good fun at the party—at my expense. Not this time. Besides that, I'm going with Minerva this year!"

She sat on my desk! And she leaned down and looked into my eyes. "I don't think so," she said in a sing-song way.

A sick feeling came over me, "You've not done something to her."

She leaned back and laughed, "No, of course not. She's just going to WETTING."

I was surprised that she hadn't said anything about it. So, I asked, "Whose wedding?"

She laughed again, "Not whose WETTING. Which WETTING."

"Is there more than one wedding that day?"

Something about it struck her as terribly funny. She could hardly breath she was laughing so hard. Between the gales of laughter she forced out, "No. No. Not wedding. WETTING—W, E, T, T, I, N, G. It's the Western Europe Thaumaturgy Teachers and INstructors Gathering. It's a convention every year. We take turns going. I'm surprised that you haven't heard of it."

"Well, maybe the fact that I don't teach Thaumaturgy might have something to do with that."

"Anyway, she'll be gone most of the week, including Halloween."

"Well, good for her. I hope she enjoys it."

"Oh, it's lots of good fun as well as being a source for lots of tips about teaching. They're holding it in Paris this year."

I thought to myself that I wished Sinistra were going to WETTING, but she had gone on to her big idea for Halloween this year.

"Why don't YOU pick whom we go as this year."

"In the first place, if Minerva's not going to be there, I'm not going. In the second place, I wouldn't go with you again if you were the last female teacher at Hogwarts. Finally, in the third place, Halloween has always been bad luck for me, and I'm holing up in my rooms, full stop."

"Oh, you are a spoil sport. How about this: the two of us just go as ourselves?"

I got up, walked over to the door and said, "How about this: you just walk yourself back to your office and let me finish the *Scientific American* in peace?"

I decided that I had to make sure that Sinistra was being honest when she said that Minerva would be gone for Halloween. The next time I saw her I asked Minerva about WETTING. She confirmed that everything that Sinistra had said was true. She was going to WETTING. She would leave early on Oct. 31 and would be at the convention for the opening feast and keynote address while Hogwarts was celebrating Halloween.

She was sorry that I couldn't come. "If only Halloween were on Friday, you could come down and spend the weekend with me, but I'll be back Sunday morning. Halloween will be on Wednesday this year."

"I suppose there's no way I could get out of school those days?"

"No. If you were a magic teacher, I could probably magic you an invite, but as it is. . ."

"That's all right. Halloween has always been sort of bad Karma for me. I'm just going to 'hole up' in my office that night and not open the door for anyone."

"Not even Sinistra?"

"Especially not Sinistra." But I didn't dare mention that Sinistra had paid me a visit and talked with me about Halloween.

▽

I didn't hear anything more about Halloween until the day of. It was a crazy day. Even though Halloween was on Wednesday, all the students were treating it like a holiday. There were a number of absences, and there were students constantly wandering the halls. Wednesday was my heaviest day with almost continuous classes. Hogwarts was experimenting with "block" scheduling where students could have double length classes. Wednesday, all my classes were double length except one.

By the evening, I was exhausted and could hardly drag myself into the Great Hall. Also, I was a little worried that Sinistra might have some last minute appeal to make, so I quickly filled my plate and headed off to my office to lock myself in. I got there and had a pleasant little dinner by myself. I enjoyed it so much, I thought I ought to do it every now and then. I could read and eat at the same time—something that I could never manage in the Great Hall.

About eight o'clock, there was a knock at my door. I said as firmly as I could manage, "Go away Sinistra, I'm not buying anything you're peddling."

The voice that answered me began with a distinct clearing of the throat that I immediately recognized. It was Minerva's voice. "Ok. Ok. I'm on my way." I got up and walked around the desk and briefly thought about my Glock. This was crazy, but I pulled out my purse, retrieved my Glock, slipped a loaded clip into it, made sure the safety was on, and slipped it into an inside pocket of my robe. Then, I unlocked and opened the door.

Minerva shook her head and said, "Why lock the door? And what's the point of it anyway. Any decent wizard or witch could use 'Aloe Amore' and open that lock?"

In my turn, I sneered. "Simple. The lock gives me some time to take precautions in case someone does use that spell.

"But what in the world are you doing here? I thought that you were in Paris living it up on an expense account?"

"I was, but I just didn't trust Sinistra alone here on Halloween. It's OK. I'll go back tomorrow early and all that I'll have missed is a boring keynote address and rubber chicken and overcooked vegetables at the opening feast."

"Well, I have to admit that I was 'looking forward' to a boring evening holed up here in my office. I can't complain that you decided to return for the evening."

She smiled and said, "Well, why don't you put on dress robes and we'll head for the party."

I did and we walked down to the Great Hall hand-in-hand. That was a little unusual. Minerva almost always walked briskly—too briskly for held hands. The halls were decorated with great orange globes that glowed warmly.

The Great Hall itself was packed with upper class-men and a smattering of 4th years, as usual. The theme for the party was Phantom of the Opera. Everyone was wearing a mask. In all cases, no one's identity was hidden, but Minerva and I were kidded by a number of other teachers because we didn't have masks. I was not surprised that Snape wasn't anywhere to be seen. He always avoided these parties—except when he was one of the chaperones. I didn't see Dumbledore either. He usually put in an appearance at these events, but it might have already happened.

In my second year, one of the teachers had advised me that it was important to be seen by the Headmaster at all social events sponsored by the school. I usually tried to do that, but it's a little difficult with Dumbledore because you'd have to be there at the beginning of the event to the very end to ensure that. I hadn't taken it to heart, but whenever I was at a social event and noticed Dumbledore, I would speak to him.

In line with the theme of the party, there was a great chandelier seemingly suspend from nothing. The sky above was dark, cloudy, and without moon or stars.

Minerva and I found a table. I got some pumpkin juice for us. We talked for a few minutes about the convention that she was missing. She commented that the conversation we were having was much more entertaining than any keynote address.

She asked me to dance and I agreed. The band was playing a slow dance, or at least, a dance that was not frenetic. Neither of us danced a lot but she seemed to be particularly comfortable dancing tonight. She leaned in close every time she had something to say. She had to, the band was that loud. Even so, I only caught half of her comments which were all about couples that she noticed as we danced.

The night went on without my noticing the time. Suddenly, Dumbledore was there at the podium. His amplified voice announced that it was 11PM, and all students should be in their OWN dorms and in bed before midnight. Those who didn't were liable to end up in detention with Mr. Filch. I found myself regretting that it was the end. However, the band had one last good slow dance in them. Minerva and I took to the floor. I found her leaning her head on my shoulder with both arms around my waist. I guess my arms were around her waist too. The lights had been low for the last half-hour, and I found myself day-dreaming.

The dance ended and the crowd reluctantly broke up. We had to help shoo people out of the Great Hall and then we went back up to my office. We got there and Minerva said, "I think that was a good idea— locking the door."

I took the hint and locked the door. In the meantime, Minerva had sat down on my sofa. I joined her and there was no surprise that there was not a word exchanged before we were snogging. In a break when we stopped for breath she commented, "You know, I don't have to spend the night in Gryffindor tower. I've already got a substitute to supervise them."

"How nice! Would you like to spend the night here?"

"I thought you'd never ask." Then, we resumed lip-lock.

Even though Minerva said that she had to get up early the next day, she really didn't have to. But I had classes the next day. So eventually I said that it was time for bed. Minerva perked up and said, "I thought you'd never ask."

I hadn't been thinking exactly the way she had, but I wasn't sorry that she took it that way. We immediately headed for the bedroom. Minerva was constantly being helpful, by magically removing clothes—mine. Frankly I got one or two of her things off her when we fell into bed.

I managed to remove her hairpins by a miracle of concentration while she was trying to distract me from my goal. As soon as I did, her hair cascaded down over her shoulders and back. It was soft, silky, and made caressing her even more sensual that it normally was. We were busy caressing and kissing when she said, "Sorry to disappoint. I'm having my period, but that doesn't mean that we can't enjoy the evening."

That seemed a little strange. "I thought you had your period three weeks ago."

"I don't know, I just know I'm having it now."

Which was really—for once—OK with me. I was pretty exhausted after the full day of classes some of which were doubles, followed by the party, and followed by—well, followed by some moderately strenuous or at least stimulating kanoodling. Now, why did that word come to mind? It was hardly a Briticism. But I accepted it, and we just enjoyed some wonderful caresses. I ended up spooning her.

My face was buried in her cloud of fragrant hair. Every warm breath reminded me with whom I was lying. I mumbled through that cloud of hair, "I'm so lucky to be with you. I love you."

She responded with a surprisingly soft answer, "Me too." We were on our left sides and she drew my right arm across her body slowly down and down ending with my caressing the inside of her left thigh. I was so exhausted that I drifted off to sleep slowly with my hand held in place between her thighs.

Sometime during the night my sleep was disturbed, but I didn't truly wake. When I finally was awakened by my alarm, I was disconsolate that I was alone in bed. I got up to see if she were still in my apartment, but found that she'd left. I guessed that she'd been serious about wanting to go to that conference early. Suddenly it seemed very lonely.

Thursday was a light day. If I had been willing to miss breakfast, I might have gone back to bed. But, breakfasts and indeed every meal are not to be missed at Hogwarts. I had a good breakfast that somehow didn't satisfy. The day dragged on and finally ended. The next went nearly as slowly.

Then on Saturday, I tried to keep in mind that Minerva would be back the next day. After breakfast, I wandered out to the courtyard, where students were lined up to go to Hogsmeade. The weather was cool, and there was a bit of snow in the air with the appearance of more to come. As I stood enjoying the cool crisp air, someone spoke my name.

"Professor Wendt, may I ask you a question? Why yes. What can I do for you Mr. Potter?"

He handed me a piece of paper and asked, "Would you mind signing this permission slip?"

I scanned through it quickly. It gave permission for one Harry Potter to visit Hogsmeade when there was a Hogsmeade weekend. It required a parent, guardian or house head to sign it. I had to give Potter the bad news, "I'm sorry. I can't sign this. It has to be signed by a guardian or house head. I'd send you to Minerva, but she's not back yet. Maybe another house head would sign it for you, maybe Sn.-.-."

Potter resignedly said, "Yes, Yes. Snape is not exactly a buddy of mine. And the others, well they pretty much follow the Minerva line—I'm not safe in Hogsmeade."

"You're quite right. I don't think that I'd sign it even if I had the right to sign it."

"But that's so unfair." Harry's mouth was set in a hard line and it was pretty easy to tell that he was angry.

"It sure is. Look, Potter, do you know the expression, 'permission to speak frankly'."

The completely unexpected question seemed to have knocked him out of his funk for a moment. "I don't .. . I've never heard of it, but I guess I know what it means."

"I think you do."

He stopped for a minute trying to compose a good definition, "It means that what you say won't be held against you."

"That pretty much is it. I'm going to make you an offer, perhaps never to be repeated. We'll each speak with permission to speak frankly. What do you say?"

Potter seemed confused. "Are you saying that I can say anything and you'll not remember it?"

"Pretty much. I can respect confidentiality. Can you?"

He looked up into my eyes for the first time and hesitated. Then he said, "Yes. Let's do it." Now he spoke with determination. "You don't understand what it is to be left out of everything. To be a captive in this castle."

"Do you know that I can't leave the castle either?"

"What do you mean, you're a teacher. You can go anytime you want—even weekdays."

"No, I can't. Dumbledore doesn't want me to leave. Do you know that I can't defend myself from Dementors in any way? I can't even see them. When they're around I can sense the feeling of dread and despair, but I can't even know which direction to go to keep out of their way."

Potter started to say casually, "Well, you're a Squibb like Fi.-.-." But he stopped and seemed to be trying to work out how to proceed. "Yea. OK. I get it, you're a victim of circumstances that you don't control. But.-.-. But.-.-." He was stuck again.

I broke in, "But nothing. We're both screwed."

"But, you're a teacher. You enjoy sitting around in your office grading papers."

I just stared at him and after a bit he said, "OK. So, you don't like being cooped up here any more than I do. What are we supposed to do?"

"Why don't you tell me how bad it is for you?"

He stared at me for a minute and said, "It's, it's unfair and evil and bloody wrong!" He went on like that for a while. Finally, he fell silent.

I asked him, "Anything else that you want to add?"

He looked down and said, "No."

"Then, I'll be seeing you around." Just then I noticed the Weasley twins walking across the courtyard in our general direction. I added, "Yon, Fred and George have a lean and hungry look. They're still here, so they must be serving a detention."

Harry turned and said, "Are you sure?"

I laughed and asked, "Aren't you?"

He laughed and headed into the castle.

It was a boring day. I went to bed early and took my time getting up. But I made it to breakfast. I was speculating idly when Minerva would get back. I decided that she'd be back in time to have dinner at Hogwarts if it were at all feasible. She didn't disappoint me. I was early for dinner and was sitting at the head table in my usual seat when people started wandering in. After a good number of students and teachers had arrived, I saw HER enter through the main doors. I leapt up and trotted down to her, made sure there wasn't anyone in sight, hugged her and gave her an enthusiastic kiss.

She seemed a little surprised and said, "Well your impetuosity is definitely up this evening."

"Well, you should hardly be surprised."

"I've only been gone a couple of days." As we walked back to the head table, she said, "I'll see you in your rooms after I unpack."

The dinner couldn't finish quickly enough for me. I sprinted back to my office and looked for something to keep myself occupied until Minerva arrived. I finally decided to try reading. I had the Sunday

245

Times and had not had the concentration earlier to try the crossword. And truly, I didn't have any better concentration, but it was the only thing I could think of. I started working it and had maybe found two words when there was a knock on the door. I leaped up and said, "Come" at the same time that I trotted to the door. She opened it and had hardly crossed the threshold when I had her in my arms and was giving her a serious kiss. She seemed a bit surprised at my ardor but was not unappreciative. When we finally broke, she commented on the pascion of my greeting. I started to reply that after Halloween she could hardly be surprised, but before I'd gotten that half-way out of my mouth, I had another thought—a terrible, scary, impossible thought—maybe it hadn't been Minerva on Halloween. Maybe, it was Sinistra!

With that thought came the realization that I was in a boat-load of trouble. I thought feverishly about how to deal with it. As I saw it I had three options—one of which was slow suicide and the other two weren't much better.

One option was to maintain an appearance of ignorance. The thought had never occurred to me and I'd say what I'd been about to say with perfect openness and candor and let Minerva point out that she'd not been here at Halloween and let come what would come. That was not a bad idea, but I wasn't sure that I could pull that off well enough to fool her into thinking that I'd never had the thought that it was anyone but Minerva on Halloween.

Another option was to pretend that nothing had happened. That was pure suicide. Eventually Minerva would find out and then I'd better be out of the country.

The third option was to right away be completely open and honest, tell her what had happened on Halloween and admit that the possibility that it hadn't been Minerva had just occurred to me. The problem with that is that she would probably not want to believe me. Only the complete purity of my heart in this could convince her that I was telling the truth. BUT then there was the fact of my having spent most of the night with the imposter in bed. Did I dare fess up to that? On the one hand, Minerva might never learn the complete truth and might remain blissfully ignorant of that detail. On the other hand, it would be just the sort of thing that Sinistra would do to save that little detail up for a rainy day when she could open the bag completely and get some satisfaction from Minerva or more likely blackmail me.

All that flew through my mind in a few seconds but Minerva had certainly noticed the pause in my conversation and asked me what was wrong. I pursed my lips and decided in that moment that my best strategy was to open the bag completely and take what might come. So, I said, "Minerva, I'm going to tell you a little Halloween tale—a true Halloween tale.

"I was holed up in this very office with the door locked and hoping to survive the night without a disaster happening, when there was a knock on the door followed by your voice asking to be let in." I paused for effect. Minerva was completely deadpan. She just did a little nod to show that she'd heard what I'd said.

I went on, "As, I'm sure that you've already surmised, it was actually Sinistra." A faint and hard smile formed on Minerva's face. "But she claimed that she, uh, that is you had decided that she couldn't be trusted and she'd—or—you'd returned for the night."

Minerva stopped me, "So, you believed that I would miss a night in Paris and return for one night here."

"Well, she said that the events of the evening were a keynote and rubber chicken for dinner."

"Absolutely right, but nobody attends the opening dinner and keynote address."

"Anyway, she suggested that we should go to the party and enjoy ourselves."

Minerva's eyes rolled and she said, "Which I'm sure you did."

"Well, yes." Here I rushed on because I was afraid that Minerva would surmise what happened next, and I thought it would be better for me to voluntarily say it than to have her force it out of me. "And after the dance was over, I .-.-. or I guess it was actually she invited herself up to my office because she—er—you had arranged for someone to take her duties in Gryffindor tower."

I couldn't talk fast enough because she broke in and in a sarcastic voice said, "And of course, that meant that the two of you had to share your bed."

Here was the moment of maximum dynamic stress, I tried to resolutely and with dignity say, "Yes, Minerva that's exactly what

247

happened, BUT she said that she was having her period, so it was platonic—pretty much."

Minerva seemed frozen on the spot; she just stared at me and moved not a muscle. I was terrified that she was going through her entire repertoire of curses, looking for the one that would cause me the maximum amount of pain. What she did next completely surprised me. She simply walked to the office door and went through it.

I called after her, "Minerva!"

She said, "Don't you dare speak to me again." She used a voice that I'd never heard before and I suppose she reserved for the Weasley twins.

I said to myself, "Well, you're still walking and talking."

The next several weeks were the most miserable that I'd ever experienced in my life. I barely ate—even the superb food served at table in the Great Hall. I mechanically went through the paces of planning lessons, grading papers, conducting classes. At one point, Filch noticed that I was off form and suggested that I join him in his office and share a nip with him. It's a sign of how depressed I was that I went along with the idea and didn't even suggest having something decent to drink in my office.

The turning point was just then. Sitting in Filch's office taking that first swallow of that infernal fire whiskey woke me up. This might be the end of my world with Minerva. If it was, I'd better wake up and get on with life. I genuinely thanked Filch for the drink and was ready to go.

Filch stared at my glass and noticing that I had left some fire whiskey in it, he expressed shock.

I replied, "Filch, you've done wonders for me. I was depressed because Minerva threw me over, but you made me realize that the world is wider than one relationship. I can't thank you enough. I've got to get going. I'm burning moonlight."

Filch stared at me and said something like, "Whut?" But I was gone.

Minerva and I rarely crossed paths over the next couple of weeks. We had become expert in unconsciously anticipating the other's movements and avoiding them. Those rare meetings in a hallway or in the Great Hall were ones of averted eyes and care to avoid accidental brushes.

The end of the term was approaching. One day after class, I was cleaning the blackboard and had my back turned toward the door to the classroom. Suddenly, I was aware of another presence in the room. I was about to turn when a familiar voice asked, "Professor, do you have a couple of minutes."

"Of course, Cedric. What can I do for you?"

He was a bit shy when it came to making requests. He glanced at his feet and said, "I was wondering if you'd fancy helping me get into that Chess tournament at Christmas?"

I had completely forgotten that it happened every year. And I'd rather lost track of everything except what I absolutely had to do to keep classes going. "Sure Cedric. I'd meant to bring the topic up myself. So, I'd better get moving. I'll get a letter off to the Tradewise Trafalgar people today."

"Thanks, sir. You know, I've been reading *Modern Chess Openings*. I haven't finished it, but I've got a lot better idea of how the openings work. You know, the more I read it, the more sense it makes to me. I play a little game where I try to anticipate the best path for white and black as I read and I've gotten fairly good at anticipating what the book has to say."

"Good for you. I'm anxious to see if it has any effect on your game." I added, "I hope you're not neglecting your classes to do this."

A sly smile crossed his face. "No, I've been keeping my grades up—though I have to admit that I am sometimes tempted in Professor Bins classes to sneak out the MCO during one of his boring lectures."

"I give you Professor Bins. I've never had the misfortune to sit through one of his lectures, but they're famous throughout the school. Now, get along. I've got some grading to do."

I thought to myself that maybe I ought to sit in on one of his lectures—to get a list of tips of things NOT to do.

In the evening I wrote the letter and then was faced with a little problem. I didn't have an immediately apparent way to mail it. Mail to

Muggles was handled by putting the letter into an outer envelope that was addressed to the Wizarding Post Office that would strip off the outer envelope and put the inner one into a normal post office box. The catch was that you had to send the outer envelope by owl post, but I couldn't do that. Normally, I'd just pop off to find Minerva, but we weren't exactly on speaking terms. So, I had to think. Who could help me?

Well, there were lots of people that I could ask, but I hated to do that because inevitably the question would come up—why hadn't I just asked Minerva? Finally, I came up with a name—Snape. We weren't great friends, but he had discretion and I thought he'd do that for me. I went down to his office in the dungeon and found him there.

He asked, "Well, this is an unusual caller at an unusual hour. What can I do for you?" He put emphasis on the "can".

I was beginning to be sorry that I'd come, but I was there. So, I went on with my prepared speech, "'I have a letter that I want to send to a Muggle. I was wondering if you could send it by owl."

Snape raised one eyebrow and said, "Do I take it that you and Minerva are out of tune?"

"Yes, and I'd appreciate it if.-.-. "

"If I didn't say anything? I won't, but it hardly matters. I think practically everyone in the school understands that you and Minerva are at odds. You enter and leave the Great Hall separately. You're never seen together. Even Mr. Filch is coming to understand that all is not right between the two of you.

"I will mail your letter. You have it properly enveloped and addressed?"

I nodded and handed it over to him. He glanced at the address and said, "Fine. Is it urgent? Does it need to go out tonight?"

I told him that tomorrow would be good. He assured me that he had a couple of letters to post tomorrow, and that he'd include this with his. I thanked him and was about to leave when he had a question for me. "Wendt, we both know that the real reason that you are here is your relationship with Minerva. Does this mean that you're going to leave Hogwarts at the end of year or even the term?"

He seemed to be asking the question out of genuine interest. I thought about it a minute. The thought had never occurred to me, and I said as much. "I came here to work because it was a teaching opportunity, and I think I've been successful here as a teacher. Even if I wanted to leave, I think it would be hard to get another post on the strength of the references that I'd get from a Wizarding school—even if I dared to offer them to a Muggle head. I like Hogwarts. I like the students —mostly. I like the teachers—without qualification. Why would I leave?"

He smiled the first smile that I'd seen since I entered the room, "Then I hope that you and Minerva work out your troubles. Good luck."

The next several days were quiet with no mail arriving. I had almost forgotten that I was expecting some mail, but after a couple of days, Cedric approached me after every meal to see if a mail had arrived. It was cute the first couple of times, and then it began to become boring.

Then one morning at breakfast, among the flocks of owls delivering mail to students and teachers, one large snowy owl flew right up to my plate and dropped a large envelope onto my eggs sunny-side up and hash browns. I looked at the unappetizing mess. I picked up the envelope gingerly because the bottom half was soaked with egg yolk. The return address was obscured, but I thought that there was probably only one source for it. I used the table knife to open the envelope. The interior envelope was unaffected.

Just then Cedric appeared and started to ask, "Is that.-.-. "

I answered, "Yes, yes. It's from the tournament." I handed it to him and he stared at it. "Well are you going to open it?"

Cedric said, "This is crazy. I got in last year. Why wouldn't I get in this time?" Then, he slit the envelope and pulled out the thick sheaf of forms. The cover letter said that Cedric would have to fill out the forms and send them in. In a PS, the Tournament Director said that Cedric would certainly be accepted, and the fee would be waved if necessary. Cedric whooped and almost left his feet.

"Well, I can tell that you're bored silly."

Cedric smiled a shy little smile and said, "I guess I'm anxious to take on the upper division of the Trafalagar."

"Well, I guess that I've got to tell you that I'm not able to provide transportation to the tournament. Please get in touch with your parents and see if one of them can get us there. As a matter of fact, I can't even get myself to your home."

Cedric turned a light shade of red and glanced down at his feet for a moment. He asked, "Is there.-.-. uh.-.-. a problem between you and Professor McGonagall?"

"I really can't discuss that, but don't worry, we'll figure out ways to get you to the tournament—even if we have to ride Muggle trains."

That made Cedric smile, and he turned to go. Then, he whirled around and asked, "Are you planning on going to the Yule ball? With anyone?"

My mouth dropped open and I stared at him. I'd completely forgotten the Yule ball. What if Sinistra tried to get me to go with her? What—and this was really a scary possibility—if she disguised herself as Minerva again and pretended to make up with me. But I just shrugged at Cedric, "Who knows." Who knew indeed? How could I be sure whom I was going with?

I added, "Maybe nobody."

"Oh, come on Professor. You're always the life of the party."

"You mean the joke of the party. Whichever, I wish that I could just show up, and nobody would pay any attention."

Cedric shook his head and walked away. I went on to the first class of the morning. That evening in the Great Hall, Sinistra came over to sit next to me. I was sick. It was enough to make one want to take his meals in his office. She leaned over to whisper in my ear, "Do you know what ball is coming up in less than a week?"

"I'm afraid I do. And let me save us both some time." I decided that the only way to sanity was to declare right then and there, "I'm not going to the Yule ball. I'm sick of balls, and I don't think I'm ever going to another ball in my life."

She just shook her head and "tsked" with her tongue. "Oh, you'll think better of it. Let's not make rash decisions."

The rest of the meal, I just sat staring down into my plate and nibbling unenthusiastically while Sinistra prattled on about how wonderful the ball was going to be this year. She was on the decorations committee. She was having a wonderful time.

I didn't have the heart to try to deflate her exuberance. She was not an awful person. I was just tired, and come to think of it, it had been a long, hard semester. I deserved a little rest before the Christmas holiday.

There were finals to give and grade. That kept me busy until the night of the ball. I spent the day of the ball packing and making a Christmas list. I'd have to get my presents for friends and family in Ohio off in the mail quickly if I wanted them to arrive by Christmas. That used to be a big problem for me, but I'd solved it recently. Before I came up with the solution, I had to go shopping immediately after getting back to London. Then, I would hurriedly wrap and mail them, spending a fortune on air post. And even then, I was lucky if presents arrived at their recipient before New Years.

But this year, I had a much better plan. I had my Mom send me some American Christmas catalogs, including the JCPenney Christmas Catalog. It arrived in early December. I'd spent hours poring over it and other catalogs to find something for every relative and friend in the States. When I got to London, I'd find a pay phone and make a couple of expensive long distance calls to the catalogers in the States to place orders and have my presents delivered on time for a change!

I had spent the afternoon making final decisions, having a backup gift for each person—just in case Penney was out of stock in what I wanted. It's harder than you might think—. shopping for a dozen or so people by catalog, recording all the lot and sku numbers, sizes and colors, getting it all right.

I was suddenly almost late for supper. I ran down to the Great Hall and arrived before all the food was gone. I loaded my plate with the last dregs of scalloped potatoes and roast beef, steamed vegetables and a few cold rolls. I looked around and didn't see anyone that I was especially interested in talking to, so I did something that I'd rarely done before. I took the plate up to my office.

When I arrived there, I lit a fire in the fireplace. I watched as it sputtered into life and then caught hold. I sat at my desk and leisurely ate as I watched the fire. I had a few minutes to think about what I would do tomorrow on the train ride to London and after. Oh, I supposed there was lots to do. I had my presents to take care of. I had to arrange for the tournament and get Cedric there somehow.

I was deep in thought when there was a knock on the door. At first, I didn't quite understand what it was. Then I realized that someone was knocking on my office door. I looked up and said, "Yes?"

"Aren't you coming to the Yule ball?" It was Minerva's voice. Oh, shit, I thought. Is it Minerva or not?

I said, "Uh.-.-. " What I was going to do was dangerous. "Can you prove that?"

Minerva's voice said, "Well, if you can't tell the difference then you'll have to guess. I'll be at the Yule ball. If you want a kiss under the mistletoe, you've got to get moving."

What had started off as a really pleasant quiet evening before the rush of activity of the Christmas Holiday now had turned into another test of my judgment, resolution and strength of character. Well, I decided to take a pass on this one. I stayed in my office but it had ruined the evening for me.

The next day, I had breakfast—a sad, cold affair and made my way down to the train station. It was a cold, dark morning—overcast with the threat of snow. I boarded the train and made my way to the Teacher's Car. I stopped at the door. Hoping half-way that I would find Minerva on the other side of the door and fearing half-way that I would not find her there. I turned the door handle and found—an empty car.

I walked in and chose a stuffed armchair, opened my bag and pulled out a *Scientific American* and started reading. Later, the door opened. I immediately shot up and, hoping against hope, waited for the entrance. It was Grubbly-Plank. I said hello and she complained about drawing the duty of riding back to London. I toured the cars with her. The only bright spot in the trip was when we went through the Hufflepuff car. Cedric stopped me. He asked me if I would like to play a game of chess with him.

"Are you kidding? I wouldn't last a dozen moves against you."

"Nobody else will play with me," he complained

"Well, why would anyone? You'd make mincemeat of them blindfolded."

"It was worth a try." He went back to the book that he was reading—MCO.

The rest of the trip was boring. The one strange thing was that I didn't notice Potter on the train. He'd stayed at the castle before for Christmas. Grubbly-Plank hadn't seen him either. I was a little concerned with the possibility that we would be visited by Dementors but no such visit happened. I supposed it was because the Dementors somehow knew that Potter wasn't on board. I asked Grubbly-Plank about that speculation, but she was totally uninterested in the question. Ah, I reflected another reason that I missed Minerva.

We arrived at King's Cross, helped get kids reunited with parents, and checked the train twice through to be sure that we'd not missed out anyone. At the end of this, I realized that I had a problem. I needed to get into Diagon Alley in order to draw money out. There was another problem that I'd not thought of in my planning that could only be addressed through Gringott's—if at all.

So I asked Grubbly-Plank if she would help me go to Diagon Alley. She was surprised at first, but then realized that I had always gotten to Diagon Alley with the help of Minerva. Somehow she seemed to be the only person at Hogwarts who didn't realize that we were not "together". When she realized that, she agreed that she would be happy to take me there. We agreed that I'd meet her on the street outside the Leaky Cauldron the next day around 10 AM.

In the Muggle world, I was pretty proficient. I had no trouble making my way to the rooming house where I usually spent summers. I arrived and set to moving into the loft that the landlord kept open for me. I had bought a floor lamp that had a very bright bulb in it. That provided decent light for writing. I realized that I'd have to send word to the Diggory's so that I could arrange their meeting him. Fortunately, King's Cross was easy to get to by wizards and, of course, easy for me to get to. I wrote a letter in which I laid out my plan for the tournament. Diggory would get himself to King's Cross, and I'd get us from there to the Trafalgar Tradewise Tournament.

The next morning I was up early—for me—so that I could have breakfast and get on my way to Diagon Alley. My landlord was truly surprised to see me up at that early hour before 8 AM. I feigned ignorance of why he would regard this as early for me. He laughed and said, "I never hope to see you up before 9 when you're on holiday."

"Well you've seen it already." I finished my breakfast and was off to the Cauldron. It was a cool, crisp late autumn day—such as one rarely finds in London. The skies were clear and the sun had just risen. I arrived at the closest tube station and set off for Trafalgar, which was the closest station to the Cauldron. It was almost nine-thirty when I arrived in the street where the Cauldron lay. but, I couldn't see it. I simply walked to and fro, up and down the block waiting for Grubbly-Plank to show up. She did show up about ten minutes after I arrived. We went into the Cauldron and bid Tom Merry Christmas. He asked us to stay and have a beer with him. I suggested that after our business that we might just do that.

We proceeded via the back door, through the alley wall and into the largest collection of magical shops and businesses in England. I arranged with Grubbly-Plank to meet her at 1PM, promising to stand her lunch at the Cauldron.

We parted, and I went directly to Gringott's. That was always an ordeal. This time promised to be worse than normal. The goblins are always so greedy, I have the feeling that I have to watch what I say, lest I agree to some trap they lay for the unwary. And this time, I had to negotiate with them for something difficult.

I started by withdrawing some gold from my vault. It's always fascinating traveling to one's vault. Taking the car down into the depths under London is always impressive. You fly through the caverns at break-neck speed and stop fast enough to almost throw you out of the car. We stopped at my vault, which must have been the smallest they have. I could barely step into it. Even so, it was far larger than I needed for my modest pile of gold. I pulled a couple of thousand pounds worth out and put it into my capacious purse.

When we got to the main lobby, I exchanged about half of it for pounds sterling. Then the hard part came. I asked to see a bank officer. The teller who had been helping me looked at me quizzically and asked what it was that I wanted to talk with a bank officer about.

I simply said, "I have a business proposition."

The teller shrugged and said, "I'll see if one is available for a 'business proposition'." The way he said it was just short of a sneer. It was as though a Muggle couldn't have a legitimate business idea.

He came back about a half hour later and asked me to follow him. We went into a part of the bank that I'd never seen before. It was a corridor between a series of nondescript doors. There were characters on the doors that I guessed must be in the goblin language. I suspected that this was a part of the bank that very few humans had ever seen. About halfway down the hall, we stopped at a door, which he opened. He gestured me in and closed the door behind me.

Behind the desk that filled a great deal of the small room was a goblin dressed in what must have been an expensive hand-tailored suit. He wore a small pair of wire-frame glasses. I didn't know enough goblins to guess his age, but he struck me as young. He introduced himself as Grabborn. He was a junior vice-president of the bank.

"Now, what kind of a business proposition do you have to offer?" He asked as he leaned back leisurely. "Do you know that you are the only non-wizard human who has ever been back here, besides, that is, human employees of the bank. I want to know what the only Muggle ever to have a vault in Gringotts could possibly have in mind in the way of a business proposition."

"I beg to differ; I am not a Muggle, but a Squibb."

He laughed. I'd never heard a goblin laugh before. I might not have recognized it for a laugh, but he gave me a hint, "I have to admit that you have a sense of humor. There's no way that you could be a Squibb."

I didn't say anything for a moment and then I said, "Well, do you want to hear my proposition?"

"Oh, yes. This should be fun."

I nodded. I was tempted to suggest that his idea of what would be fun might be a bit peculiar, but remembering that I had to pitch a business deal to him, I reserved that idea for myself and went on. "My proposition is simple. I wouldn't have troubled a bank officer except that I don't think that anyone who doesn't deal with Muggle banks and bankers would likely understand it."

He nodded and said, "Go ahead."

"It's really simple. I'm offering a fee for helping me to be issued a credit card by a Muggle bank."

"Credit cart? What in the world is that?"

"No, it's credit card with a 'D' at the end. It's a sort of letter of credit that allows the owner to get credit from most businesses rather than having to pay directly with gold."

He smiled and said, "And those 'credit cards' are issued by Muggle banks?"

"Exactly. I don't have any standing with Muggle banks. Ordinarily, you have to have a job and an account in some bank to get a credit card.

"I have both, but not that Muggle banks would recognize."

"Well, what can we do about that?" I couldn't make out his expression, but I was pretty sure it wasn't amusement now.

"You have relationships with some Muggle banks. How else are you able to exchange galleons for pounds sterling? I'm willing to pay you a reasonable finder's fee for attesting to a Muggle bank that I've got a job, that I've got resources and that they should issue me a credit card. It would be nice too, if you would be willing to receive credit card statements and pay my debts on the credit card from my account."

Grabborn smiled but somehow it didn't make me feel that he was friendlier. He said, "Certainly. That's an interesting proposition. Just how much do you propose to pay us for this estimable service?"

"I was thinking that it would probably require a couple of hours of work. Maybe a day's salary for someone at your level."

"HMMM. Let me suggest an alternative. I'll do it for free, but I'll take a percentage of the debts that we pay from your account. Shall we say 10%?"

That was an interesting suggestion. Clearly it would make them more money in the long run. 10% seemed a bit stiff, but he knew that he had me over the proverbial barrel. He had judged it finely. If it had been only a percentage point or two higher, I'd have definitely haggled, maybe threatened to go elsewhere. All I could do was agree or try to find someone else to help me. I agreed. He called in a secretary and dictated the terms of a contract in Goblin. At least I thought it must be Goblin.

I offered to leave and let him get on to more important business. I'd review and sign the contract in the lobby. He insisted that I stay. It wasn't long before the secretary returned with a pair of parchments—one for each. I was surprised to see that the contract was fairly simple, but I knew that I'd have to read it very carefully. I couldn't see any "catches" in it. We signed, and it was witnessed by the secretary. He said that he'd get to work on the credit card negotiations immediately. I thanked him. He stood as I left and said, "I imagine it will take a couple of days. Check back on Thursday."

It was necessary to get that credit card so that I could follow my plan to order Christmas gifts over the phone. It may seem like a trivial effort to you, but when you've been off the grid for almost four years, even the simplest tasks of the modern Muggle world are challenging. In this case, it seemed an almost insurmountable obstacle.

When I left Gringotts, the sun was high in the sky, and the time was shortly after noon. I glanced up at the clock on the corner and found that I was already five minutes late for my meeting. I rushed down the street and rounded a corner to see that Grubbly-Plank was not yet at our meeting spot. I walked briskly toward it. Suddenly Grubbly-Plank walked out of a small crowd and approached the meeting point. She reached it and looked around for me. Then, she saw me and waved.

We went through the wall to the Cauldron's back entrance. Inside there were a few late lunchers, but we had the choice of tables. Tom came over to us and asked where we'd like to sit. We picked a spot near the fire, where most diners were seated.

We each had a simple lunch—stew and a half-sandwich. I asked if she minded helping me get into Diagon Alley again on Thursday. She was very gracious to agree, and we finished the meal comparing our luck shopping. Of course, I hadn't had any. She had done fairly well. We finished lunch and parted company. I was sure that I could get into the Cauldron after I'd finished shopping on my own.

I looked at my list of gifts that I wanted to get for Hogwarts staff. Some had been easy. There was Filch. All I had to do for him was to drop in at McGinty's wine and Spirits close to the east end of Diagon Alley. I bought him a fifth of really good Scotch whiskey.

259

Professor Dumbledore was a little harder. I couldn't get the present that I wanted for him from Diagon Alley. I usually got him a ticket to a good chamber music concert in London.

In a way, Snape was easy too. I had no idea what he would like, so I simply got him something that I would like. This year, I decided it would be clothing. I got him a fur cap at Madame Malkin's.

Minerva was the real puzzler. I had thought and thought about what to do about her and decided that I'd buy a Muggle gift as I usually did. I decided it had to be a "nice" gift. So, I went to the jeweler, Noble and Sons. I went in with the idea of a necklace. I started looking at necklaces and suddenly saw IT. It was a necklace with a small number of white jade stones set in silver and connected by fine silver chain. I bought it and had them wrap it.

The next couple of days were quiet. The tournament hadn't started. I wasn't able to shop yet from the catalogs. I fulfilled my landlord's expectation of sleeping late. I went for long walks in the parks.

Then Thursday came. I again was up early. I again amazed my landlord. I again landed somewhere in the neighborhood of the Cauldron before nine.

When Grubbly-Plank arrived, we went in, and I thanked her profusely for helping me out. She "poo-pooed" it. She claimed she still had some Christmas shopping to do. I didn't know how long my visit to Gringott's would take, so I suggested that she return to Gringott's every hour. When I was out, I'd just go along with her or she could let me into the Cauldron.

I entered Gringott's and approached the information desk. The goblin there seemed to recognize me because he signaled me over. When I approached him, he said, "Mr. Wendt. You're expected in the back office." He then signaled to another goblin who came over and the Information Booth goblin said, "Please take Mr. Wendt to the office of Mr. Grabborn."

He led me there. When I entered, Grabborn smiled and said, "Good to see you Mr. Wendt. I've got something for you, please sit down."

After I had, Grabborn handed a sealed envelope over to me. As he did so, he said, "Your new credit card will not be delivered until after Christmas." My face fell so that even a goblin could tell that I was unhappy. However, he went on, "However, in that envelope are the details of your credit card."

While he spoke, I slit the envelope open. It was not addressed but there was a return address of Barclay's Bank, PLC. The interior contained one sheet. Grabborn was going on. "The paper contains the account # of your MasterCard, the expiration date, its PIN—whatever that is, and your name as it will appear on your credit card.

"With that information, you can use your credit card over the telephone or in most Muggle banks." With that intelligence, my frown turned into a smile. He went on, "I think that satisfies your requirements."

I had to admit that he was right. He turned serious and said, "I think that concludes our business.

"The card itself will be delivered here. You can check here after Christmas. If it doesn't arrive before you leave for Hogwarts, we'll forward it to you there."

I thanked Grabborn profusely, offered my hand (refused), and left the way I came. This time, when I left Gringotts, I found that I'd hardly spent a half-hour there. I tried to think of something to do for the next half-hour until Grubbly-Plank was supposed to show up. I finally settled for looking for a food cart somewhere on the street. The only one that I could find was the ice-cream cart. Frankly, I wasn't in the mood for ice cream. I just wanted to get to a telephone and start ordering gifts from JCPenney.

Eventually Grubbly-Plank showed up. I tried to convince her to let me stand her lunch again, but she was having none of it, so we parted ways. I stopped for a beer in the Cauldron and she continued shopping. After leaving the Cauldron, I searched for a little while and finally found a hotel that had payphones in the lobby that one could sit at while phoning.

I got out my purse, pulled out my list and a stack of coins and started dialing. I'd done enough transatlantic phoning that I only had a wrong number once, and then I was on the phone with an operator at Penney. I went systematically through my list. Only once or twice the connection deteriorated and there was confusion over whether I wanted a set of towels or a set of trowels. I finished ordering and headed for home. I was determined to get to bed early because the next day was the first day of the tournament.

Trafalgar

The next day, I showed up at King's Cross early. I took a seat on a bench next to track 9. I watched the barrier where people disappeared on their way to Hogwarts. I know that they wouldn't emerge from it, but that's where we'd arranged to meet. Shortly after 10 AM there was a tap on my shoulder. I jumped as though I'd sat on a hot coal. It was Cedric and his mom. I was a little relieved that he'd made it and was happy that his mom had come. She apologized for being late, but I assured her that it wasn't a problem at all.

I suggested that we take the tube to the tournament site. She was a little reluctant. "I've heard stories about crime on the 'Underground'."

"There can be crime anywhere, but in broad daylight on a weekday, we're pretty safe." We went down to the tube level and I bought electronic tokens for us all. Cedric found that fascinating as always.

Mrs. Diggory asked, "Just what do you do with those things?"

"Come along and I'll show you." We approached a turnstile and I told them to go through first. I'd help them with it. "Just put the token in through this slit on the side and it will pop up on the other side of the turnstile. Then walk forward and through." Cedric went first without problem. His mom was more tentative, and I was afraid that she might somehow get stuck. She had trouble feeding it into the reader and then was reluctant to walk through, but we got her to do it. Then I went through.

Cedric was having fun watching his mom navigating the turnstile. "Come on Mum, you'd think that you were a Muggle trying to go through the barrier to track 9 ¾."

We had another little adventure when our train arrived. The doors opened and people left the car. Then I made the mistake of going on first. Cedric hopped on next, but his mom hesitated at the door. The automated announcement that the doors were about to close came and that flustered her more. I stood in the door to keep it from closing, and Cedric helped his mom in. He asked her what had happened.

"Well, the door started talking to me and told me that I should stand back."

Cedric rolled his eyes and said, "Just follow us and do what we do."

"Well that's easy for you to say!"

Fortunately, we didn't have any trouble getting off. Then it was a short walk to the tournament hotel. We entered and found the registration desk. Cedric picked up his tournament ID and the registration person said, "You and a guest can attend the kickoff luncheon in the Scarlet Room just through there." He pointed off down a corridor.

That was another problematic point for his mom. She wanted me to have the luncheon with Cedric. I insisted that she do it with Cedric. I pointed out that I'd done it with him the last time and that I had some other business that I wanted to do. I had someone to find here. She accepted that, and they headed off for the Scarlet Room. I went to the coffee shop to have lunch.

Afterwards, I found out where the upper division was playing, headed off there, and found most of the entrants at their tables already. Cedric was sitting at a table opposite someone who I supposed must be his opponent. His mom was standing behind Cedric's chair. I joined them. As I did, I checked the tournament pairings and found that Cedric's first opponent was a Frenchman, Jacque Toulouse. He had a rating of 2274, substantially above Cedric's, but Cedric was playing white.

When I arrived, I patted Cedric's shoulder and said, "Bon chance!" The Frenchman looked up and said, "Merci". Shortly afterwards the Tournament Director signaled that play should begin and Cedric made his first move.

The play proceeded quickly. They were apparently following a well-known opening because they both moved rapidly. Cedric took slightly longer than his opponent, seeming to want to be sure that he was following the opening correctly. Soon, Toulouse was moving, seemingly without thought. He was slowly accumulating a small time advantage. Then after one of Cedric's moves, the Frenchman instinctively took a pawn in his hand and seemed about to move, but didn't. He stared at the position.

I realized that he really didn't have a choice about his move. He'd touched the piece. It was a pawn. The only option that was open to him in this position was to advance it one square. But he held on to it and then finally placed it carefully on the next square. From that point on, the moves were deliberated over on both sides.

Cedric's mom tugged on my shirt sleeve and wanted to say something. I pulled her off to the side so that we wouldn't disturb players.

"What was that about? Both Cedric and the Frenchy were moving rapidly, and then they both started taking lots of time over their moves."

I explained about "canned" openings and that players didn't take time as long as the opponent stayed on the known path. Once one of them diverged, it became slow slogging. She nodded and we returned to Cedric's table. When we arrived, I saw that Cedric had picked up a slight advantage in material—a knight exchanged for a bishop. He was still behind in time by a small margin, but it was small. The moves proceeded more and more slowly, particularly on the part of Cedric's opponent.

I thought there was no positional advantage, but I wasn't a fit judge of that. Cedric's mom watched closely but seemed to be as mystified as I. As they reached the end of the forty moves, Cedric had ample time, but Toulouse had only a minute and a half. On Cedric's next move, he took one of Toulouse's pawn's with a bishop. It seemed to me that he put that bishop in a great deal of danger. But Toulouse hesitated. He stared at the tantalizing bishop, but he must have thought that there was danger. He was quite aware of his time problem, but he kept hesitating. Finally, he picked up his knight but still hesitated and the clock rang. He dropped the knight—lost. He'd lost the game. The Director came over and everyone signed scorecards.

Toulouse extended his hand and said, "C'est le bon jeu. Congratulations, Mr. Diggory."

Cedric shook the hand and thanked Toulouse. We immediately left the room, and Cedric whooped as soon as we were outside. I congratulated him, and his mom hugged him. We went back to the Cauldron and had dinner there, happily.

As we spoke, I asked about his analysis of the game and his strategy.

Cedric smiled, "Well, I decided that I would try a little trick on my next opponent. I'd follow the opening game slavishly for most of the way into it, but I'd take longer than really necessary, enough longer that he might be tempted to follow the opening slavishly with little thought. If he were doing that, I'd deviate and hope that he continued the opening.

"He almost didn't do it, but he touched the piece and was committed. That allowed me to set up that little advantageous exchange. Then he became much more cautious—overly cautious. I worked that caution as much as I could. He eventually ran short of time.

"Then I took a risk, I made a move that was bad. I was hoping that he would think that I'd some trap in mind. He hesitated looking for it and that cost him the game."

His mom laughed and exclaimed, "Oh, my clever boy. That was a dangerous thing. I hope you don't think that you can get away with it again."

Cedric shook his head and said, "Oh, I know, it can only be used once. From now on, I'll have to win the old-fashioned way—by playing a better game."

We agreed to meet at the same time tomorrow morning and this time, Cedric's mom would handle the "Tube" better. We parted and I went home quite happy with myself.

$$\triangledown$$

The next morning, I was again waiting at King's Cross between track's nine and ten. I heard a harrumph behind me and realized that it was neither Cedric nor his mom. As a matter of fact, it sounded a lot like .-.-.

I rose, turned and discovered Cedric with Minerva. My mouth fell open.

She said, "Well, don't just stand there like a babbling baboon. Come over here."

What could I do? I walked over and she hugged me and whispered in my ear, "We'll talk after the tournament." Aloud, she said, "You don't think that I'd miss out on seeing Cedric play in the tournament, did you?"

I shook my head no, mutely. She held out her hands to Cedric and me. We took them and disappeared. An instant later I remembered afresh how much I hated disapparating. I'd not disapparated anywhere since the beginning of the last term. We appeared close to the hotel and walked in. She remembered the layout from the last tournament, and we walked directly to the game hall. There were hardly any players there. We quickly found Cedric's table, and we discussed the next match briefly.

The next opponent was Thomas Harding. He was an international grand-master—barely. He had a rating of 2440. I shook my head when I saw that Cedric had to play black. All we could do was wish him luck.

Cedric simply said, "I'll play my best and not try any 'tricks' with Harding. Then, things will land wherever they do."

Most of the players had arrived and set up before Harding arrived. He was a short stocky man with dark red hair. He looked over his opponent and introduced himself. He shook hands and quickly set up his score card. The signal was given, and dozens of clocks started nearly simultaneously.

The game began much the same as the day before. Both sides apparently following a standard opening. But this time differences began to show. When they approached fifteen moves, they were still following a standard opening. By contrast, yesterday Cedric had deviated from the standard by this point. But they kept on going.

When they approached thirty moves, and there was still no sign of deviation from an opening, I began to wonder just how long they could keep it up. As they got beyond move 30, it began to seem like a game of "chicken"—each daring the other to keep on this opening. By this time a number of people had gathered around Cedric's table. There was an unspoken, silent tension that seemed to grow with each move. I began to think that the crowd would not be able to hold off from cheering one side or the other along much longer despite the fact that the Tournament Director was standing there along with the rest.

Finally on move 32, Cedric spent a little more time in developing his move. Then Harding huddled over the board for a full two minutes. After Harding's next move, Cedric also studied the board carefully before moving. They had reached the middle game. Action was much slower now, but both sides had lots of time left on their clocks and could afford think time. However, neither side seemed to gain any sort of advantage. The pieces moved and occasionally were exchanged, but there was no discernible change.

As the afternoon wore on, it seemed to me that Cedric was gaining a little advantage in position. It was probably wishful thinking, but Harding was definitely taking more time on each move than Cedric was. However Harding was not in time trouble yet and didn't seem like he was going to get into time trouble, either. As a matter of fact, it looked like they would reach the end of their 40 moves each with time left on his clock.

They reached the end. The Director came over again and asked what they would do. They could either take a break for dinner and return afterwards with a reset clock and another 40 moves each, or they could decide to call it a draw.

Cedric didn't say anything in response. He appeared ready for another 40. As a matter of fact, he seemed almost rested. If neither side made an offer of a draw, the game would procede after dinner. Harding sat gazing at the board, scratching his left ear with his right hand.

The Tournament Director cleared his throat and said, "In that case, you can return at.-.-."

Harding interrupted him and said, looking over at Cedric. "What think you of a draw?"

Cedric didn't hesitate but he gave an affirmative nod with the slightest motion of his head. The Director asked, "You're both agreed then that it's a draw?"

Harding nodded and said, "Certainly." Cedric drawled, "Sure."

"Very well, then. Please so indicate on your score cards, Mr. Harding offered draw, and Mr. Diggory accepted. Then sign your cards." They did so.

We all left the hall together, and I suggested celebrating. Minerva harrumphed and said, "Why would you celebrate getting a measly tie?"

I was speechless for a moment and then said, "Minerva, the person Cedric was playing was a Grand Master. Cedric was playing black—two substantial disadvantages for him. He did extremely well to get a draw."

Cedric had been listening to the conversation but he added his own comments then, "Well, I really think that I could have taken him, but there was a way that he could force a draw if he wanted to, so I thought it wasn't worth slogging on for another hour or so just to end up with a draw at the end."

Minerva wasn't entirely convinced, but I was happy, as was Cedric. We found a small Italian restaurant. It was actually a little early for dinner, but I wanted to sit down somewhere and I didn't mind doing it in an empty restaurant. The staff wasn't especially happy at our early arrival. I decided that I'd give them a good tip and I didn't sweat it.

Minerva was being pretty cagey about how she felt and why she had really come along. I figured we'd have dinner, take Cedric home, and then we'd have the shoot-out or whatever we were headed for. But for the time being we were all being convivial. By the time it was an acceptable time for the evening meal according to the Italians, we'd pretty much talked out all the topics that were sensible: What are our plans for the Christmas holiday? Have you finished your Christmas shopping? Who are you having over for Christmas? Are you traveling over the holiday?"

There were a couple of topics that nobody seemed to want to talk about: How long will the Dementors be haunting Hogwarts grounds? Will Sirius Black ever be caught? Will the Express be visited by Dementors on the way back at the end of the holiday?

Another topic that wasn't broached was a discussion of Cedric's game. It wasn't that Minerva and I weren't interested in hearing more about it, but we'd learned that the higher the level of play, the less it was likely that anything that Cedric said about it would make sense to us. So, we had pretty much become satisfied with general congratulations on his wins and condolences for his losses.

We spent the actual meal mostly eating in silence. But it wasn't an uneasy silence. It was the silence of having said everything that mattered and being comfortable with each other It brought back memories of other similar dinners during the past year.

After it was over, Minerva disapparated us to Cedric's house. We dropped him off with a few words of congratulations to his parents. His father was dissatisfied with the draw, but his mom was happy with our opinion that it was probably the best game that he'd ever played. Cedric seemed to agree with that assessment.

As Minerva and I left the house, Minerva stopped walking after we were out of earshot of the house. She watched me for a moment and then simply said, "Well?"

I decided that complete honesty, as usual, was the best policy and said, "I wish you'd let me take you out to dinner on Christmas Eve."

"There's no one else that you'd rather be taking out to dinner that night?"

"No one in the world."

She seemed to consider that for a long moment and then said, "Then, what are we waiting for." She seemed somehow to melt into my arms and we kissed. When we broke, she kept me in her arms and said, "You always were a great kisser."

I was ecstatic and simply said, "It's the inspiration."

"AND, you were always full of the blarney."

I couldn't think of anything to say. My rule of thumb with Minerva when I'm at a loss for words is just to kiss her, which keeps both our lips busy. So I just kissed her again.

The next day was the 23rd and another tournament day. Minerva picked me up at my loft, and we then went to get Cedric. His father wanted to come along for this game. We were all satisfied with that, but Cedric gave him a refresher course in polite behavior at tournaments, especially remaining silent.

By the time we arrived at the tournament, Amos seemed almost contrite. Cedric's opponent was a weaker player. The game went south for that player almost as soon as they entered the middle game. Cedric forked a bishop and pawn with one of his knights. The opponent chose to lose the pawn, of course, but things just keep getting worse from there on. He finally resigned after 25 moves. He wasn't in any imminent danger of mate, but he'd lost a lot of material and his position was fractured. He was not gracious in loss, which was probably not surprising. I looked at his record so far in the tournament. He'd not even drawn a single game.

After we left the hall, Cedric's dad clapped him on the back and proclaimed, "Now that's what I'm talking about. Why didn't you do that yesterday?"

Cedric stared at him incredulously, "Well, dad, it was like the Hufflepuff team playing the Chutley Cannons yesterday. And I was Hufflepuff. I was lucky to get a tie."

His dad just said, "Oh." and was quiet the rest of the way to their home. The Diggory's insisted that we join them for dinner. After some protests, they convinced us.

Mr. Diggory innocently asked, "So, are you two ever planning on getting married?"

Minerva blushed, and I probably did as well. Truthfully, I have to say that everyone except Mr. Diggory blushed. I answered him, "I don't think that I'm mature enough for marriage yet."

Minerva enthusiastically seconded the opinion and added that I needed at least another 5 years to season me well. I responded that I was just fine, taken plain.

When we left the Diggory's after begging off any parlor games, Minerva commented, "Don't you dare repeat that question about our getting married."

I pretended innocence. "Why would I want to do that?"

The next day we arrived at the Diggory's and I found myself reluctant to say anything about the day's match. Cedric had to play Moise Bresnev. He was almost an international grand master with well over 2500 points. I didn't want to jinx him but on the other hand, since this might be the last game of the tournament for Cedric—if he lost—I felt required to say something, especially to his parents. So, as we walked up the lane to his house, I pondered.

I took Minerva by the arm to stop her and asked her, "Do you know who Cedric is playing?"

"No, should I?"

"He's just this far," and separated my thumb and forefinger by about a centimeter, "from being an international grand master."

She shook her head slowly and said, "Nooooo." in mock shock.

"You needn't be flippant. I think Cedric will probably lose. If he does, that will be the end of the tournament for him."

"OK. So what does that mean for us?"

"Well, I don't know whether we should talk about that with Cedric and his family. Should we urge them to go because it'll probably be his last game in the tournament? Or should we try to shield him from the extra pressure of having his parents at his elbow while he's playing?"

She sneered, "Don't be silly. Of course, they'll want to go, and he'll want for them to be there."

"OK."

We reached the door and found Cedric waiting for us. I asked if his parents were around. He said that his mom was, but his dad was at work at the Ministry. I asked him to bring his mom, and I explained about Cedric's next opponent and the likelihood that it would be the last game for Cedric in this tournament.

His mom said, "Well, then, I definitely want to go." Then she dithered about whether to bother his father at work and finally decided not to. So all three of us disapparated and appeared in an alley near the hotel.

Bresnev was a wiry man in his thirties. His hair was cut in a crew cut. He wore a sweater vest and tie over a blue button down shirt. He introduced himself and shook Cedric's hand warmly. He guessed that Mrs. Diggory was his mom and thought that I must be his dad. I corrected that misapprehension. He and Cedric sat and prepared the board to their liking. Bresnev seemed to have a ritual of straightening every one of his pieces and placing each precisely in the center of its square.

Cedric glanced over the pieces, seemingly making sure that each one was in its proper square.

Then Bresnev took a cigar out of a small pocket humidor and placed it on the table to his right of the board. Cedric shook his head at that and asked if the rules of the club didn't forbid smoking during matches. Bresnev replied, "Oh, it's my victory cigar. I won't smoke it until the match is over."

With those rituals completed, the two waited for the signal to begin. Cedric was playing white, which was a small blessing—I hoped. Cedric opened pawn to king four and the game was off. Both played down a standard opening for a number of moves and Bresnev deviated from the opening first. It was clearly the hardest game that Cedric had played so far. His moves were long deliberated over, but he seemed to be holding his own for a while.

As the game wore on, it turned more and more to a defense struggle for Cedric. He seemed to have drawn a line on the board and was determined that Bresnev wouldn't encroach without losing material. His strategy had become purely defensive. He lost a small material advantage that he'd developed but was not yet in danger when the end of the 40 moves had come. And it had come just in time—he had less than a minute left on his clock. The Tournament Director came over as before and posed them the question. In this case Bresnev didn't hesitate, "We'll take an adjournment and resume." And then he added, "Unless of course, Mr. Diggory, chooses to resign."

Diggory returned quickly, "No, sir. We'll resume."

We gathered ourselves and left the hall. Minerva suggested that we go to the coffee shop of the hotel and have an early dinner. But, I suggested, "No, let's go to some familiar place—maybe the Cauldron."

Cedric agreed heartily, and we went outside and disapparated there. We arrived and found the Cauldron nearly empty. Of course, it was Christmas Eve, and I think Tom was thinking of closing early. However, our appearance caused him to hold off. He seated us and then said, "Oh, what the hell. You're probably my last and only customers tonight. I'll pull out everything that's left, and we'll have potluck together."

He set up a table near ours as a buffet, and his staff brought out three tureens of soup, a Christmas goose, Yorkshire pudding, smashed potatoes, three kinds of cooked vegetables and two varieties of bread. He told us that he was holding out the desert because he didn't want us to have only desert. He stoked up the fire and we all sat around a long table, ate, drank, and even sang carols. A few witches and wizards finishing last minute Christmas shopping in Diagon Alley joined us and were welcome to the party.

Everyone was so merry that we almost all forgot that Cedric had to finish a game. We were only about 5 minutes from the deadline when we quickly apologized for eating and running and left, immediately disapparating to the hotel. We ran into the hall and found the Director about to declare a forfeit. Cedric quickly took his seat, and the game was begun. He seemed to take a minute to get himself re-oriented, losing valuable time off his clock, but after about five minutes, he made his first move.

The break had seemed to re-invigorate Cedric in a way that Bresnev wasn't, but Bresnev's attack was relentless. Cedric's position seemed to constantly be on the verge of collapse, but somehow there was always one of his pieces available to threaten a counter-attack to blunt the onslaught. Then Cedric began forcing even exchanges. Apparently, he was trying to force a draw. Nonetheless, Bresnev seemed to gain slightly by these exchanges.

Eventually, we neared the end of the 2nd forty moves and suddenly, Bresnev extended his hand across the board to Cedric. For a second Cedric hesitated and then accepted it. The Director signed cards and declared the drawn game. Then he said, "Gentlemen, all the other matches are complete, and, I am ready to post the matches for the next round. Congratulations, Moise, you'll be playing the American."

Then he turned to Cedric and said, "You've played amazing games. You should be extremely proud." It was at that moment that I realized that Cedric hadn't made it to the next round. "You've missed qualifying by ½ point. I hope you realize what an achievement you've made by coming this close after playing in tournaments for barely a year. Frankly, you were in the toughest first round group, and I thought you would be extremely lucky to come away with one win."

Cedric nodded and said, "Thank you, sir. I appreciate the opportunity to play with such inspiring players."

The Director added, "Personally, I hope that you'll promise to return next year. I am hoping to see you compete in the medal round."

Cedric smiled and said, "You couldn't keep me away with wild festrals."

"Pardon, young man. I didn't quite catch that."

"Oh, nothing, sir. Just a little private joke. I look forward to seeing you next year."

We left the hotel and felt the let-down of not having anything to celebrate but feeling like a celebration was called for. Mrs. Diggory invited us to spend Christmas Eve with her family. Minerva declined with thanks. She said that she had her own family to spend Christmas Eve with. Mrs. Diggory turned to me and asked if I'd join her family.

Minerva ran her arm through mine and took my hand warmly, saying, "This is what I mean when I say that I have family to spend it with."

I looked over at her and said, "You are very sure of yourself."

"Yes, I am." and she began walking off with me in tow. We hadn't gone far when we disapparated. We arrived outside Minerva's sister's house, and I gulped wondering how much her sister knew of our recent spat.

As it turned out, she knew nothing. She greeted me, but not effusively—nothing unusual for her. In that instant, it suddenly occurred to me that although I had a gift for Minerva, I didn't have one for her sister. I desperately sought mentally for something that could stand in for a Christmas gift.

We sat around the Yule blaze in the fireplace and listened to music on Wizard radio. It was mostly Christmas-themed music, although I didn't recognize a lot of them. Of course, there were the perennial favorites—Good King Wenceslas, O Holy Night, I'm dreaming of a White Christmas, etc. Unfortunately, there were a lot by a Celestine Warbucks that I'd never heard.

Minerva asked me what Muggles did on Christmas Eve. I answered, "Well, they do a lot of things that Witches and Wizards do.

275

They listen to Christmas music. They go to church services. They also do some things that are unique.

"You don't have anything like Television. It is rather like one of your moving photos, except that there is sound and you can have this sort of moving picture that goes on for up to a couple of hours. They are like plays. So, you can think of it as a kind of elaborate stage play visible on a flat screen."

Maggie commented, "That seems boring—watching a moving photo for hours on end."

"Well, I'm not doing it justice. Anyway, there are quite a lot of these plays about Christmas stories. There are all sorts—serious, funny, and romantic. One of the most popular is Dicken's "A Christmas Carol"."

"You mean a two hour play about one song?"

"No, no. It's really a story about a scrooge, who.-.-.."

Minerva asked, "A what?"

"Oh, yes. I forgot that the word 'scrooge' actually comes from a character in this play. He's someone who doesn't believe in observing Christmas. He has an encounter with some ghosts who convince him otherwise."

Maggie said, "I can see why that's popular. Ghost stories are usually good."

"Yes, well, another is a comedy about a typical American family that is preparing for Christmas in the 1950's. Then there's a serious play called, 'It's a Wonderful Life.' That's probably the most popular with Muggles."

"What's it about?"

"It's set in the great Depression and is about how even a seemingly inconsequential life can change a community."

Maggie said, "Too serious if you ask me."

"Well, I warned you it was serious."

Then the moment that I dreaded came—exchanging gifts. I'd brought my gift for Minerva along to the match, thinking I'd pick an opportune moment to give it to her. This was certainly an opportune moment, but I didn't have a gift for Maggie.

I chose to go last, and it was fortunate. First, was Minerva and Maggie. We immediately said that the gift was a joint gift from both us for Maggie. She eagerly opened it and found a set of Hummel figurines. I wondered if Minerva had actually thought about me when she'd selected it or if it was just a case of thinking on her feet. It didn't matter because Maggie loved them and profusely thanked both of us.

I honestly said that I could claim little responsibility—that it had been Minerva's idea. Maggie was overjoyed and couldn't have cared less.

Minerva gave me my gift. It was in a small box. I ripped off the wrapping and discovered the last thing in the world that I would expect. It was a portable CD player with headphones. Minerva smirked and said, "I thought that would surprise you. You've been talking so much about these new DC players that I thought that you'd like one. It's powered by bacteria."

I stared at her and guessed, "I think that you mean batteries."

"Oh, yes. Something like that. Anyway, it's supposed to work without electricity. Which is important at Hogwarts. You'll still probably have to be on one of your walks off into the hills for it to work."

I was so excited that I threw my arms around her and kissed her enthusiastically. Maggie pretended to be checking the fire in the fireplace while I did that.

Then Maggie gave her sister a ticket to the World Quidditch Cup finals. Minerva was impressed. She'd never attended before. Her gift to me was in a large box. I opened it and worked my way through a lot of heavy packing material to a much smaller box. Within it were more packing material and a smaller box still. Finally, in the heart was a small envelope. When I opened it, I discovered the twin to the ticket she'd given MInerva. They were adjacent seats. I impulsively gave Maggie a kiss on the cheek.

Finally, it was my turn. I handed Minerva her gift. She unwrapped it slowly. I think she may have wondered that I had anything for her, but she finally got to the inner box. She hesitated before opening it, saying, "I suppose this is one of your DC things that you play with that DC player."

"You're thinking of CD's. Just open it and see what it is."

She opened the box and just stared. Then she picked the necklace up and stared at it some more. Maggie gasped and said, "That's beautiful!"

Minerva unlatched the hasp and put it around her neck. She asked me to secure the hasp, so I got up and went behind her chair and tickled her ear a little before I closed the hasp. She got up and walked to a mirror over the mantle and slowly turned, viewing it from all angles.

Maggie sighed and said, "You did well, Wendt."

The rest of the holidays were really happy. On Christmas day, their aunt Beryl came. We played games, ate, and talked about the last year and the year to come.

I talked about the new professor at Hogwarts, Lupin. I said that the apparent curse of the Defense Against the Dark Arts professor seemed to be carrying on. Lupin had had a lot of absences due to illness so far this year.

Immediately on saying that, the room became very quiet. I noticed immediately and said, "I seem to have conjured the elephant."

They all stared at me and asked what I meant. I replied, "Muggles have an expression for situations like this when there's a topic that no one wants to talk about. They say, 'There's an elephant in the room.'"

Minerva said, "Well, I guess we all know about it, so you should as well.

"The elephant is the fact that Professor Lupin is a werewolf."

I stared for a few seconds and asked, "Is he dangerous? Is it catching?"

Minerva tsched a few times and said, "You Muggles are so ignorant of these things. The only way you can 'catch' lycanthropy is to be bitten by one while in the wolf stage.

"Secondly, it can be controlled by a drug. However, if the drug isn't administered in a timely manner, the transformation can happen, and then the werewolf is dangerous. However, Professor Snape has no problem brewing the medicine, so Lupin's affliction is under good control. However, for a couple of days around the full moon, Lupin stays in his office and is weakened."

I had mixed feelings about the situation. I liked Lupin. There were many times that I thought that he was the most reasonable and intelligent teacher at Hogwarts—not excepting either Minerva or Dumbledore. However, the idea of having such a potentially dangerous teacher around made me wonder at Dumbledore's wisdom.

Minerva sensed this unease and when we went to bed that night asked me about it. I said, "I have to admit to being worried about the situation. Lupin's a good man, but has a serious illness. It worries me having him around children."

We were lying in bed with the lights out. I couldn't see Minerva's face, but I could feel her body tense. She said, "I had him as one of my first pupils when I came to Hogwarts. I can't help but remember that stricken youth who hardly deserved what happened to him. I trust him."

I decided that I had to trust her judgment. As she said—you Muggles don't really understand what's going on with lots of magical things. However, neither of us felt like doing anything other than spooning that night. I think we both wanted some comfort and assurance that nothing bad would happen as a result of Lupin's being on staff.

We managed to put it out of our minds for the rest of the holiday and pretty well enjoyed ourselves. I convinced her to go see "Forest Gump". She was astounded by the movie.

We had gone to a Starbucks for coffee after. She asked me if such a person really existed.

"No, I don't think so, but I do think that the character is a composite of several people who really do exist.

"More than that, the movie is a parable about life in the States. It's about how simple people of good intentions eventually have good karma that defeats even the worst intentions of smart evil people. That's the fairy tale that most Americans believe in. That's why most Americans feel that government intervention is a poor second to the nature of Americans."

She stared at me in amazement, 'Really! Do Americans really believe that?"

"You bet they do."

"And I had such a high opinion of Americans."

"Don't give up on us yet. We may still surprise you."

She shook her head in mock derision. We had a good laugh at ourselves. She allowed that movies were entertaining and she wouldn't mind going to another one—maybe for her birthday.

The days passed quickly and pleasantly. The nights were even more pleasant. They ended with happy exhaustion in each other's arms or spooning ourselves to sleep.

Eventually, the end of the holiday came, and we had to take the Express back to school.

The Werewolf

The trip back to Hogwarts on the Express was a cold overcast day with enough humidity in the air to make you think that snow was about to fall at any moment. Everyone on the train was wearing heavy cloaks or layers of sweaters. I set up shop in the Teacher's Car, but today, Minerva and I were the only ones there, so we had to do all the tours of duty patrolling the passenger cars. The first time through, I kept alert for any sign of Professor Lupin. He was apparently not on the train.

Minerva noticed that I had been looking for something or someone. She asked me whom or what.

I admitted that I was looking for Professor Lupin.

"Why in the world? Are you expecting him to change form on the train?"

'No, "

She looked exasperated, 'Well? Why?"

I was a little ashamed to admit the crazy theory I had, but I told it to her anyway, "The only time that the Dementors entered the train was when Lupin was on board." And then another idea occurred to me, "And, come to think of it, the only compartment they stopped at and entered was the one with Lupin in it.

"Do you suppose they are attracted to werewolves?"

She stared at me and then appeared to consider it. "Who else was in that compartment?" She added, "Besides Potter, whom I know was in there."

"Well, there was Ms. Grainger and the Weasley kid—uh, Roland, is it? No. Ronald."

"Yes. Hmmm. Well, neither Lupin or Potter is on this train, but Ron and Ms. Grainger are."

"Well, then, maybe we can find out if Dementors find them interesting."

Minerva said, "I suppose it must be .-.-.", but I interrupted her and finished the sentence for her.

"Potter. Yes, the Dementors found him interesting at that Quidditch match as well."

Minerva ran a hand absently through her hair, "But why would they be interested in Potter? He's never been to Azkaban." She seemed completely engrossed by the question and then shook her head. "I don't get it. Hundreds of kids on the train and the only people they're interested in are Potter or Lupin or both."

I had another idea, "Do werewolves ever end up in Azkaban?"

She looked up and said, "I don't know of any. It's a disease, not a crime."

"OK. I get the idea. No prejudice against werewolves."

"I should think not, but, of course, a lot of people are prejudiced against werewolves."

The rest of the trip was uneventful. No Dementors showed up. No nothing. I did drop by to say hello to Cedric. He was talking with a couple of his classmates, and I just waved at him, but he got up. He came over to talk for a minute. "Professor, are you getting excited by the Cup?"

I was puzzled and must have shown it. He amplified, "The World Quidditch Cup."

"Oh, yes. I guess so. I've not ever gone to a professional Quidditch game, but I've got tickets for the finals."

Cedric said, "Lucky!"

"I bet I see you there."

"Why?"

"You're a pretty good Quidditch player yourself. I'm betting that your dad will want to take you. It's a good father-son bonding opportunity."

"We'll see."

After we arrived, there was the usual end-of-holiday banquet. Dumbledore gave his usual speech, but this time it went a little differently than before, "I want to remind you all that despite all our hopes that our guests the Dementors would have completed their task and returned to Azkaban by now, they are still patrolling the borders of Hogwarts. This is an ever-present source of danger for us all.

"I urge everyone to take the greatest caution when Dementors are present. They are absolutely unforgiving in their behavior. If they believe that you are impeding their search for Sirius Black, they will not hesitate to attack. Do not assume because you are a student that you will be afforded mercy.

"Now, on to happier subjects." Everyone breathed a sigh of relief until Dumbledore continued, "Please don't let the frivolities of Christmas holiday let you relax your pursuit of academic excellence."

He finished with a little side note, 'Oh, yes. One more thing. Would the staff please join me after this excellent repast for coffee in the Teacher's Lounge?"

We all sighed because we knew that there would be some request that we would have to work on in addition to lesson plans and grading and school discipline. We all trudged up to the Teacher's Lounge, where there was indeed coffee and chocolates. Dumbledore, as usual was the last to arrive and took his place at the front of the great fireplace.

He began, "We've had our guests for many days now, and I, for one, am anxious to see them gone." There were general murmurs of agreement.

As they quickly died down, Dumbledore went on, "I think that we should lend a hand and help them find their quarry." This was followed by a general sound of resignation—except for Professor Snape who said a soft, but clear, "Hear. Hear".

"So, I want you all to think over how we might discover this most elusive Black."

A babble of conversation began. Minerva bent over toward me and whispered, "I think that means you and me."

I laughed and said, "After this is over, let's have a little council of war and see what we can come up with."

283

Dumbledore divided us up into little teams to come up with ideas. At the end, some people noticed that neither Minerva nor I had been assigned to a team and objected. Dumbledore simply replied, "I think they've already formed their own team. Am I not right, Minerva?"

She simply smiled and nodded. Dumbledore "invited" us to another little coffee after dinner on the next Sunday night.

Minerva and I went to my office, and I pulled out a bottle of my best scotch. I commented that it looked like a Dewar's White Label problem. She laughed and took the tumbler that I offered.

I started the serious part of the conversation, "OK. What do we know about Black? Who were his friends, what about family? What were his interests?"

Minerva stood and started to pace the floor. "Well, he went to school at the same time as Potter—Harry's dad. As a matter of fact, there was a little gang of them that hung out together. There was James Potter, the Pettigrew boy (I can't remember his first name), Sirius, Lily Potter—although she strictly speaking wasn't part of the gang—and Remus Lupin—our Professor Lupin.

"Come to think of it, none of them has survived except for Professor Lupin and Sirius. They were always getting into trouble, and they always seemed to get away with things because no one could catch them at it. I don't know how they managed it to this day. Sirius seems to have his old knack of staying away from authorities."

"Well, I'd say that it's high time that we had a talk with the only surviving member of that gang and see what he has to say about that 'magical' ability of theirs." I had an idea then, "Do you think that Lupin might be helping Black still? That might explain the Dementors' apparent interest in him?"

"Lupin? No, I don't think that Black would be helped by Lupin. Did you know about how Harry's parents died?"

I had to admit that I didn't. Minerva enlightened me, "The Potters were in hiding because there was this prophecy that Harry Potter would be Valdemort's downfall. The Potters were hidden magically, and only one person knew where—Sirius Black. He betrayed them to Valdemort.

"Anyway, up till that point, the old school gang had hung together and they all knew each other very well. Apparently, though,

284

Black must have developed some new friends among the Deatheaters. We don't know who any of them might be."

I went on to another topic, 'What about family, then. Have any of them survived?"

Minerva shook her head, "Wait till you hear. The Blacks were supporters of Valdemort from way back. His brother Regulus was a known Deatheater almost from the start. His cousin, Bellatrix is still in Azkaban for being a notorious Deatheater. He's related by marriage to the Malfoys through Bellatrix's sister, Narcissa. Her husband Lucius Malfoy has long been believed to be a Deatheater, but due to wealth, influence and luck, it's never been proven well enough to send him to Azkaban.

"I don't think that we'll get any information from Black's relatives that would help us."

We were striking out at every turn, but we couldn't give up, 'What about his interests when he was at school. Is there anything that might give us a clue about him?"

Minerva stared down at her left foot, slowly shaking her head. Eventually she said, "I was a teacher when he was here, but transfiguration was not one of his strengths. I never got close to him. He didn't have any extracurriculars that I know of."

"Well, then, were there any professors that he did get along with?"

Minerva was quicker about this answer, "Well, there was the Potions master, Horace Slughorn. Of course, he's left Hogwarts long ago —replaced by Professor Snape."

"Do you know how to get hold of him?"

Minerva just shook her head "no".

"Well, we've got to try to. He can't just have dropped off the face of the Earth. Is he retired?"

"Yes, he does have lots of influential contacts, but I think he's been using them to stay out of public view—which isn't hard if you're retired."

"Well, shake the tree and see if you can come up with a lead."

Minerva agreed to. I asked her if she was interested in coming along when I talked with Lupin. She said, "No, I'll be busy shaking the tree."

I grimaced and called her a coward which she readily admitted.

I took a day or two to think about my approach to Lupin. He and Black had been close friends. I would probably have only one real chance to get him to talk about Black. He might be willing if he valued his friendship with Potter, but then again, he might not want to be a "snitch". I pondered long about the right tack to take, wavering between appealing to his friendship with James Potter whom Black had betrayed and his duty to James' son,.

Then I remembered that Lupin had been in Potter's compartment in the Express. Had that been totally a coincidence or was Lupin consciously or unconsciously trying to protect James' son? I decided that that was the approach to take.

The next day at lunch I approached him as the teachers table. "Professor Lupin, may I have a word?"

He turned to me and this was the first time that I'd seen his face full on that day. He looked terrible. He was white and haggard. But he managed a small smile and said, "Of course."

"I'd just like to see you sometime in the next day or two. Would there be a time that might be convenient for you to come to my office. I've got a rather nice bottle of scotch that we could sample."

His smile grew a bit wider, and he said, "Well, I'm glad you said so. I'd walk a mile for a good glass of scotch."

"Excellent. I'm free most evenings and you could just come in any time."

His smile dimmed a bit and he said, "I'm recovering from a little illness. How about tomorrow night? I should be feeling better then."

"Thanks. That would be fine. I wouldn't want to cause you to have a relapse. Just come when you feel up to it."

"Thanks. What's the topic of our little talk?"

"Oh, I'd rather reserve that until we can actually talk about it at some length."

He nodded assent and walked off. I internally gave a sigh of relief that I didn't have to put any pressure on. It would be tough enough when I actually broached the topic.

A couple of evenings later, there was a knock at my door, which turned out to be Lupin. I invited him in, got out my Dewars White Label and poured us each a glass. He was looking better than when I'd invited him to my office. His smile seemed genuine and unforced. He accepted the glass and offered a toast, "To old friendships."

I responded, "Never forgotten." It didn't seem auspicious, considering that I was about to ask him to betray an old friendship, but I could hardly say anything else. He turned his head quizzically and asked what I wanted to talk about.

I tried to be as nonchalant as I could manage and said, "Has it ever occurred to you that you may be the only surviving friend of Sirius Black?"

He nodded his head knowingly and replied, "That's an interesting way to put it, but I suppose that you are exactly right. I am his only friend, excepting, of course, the possibility that Deatheaters can have other Deatheaters as friends."

"I don't know any Deatheaters, but I suspect that Deatheaters have associates—not friends. I hope that you consider yourself a friend of James Potter and his son." Here, Lupin nodded and took a sip of the scotch.

"Yes, it's sad when friends force you to choose between them. I suppose that you want to understand Black better?" and sipped appreciatively at his tumbler.

"Right. We—uh, that is Minerva and I—would like you to tell us everything that you know about Black: how he might be evading detection, who his Deatheater buddies might be, what his interests were, if he had other friends outside your close circle of friends at school."

Lupin took a long slow sip and stared straight ahead. After a moment he said, "I suppose that the thing that was the glue that bound us together was the shared abnormality that we all had."

I stared at him incredulously, "You were all werewolves!" I couldn't believe it.

He laughed a real laugh that seemed to release the tension that he felt. "Oh, no. Not that. Although you're on the right track. We all shared the ability to turn into animals. James could transform to a stag.

"Peter Pettigrew—little Peter—he could transform into a rat. It's funny isn't it, how these things seem to define the person. Did Peter transform into a rat because his character was small and pusillanimous or did he become small and pusillanimous because he could turn into a rat?

"I, of course, had no choice about the timing. I'd gladly not have had that 'ability'."

"Then there was Sirius. He could turn into a dog—a big shaggy black dog.

"People pretty much kept those things quiet. There's nothing really wrong with it—except turning into a wolf, of course. But somehow, people don't trust other people who can turn into animals."

I interjected, "You know that Minerva can transform into a cat?"

Lupin smiled again, "I'd forgotten that. I suppose somehow cats don't seem threatening in the same way that rats or werewolves or even stags and dogs do. No, we all kept our various secrets zealously. No one at school outside our group even suspected. Even now, I think that only my 'ability' is known."

"The great bond between us was that we all had a secret that we desperately wanted to keep but we also needed to tell someone— someone safe. That was the group."

"What about other friends?"

Lupin took another long sip on the drink and looked up from it. "I'd have said that the only good friends that he had were in the Order of the Phoenix, but that was before."

"What's the Order of the Phoenix?"

Lupin stared at me and asked, "You don't know about the Order of the Phoenix?"

I shook my head innocently because I really didn't. He said, "Well, I suppose you were in school in the States when it all happened.

"The Order of the Phoenix was an underground organization that opposed the Deatheaters."

I asked, 'I thought that was the Aurors?"

"Oh, the Aurors were the official group that opposed him. We thought that they were probably infiltrated, so Dumbledore formed the

Order. Sadly, we weren't that successful. We kept a few people from being killed and slowed things down for the Deatheaters, but we were losing. Then Potter defeated Valdemort.

"Anyway, most of his friends died in the war and then he showed that none of them were really his friends anyway."

"How was that? I know that he was in Azkaban because he was a Deatheater but what did he do?"

Lupin lifted his glass to his lips and noticed that it was empty. He glanced over at the bottle. I took the glass and filled it again. This time he took a big swallow and stared off into the distance.

Then he went on, "Where do you begin with his perfidy? To start with, he revealed the location of the Potter family to his master."

I interrupted, "You mean Valdemort?"

Lupin nodded and continued, "Valdemort went to the Potter home and killed James and Lily. He tried to kill Harry, but he failed. I suppose that you know that story pretty well."

I nodded.

"So, his master was gone, and I guess he went crazy. He met Peter Pettigrew on a public street in London. He somehow created a massive explosion that killed Pettigrew and dozens of Muggles. He was the only survivor."

"Yes, crazy. Why do that? If he had to kill Pettigrew, why not do it in a secluded place? It's absolutely crazy." I shook my head in disbelief.

"You've seen the posters. He's as mad as a hatter."

"So, did you go to his trial? Did anyone show up to watch? Was anyone interested in him?"

"No, I didn't. I couldn't stand to see this man who used to be my friend show his real nature. I've not seen him since before James Potter's death.

"IF he had Deatheater friends, I doubt that any would be anxious or able to help him. Many are in Azkaban. The ones who aren't are pretty much trying to stay out of sight. They don't want to attract attention to themselves."

"OK. What about relatives?"

Lupin laughed. "They're pretty much all Deatheaters. His brother Regulus was one. His parents are dead."

He paused as if reconsidering and went on, "I guess Regulus is dead too. His cousins are Belatrix and Narcissa. Belatrix is in Azkaban. Narcissa is married to Lucius Malfoy—another Deatheater who never went to Azkaban and who wants to stay out of Azkaban. They won't help him.

"I can't think of anyone who would help him." Lupin glanced down into his glass and then looked up again, "No, wait. There's actually a Deatheater here at Hogwarts."

"What! You're kidding, surely?"

"No. He was a bona fide Deatheater who spent time in Azkaban, and he might just be willing to help Black except for one thing." He smiled for the first time since he'd entered my office.

"Which is?"

"He hates Black's guts."

I was becoming intrigued. Who was this Deatheater? And why did he hate Black's guts? Black ought to be his hero. "OK, I'll bite. Why?"

"He was at Hogwarts at the same time as our gang. It was Snape. We all hated him, and the feeling was mutual. We pretended to hate him because he was a supercilious know-it-all who liked the dark arts."

"But..."

"But the real reason was that the leader of our gang—James— and he both had a thing for Lily Evans."

"Was she the same Lily who. . "

"Yes, who married James? Snape started off with the inside track for her affections, but James stole them. The rest of us just knew that we didn't have a shot at Lily, and we didn't want Snape to get her either. I think he blames all of us that James won her, but he had it wrong from the beginning. It was all James."

I refilled my glass, took a sip, and asked, "Was Lily really that. . uh.-.-. "

"Enchanting? No question of it. If any of us had figured that we had a shot at her, it would have been the end of the gang. She was beautiful, charming, sweet, smart, great at magic, you name it, that was Lily." He looked at me speculatively, "I know that you have a thing for Minerva. I wonder how your relationship would have fared had you known Lily then."

That was a topic that didn't bear much thought. I went on, "Let me just repeat this back to you to be sure that I've got it all right:

- o   Black has no friends that would help him
- o   no relatives to help him
- o   no Deatheaters to help him
- o   He's able to become a shaggy black dog."

"That's pretty much it. I figure that he's hiding out most of the time as a dog and biding his time. He's waiting for an opportunity to strike."

He thought a moment and added, "Oh, just one more thing. Although I can't think of any Deatheaters who would help him, that doesn't mean that there aren't any."

"Understood."

This time I looked into my glass, which was empty. I supposed it was time to end. "Thanks for talking with me. I'll keep it confidential except for what I have to share with others to help catch Black. I guess, I'll have to be completely open with Dumbledore.."

Lupin added, "And Minerva?"

"And Minerva."

He finished his glass and said, "I've got one question for you. Why Minerva?"

It was the first time that anyone had asked me that question point blank (other than my parents), "Well, can't you imagine anyone falling in love with someone who doesn't seem attractive, brilliant AND young?"

With that he got up, walked to the door, and walked through. At the last moment, he turned and thanked me for the scotch. I told him that it was the least that I could do.

He almost closed the door, but he then opened it and bowed my next visitor in.

Minerva greeted me in a most cordial way and sat in the red leather chair. She saw the bottle and said, "As long as you've got that out, why don't you pour us a shot each?"

I did. She sipped it appreciatively and said, "Have any luck?"

I admitted that I had and gave her a quick resume of the discussion that I'd had. She smiled at the story and then said, "I've had some luck too. I found Slughorn."

I perked up immediately. "You did? How?"

"Oh, it wasn't that hard. He always liked to write letters to the editor of the Daily *Prophet*. I just asked the editor. Then I sent Slughorn an owl, asking him to meet us. Slughorn agreed."

"Does he know what we want?"

She almost sneered, "Of course, he does. I wouldn't talk with him without being honest with him about our intentions." She hesitated and added, a little sheepishly, "But there's a price."

I groaned inwardly. There always was. "Ok. What is it?"

"We're going to meet him for lunch at Claridge's."

"I suppose that's expensive?"

Minerva named a price in galleons for a typical lunch entree. I gagged and assented to the highway robbery that Slughorn was about to practice on us. It turned out that we would meet him the next Saturday. At least Slughorn had agreed to make the reservation.

That Saturday morning I decided to go without breakfast so that I would have a good appetite for lunch. Minerva and I met at the main gate at 11 AM, and we walked the short distance to where we could disapparate to London. Minerva had given me a choice of modes of travel—floo powder or disapparation. I asked if the Express were available, but she only frowned. We arrived in a little narrow lane about a block from Claridges. That was a thing about traveling wizarding style. You either traveled in alleys or sooty fire-places.

After we arrived, she insisted on remaining in the alley to give me some preview of what Slughorn was like. She said, "There are a few things that you need to know about Slughorn. He's always curried the favor of the powerful and rich. He did that when he was at school by gathering to himself students that were either brilliant students or came from rich and influential families. He used to have little parties and symposia for his favorites. He expected—and mostly got—little preferences from them when they graduated and came into positions of power."

I asked, "And the Black family was a powerful family?"

"Yes, and also generally very good wizards and witches. But I don't know if Sirius was one of his inner circle or not. When he was at Hogwarts, I was just a new teacher and wasn't well acquainted with Slughorn."

I nodded and prepared for the worst.

At least, it was a short walk to Claridge's. We entered the fairly un-imposing entrance and found that it was indeed luxurious. We asked for Slughorn's table and found him at a small private dining room called the Davies room. When we arrived, we were immediately attended by waiters. Minerva looked over the menu *du jour* and pondered over the options. I simply asked Slughorn what he was having and decided that he probably knew what he was doing gourmet-wise if he knew about this place.

After we'd placed our orders, Minerva came immediately to the point. She introduced me as a new professor and asked "Professor Slughorn. I've told you that we are trying to get some information about Sirius Black, who's escaped from Azkaban Prison, as I'm sure you know. Was he part of the Slug Club?"

I happened to be drinking some water and almost gagged. Slughorn was solicitous, "Did you get some down the wrong pipe?"

I cleared my throat and said, "I'm afraid so, but do go on."

Slughorn leaned back and gazed up at the ceiling to his left. He seemed to be contemplating something, "No, I'm afraid not. He's one that I would like to have collected. I had his brother, Reggie, and would have liked to have had the set.

"Sad story. They were both brilliant students. Reggie was by far the more serious than Sirius," he chortled at his little pun and proceeded, "but I really think that Sirius was the brighter and more talented of the two. Reggie died a few years after graduating and Sirius, well, we all know what happened to Sirius."

I leaned over toward him and asked, "But what can you tell us about Sirius?"

"Oh, Sirius was a real joker. He was one of the top students in my potions class. The only one in his year who was better was Professor Snape. Now, there was a serious student. He was unequalled at potions, but, you know, I think Sirius could have given him a run for his money if he'd set his mind to it.

"If a problem fascinated him, he would stay in there with Snape, but most of the time, he finished the assignments with the minimum work that he could manage and spend the rest of class doodling or working out pranks.

A fit of laughing overcame Slughorn and he controlled himself and said, "I recall one class period. We had been studying the formulation of magical inks—like those used in quick-quote quills. Sirius finished the assignment quickly and then began working on a different ink formulation.

"It usually did little good to get Sirius back to the problem at hand, but I decided I'd see what he was doing with his new ink. I went to his work bench and looked over his shoulder. He had been drawing on a parchment, but there was nothing visible on the parchment. I asked him if he were working on some form of invisible ink.

"He seemed rather excited and anxious to share his discovery with someone—even me. He pulled out his wand and muttered a spell over it. The ink drawing appeared. It was a crude but easily recognizable drawing of the classroom. All of the students and I were in the drawing, represented by stick figures with little balloons over their heads that had initials in them. They turned out to be the initials of the names of the persons, and the ones that were moving were duplicates of the motions of the people they represented in the room. Little Denton Quillby (DQ) was walking to the supply cabinet, just as his stick figure was on the parchment.

"Sirius turned the parchment over and showed me stick figures with initials in balloons over their heads just like on the other side. But these were not moving.

"I'd never seen a map like that before and I congratulated Sirius on it. I suggested that he might want to write it up in a paper. I'd help him get it published. As soon as I mentioned my helping it get published, he immediately became as quiet as the tomb and refused to say anything further. He put the parchment in the flame of a cauldron burner, and it disappeared as I gazed in horrified silence.

"Oh, yes, I'd like to have collected him. I might have been able to keep him from going wrong."

It was a fascinating story, but it didn't get Minerva and me any closer to our goal, so I tried to bring him back to the subject at hand. "But can you tell us anything about his family or friends or anything that might help us find him?"

Slughorn considered that for quite some time as he finished his salad and waited for the next course to arrive. After the tournadeau bourguignon arrived, he looked up and said, "Well, you know, MInerva, about that trio that he hung around with. They were all at least capable wizards. But they weren't quite the sort that I sought out for the Slug Club. I guess they're mostly dead now. His family, come to think of it, are pretty much all dead or gone wrong too. Sad. Sad."

He became even more contemplative. "And then there was Lily —Lily Evans. She spent a good bit of time with them, and she WAS in the Slug Club. But she's gone. Gone."

I was beginning to get impatient. We'd sunk a lot of money into this lunch, and I wasn't especially happy with the meager outcome. "Do you not have any ideas?"

He just shook his head and then he brightened, "Now wait. If he'd only given the secret of that tracing map of his to someone, you could draw a map of the area that you wanted to search and put him on the map. Then you could figure out where he was."

I looked at Minerva and asked the question silently with my eyes. She nodded her head, and I asked Slughorn, "And you don't have any idea of anyone that he might have given the formula for that map thingee to?"

Slughorn said, "Oh, I only wish I did. Do you realize the amount of galleons to be made with such an invention?"

MInerva sneered, "Yes. Lots."

Slughorn admitted that the only people who might have the secret were the ones that he'd mentioned as friends of Black. Great lot of good that did us! The rest of the lunch he reminisced about the good friends he had in the Ministry, sports figures, wealthy, or brilliant wizards.

After we left him, I asked MInerva, "Do you have any idea of anyone reproducing that fascinating map technology that Slughorn described?"

"No. I'd no idea that such a thing existed. It's hard to believe that such a thing could exist, and I not know about it."

We returned to the castle and decided to go directly to Dumbledore to report our success or lack of it. He was in his office. As soon as we entered and he'd offered us tea, he asked us about our luck.

I gave him a quick resumé of the various results that we'd obtained. He shook his head and said, "I'd no idea about either of the two main results you bring back—that Sirius was an animagus who could become a dog or that he had this interesting map. I feel quite certain that if someone else had invented such a thing, I'd know about it."

He went on, "So, what's your suggestion on how to proceed?" He looked at Minerva, who turned to me and simply said, "Well?"

I asked, "ME? I don't know anything that you don't."

Dumbledore smiled and said, "That hasn't stopped you in the past."

I wracked my brains for a while and finally said, "I've only got one suggestion, and it's not exactly what I would call a brain storm.

"I'd suggest walking the countryside, pointing your wand at random and using the spell, 'Asio black dog.'" I shrugged and Dumbledore shrugged as well.

He said, "I suppose that must be it. It's crude, but it's the only sensible idea that I've heard so far." He turned to Minerva and asked, "What do you think Minerva?"

"I'm ashamed to admit that I've not got a better idea."

Dumbledore eventually said, "Then, go sleep on it. Maybe one of you will come up with a better idea. If you don't soon, we'll have to use this one."

I added, "At least, it's an idea that we can organize and use lots of people to do. That will make it more likely to succeed."

Dumbledore shook his forefinger and said, "I'm afraid we can't. If we let many people know about this idea, somebody will report it to the *Prophet.* Then it will be on the front page, and we won't be able to use it."

I completed the thought for him, "Because Black will never transform into a Black Dog again."

Dumbledore dismissed us, and we walked back to my office. For some reason, Minerva sat in the chair behind my desk, and I sat in the red leather chair. She steepled her fingers as she lent on my desk and shook her head. "I don't know. I just don't know."

"I do. We need to take our minds off this. Let's do something completely different and sleep on it. Then in the morning maybe something will occur to one of us."

"And if it doesn't?"

"Well, we'll have had a good night of it."

She smiled and I smiled.

The next day, we joined Lupin at breakfast. He asked what had resulted in his being honored by our presence.

I asked him, "Do you know that Black invented a special sort of map that .-.-."

He interrupted me and finished for me, "That tracks people?"

Minerva nodded, "Exactly."

Lupin asked, "How did you learn about that? I thought it was a secret that we never revealed to anyone."

"Well," I glanced over at Minerva. She rolled her eyes and said, "Just go ahead and tell him."

"Well, we talked to Professor Slughorn. Apparently, Black invented it in his Advanced Potions Class."

Lupin nodded, "We wondered how he'd gotten the idea.

"You see, one day—or actually night—he showed up with this piece of parchment. He'd drawn a map of the castle and it had little. -.-.uh .-.-. I don't know what to call them."

I supplied, "Icons."

"Yes, I suppose you could call them that. Anyway, they stood for people, mostly teachers. With that map, we could avoid the teachers and Filch on patrol in the halls, when we were having our little excursions.

"Later, he made more innovations. We all contributed to the map." Lupin smiled and sat a little straighter, "I contributed the idea of generalizing the map to track any person in the castle. He had specific people on his map, but I showed him how it could track anyone and any number of people."

Minerva said, "Great! No wonder you hooligans were never caught. We knew you were out—up to no good, but we could never catch you at it after early in your 6th year."

Lupin laughed and said, "Yes, we ran you teachers a merry chase. Anyway, I don't know what happened to that map."

Minerva said, "Forget about that map. Do you know how it worked? Could you create a new one?"

He shook his head no, "Only Black knew the central secret to the ink of that map."

I brought things back to the problem at hand, "Then, we're still stuck with going out and trying to find him by looking for black dogs."

Lupin nodded and said, "I'll help."

Minerva thanked him and tried to set up a time for us to go at it. That turned out to be harder than we could have guessed. It turned out that Lupin was always very weak for a couple of days around the full moon. He explained, "Even though my lycanthropia is controlled by medicine, I still suffer around the new moon. By the weekend I should be OK." So, we agreed that the next Saturday we'd have breakfast together and then go searching.

The week passed altogether too slowly. I thought that I could forget about our "date" on Saturday, but every night when I went to bed, I found myself automatically counting days and then hours until Saturday breakfast. The night before I tossed and turned all night, and it felt like I'd only gotten a couple of hours sleep.

The normally luxurious and wonderful breakfast on Saturdays, when teachers could count on having the great hall to themselves, was as hard for me to appreciate as it is for any student worried about an upcoming exam. It was strange to me that both Minerva and Lupin seemed to be fully enjoying the croissants, bialy's, eggs Benedict, and all the other delightful things that appeared on the breakfast menus on Saturdays. So that Feb. 19, I found myself playing with the soufflé on my plate unable to force any of it into my mouth.

Of course, Minerva and Lupin were having a hearty breakfast and joking about what we'd get when we started using the "Asio" spell. They wondered if I had the flu or a cold. Finally, I couldn't stand their good spirits any longer and asked, "Just what are you planning to do if we do pull in Black?"

They were unfazed. Minerva said, "Well, we just stun him with *petrificus totalis* and disarm him. Then we send for the Aurors, and we're off."

"Well, I'm glad you've done some thinking about it. I guess I should be happy that there are two of you with wands, but I've got a bad feeling about it."

They assured me that there wasn't going to be any serious problem. And countered by asking them to leave right now if they were so confident. Lupin said that he wanted to finish his croissant first, and then he'd be ready to go. So, in fifteen minutes we found ourselves walking out the main entrance. We debated a bit as to where we should go to try the experiment. Lupin wanted to go toward the village of Hogsmeade, but Minerva wanted to go toward the Forbidden Forest. I wanted to go toward the low mountains. Minerva won in the end, so off we went. I think she just wanted to go a direction that would get us to an uninhabited area the fastest.

So, we soon got away from everyone, and Minerva was ready to try the spell immediately. I put a quick halt to her plans by objecting, "Wait, wait. Wait. Let's do a little thinking first. You do your spell and we're going to be inundated in black dogs. How are you going to know which—if any—is Black?"

Minerva shot back, "I'm going to use the 'Revellio' spell."

Lupin weighed in, "How do we know that will work? Have you ever tried it with an animagus?"

Minerva shot back, "Well, of course it will work. Why wouldn't it?"

I put in my thought. "Why don't we test it?"

She looked daggers at me, "So, who do we experiment on, eh? I just know one animagus here—me."

I nodded. She grumbled a little and admitted that it was something that maybe we ought to do. She added, "I convert to a cat. Black turns into a dog."

"Well, we can only work on what we've got."

Lupin was amused by the little "cat fight". He said, "Well, we seem to have just enough people. Minerva, you disapparate off a distance and transform into a cat. I'll do the "ascio" spell and use the 'Revellio' spell to see if we can tell which one is you."

Minerva reluctantly agreed to that. She said to give her two minutes after she disapparated and then use the "ascio" spell. She disappeared, and I watched my watch. After two minutes, I nodded to Lupin and he used the spell. Nothing happened for about a half minute, and then it started to rain cats. They were falling all around us. Lupin did his best to use the "Revellio" spell on them all, but they were scattering faster than he could swing his wand around.

After a few minutes there were still a few cats wandering around, and he started using the "Revellio" spell on all of them until one flashed a bright green. He said, "Ah, ha! Minerva, I found you."

She transformed back to herself and said, "Well, that could have gone better."

I agreed, "If we get that many dogs, we might as well give up. Black could be in the next county before we got around to him."

Lupin wasn't ready to give up. "But my spell wasn't specific. If I'd known what kind of cat you were, I could have been more specific. Then, there would have been a lot fewer cats. What kind of tabby are you?"

"A silver tabby."

"OK. Let's try again, but this time, I'm only bringing tabbies."

Minerva disappeared. I timed off two minutes, and then Lupin summoned tabby cats. This time the cats came down not as a downpour but as a drizzle. He could use the "Revellio" spell on them, one at a time, and he caught Minerva almost as soon as she landed. She declared that it might just work.

We were almost ready to proceed when Minerva hit her forehead with the palm of her hand and said, "I'm being really stupid."

I commented that one hardly knew how to respond to that. Did one agree or disagree? She didn't even pay attention to the comment but said, "Lupin. Let's try that one more time."

He shrugged and agreed to the test. She disappeared. I counted off the minutes and told Lupin to go. He did the spell and cats started to rain again. But this time it was different. Lupin tested all the cats as they appeared, but none of them were Minerva. The drizzle slowed to a few drops and then stopped all-together. Lupin looked around at the cats and said to them in general, "OK. Minerva, you've made your point. Transform back." None of them did.

Then she disapparated in front of our noses. Lupin said, "OK. What did you do? Did you disapparate so far away that the ascio spell couldn't summon you?"

She shook her head vigorously. "No, I did something completely different. When I started to fly through the air, I disapparated to Birmingham."

Lupin nodded sagely, "Clever. Yes, I didn't know that you could disapparate while transformed. I supposed that like werewolves, you couldn't do much magic while transformed.

"But, the only reason that you knew to do that was because you knew what was happening. The first time, you didn't think of that."

Minerva said, "I'm not so sure. Black is obviously very smart. He could probably figure out what was happening the first time and think of a way out while he was still being summoned. I'm beginning to think that that this is a really long shot, now."

My contribution was to note that we could at least try for a while and see what happened.

The two reluctantly agreed to that idea and we set up to start trying the spells on black dogs. It was agreed that Lupin would use the ascio spell and Minerva the Revellio. I got out my purse and pulled my Glock out. I began checking out the clip and the safety. Minerva asked, "What the heck is that?"

I stared at her, "You know perfectly well what it is. I just wanted to be prepared for anything."

Lupin asked, "What is that that you have there?"

"It's a Muggle gun—just in case."

He frowned and said, "I don't think that's really necessary."

I said, "Well, I do." No one was happy, but there was an uneasy truce. It was agreed that I could keep it if I really held it in reserve until there was absolutely no other alternative. So, I had the Glock out and had the safety on without a bullet in the chamber when Lupin used the ascio spell. Then there was a deluge of dark dogs. No one realized just how many black or dark dogs there were around. The ascio spell wouldn't land something on the head of the person who was using it, but it didn't protect the people who happened to be standing nearby.

The dogs, some of them pretty big, pelted Minerva and me—seemingly from all directions, except down. We were both knocked down several times. Lupin had all that he could do to help with the Revellio spell. Minerva didn't have much opportunity to use it. By the time the downpour was over, there had been a couple of what looked an awful like wolves to me fall from the sky. I had my Glock trained on them, but they decided that they didn't want to have any more to do with us than they already had.

When the dust cleared, we weren't at all sure that Black might not have been there and just missed in the melee. We all agreed that we'd had enough for the day and that we'd go back to report to Dumbledore to see if he had any suggestions before we tried that again.

When we got back, Dumbledore was nowhere to be found, so we left a note for him in his mailbox in the Teacher's Lounge saying that we wanted to see him about our experiments.

He was back later in the day but left a note in Minerva's box that read, "I know about your experiments. I have no further ideas for the moment. If you want to proceed with your plan, please do. I don't hold much hope for it." That was good enough for us. Our only real hope was that Dumbledore would propose some change in procedure that would give us a better shot at catching Black. We agreed to keep thinking.

Buckbeak

Life went back to normal—sort of.   That is if you consider the surroundings of the castle being haunted by Dementors as normal. I'd heard descriptions of them but had never and would never be able to see one, so I had to depend on descriptions from every magical person that I knew. What I heard was bizarre. They look like hooded figures, but the hooded robes are actually part of the creature—not something added on. They have almost normal faces—including eyes and mouths but no one could say whether they had ears or even noses. Everyone was agreed that you never wanted to be close enough to one to allow you to know for sure if they had those things.

No one who was willing to talk with me knew or would say how you communicated with them. It was doubtless that people did. How else could they be guards at Azkaban? How else could they be given directions? Dumbledore flatly refused to talk about them in any more detail than those that I knew. His standard reply was that it was dangerous to know too much OR too little about them, and apparently, I knew enough. So, he didn't want me to know more.

Other than their presence, life at Hogwarts settled down, and things seemed OK, that is, until I heard about Buckbeak's "trial". I'd not talked with Hagrid more than to say "hello" and "how are you" since before Christmas. However, one evening I could tell that he was disturbed about something. He sat the entire dinner, just staring dejectedly at his plate and playing with the haunch of lamb there. His plate was actually a serving platter. He just took a nibble or two at it, and after Dumbledore dismissed everyone, he just continued to sit there while everyone else filed out of the Great Hall.

I walked over and sat down next to him and tried to get his attention. The only way that I succeeded was to walk around the table, position myself in front of him and throw an apple at his forehead. It bounced off. I was afraid that he wasn't going to notice even that, but he slowly looked up and sniffed a huge gout of air through his nose and then pulled out a tablecloth from an inside pocket and blew his nose. Up close, I noticed that he had been staring down at a parchment.

He stared at me for a moment and then said, "Oh, it's you, Professor Wendt. Is there some'at that I can do for you?"

I said, "Well, that's what I was going to ask you. You seem to be pretty disturbed. Has something happened?"

His body seemed to slump even more than it already was, and he seemed on the verge of bawling. He pulled out his handkerchief again and dabbed at his eyes. Then he said, "Oh, I suppose it's nothing important. Do you know my Hippogriff, Buckbeak?"

I had to admit that I'd not had the honor. He explained that he, as Buckbeak's owner, had been summoned to a hearing at the Ministry to decide if Buckbeak would be destroyed. "You see, I just got this summons by owl during dinner." He held up the parchment.

I expressed some surprise and asked what had happened to cause that. Haggrid explained about the incident early in the Fall term when Draco Malfoy had been injured by Buckbeak following Draco's gross incitement of the creature. Apparently, Malfoy's father had appealed to the ministry to have Haggrid fired over the incident. When that was blocked by Dumbledore ("great man that Dumbledore"), Lucius had worked to get Buckbeak destroyed under the Dangerous Magical Creatures act.

I nodded and asked if he thought that would happen. Haggrid said, "Oh, Malfoy has lots of money and influence. Of course, he'll get that done." This time he broke out into gales of tears.

I asked Haggrid if he had legal help. Haggrid just stared at me and said, "Well, of course, Dumbledore is going to go with me and help me, but I just don't think that it will make a difference."

"Well, I hate to see a character like Lucius get his way ALL the time. Do you mind if I have a look at that summons. I'd like to come along to the hearing to give you moral support at least."

Haggrid sniffed once and thanked me. I glanced at the summons. It listed the complaint against Buckbeak and details of the hearing. I asked Haggrid, "Do you mind if I keep this for a while—maybe a couple of days. I see that the hearing isn't for another 40 days."

Haggrid didn't object, but he asked why I wanted to borrow the summons. I answered that there might be a legal loophole that we could use to get him off.

It was a couple of days before I had a chance to look at it in detail. When I did, I realized how ambiguous it was. It had a brief description of an attack by Buckbeak on Draco Malfoy. There was no description of what happened prior to the attack, no detailed description of the injuries suffered, no discussion of other attacks that had occurred involving this Hippogriff. The entire document was hardly more than 11 inches of parchment, and most of it was taken up with details of when, where and how the hearing would be. It also discussed the appeal procedure—there wasn't any.

It said that the review process would be "informal." I reflected on the word. I laughed to myself. They'd discover some of the disadvantages of informality.

At the next meal, Minerva and I talked about the hearing. I asked her, "I want to understand what's normal for hippogriffs. Have you got a good text that I can consult?"

Minerva laughed. "The best simple text is the *Monster Book of Monsters*. There's just one little problem with it. It's tough to read if you're not a wizard."

"Oh, I knew there would be a catch. What's the deal with this Monster book?"

"Well, it'll try to eat you if you don't know how to handle it."

"Great. Well, can you help me with it?"

Minerva smiled a wicked smile and said, "I thought you'd never ask. There's a copy in the library. Why don't we get together in your office, and we can snuggle up over a good book."

So, we went to the library. Ms. Pinz was unhappy to be dragged out to open the library, but she went with us to the Library and looked over our shoulders as we selected the book. She begrudgingly checked it out to Minerva. The book seemed OK, but by the time we reached my office, it had started to snarl. Minerva stroked the binding and it calmed down. I commented, "Great. I don't know why I doubted you. I guess it was just wishful thinking."

We took it to bed for some light bedtime reading.

The next day, I started making notes for my appearance at the hearing. In a week I returned Haggrid's parchment. Then I waited.

▽

The day before the hearing, I asked Minerva if she'd drop me off at the Ministry. She said that she'd do more than drop me off—she'd go with me to the hearing and back me up if it were necessary. I smiled, "You won't need to do that. Just sit back and enjoy the show." That night I didn't get much sleep. The next morning at breakfast, Dumbledore joined us and asked if I needed a lift to the hearing.

"Are you going too?" I asked.

"Certainly, I'm going with Haggrid. I always support my staff in their times of need."

Minerva said, "I hope you know that I support my man."

"Well, then we'll all go." Dumbledore smiled and led us to the big fireplace. We all joined hands including Haggrid, and we stepped out of the fireplace into the Ministry atrium. We checked in at the Reception Desk to get visitor's badges and the site of the hearing. It was in the Auror's Office rather than the Courtroom. Apparently, Dumbledore knew his way around pretty well because he declined with thanks the offer of a guide to get us there. We found an elevator and went to the top floor. When we got there, we found Room 822 where the hearing was to be.

We were there about fifteen minutes early, but the room wasn't locked. We were the first to arrive. It turned out to be a meeting room with a large, mahogany table that would seat 16 easily. We chose seats on one side and sat. Haggrid was wearing a suit that I couldn't believe it was possible to find in any sane Men's Department Store. It was checked with the broadest tie, I'd ever seen. I wondered if it were actually a flag in an earlier life. Minerva was wearing emerald green robes, matching earrings, and the necklace that I'd given her.

Shortly after we arrived, there were several people who entered. I recognized the Minister of Magic, Fudge. None of the others I recognized. They were introduced as McNair, an officer of the Magical Animal Control Board, an auror by the name of Finney, and a judge in the small claims court, Michaels.

Shortly afterward, Mr. Lucius Malfoy and a lawyer named Raymonds arrived. Michaels announced that since all interested parties had arrived, the hearing would begin. He explained that the hearing would be informal, that he just wanted to get to a full understanding of the case, and that he would deliver his decision quickly.

He invited Malfoy to state his case. Malfoy essentially restated what was in the summons parchment. He emphasized the serious injuries that his son had received. The judge made a few notes and asked if anyone had anything to add.

Haggrid raised his hand. The judge told him to proceed. Haggrid simply listed all the virtues of the good Buckbeak, including being strong and clean and being a good hippogriff that had never harmed anyone before. He'd even let Harry Potter ride on his back.

Malfoy simply sneered and commented that it was just the sort of thing that an oaf like Haggrid would say. The judge asked if there were any others who wished to speak. Dumbledore was preparing to speak but I beat him to it.

"Your honor, I'd like to make a few comments." The judge assented and I began.

"I have a few questions that I'd like to ask some of the people present."

"Go ahead, but who are you?"

"Your honor, my name is James Wendt. I work for Hogwarts school as a professor."

"Please go ahead."

"First, Mr. Malfoy, I don't recall you saying how long your son was in the hospital."

Malfoy swung around toward me and said, "I didn't."

"Well?"

"Well, what?"

"How long was he in the hospital?"

Malfoy looked around furtively at the judge. Apparently he was hoping for relief from this line of questions. The judge just shrugged and said, "Go ahead and answer."

Malfoy said, "I think it was two or three days."

Dumbledore interrupted and said, "I believe that it was one day and he wasn't kept overnight."

Malfoy said, "Perhaps that's true."

"I believe that Quidditch injuries frequently involve longer hospital stays than that, don't they Headmaster?" I asked.

"Yes, why only last year Mr. Potter was in the hospital overnight after the bones in his right arm were crushed."

"Then Draco Malfoy's injuries and their severity were not at all unusual for Hogwarts students? I believe young Mr. Malfoy plays seeker on the Slitherin quidditch team doesn't he, Mr. Malfoy?"

Smiling, Dumbledore agreed, and Lucius was forced to as well.

"Then these sort of injuries are not unfamiliar to him?"

Dumbledore said, "They shouldn't be."

"Your honor, I have a question for you, if I may."

The judge stared at me but said, "Go ahead."

"What are the criteria for deciding to destroy a magical animal?"

The judge was taken aback but answered, "Well, there are several reasons. Some species are simply so dangerous that they are never permitted to survive. For example, basilisks are so dangerous that they are always destroyed when found.

"But for most species, it's necessary to prove that the individual animal is unusually vicious."

I repeated his phrase, "Unusually vicious."

"Yes."

"I'd like to quote from a standard book on magical animals—*The Monster Book of Monsters*.

"'The Hippogriff is a proud animal, which must be approached with great care. They are very proud animals and susceptible to being insulted. It is necessary to approach with head bowed, and only if the Hippogriff signals acceptance should the wizard come closer than two meters.'

"I submit that there has been no evidence presented that young Mr. Malfoy treated the Hippogriff with respect. Therefore it is necessary to conclude that the Hippogriff, Buckbeak, was acting perfectly normally for a Hippogriff."

Malfoy leaped up and shouted, "That thing attacked my son and can't be let off without punishment."

I went on undeterred, "I think that Mr. Malfoy is correct in one regard. Someone should be punished for what happened. The real fault here is the teacher who brought a member of a hard-to-control species into a classroom experience. That teacher should be disciplined, not the Hippogrith. That teacher needs to do penance for his gross stupidity in this case.

"I rest my case."

The judge asked for other comments. No one had anything to add. He instructed us that his opinion would be rendered within a week. It was very anti-climatic. We wandered out of the meeting room and went our separate ways.

I patted Hagrid on the back and said, "Hagrid, I'm sorry that I had to be so hard on you. I thought that was the only way to deflect from Buckbeak the wrath of Malfoy."

Hagrid sniffed, "I know Professor. I didn't take it personal-like."

Minerva asked, "What do you think will happen?"

Dumbledore shook his head negatively. "I don't know, but I fear that the Malfoy family has very much power and influence, and despite your vigorous defense, Mr. Wendt, I think that Buckbeak's days are numbered."

Haggrid shed a tear and then sighed.

A few days later an owl arrived with the verdict on Buckbeak. The time for the execution had been set. Haggrid was grief stricken. He could be seen on the shore of the lake gazing off to the distance for hours on end.

The first free evening that Minerva and I had together I asked her if she could think of anything to avoid the execution. She said, "As Buckbeak's owner, he's been make the jailer. If the hippogriff disappears for whatever reason, Haggrid will be responsible."

"Great, then everyone's stuck. We can't do anything like 'spring' Buckbeak." After a moment, I had an idea, "What about faking Buckbeak's death?"

Minerva shook her head. "No, the execution will be by decapitation. Hard to fake that kind of death, and even if we faked Buckbeak's death before the execution date, Malfoy has the right to have it's head on a platter. Don't you think he won't ask that."

"No kidding. Well, we can always turn to that other hopeless case, trying to catch Black."

Minerva grimaced and said, "Thank you, no."

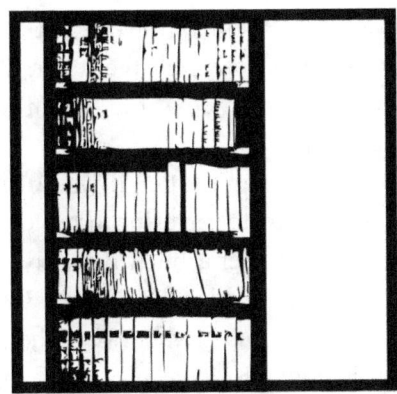

Paris in the Springtime

The next week or so had nothing unusual happening. I'd begun to make peace with the idea that Hogwarts might become a sort of branch office of Azkaban with Dementors continually guarding the school.

Then, one day, as I was leaving a 2nd-year English class and was hurrying up to my office, I almost knocked Cedric Diggory off his feet. "Sorry Mr. Diggory, I should have been paying more attention to what I was doing."

"No problem, Professor, I was just wondering, what with the Easter Break coming up soon, if you'd .-.-. well, you know. maybe you could." During this rambling discussion, it dawned on me what he wanted.

"Do you want to ask me to find a tournament for you during the spring break?"

"Yes, sir. Would you please do that?"

"Of course. I should know something in a few days. There should be something interesting going."

Cedric trotted off happily, and I was happy that I could offer someone what he wanted for a change. I hurried back to my office, looked up the address of the British Chess Association, and wrote a quick note asking for the list of available decent tournaments during Holy Week. I got Minerva to send it off by owl, and all I had to do was wait.

The response came in a couple of days, but it wasn't quite what I'd expected. There was a one page letter and a couple of tournament brochures. I pulled a scrap of parchment out of my desk in my classroom, where the owl had delivered the letter. I wrote a quick note asking Diggory to come to my office at the end of the next class period or as soon as he could.

I was monitoring an exam. After it was over, I surprised a 2nd-year Hufflepuff by asking him to give the note to Diggory. I took the tests up to my office to grade them, but I'd barely set up to get started when there was a knock on the door, followed by the appearance of Diggory's broadly smiling face inserted between the door and jam.

"Hi, Professor, is now OK?"

"Sure come in." I gestured Diggory to take a seat in the red leather chair. He did so, and then I began. "Well, things didn't go quite the way I expected. I just got a letter from the British Chess Association and. . ."

Cedric anticipated me, 'there aren't any tournaments?"

"Well, not exactly. You've got choices. There's the usual low level and Junior British tournaments. They'd bore you to tears, and you'd probably get a reputation for stealing papers from blind newsies."

Cedric was confused by the phrase, so I explained. "In Muggle cities, there are 'newstands' where newspapers are sold. The people who run them are known as 'newsies' in some circles. The idea is that there's hardly anything easier than stealing a newspaper from a blind man."

Cedric nodded and then shook his head, "That's what you call a joke, right?"

"Yup, in my circles that passes for a joke. Anyway, there are a couple of good tournaments, but they're pretty far away—Western Russia; Chicago, USA; Venezuela and Paris. Right now, a decent tournament is going on in England, but you're still in school."

"There's no way that I could get out of school to go to that tournament?"

"As your faculty adviser, I'd have to agree to it. And frankly, I don't think that I can go along with that."

"I was afraid of that. So, where does that leave us?"

"There's a couple of good tournaments in the summer—you know a lot about one of them. So, you just have to be patient."

Cedric leaned back and said, 'Hmmmmmmmmmmmmmmmmmmmmmm. I'm not sure that I can make those. Do you know that the World Quidditch Cup qualifying rounds are just now starting and that by the time our Summer holiday starts, they'll be in full swing?"

"Yes, I knew that. You know, I missed them last time around." I didn't tell him that I didn't even know they existed the last time around.

"Oh, you missed a great Final. Wronsky was seeker for Poland. In the final, he introduced a surprise play, the Wronsky Faint. It was the turning point in the final game."

I nodded, trying to seem knowledgeable.

"I don't know if I'll be able to play in any of those tournaments during the summer."

"OK," I smiled, but didn't really feel happy about it. There seemed to be something ominous in it, but I couldn't put my finger on what it was. I thought nothing more about it for a long while.

For a few days I didn't think further about it, but one evening Cedric came to visit. He had a big smile on his face. I invited him to sit in the red leather chair and waited expectantly.

"Sir, I've been doing a little talking with my parents. That tournament in Paris. I think I can play in it." He hurried through the rest of what was apparently a prepared speech, "It happens during the Spring Holiday at Hogwarts, and I've written to my parents to see if I could play. They've approved it." He pulled out a small parchment that was addressed to me from the Diggory's. They simply gave permission for me to take their son to a tournament in Paris during the school's Spring Holiday.

I examined it very carefully, which gave me time to think. I finally decided that it would be a good opportunity—if all the stars lined up properly—for Diggory. I asked him about details of the tournament like how far in advance you had to register for it.

He turned red and said, "Well, actually, I already applied to the Tournament Director. AND I've been accepted—if I have permission from my parents." He handed over a letter. It was written in French, but my college French was up to getting the gist out of it. The gist was that Mssr. Diggory would be welcome to compete in the tournament—with permission of parents or guardians. It listed the dates of the tournament and the location, including a list of appropriate hotels that contestants could stay in. There was an entry fee. It was quoted in Euro's.

"Well, it looks like you've done your homework. I need to work out transportation and other details.

▽

The first thing that I did was to talk with Minerva. I wanted to settle whether she'd be willing to travel with us to Paris and help us get around.

When I proposed going to Paris for a chess tournament and asked if she'd like to go along and help with transportation, she just stared at me and then said, "Let's see. Would I like to go to the most beautiful city in the world, the City of Lights, the City of Love? I don't know why in the world you'd think that I might be interested in that."

"OK, drop the comedy and just answer with a simple 'yea' or 'nay'."

She looked at me askance and said, "When do we go?"

"During Spring Break."

Her gaze drifted far away and she said, "Paris in the spring. Where else would one go?"

"I'll take that as a 'yes'."

"You certainly may. I suppose that you're planning on Cedric going and maybe a parent or two."

"Yes, if they're interested."

"I think that you can count on Reina being interested even if Amos isn't."

It turned out that Reina was indeed interested, and that made Amos interested—if only to defend his wife from the Parisian Lothario's. The tournament began on Sunday and our Spring Break began on Friday. Minerva had done a little research and found a Wizard inn off the Rue Jean-Jacques Rousseau. It was one of these hidden buildings that only wizards could see.

There was some dispute about how to get there. The first step was easy enough. We took the Hogwarts express back to London. That was where the dispute began. Amos and Reina Diggory picked up their son at platform 9 ¾ and arranged to get themselves on to Paris.

Then, Minerva and I wrangled about how to get there. I wanted to go via the Chunnel. It had just been completed, and I wanted to ride a train under the channel. Minerva on the other hand was adamant. She wasn't going to ride a train through any Muggle-built tunnel that was so long that she couldn't see both ends at the same time.

She tried cajolery, pleading, threats and anything else she could think of. I just rebutted with one argument, "Minerva, I've gone along with all your wizarding hare-brained travel schemes. I've disaparated with you, I've gone through floo's with you, I've agreed to travel by port key—whatever that is. I've thrown up, been so dizzy that I couldn't stand for half an hour, and come away covered with soot. But you've never gone a single Muggle way of travel with me!"

She looked around desperately as though an idea would pop out of thin air, and then she had an "ah ha" moment. "Oh, yes, I have. You're forgetting all the times we rode the Underground."

I wasn't giving up that easily, "Oh, I suppose one time that you humor me makes up for all the times that I went your way. However, this will be a wonderful trip. They say the Chunnel ride is as smooth as silk. You won't spin around. You won't nearly throw up. You can go to the dining car and have a gourmet meal. What's not to like about that?"

She just shook her head, "How about being a hundred meters below the ocean?"

I was so exasperated that I paced back and forth trying to come up with an argument. Finally, I just said, "Well, I'm going by chunnel. You decide how you're getting there."

She just nodded and said, "Well, why didn't you say so. Of course, I'm going with you."

I was stunned. If I'd know it would be that simple, I'd have done it a long time before. However, she did raise a good point. If we went by chunnel rather than by floo powder to the Beaux Batons academy near Paris and then by disapparation to the wizarding inn that we'd selected, she'd have to go through customs.

I was stuck. I could suggest that after we arrived on the French side that we disapparate directly to the inn, but that would defeat the purpose of traveling by train. Her superior smile began to creep over her face and she nodded and hummed quietly.

"Well, there has to be a way." I thought desperately and then an idea occurred to me. I got my passport out and showed it to her, "Do you think you could duplicate this?"

She looked at it, thumbed it open, seemed to read a few pages and said, "Yes, I suppose so. But it would just be a copy of your passport. By the way, that's an awful picture of you."

"Never mind my picture, could you alter the picture so it's a picture of you?"

She shook her head but finally said, "I suppose so. I'd have to use a photochop spell to do it, but I think so."

"And change the name, date and place of birth?"

She growled lowly and said, "I suppose so."

"Well, then you'd have your own passport."

She took out her wand and made a couple of loops around my passport and then a second passport appeared on the table in the restaurant where we were sitting. Then, she opened the faux passport to the page with the photo. She looked at me and said, "Please give me the photo of me that you keep in your purse."

She took it and seemed to use her wand like a brush. The photo of me slowly altered to match my photo of her. It appeared to be Minerva in her very jaunty pointed hat and with an arch expression on her face.

I looked and said, "OK. You'll have to change that. They don't allow you to wear a hat when you're photographed and you have to see your eyes very clearly in the photo."

She sneered and said, "No wonder your photo is so awful. I guess I can ruin my photo too." She made a few more passes. The hat disappeared, the arch expression left her face, and a rather bland, silly expression replaced it.

"I suppose that will have to do." Then armed with her new US Passport, we picked up our bags and hailed a cab to take us to Waterloo station. We bought tickets and boarded the train. Minerva wasn't very impressed by it.

"We won't board the actual Chunnel train until we change trains in Folkestone." When we did, she was appropriately impressed. The trip was uneventful and Minerva even enjoyed it, although she would never admit it. At the French end, we went through customs pretty

316

uneventfully, although the Customs Agent who reviewed her passport decided to ask her a few questions:

"You're from America?"

"Yes."

"You have a very strong English accent you know—not like your companion."

"Oh, he's not my companion, he's my hubby. We've lived in America for a long time, but I've never lost my British accent. You'll notice that I was born in London."

He glanced down at the passport and nodded, "Yes, Madame Wendt. I hope you enjoy your stay in France." Then he added, "Why are you visiting?"

She immediately answered, "Why for the chess tournament. We have a friend who's competing. Do you play?"

He shook his head and said, "That game is one that never interested me. Not enough attractive women play."

As we left the station, I said, "Well, he's right about that." We then took a train to Paris. When we arrived, we took a taxi as close to our inn as we could. We had to walk a block or two because the inn is in the part of central Paris where motor vehicles are not permitted.

When we arrived, we discovered that the Diggory's had already arrived and were in their room. We joined them for dinner. It was good French cuisine. The sauces were not too heavy and the wine excellent.

The next day, we made our way to the hotel where the tournament was being held. Cedric signed in and received a handbook with tournament rules, initial pairings and a map of the hotel. The rest of us had to buy copies. We found that Cedric's first opponent was a French woman. Her name was Helene du Bois. We had a light lunch in the hotel and made our way to the Salle de Jeux and found Cedric's first table.

Helene took her seat opposite Cedric and held out her hand. She was wearing a bright sun-dress that was flimsy but somehow revealed nothing. Her blond hair was drawn up into a simple twist at the back of her head. It was impossible to know how long her hair was—whether barely shoulder length or much longer. She wore hardly any makeup—perhaps a bit of lip gloss.

Cedric, who'd never played against a woman before in serious competition, seemed rattled. Not only had he not played a woman, he'd not played against a lovely woman at any level of competition. Not only was she lovely, but she was older—perhaps just at the sunny beginning of middle-age. She still exhibit a sensuality that she seemed half aware of and that was half muted by innocence. He seemed not sure what to do about the extended hand. He eventually held out his hand just as she seemed ready to withdraw hers. Their hands clasped briefly, and Cedric withdrew his hand but slowly from the contact. At sixteen—almost seventeen, he'd never met a mature woman on terms of equality—in any field of endeavor. This meeting seemed to have shocked him into a realization of the seriousness of maturity—in a way that no lecture from his parents or any teacher was capable of. He perhaps saw for the first time, the reality of aging. He'd played against much older competitors, but somehow he'd imagined that they'd all been their apparent age forever and would remain that age forever—certainly never as young as he was.

This obviously beautiful woman who equally obviously was beginning to age proved to him the reality of change and even death for everyone—even for him. He seemed to feel it viscerally. In a way much more real than intellectual reflection could ever produce, it convinced him of the reality—one day—of his own death.

In a surprising turn of feeling, it also led to his desire for this strange woman. It was a desire to tell her that she was still beautiful and that she could still excite any man she wanted. For that moment, he desperately wanted her to want him.

The feeling lasted not much longer than the brief hand-clasp had, but it would never leave him for the rest of his life—that he was sure of. In the next moment, he realized the danger to him in this game of letting his concentration slip, and he returned to the moment. The lapse had, if anything strengthened his determination to win. He must prove that he was worthy of her—that he could defeat her on this 64-square field.

As Cedric sat, there began to be a crowd gathering around his table. Cedric didn't really have a ritual that he went through in preparation for a game. Instead, he glanced briefly over the board, the clock, sometimes adjusted his chair for comfort and was ready to play.

This opponent was no more fastidious than he. She glanced about the crowd that was gathering, perhaps to see if there were a familiar face. She noticed mine and smiled companionably. She seemed about to speak, but we were all interrupted by the Tournament Director who announced that play would begin momentarily. She turned her attention to the table and frowned slightly.

In the meantime there was quite a lot of talk going on around the table. Some was in French, some in Spanish and, of course, some in English. This came to silence as the Tournament Director signaled, "Commencez."

Cedric's full attention went to the table, where his opponent opened with pawn to Queen 3. He responded and just then I was interrupted by a tug on my elbow. I looked around and found that Amos Diggory was trying to pull me aside. I went with him and the two ladies followed. He led us into the spacious lobby, where he found a grouping of four chairs around a table. We sat.

Amos immediately asked, "What are those Frogs playing at? Why the big crowd watching and what were they saying?"

I admitted that I didn't have very good command of French, but I'd tell him what I understood from overhearing conversations. "His opponent."

Diggory interrupted, "You mean the lady Frog."

"Her name is Helene. I don't know a lot about her, but what I've heard is that she has only been in one tournament—and she won it. It was in Barcelona—a decent tournament. Which, I'd like to point out to you is more than Cedric has done."

Again Diggory interrupted, "But he's a great player."

"Oh, I agree. He's done amazingly well, considering his age and the amount of experience he's had. He's rated a Master and not far from Grand Master rating. But, he hasn't won a major tournament. She has won a decent tournament. She's not rated as highly as he is, but I wouldn't underestimate her."

Mrs. Diggory asked a question of her own. "I didn't know that women are allowed in these tournaments."

"Oh, yes. They are. It's just that there aren't a lot of women who try to become world class chess players."

Minerva nodded sagely and asked, "How did she become one then?"

"Well, I don't know. I did overhear some talk from the crowd. It seems that there are two theories about how she became a good chess player.

"One theory is that she learned completely by playing chess against computers."

Diggory looked puzzled, "Who are these 'compoosters?'"

"It's not who. It's what are they." I hesitated as I considered just how hard it would be to try to come up with a meaningful explanation, but Minerva broke in on my thoughts with her own answer.

"Computers are thinking machines. They are made of gears and wheels by Muggles, and they can solve all sorts of problems." She beamed with pride at understanding something so abstruse as Muggle computers. I had to admire her for coming to the nub of an answer.

Diggory stared at her, unbelieving, "gears and wheels can learn how to play chess?"

I stepped in to help out, "Computers aren't usually made of gears and wheels these days, but the original ones certainly were. And, in principle, you could make a chess-playing computer with gears and wheels.

"Computers can do anything that you can make up a set of simple rules and instructions to do. The best computer chess programs can beat almost any Muggle," and then I added, "Or wizard.

"Computers aren't considered to play particularly good chess, but they are very good at avoiding bad moves. I personally doubt that her chess tutor was a computer program, regardless how good it was." I stopped again, trying to decide whether I wanted to repeat salacious hear-say. Minerva intuitively understood my hesitation and asked me a question.

"Do you have a bit of juicy gossip that you're trying to decide whether or not to share with us?" She arched an eyebrow but only I could see the gesture. She wanted to hear it even if I didn't share it with the others. I decided to go ahead and share.

I nodded to her and then spoke to everyone, "Well, it's hard for me to be sure, because this was a French conversation from the crowd, but it seemed pretty clear that the speaker was claiming that she had learned at the knees of an old Grand Master and that his price for the lessons was .-.-." I hesitated, and Minerva completed the thought for me.

"Was it possibly .-.-. uh .-.-. sexual favors were traded for chess lessons?"

"That was the implication." I said.

Amos hooted and said, "That's the Froggies for you. Everything can be traded for 'sexual favors'."

I had hoped to avoid that kind of response.

Trying to turn the topic elsewhere, I said, "But to answer your original question, the chess fans expect that this will be an amazing struggle. Both players are pretty inexperienced. They think that they'll deviate from the standard openings early and quickly enter unexplored territory where there will be lots of unexpected and exciting developments. The crowd recognizes that they are brilliant players and hope there to be brilliant play."

Amos said (under his breath), "Exciting developments, my foot." But he added more openly, "Let's go back in and see these exciting developments."

We did, or at least we tried to. The area around Cedric was so packed with people that we couldn't approach it. Amos was a little put out, "Well, I came all the way to Paris to see my son play chess and all I can see is the back of somebody's head. We might as well just go see the Eiffel Tower or something."

I shook my head and said "There'll be a room where we can see the boards on video screens and maybe the moves as well." I started looking around and found a sign that said that the Salle de Provence had viewing or something like that in French.

We found the Salle de Provence and inside were a couple of dozen monitors that showed the positions of all the boards along with a list of moves on the right side. There was a small crowd around Cedric's monitor, but we could at least see it. I looked at the position and the moves. They were only on the eighth move. If they'd been playing a standard opening, they'd have probably been twice as far into the game. I commented, "It looks like the expectation is right. They seem to already be in the middle game."

Reina asked, "Will they be done soon then?"

Minerva supplied an answer, "No, Reina, it's more likely to be slower. The farther into a game, the slower the moves come—usually."

I agreed, "Yes, that's it. It's strange, but the fewer pieces on the board and the closer to the end, the more thought is necessary, but there is a limit. They won't go longer than four hours—that's the rules. Each side gets.. . "

Amos interrupted, "Yes, I know that much. Each side gets two hours to make 40 moves."

After that we mostly watched in silence. Every now and then Amos would leave the room—to smoke a cigarette, I think. His wife just found a chair and got into a conversation with Minerva. I watched and tried to understand what I probably wouldn't be able to understand. The moves were mostly pointless to me. There was nothing new about that to me, but for some reason this game seemed like it might be a turning point for Cedric.

He had a slight advantage in material but I couldn't begin to guess whether he was ahead or not in position or tempo. He had a little less time left on his clock but not enough to be concerned about.

I suddenly realized that I felt more lost in this game than I had in a long time. And then it occurred to me. I had been depending on body language to help me understand how the games were going. I couldn't even see their faces.

I watched the moves proceed. An amazing thing happened. The further into the game that play proceeded, the faster BOTH players played. It was as if they both had seen a goal and were racing for it. Much more likely I thought, each player thought they saw some advantage that they hoped to keep from their opponent by moving too fast for full analysis on the other side. Whatever the reason, it was beginning to look like the game would finish long before the end of the time limit. Each had a ridiculous amount of time on their clocks. It was become like a speed chess game. Before long everyone in the room had begun to congregate around the monitor for Cedric's game. I found a hand had been squeezing my right forearm. I looked over. It was Minerva. The room had become hushed. Outside the hall of play, there was always a constant murmur going on, but here now, there was absolute silence—as though no one wanted to break the concentration of the players in the other room. They were well past the 30th move. Then there was a gasp in the room with a move, and I heard someone say "escheque decovert." In the other room, the speed play had ended, and Helene sat motionless, a mask of concentration distorting her features. Then she leaned back and gave one silent laugh, smiled, carefully set her king on its side, and extended her hand to Cedric.

We didn't realize this had happened in our room until later, but suddenly one soft voice said, "C'est fini." With that there was a chaos of sound mixed with applause. After a moment or two, the two came into the spectator's room, and both players were surrounded by the crowd who were bombarding them with questions. Amos punched me in the ribs and asked urgently, "What happened."

I had been assuming that everyone realized that Cedric had won, so I quickly told him.

"Good. It was a little hard telling from the crowd. They seemed to be as interested in the woman as they were in Cedric."

I looked around and realized that he was right. Eventually, the crowd broke up and we walked over toward Cedric. However, I went to his opponent and asked her, "Parlez-vous Anglais?"

She responded that she spoke a little. I tried to tell her that it was a magnificent game, which she seemed not to understand, so I tried French, "Je pense que vous avez jeuxer, le jeux magnifique."

She seemed to be puzzling out my broken French, but eventually she seemed to get it and nodded. "Merci beaucoup. Vous etes tres gentile."

'Bon chance avec vos autre jeaux."

"Merci." Then she had another idea. "Etes vous l'ami de Mssr. Cedric?"

"Oui."

"Il est le gentilhomme, tres espece." She then switched to English. "I wish to him the good luck."

It was my turn to thank her.

I then walked over to the small group around Cedric. Amos asked me, "Did you ask her how she learned to play chess so well?"

Minerva answered for me, "I know very well that Wendt didn't ask any such question." Then she turned to me and asked, sounding somewhat suspicious, "Just what did you ask her?"

I couldn't help sniggering as I answered, "I asked her if she spoke English."

Everyone stared and Cedric said, "And .-.-."

"Oh, she speaks a little English but we stuck to my college French."

Minerva asked pointedly, "And .-.-. "

"Oh, I just told her that she'd played a marvelous game and wished her luck in the rest of the tournament." Then I turned to Cedric and asked him, "What in the world was going on at the end of the game? You both seemed to be playing speed chess."

Cedric smiled in relief that I didn't have a more difficult question and answered, "We were both trying to promote pawns and the moves were all about clearing the path. We both knew perfectly well what the other was doing."

"But, why the flurry of moves."

"Well, I think we both knew that I had a 'move' on her and that I'd promote first. I think that she was just hoping that I'd make a blunder if she hurried me along enough, but the moves were so obvious that I just made them. So I suppose we both were moving kind of fast."

Amos suggested that we all go to the bar in our inn and celebrate. I objected that as Cedric's faculty advisor, I had to enforce curfew. Amos grumbled and we ended up agreed that one drink in the bar would be OK with the understanding that immediately afterwards Cedric would head for bed. If Amos wanted to keep celebrating, it was between his wife and him."

Reina nodded and said, "One drink."

Amos said, "One more drink for the two of us." It wasn't clear if it was a question or a request or an order, and I didn't care to know which.

We each had our preference. Cedric had a butter beer. Amos, a fire whiskey; his wife, a glass of white wine; Minerva, a gin and I had a Dewar's. After Cedric had been sent off to bed, Amos and Reina found a small table for two, and I suggested that Minerva and I go out for a walk. She seemed satisfied with the suggestion, so I led the way.

We found our way to the left bank of the Seine, and we gazed into the river strung with the lights of the city like a pearl necklace on the neck of a dark, mysterious woman. We were silent for a while, simply enjoying the cool night air, which was not quite cold enough to require a jacket, but which made being close very comfortable.

She pulled a napkin that she'd carried from the bar apart slowly, dropping the fragments into the Seine. "What do those represent?" I asked.

She had been conducting some internal discussion that she was startled out of. She looked up and asked, "I'm sorry. What was it?"

"Oh, it looked like those little pieces of napkin mean something to you. Just wondering what it was?"

"I was thinking about the tricks of fate. We are here standing in the most romantic city in the world, enjoying ourselves, being together. I was just thinking that it would be so easy to forget all the problems that we have and just go off to your America and be lovers."

I was not expecting such deep thought and I tried to think whether I should suggest that we do just that. Leave Cedric and parents here. They could take care of themselves. We could definitely take care of ourselves. We had our passports. We could just get on a jet plane and go, but what I said was,

"What problems do we have?"

"Oh, think." Her mood suddenly changed to that of the instructor reminding a slow student of all the basic facts of the course. "Sirius Black is haunting—almost literally, the castle. We're stuck with the Dementors—maybe forever. Nobody has any good ideas how to fix this situation. Wouldn't you call those some serious problems?"

"Well, if you put it that way, I suppose we do have a few problems."

"You're right we do."

She'd turned to face me rather than the river. I slipped both arms around her and pulled her closer. "Well, if we can't solve our problems and we're in the city of.. . "

She interposed, "Light."

I added, "And Love, then we should make full use of both the Lights and the Love." A smile crept across her face and staying in my arms, she turned back toward the Inn. We slowly walked back, not wanting to destroy the fragile moment. We both enjoyed that night.

The next morning, we joined the Diggory's for lunch. Then, we made our way to the hotel that hosted the tournament. We found that Cedric's next opponent was a Russian who was on the decline. He once had been an international grand master, but he still was a formidable enemy across the board.

Cedric had drawn black against him. I thought it would be another struggle, but somehow, his opponent seemed dispirited. Had he heard the details of Cedric's win against Helene? Or was the phlegmatic way that he played just his normal style?

There was no particular crowd at Cedric's table. I supposed that no one thought that it would be an interesting game. There were several people around Helene's table. She seemed to be bright and active as she was in Cedric's game. I thought, "Good for her." I just hoped that she wouldn't show up in the next level of play.

We took a break in the middle game, and I wandered over to her table to see how she was fairing. She was clearly well on her way to demolishing this opponent. Cedric's game was not quite so one-sided, but it seemed that he was moving to a victory. I came back to Cedric's table and watched the end of the game. It finished quickly with a polite victory.

The next couple of days ended with Cedric picking up all wins. He would advance in his division, and there would be two wild card players advance as well. One of them was Helene. The night before the single knockout round, there was some discussion around the dinner table as to whether it would be good or not to have to play Helene again. Amos' view was that it didn't matter—that he'd beaten her once and the next game would be just the same. Cedric declared that once was enough as far as playing against her was concerned. He'd beaten her by a heartbeat, and he personally didn't want to take a chance on a rematch.

Reina was mostly silent on the topic other than saying that she had confidence in Cedric whomever he had to play.

Minerva simply said that she was happy to be in Paris, and she stroked my shin with a toe through her open-toe shoe. I was in danger of turning red. However, I managed to say that whatever happened, it would be a good experience for Cedric to play in the tournament.

The next day at the tournament, we discovered the pairings for the knockout round. Cedric would play a Frenchman in the first game. If he won that, he would then play the winner of the game between a German and a Spaniard. That would be the semi-final round. If he made it past that to the final, he'd play for the championship. That was the round where he had an opportunity to play Helene but only if she made it to the finals as well.

The first round play was difficult for every pair. Cedric's game was a drawn-out affair with no quarter asked or given. Every move seemed to be agonized over by both players. There was hardly any time left at the end of the first 40 moves on either clock. His game had gone the longest of all the pairings. The rest of the players gathered around Cedric's table at the end. Helene had joined the group around his game. Her eyes were wide as she took in the last moves before adjournment.

We went to a non-magical restaurant for dinner that evening, but before we left, Helene came over to Cedric and said a few words. The only thing that I could understand was, "Courage." Everyone noticed the exchange, but no one asked Cedric about it. Eventually he mentioned that she had simply wished him good luck.

Amos snorted and said, "Of course, she's hoping to get another shot at Ced."

I replied, "Yes, that's what I'm afraid of."

Amos snorted again.

Minerva and I went out for another stroll after dinner. There was a light rain falling—more a mist than a true rain. It surrounded all the streetlights with a diffuse glow that in another context might even have been threatening. But neither of us felt any fear whatsoever. We strolled hand-in-hand along the left bank, and I think that we both wished that we could stroll that way until the end of the world.

She asked me if it weren't sad that the tournament was coming to an end.

"Yes, I suppose so. We'll still have a couple of days if Cedric keeps winning, but even then, this time has to come to an end." She drew me a bit closer and stopped walking. Our lips met by common consent. I drew my arms around her and the kiss was deep.

She then said something that was spooky, "Just in case.-.-. Oh, you know.-.-. just in case something happens back at Hogwarts, I want you to know that this trip has been the happiest of my life."

What do you say in response to that? "Me too," doesn't begin to say what you want to, but anything more would seem like it was contrived. I just nodded and hoped that body language would do.

But I did ask, "Do you expect something to happen?"

She shook her head and the bun that she usually wore her hair in reverberated loosely after her head stopped its nod. "No, I don't think so, but you just never know what will happen. I didn't want that to go unsaid."

"OK. Just don't ever keep anything from me that worries or scares you."

She laughed, and the magic of the moment changed. She glanced at her wrist and declared that we needed to get on our way back to the inn. Her usual definite, no questions asked attitude is one that I enjoy, but these rare moments of uncertainty were reassuring. I liked to think that she occasionally had doubts and wanted the presence of someone else—like me.

We were brought back to the current circumstances and ran to the tournament site to see what had happened. We arrived just as Cedric and his parents were leaving the Salle de Jeaux. There were big smiles all around. Amos reported that the opponent had resigned almost as soon as play started again. Apparently, he was hoping that the pressure on the inexperienced player would cause him to stumble. Since that didn't happen, he himself had made a serious mistake on the fourth move and had resigned soon after.

The morning was clear. The rain of the previous evening had seemed to clean the air. We decided to walk to the hotel where the tournament was held rather than disapparate there. Minerva and I discreetly held hands. When we arrived, neither of us was anxious to release the other's hand.

Cedric's competition the next morning was an old Frenchman whose beard had more salt in it than pepper. He was dressed neatly but casually. He left his cane hooked over the back of his chair. He hardly glanced at the board before the beginning of the game. There were no superstitious preparatory habits for him.

He greeted Cedric pleasantly and acted as if this were just a meaningless game at a park bench near the Tuillery or the Tower. He noticed Cedric's friends and nodded politely but didn't attempt to engage us in conversation. There was a small crowd that gathered around the table as the game began. No one had trouble seeing the board but if there had been a few more, seeing would have been a problem.

The Frenchman seemed to pay no more attention to the board than he had before the game commenced. He hardly watched the board. However, as soon as Cedric moved, he would nod slightly or shift position. He'd spend a minute or two staring off into the distance, and then he would glance down at the board seeming to have just discovered that he was sitting at chess board.

He gazed at the board for another minute or two and then would reach out and make a move without any excess movement or force. He seemed to barely touch the pieces. There was never any hesitation or apparent second thoughts. The move was simply made as though he were recreating a chess problem from a book.

Cedric, on the other hand had a look of intense concentration on his face, little different from the previous game. Once or twice after picking up a piece, he seemed to wish that he could change his mind.

The pieces disappeared off the board as though they were not of any value to either player. The actual capture seemed to be anticipated by both well in advance and were not surprises in the least.

Cedric actually began to sweat toward the end of the game. At one point he had just wiped some sweat from his brow. Then he seemed about to move a piece, and at the last moment realized that he was about to get the piece sweaty. Then, he pulled a handkerchief from a pant pocket to wipe off his hands.

The game ended suddenly when the Frenchman extended his hand to Cedric who seemed to fully be expecting the gesture. They shook briefly, and the Frenchman inclined his head slightly toward Cedric. He then said in precise English, "An excellent game, young man. I wish you much luck in your career. Just remember to be gracious to your opponents at the end of your life when they defeat you."

Cedric nodded and said, "It was a real pleasure sir. You should remember that advice when you come to the end of your career, as well."

The Frenchman laughed briefly—almost more a cough than a laugh and rose to go. The Tournament Director who was recording the result asked Cedric, "Do you know who that is?"

Cedric admitted that he didn't. The Director nodded in the direction of the retreating figure. "He was rated second in the world, briefly, ten years ago. At one point early in his career, many regarded him as the heir apparent to the world championship."

Everyone in our group was impressed by him, and even Amos allowed that he was a true gentleman—even though he was a Frog. Since Cedric's game had finished fairly quickly, we went over to Helene's table where we found her engaged in a tight game. The battle raged on as we watched. Finally, her opponent made a move that seemed trivial to me, but she stared at the board for five motionless minutes before a single tear slowly streamed down from her right eye. Then she extended her hand and upset her king.

There was a profound sigh that filled the room as this happened. She was clearly the popular favorite of the tournament. There were expressions of support that seemed to come from the crowd spontaneously as she rose.

Cedric hung back waiting for the crowd to clear. We stood off respectfully. When she was free, he extended his hand and said in a clear unmistakable voice, "Ma'am, I wish we had a chance to play again."

She smiled and said, "Moi aussi. Perhaps at another tournament."

Cedric nodded and said, "I hope so."

This cleared the way for the final round. Her opponent would be Cedric's tomorrow. We returned to our inn. Everyone was quiet at that meal. We realized that it would undoubtedly be the last evening meal of the trip.

Minerva and I spooned that night, and I felt a tear on her cheek as we kissed goodnight.

The next morning, she was all business. She packed her bag efficiently and had it delivered to the concierge quickly so that we could pick it up on our way out of town.

We were out early enough that Minerva suggested some shopping in the neighborhood before going to the tournament. She found a furniture store that seemed to me to be a strange place to shop since there was no point in our buying furniture. Reina seemed happy to shop there as well. Amos, Cedric and I wandered about in the shop briefly and then stepped outside to see if there were something worth looking at in the neighborhood. We spotted a patisserie and stuck our heads in to buy something sweet. The shop-keeper was talkative and wanted to know what brought three Englishmen to Paris.

I explained about the tournament, and she was charmed. She insisted on asking if any of us were playing. Cedric admitted that he was. She "oohed" and "ahhed" about such a young player being involved in such a tournament.

We eventually escaped from the Patisserie and went back to the furniture store, where the ladies had hardly noticed that we had been gone.

No one was hungry for lunch. I tried to convince Cedric to eat some pasta to help with blood sugar levels, but nobody was interested in food.

We went on to the tournament. For the final games, no one was permitted in the Salle de Jeux except the players and tournament officials. We went to the viewing room where there was a huge chess board set up on a wall. Cedric was playing against a Russian who was in his thirties and was in good physical shape. He wasn't quite in the same shape as a young, athletic Cedric, but he looked pretty good. His entourage had two truly athletic men along with a couple of much older advisors who were probably former chess greats.

I decided that I didn't want to go through the agony of watching hour after hour without having an idea how the game went until someone actually lost. So, with the first move, I got up and walked out to the

Lobby of the hotel. I couldn't bring myself to do anything there but I couldn't bring myself to go back and watch the game either. The seconds dragged by gradually turning into minutes and eventually into hours. I walked slowly from one side of the lobby to the other.

Then, suddenly, a rush of people leaving the Spectator Hall let me know that the game was over. I couldn't see any of the Diggorys or Minerva. Finally, I worked my way into the room and I found them standing around Cedric, clapping him on the back and talking excitedly.

I joined them and just listened. Amos was asking, "Were you worried by those fancy advisers?"

Cedric shook his head and said, "During the game, it was just Dimitri and I. He was a very good player, but I didn't think that this game was as hard for me as yesterday or, maybe, even the one against Helene."

He went on, "There was just one point where I was concerned about the outcome. He took a very aggressive line of play and was betting that his force would overwhelm me quickly. When that didn't win the game, it was all over for him. AND I think that he realized it. After the middle game, he was just trying to force a draw."

Cedric had played black. The next game, he would play white. If he won or tied, the tournament would be over. If not, we would proceed to the third game in the evening. Amos was optimistic as ever. His advice to Cedric was, "Let's get this over quickly and get home. Just finish him off in the next game."

Cedric rolled his eyes but said nothing. We dropped into the coffee shop in the hotel and had some carbs, though goodness knows I didn't need them.

Back in the Spectator Hall, I determined that I would stay for the whole game and watch it through to the end—good, bad or a tie. I wanted to sit near the back, and Cedric's folks didn't object nor did Minerva.

As we watched the game unfold, I lost all sense of my surroundings. At one point, Minerva's fingers dug into my forearm, and I remembered that I was sitting among friends. She whispered into my ear, "Doesn't that seem like a bad move?"

It was then that I realized that I hadn't really been trying to do analysis of the game. I had to think carefully to remember what the last move had been. I was tempted to snap at her that I hadn't the slightest idea whether it was a good move or not. While I was thinking about that, she whispered, a little more insistently, "Well, what do you think?"

I whispered back, "Give me a minute to think." I used that minute to try to do a holistic analysis of the position. Cedric was dead even on material and seemed to have a slight positional advantage—if controlling the center were really important. I glanced at the clocks and was shocked to see that he must have been spending a lot more time than his opponent. What about his move? He had advanced a bishop in what looked like might be an attack forming on the King's side.

I whispered, "It seems like a move that's threatening an attack Kingside. I don't know if that's good or not." Minerva's grasp on my arm tightened, but at least, it wasn't her nails biting into my flesh. My lips were next to her ear, and I couldn't help noticing that her hair was drawn over the shoulder under that ear and then down over her breast. She almost never wore her hair down. Strange that I'd only just then noticed that.

I returned my attention to the board. In that moment, while I'd been noticing Minerva's hair, it had ended. Cedric and Dimitri were shaking hands. The Tournament Director had raised Cedric's hand in the universal emblem of victory. It was all over. People were getting up and talking in small groups. The hush that had reigned in the Spectator Hall was broken.

We went to the closing banquet. Surprisingly few people attended. Most of the contestants were gone. Even Helene had left. The hall had seemed empty—not only of people but even of meaning. The presentation was short—no speeches other than congratulations to both finalist for excellent games.

We went back to the inn and picked up our luggage from the concierge and then separated. The Diggory's disapparated to the French coast, and I tried to talk Minerva into taking the Chunnel back to London, at least. She felt that going under the Channel once was once too often. So, we took the French Floo Network to Cherbourg, and from there, we disapparated to London. Then, mercifully, the next day we took the Hogwarts Express back to Hogsmeade.

We stayed the night at the Leaky Cauldron, and there was a little celebration with a few people who knew about Cedric's tournament appearance. Tom, the barman, was handing out steins of ale. There were some Hufflepuff families there, and before the night was over Professor Dumbledore showed up. I was surprised—happily.

He accepted an ale and shook hands with the Diggorys giving them the congratulations that they deserved. He eventually found Minerva and me. He said, "Well, that's it. Congratulations for your student's victory. What do you project for his future chess career?"

"I haven't seen his rating, but my bet is that he's a Grand Master now. If he keeps at chess and plays in several good tournaments, he could be an International Grand Master by the time he graduates from Hogwarts."

Dumbledore nodded and asked, "And World Champion?"

I hoped that he wouldn't ask that particular question, but there it was. I said, "I don't think it's a good idea to talk about that just yet."

"But?"

I looked around to be sure that no one was within earshot, "But, it's possible."

Dumbledore nodded again and said, "Let's the three of us go up to your room."

Minerva showed surprise on her face. Dumbledore shook his head negatively and chuckled, "Come now. Let's not waste time with your discretion. This is important, and I want to talk with you discretely about something else."

We lead Dumbledore up to our room and invited him to sit at the table while Minerva and I sat on the bed. "What can we do about Buckbeak?"

He was looking directly at me, and I shrugged, "I don't know. What if Buckbeak escaped?"

Minerva said, "No one would believe that Buckbeak 'escaped' and it would be hard to keep Haggrid out of Azkaban."

I tried again, "Could we fake his death?"

334

"I doubt it," Dumbledore said. "What would we do if they wanted to bury the body—or worse, cremate it?"

"Suppose someone stole him?"

Both Dumbledore and Minerva stared at me. Dumbledore asked, "Stole him? Why would anyone want to do that?"

I had to admit that I couldn't think of a good motivation for grand theft—Hypogryff. Dumbledore stroked his beard and seemed to be deep in thought. Then he said, "That's not such a bad idea, Mr. Wendt. I like it."

Minerva was still dumbfounded, "But who would steal a Hyppogryff?"

Dumbledore was smiling broadly now, 'Minerva, you mean to say that you can't think of anyone who might want to steal a Hyppogryff and who couldn't be caught and interrogated?"

She shook her head and said, "I give up. Who?"

"Really, you can't think of someone?"

I interrupted, "Believe me, Professor, I know Minerva. You're coming close to her limits. I know the signs. You'd better just give it up." Minerva was now frowning at me.

He laughed again and said, "I'm not going to tell you yet. You'll be safer if you don't know."

I answered, "We might be safer, but I'm not so sure that you'll be safe."

Dumbledore laughed again and said, "Then, I'd better bid you two a fun night and leave while I still can."

She was still frowning, but she said a civil, "Good Night."

It was a good night.

Time Travel

As we approached Buckbeak's execution date, Haggrid's misery became more and more noticeable. With only a couple of days before the execution, he got more and more absorbed in his interior thoughts and started having little accidents—at least little for an eight foot behemoth. He knocked over a bronze suit of armor in one of the halls and didn't even realize it had happened, despite the clamor that woke the school late one night.

He hardly ate at meals. On the morning before the execution, he had only a half-dozen pancakes that he seemed to eat without realizing that he'd done it.

One evening, Minerva and I were alone in the Teacher's Lounge. She asked if I'd had any idea of who would want to steal Buckbeak but couldn't be found or interrogated. She went on, "I've racked my brains, but I just can't think of anyone that really fits that description."

I responded, "I've been doing some thinking about it too. I don't think this is a perfect answer, but here's my best guess.

"Who do we know whom no one has been able to find or interrogate?"

"Well, besides 'He Who Must Not Be Named'.-.-." She trailed off.

I said, "Yes, let's leave him out."

"Well, then, I suppose it must be the Darling of the Dementors—Sirius Black."

"Right. And doesn't he have a legitimate reason for wanting to steal a Hyppogryff?"

"How do you see that?"

"Well, think." I hesitated for dramatic effect, "How can he transport himself around?"

"Well, certainly not the Floo Network. If he used that, he'd be detected. Also, not by Port Key, but he could disapparate, right?"

"Does he have a wand?"

"We don't know, but I've been assuming that he must have. I guess I don't know that he has one and without a wand, disapparation is next to impossible."

I smiled triumphantly, "You see, he really could use a Hyppogryff."

"Well, there's some logic to that, but there are other ways that he could transport himself. There are other magical animals that he could ride."

"But, if the Hyppogryff just disappeared, and we blamed it on Sirius Black, it would be hard to deny the likelihood of that happening."

"Yes, and I suppose the real Black wouldn't walk up and deny being wrongfully accused."

"Right."

She looked down at her feet as if consulting something she'd seen or heard before. After a moment she shook her head and said, "I suppose that I can't come up with a strong objection to that idea, but who would take him and what would they do with Buckbeak?"

"That is a little problem. Whom could we trust? Is there someplace that we could release Buckbeak and trust that he wouldn't be found and identified? Is there anyone who would keep him on their farm or whatever?"

Minerva shook her head and didn't say anything. Then she said, "I suppose that we should talk to Dumbledore and see if he can think of anyone. We've got to do it soon."

We didn't do anything more that day, but the next day we went to Dumbledore's Office and told him about our idea. He shrugged and said,

"Yes, something like that was what I had in mind. But I don't know of anyone who would willingly take that kind of risk for a giant misfit like Haggrid."

Minerva's jaw set, and I knew we were in for trouble. She said through clenched teeth, "And you don't think that we would take a risk for a good friend?"

He was immediately conciliatory, "Oh, of course, I wouldn't want to know that any of my teachers would do such a rebellious act."

Minerva was angry, "So, you object to rebellious acts?"

His eyes twinkled, and he said, "I never said THAT.

"So, are you saying that you and Professor Wendt are volunteering to take him somewhere out of harm's way?"

I put in, "Provided that you can come up with a good location that is far away and where he can fend for himself without help."

Dumbledore glanced up toward the ceiling and seemed to be meditating. But he said in a low voice, "I've heard that the Rumanian hills are a beautiful place to retire to. There're even some wizards there tending to a dragon reservation."

I snapped my fingers, "Of course, Bill Weasley!"

Minerva said, "Yes, we could ride there."

Dumbledore looked down from the ceiling and said, "What a pleasant little weekend it would make."

I frowned at him and we took our leave. As we did, I hissed, "Well, there's another fine mess YOU've got us into."

She smiled back at me and raised her eyebrows, "I got us into? I thought it was your idea to steal Buckbeak and blame Black."

"Yes, but I never imagined it would be us doing the stealing."

We went to my office and sat over my desk planning the theft. There was the question of whether to involve Haggrid in it in any way. We finally decided that it would be better if he didn't know anything. If you're going to lie, the best way is to tell as much truth as you possibly can. We decided that the time to steal him would be on the very day of the execution.

After breakfast the next day, Minerva and I asked if we could be with Haggrid when the execution happened.

He snuffled and said, "No, thanks, professors. I'll be just fine." And he broke out in a flood of tears.

After he'd moved on, MInerva said, "Well, we said we wouldn't be there when the execution happens, but that doesn't mean that we won't be there just before."

I agreed.

The next day after dinner, Minerva and I stayed in the great hall waiting for the sun to be close to setting. That was the scheduled time of the execution. We were almost as sad as Haggrid—not because we were especially concerned about the Hippogriff, but because Haggrid was a good, gentle, kind man who was going to be hurt very much by what was about to happen—even if we succeeded in saving Buckbeak.

As the sunset neared, without saying a word, we started to walk slowly out of the Great Hall and toward Haggrid's hut. When we got within eyeshot of it, we saw there was something strange going on.

We could see that there were three students leaving Haggrid's hut. They hid behind the hut and then left, followed by two other students replacing them and stealing the Hyppogryff before we could!

Shortly after that, the Executioner left the hut. The executioner couldn't find the Hyppogryff and then was leaning on his axe. There was no sign of a Hippogriff—dead or alive. I heard what I thought must be Dumbledore's voice say something like, "Search the skies if you must Minister, I'm going to have a cup of tea or maybe something stronger."

Nobody noticed us until we got very close. Minister Fudge looked up and said, "What are you two doing here?"

"We came to condole with Haggrid."

The Minister sniffed and said, "The only one who needs any condoling today is MacNair. I think he was really looking forward to this execution."

Minerva asked, "Why, what happened, Minister?"

"The Hippogriff just disappeared. One minute he was tied up securely. We went in to have the papers signed and when we came out, the Hippogriff had disappeared. Did you two see it disappear?"

I answered for us, "No, the first thing we saw was MacNair here leaning on his axe and Dumbledore gazing up to the heavens."

Fudge frowned, "Heavens, indeed. Something fishy happened here tonight, and I'm going to get to the bottom of this and pretty darn quick."

Minerva said, "Good luck, Minister," but somehow, I didn't think her heart was in it. We looked at each other, shrugged and went on into the hut where Haggrid was having a drink with Dumbledore. Minerva asked him if we could join them.

"Of course, of course, Professors, isn't it wonderful!" We agreed that it was. We had a couple of drinks

Then I asked Dumbledore if he knew what had happened. Dumbledore simply smiled and asked the rhetorical question, "I? I thought you two might have some idea?"

"No, we definitely don't. And, yes, you. You seem to know about everything that goes on here."

"Well, if I told people everything that I only suspected, I'd soon lose my reputation for omniscience, wouldn't I?"

Minerva sniffed, and I said, "Then you do know something. Well, let's see. If someone organized that, it's got to be one of the usual suspects."

Minerva suddenly smiled and said, "Well, that really narrows it down, doesn't it. That's not something that anyone from any house other than Gryffindor would do, is it? And if it's Gryffindor, the only people worth mentioning would be the the Weasley twins or Potter and his little gang."

Dumbledore just continued to smile. It had gotten dark outside with the moon having just risen. We were distracted by the sounds of the baying of what sounded like several wolves. It made me shiver as I hoped that one of them wasn't Lupin. Then, Dumbledore suddenly became quite alert. He jumped up and said, "Minerva, get Wendt back indoors and join me at the main entrance."

I was going to object, but thought better of it. Dumbledore in such a mood was not to be trifled with. Minerva grabbed my arm and urgently pulled. We barely had time to say, "'bye" to Haggrid, and we were actually running up the hill toward the castle. When we arrived, Minerva sent me to my office and said she'd be back as soon as she could. I was about to object, but she was as stubborn as Dumbledore on occasion. So, I just locked my office door and paced. Then, I had an idea. If this were serious, people would end up in the hospital wing. If I were there, I'd probably learn things as quickly as anywhere.

I arrived there in a few minutes. Madame Pomfrey greeted me, although that's perhaps not the right word for what she had to say when I arrived in hospital wing. "You don't look hurt. What are you doing here?"

I admitted that I was there to find out what had happened. She said, "Get out of the way. Go home!" Then she thought better of it. "No, wait. You might be helpful. How strong are you?"

That was a question that put me off my form. "Why do you want to know that?"

"I may want you to help hold people still while I administer first aid." That didn't sound pleasant to me, but she suddenly took the option out of it. "Yes. Stay. I want you available to help force medicine down throats."

So, we sat and waited and we didn't have to wait long. Severus Snape came into the hospital wing with Ronald Weasley in tow on a stretcher. I helped Severus transfer Weasley to a bed and Madame Pomfrey began examining his leg. She felt the leg as Weasley moaned in pain. She nodded as she worked and quickly delivered her opinion.

"He's got a fractured tibia. But we'll get him fixed up quickly. I'll be back in a minute."

Weasley said, "Professor. It's very important. We were wrong about Sirius Black."

Snape interrupted, "Don't listen to him. He's delirious with the pain."

Weasley interrupted back, indignantly insisting that he was NOT delirious. Snape just started to walk away and said, "I've got to go check on Black. I don't want him to get away when we've finally got him." He muttered, almost to himself, "Now where are those Dementors when you want them?"

For a moment, I reflected on the idea of 'wanting' Dementors. What did he have in mind? But that didn't go on for long because Weasley repeated what he'd said before, "Snape is wrong. Black is innocent."

Just then Pomfrey returned with a large bottle of evil-looking brew. She poured out a small glass of it and handed it to Weasley and told him to drink it. He took a sip and spewed it out instantly, "That's hideous! What in the world is it?"

She frowned at him and said, "It's Skelegrow. Of course, it's hideous." Then she turned to me and said, "You see what I mean. Help me get it down him."

I told Weasley, "You heard her. You'd better just drink the stuff. You're going to sooner or later and the sooner, the better for both of us."

He made a face and forced it down slowly. Then Pomfrey pulled out another bottle and said, "Here, take this. It'll help you sleep. You'd have a rough night otherwise."

I said, "I'll see that he takes it, but before he does, I'd like to talk with him a little." Pomfrey shrugged and left. Then I turned to Weasley and asked, "Just what did you mean about Black and what happened to you?"

A jumble of words poured out of his mouth. I gripped his shoulder and said, "Just take it easy! It'll go a lot faster if you just slow down and tell me what happened. Now take a minute to calm down and think carefully about what you want to say. It usually helps to talk it through from the beginning methodically." Weasley did stop babbling and seemed to be concentrating.

Then he said, "OK. Here's what happened. We'd just left Haggrid's hut, and Scabbers my rat, well, he wasn't exactly a rat but.-.-. " He seemed to be on the verge of running off at the mouth again.

I said, "Slow down. Methodical wins the day."

He nodded and took a moment to think again and tried again, 'OK. Scabbers, my rat, was trying to get away from me. I'd just found him and suddenly, something grabbed me and started dragging me off. I didn't know what it was but .-.-."

As he was saying that, an idea struck me and I interrupted him, "It was a black dog wasn't it?"

Weasley stared at me for a second, "Blimey, how did you know?"

"Oh, just an intuition. Anyway, go on."

"Well, this black dog dragged me down to the Whomping Willow and into a hole at its base. He dragged me through a tunnel, and we ended up in this dark old house. It was the Shrieking Shack, but I didn't know that at the time.

"Anyway, Hermione and Harry followed me and arrived almost as soon as I did. Then, the dog turned into .-.-."

I could see it coming, so I supplied the name for him, "Sirius Black."

Weasley was shocked for a second time, "How DID you know? I'd never have guessed that."

"Oh, it just made sense. Go ahead."

Weasley took a moment to catch his place again, and he said, "Anyway, then Professor Lupin showed up. It was beginning to be like a convention there. Then Snape showed up.

"They started arguing about who would kill him. We all thought that they were talking about Harry, but then, the craziest thing happened. There was this fight, and Harry stunned Snape" Ron paused for emphasis.

But, I now knew what was going on. I nodded and muttered to myself, "Of course, it was a convention."

Ron heard part of what I said and asked, "What did you say?"

"Oh, nothing, I know what happened next. Your rat—what's his name?"

"Scabbers."

"Right, Scabbers. He turned into Peter Pettigrew."

Ron threw a pillow to the floor and said, "How DO you DO that? How can you possibly know that he was Scabbers or Scabbers was Pettigrew or whatever?"

"Oh, it just made sense. Professor Lupin told us about the little gang that he, Black, Pettigrew and Potter had formed, and what united them. It just made sense."

Weasley went on, "Well, it was this Pettigrew who was actually the person who betrayed Harry's mum and dad. He brought 'You Know Who. And. And. . .'"

343

I went on for Ron, "And Pettigrew decided that he needed cover with Val-de-Mort gone. So, he got into a public fight with Sirius. He killed a bunch of Muggles and turned himself into a rat. Nobody suspected that it was all a frame-up."

Ron, who'd stopped being amazed at my deductions said, "Yeh. That's pretty much it. But now Snape's captured Black, and the Dementors are coming to take him back to Azkaban."

I shook my head, "Great. Well, we don't have any time to lose. I'm going to find Dumbledore and Minerv.-.-. that is, Professor McGonagall, and we'll see if we can put an end to that."

I left the hospital wing and broke into a run. I wasn't quite sure where to go to find either of them, but I ran into Minister Fudge. He was in the Great Hall, but there was something funny. The hall had turned very cold suddenly—Dementors. I called after Fudge who turned and said, "Ah, it's Wendall, right?"

"Close. Actually, it's professor Wendt. Why are you here?"

"I suppose you haven't heard. Sirius Black has finally been captured. I'm on the way with a couple of Dementors to have them administer the 'kiss' to Black."

That was a wholly different case, "Did you say the 'kiss'?"

"RIght, And long overdue."

"But." I thought quickly. How could I convince Fudge to not let that happen—at least until the truth could come out. Just then I saw Professor Dumbledore approach, "But, shouldn't you talk with Dumbledore before you take any action?"

Fudge noticed Dumbledore just then and muttered, "Damn", to himself. Dumbledore was positively running. He reached us just then and said, "Minister Fudge, please let us have a little talk before you do anything with these Dementors."

"I don't want to waste another minute. Black has escaped once; I don't want to take a chance of his escaping again."

Dumbledore said something under his voice that I couldn't quite make out, but he added, "Isn't there a possibility that Black is innocent?"

When I heard Dumbledore say that, I threw in my two knuts, "Yes. And what kind of justice system is it anyway that condemns a man to death without a hearing?"

Fudge harrumphed and said, "Well, it's not technically death, it's more like.-.-. uh.-.-."

But Dumbledore surprised me by saying, "If you must, why don't we all go up. You'll probably need a witness or two for what you're going to do."

I stared at Dumbledore and if looks could kill, he'd be on his way to the hearse right then. I came up to Dumbledore and said, "I think that we should all have a little talk before we do anything rash."

Dumbledore was imperturbable. He just said, "It will be just fine, don't worry. Come along." And he started walking up toward the Astronomy tower. I was completely shocked and could hardly find anything to say, other than, "But. But. "

Dumbledore walked faster than any of us and we struggled to keep up. We arrived at a door and Dumbledore did something with his wand and the door flew open. We all went in and found—an empty room.

Fudge threw his hat to the floor and uttered a few expletives. When he'd finally calmed down he exclaimed, "Why is it always me? Why do these things always happen on my watch? Don't tell me that Black has escaped a second time!"

Dumbledore calmly said, "I suppose.-.-." But he never finished the sentence because just then Minerva ran up, huffing and puffing.

She exclaimed, "Don't do it! Don't do it!!" She entered the room, looked around, and, not finding Black, released a sigh of relief.

Dumbledore said, "Well, I suppose that there's nothing more for us to do here now. Minerva and Wendt, would you like to join me for a little nightcap? OH, of course, you're invited as well, Minister Fudge. But the invitation doesn't extend to your friends."

Fudge looked around quizzically and Dumbledore pointed at something, I suppose the Dementors. He just excused himself, saying that he had to prepare a statement for the press.

Dumbledore, Minerva and I headed for Dumbledore's office. Minerva asked, "I hope you're going to explain all of this before we leave tonight."

Dumbledore pretended ignorance. "All of what? Oh, I suppose you mean Black's escape."

Minerva just sniffed, and we remained silent until we reached Dumbledore's office. Inside, Dumbledore offered claret, which I'd never drunk before. As soon as we were seated, I asked, "Well?"

Dumbledore took a sip and then said, "This escape was organized by students." He hesitated, and I leaped in.

"Wait! Let me guess. First of all, let's figure what house was involved. It certainly wouldn't be Slytherin. Despite the fact that nominally Black should have been their kind of guy, I don't know any Slytherin student who would've put him or herself on the line for anybody.

"So, what about Hufflepuff. The question answers itself with them.

"Ravenclaw? They've certainly got the brains to do it, but where does the motivation come from? And with Ravenclaw, you've got to have real motivation.

"So, it's Gryffindor. But who? For my money, there's only two possibilities—the Weasley twins and Potter and company. I don't see how it could have been Potter and friends. You look at all the things they were doing, and I just don't think they'd have the time to carry it out. That the Dementors were going to perform the 'kiss' on Black only came up when Ron was in the hospital wing. How could they have organized a break-out so quickly? Did they fly? Get the old Ford Anglia to fly up and rescue him? Maybe they stole a broom and flew it up to him? They sure didn't disapparate him out of there.

"So, that leaves Fred & George. They've got all the requirements, including adequate time. They even organized a similar breakout of Potter from the Dursley's. The only question is how did they find out early enough."

Dumbledore was smiling wider and wider as I went on. Then he said, "Good deductive reasoning. And you were almost right."

"Almost right? Do you mean that it was Potter and," thinking quickly I added, "Hermione Granger?"

"Right."

"But how is that possible! They just didn't have time—unless they somehow knew in advance and just did exactly the right things in the right sequence!"

Minerva got up and walked over to my armchair and sat on my lap and patted my head while she said, "Well, wittle one, let me tuck wou in and Mommy will tell wou a wittle bedtime story."

I muttered, "The first sensible suggestion that I've heard tonight." We took our leave of Dumbledore and walked back to my office. She did tuck me in, but she seemed much more interested in other activities beside bedtime stories. She was stretched out along my side with lots of skin making contact.

I insisted on hearing the story. So, grumbling, she agreed and she told me, "Well, you're always talking about Time Reversal Re-variance."

I corrected her, "Invariance."

She reached her hand someplace that was hard to ignore and said, "Don't interrupt. The sooner you let me finish this, the sooner we can get to something sensible.

"Now, there are things called Time Turners." She forestalled my interruption with her impossible-to-ignore hand. "Now, I don't know how they work, but they can send you back in time.

"Hermione Granger has been using one all year to allow her to take more classes than she could ordinarily have time to take."

I interrupted despite Minerva's irresistible insistence, "But what about paradoxes of changing history."

"Oh, we understand those very well. She was thoroughly instructed in the problems of time travel. Anyway, she and Harry went back to the time just before the supposed execution of Buckbeak. She and Potter #2 freed Buckbeak and then rescued Sirius with Buckbeak's help."

"Well, I'll be. Time travel."

She said, "Yes, you will be—right this very minute."

The Hogwart's Express

The term ended without further disasters unless you looked at it from the perspective of the Dementors who DIDN'T get their man and had to return to Azkaban empty-handed.

On the trip back to London on the Express, the World Cup was all the talk. Everyone seemed to have the sports section of the Daily *Prophet* with its lengthy coverage of the All-England Quidditch team's defeat of the Brazilian Quidditch team in a marathon 20 hour contest.

When Minerva and I toured the train, I stopped in the Hufflepuff car, I talked briefly with Diggory. He reminded me that he intended to attend the last rounds of the Cup, which would happen during the prime Tournament time in the summer. He might be interested in an earlier tournament if there were a strong one available in late June or early July.

I had already checked all the tournaments in June and July and found that the good tournaments in those months were in Kyoto, Japan and McKay, Australia. Well, so much for chess this summer.

We arrived in London and phoned my old landlord to secure my lodgings for the summer. Minerva and I pondered on the value of her escorting me there. We finally decided that disapparating there would throw any of my "friends" off the trail in case they happened to be watching for me.

As soon as we were sure that all the students had been accounted for and picked up by relatives, guardians, or whoever, we disapparated directly from track 9 ¾ to my summer digs. Minerva suggested that we go out to dinner and in for 'afters'. I always like to settle into new digs before entertaining, so I declined with thanks and gave her a "rain check" for later.

The first couple of weeks of the summer holiday were a time to unwind for me. I slept late. When I did get up, I went to the corner grocery and bought a *Times*. I fiddled with the crossword, although I rarely made much progress on it. Every day or two, I would go to a gallery or a museum, usually with Minerva. The first opportunity that I had to do that, I asked Minerva if she could subscribe for me to the *Daily Prophet*.

We were in the British Museum, one of my favorite destinations. She snorted and asked if I wanted a subscription to *Witch Weekly* as well.

"Oh, don't be silly. For my serious news, I read the *Times*, but the *Prophet* is good for one thing. They have good coverage of sports. I don't usually follow Pro Quidditch, but this is the Quidditch World Cup. I want to know what's going on and not seem like the Muggle from the country that I actually am."

She was mollified and allowed that the *Prophet* was probably all right for that. This raised a question in my mind. I asked it, "What do you read to get serious wizarding news?"

She nodded sagely and said that she generally listened to the British Bewitched Corporation radio news for current events and read a couple of journals. "Currently, I read Transfiguration Today for news in my specialty." Somehow, she managed to pronounce "Speciality" as though there were an 'I' before the 't'. I always found that very charming. I was always tempted to pinch her bum when she did that.

Anyway, she went on, "And I read, 'Magic', for general new research results."

"'Magic'—you say that as if it were the name of a journal."

She replied, "It is.

"Anyway, I'll get you a subscription to the *Prophet* for the summer and you can read about the Scottish National team's thrilling rise from obscurity to the Cup."

I myself just snorted.

I had been reading the *Times* and had noticed a concert by the Silesian Quartet at the Albert Hall. It occurred to me that it might be a good evening's entertainment.

The next day, I saw a rather unusual article in the back pages of the *Times*. It was a story about an unusual death in a small town near the English channel south of London. The body of a World War II veteran had been discovered on the property of an empty estate that he was the groundskeeper for. The locals had attributed the death to any of a variety of causes—a drug gang that had been rumored to be using the estate as a "crack" house or a local gang of tough youths or simply old age. However, there were people who had lived in the area who had not forgotten the unusual, unexplained deaths of the family that lived in the estate. These deaths had happened about 35 years before. It was a gruesome story because of the lack of an apparent cause of death—just as there had been a similar lack 35 years before.

My first copy of the *Prophet* arrived the next morning. It was delivered bright and early. REALLY early—before I was ready to get up. The owl—a tawny owl that looked like it brooked no nonsense had been tapping on the sole window in my garret so loudly that it actually woke me up—no mean feat. I finally identified the source of the noise and realized that the bird on the window sill had a newspaper in its beak. I struggled to open the window—probably the first time it had been opened in decades if not centuries.

The disgusted bird flew in and tossed the paper at my feet, squawked raucously, and flew out the open window. I immediately closed the window and went back to bed.

When I finally did get up, I decided that I'd have to leave the window open when I went to bed so that the stupid bird could deliver the paper without waking me.

I opened the *Prophet* and briefly scanned the front page. Nothing particularly interesting today. There was a little article about the Dementors of Azkaban returning there after nine fruitless months of trying to find Sirius Black in the neighborhood of Hogsmeade. I found myself thinking that it was high time and that it would be way too soon if I never saw—er—didn't see them again.

I quickly turned to the Sports section, which was fully as large as the rest of the *Prophet*. On the front page was an article about the finals of the Cup, where it was to be held, the security measures in place to keep Muggles out, and so forth. There was a picture of the construction of the stadium. The photo moved through a sort of time lapse series showing its construction from the ground up. The main structure was complete, but there were lots of finishing touches that were being added —like loos and other useful things.

There was also a photo of Ludo Bagman, the Minister of Sports. He was in decent shape although he was beginning to develop a tummy. He apparently had been a Beater early in his career. He was quoted pontificating about how wonderful the Cup final game would be. There would be far more than 100,000 witches and wizards in attendance. The pre-game entertainment would include a light show by a troop of wizards and trained Salamanders. Or was it trained wizards and Salamanders?

Most people would be camping near the stadium, although some would disapparate in during the afternoon of the game. There was some sort of technical problem with 100,000 people disapparating into a relatively small space in a short period of time. So you definitely had to have a permit to disapparate there just before the game. Most people would arrive by Port Key. I wondered if wizards had invented a new way to induce vomiting.

The security arrangements were said to be the tightest in the history of the Cup. There was a sidebar article about the Cup of 1630 when the only people allowed to see the Final of the QWC (Quidditch World Cup) were the Minister of Magic of England and the King and Queen of the Holy Roman Empire (the QWC finalists). No one knows where it was held because there was a plague of dragons that year, and the location was made unplottable, untimeable, and unthinkable. As a matter of fact, no one knows who won the Cup that year or even if the Cup actually was played.

I hoped that I could manage to arrive by car or helicopter or even walk, but I had a feeling that the chances of that were comparable to a celluloid mouse surviving more than a second or two in Hell.

I turned to the pages and found some accounts of the qualifying rounds played the day before. The Bulgarians had defeated the Soviets 250 to 30 in an eight-hour match. The defenses of both teams were so fierce that the first six hours of the match saw only a total of 12 goals scored. The Soviet team substituted their Beaters 10 times during that game. The Bulgarians only once. There was an unfortunate incident involving the Vela mascots of the Bulgarians. One of the Soviet bear mascots had mauled her and her sister Vela had nearly cooked the bear in the heat of their fury. Both sides had received penalties after the incident. The mascots on both sides were sent off the field and had to sit out the next two games.

In another match, the American team had played and defeated the Austrian team 150 to nil in 15 seconds. In a bizarre turn of events the Snitch had flown directly to the American Seeker and had been captured before either Seeker had moved from their starting position. There was an immediate protest, and an official inquiry had been started. There were protests by the Austrians that the Americans had switched a befuddled Snitch into the game. The American coach had objected that it would be stupid to make the Snitch go directly to a Seeker because the kind of inquiry that would result would not be good for the cheating team.

The only thing that had prevented a riot in the stadium was the presence of a contingent of security trolls who were itching for the opportunity to crack some heads. The article expressed doubts that either team would be cleared of culpability before the Cup final, and therefore were both effectively eliminated from second round play.

There were color articles about the many unusual players. For example, one Beater was convinced that no one could beat his team if he were wearing nothing other than blue jeans that were five sizes too large but held up by suspenders. There was nothing in the rules specifically forbidding unusual adaptations of team uniforms. Rhe player had attached to both suspenders the national flag of his country.

Even Rita Skeeter, a society columnist, had an article in the sports section. She had written an article about the love life of the Irish Seeker, Colonel Moran. He was not a military officer but had been given an honorary position in the Kentucky militia when he had visited the States a few years ago. Apparently, he never used the title himself but somehow the sports columnists had heard about it. So, he was occasionally referred to as the Colonel in the press. Rita had tried to find some link between him and the twin chasers of the Holyhead Harpies. He stoutly denied that he had ever had an affair with either of the sisters, but Rita had contrived to convince one of them, Matilda, that the other, Tina, had been seeing him secretly. The pair had consequently been having a feud that threatened to destroy the winning partnership of the Harpies.

A few days later, I decided that I'd start an exercise regimen of walking various parks. I decided to start by crossing London to walk in a variety of parks. I always took copies of the *Times* and *Prophet* along to read on the Tube.

One day, there was a follow-up article in the *Times* to the one about the mysterious death in the south of England. The article had moved a good bit closer to the front of the *Times* than its predecessor. It appeared that the CID had decided to do a serious autopsy on the victim, a Frank Bryce. The autopsy had been extremely thorough. The Coroner, Frederick Feuerstein, had claimed to have used every technique known to modern forensic medicine to determine the cause of death. He was quoted, "We've ruled out all known viruses, bacteria, hereditary diseases. There were no cuts, lacerations, microscopic pin pricks, bruising. There were no unusual drugs in his blood or tissues. His heart, lungs and brain were all intact with no sign of tumors or other abnormalities. It was almost as though he had never been alive. But, of course, there were plenty of witnesses to testify that he was spry, intellectually active and generally healthy for a septuagenarian.

"There are still a few possibilities—drugs that would break down before we got the body but those are extremely unlikely especially in an obscure rural town. He had no known enemies and we regard this as a murder by person or persons unknown."

As I read the article, I wondered if the Avra Kedavra curse would leave traces.

The next week, I was walking in one of my favorites, Hyde Park.

Without thinking about it, my brisk walk took me to the Serpentine and I suddenly discovered myself approaching the tree where I'd waited for my meeting with Professor Dumbledore almost exactly four years before. I passed it and continued on toward the boathouse, feeling progressively more nervous as I neared it. I was only fifty meters away when I felt that someone must be watching me. It was crazy. It was broad daylight on a beautiful, partly cloudy day, but I found myself doing my best to keep myself from whirling around to see who it was. There were a number of park-goers all around me.

I didn't know what I expected, but I found I couldn't resist the temptation. I felt in my pocket for the purse where I kept my Glock—as crazy as checking it seemed. When I was satisfied that it was there, I took a deep breath and rapidly whirled to see—a figure that I knew extremely well about thirty meters behind me and walking at an Olympic pace to catch up with me. I stopped and allowed him to reach me and said, "Professor Dumbledore, what a pleasant surprise."

He looked at me suspiciously and asked, "Why? Were you expecting a banshee?"

I wasn't sure whether to take it as a joke or not, but decided it was a joke. "No, I really didn't have an expectation of seeing a banshee."

He said, "It's an interesting coincidence—the two of us running into each other here again."

"Yes, do you believe in coincidences?"

"Believe in them? Do you mean believe something particular about coincidences?"

"Well, I'll give you a coincidence. Just a couple of days ago, I noticed in the paper that the Silesian Quartet was going to perform in the Albert Hall this weekend. Now, I happen to know that you are a fan of chamber music. I was thinking of going. What about you?"

Dumbledore shook his head and said, "I suppose you read that in the silly collecting card they made of me a few years ago."

"Yes. Is that not accurate?"

"Oh, it's accurate enough. It's just been quite a while since I've actually taken the trouble to attend a concert. But, going with someone makes it more interesting. Why not?" He paused and seemed to contemplate the possibility and then said, "Yes, I'd enjoy going. Do you know what's on the program?"

"No, but I'm sure it will be good."

"Oh, yes, one other thing. Will Minerva be coming along?"

I laughed, "I've tried dragging her to concerts for years, but she steadfastly refuses to attend any concert where the music is older than she is."

A whimsical look came over his face as Dumbledore said, "Well, I don't think that lets out most chamber music."

I just stared at him reproachfully.

A troubled look briefly crossed his face and he asked, "Would you like me to pick you up? We could disapparate directly there."

I declined with thanks, expressing the opinion that I'd rather be dragged there by wild horses than disapparate. I added, "I know my way around the Tube plenty well enough. The concert is at 8PM. I'll meet you there a half-hour before."

"But isn't that taking a risk that there won't be tickets available or should one of us buy in advance?"

"It's well documented that even 'sold-out' events always have a few tickets available just before show time. I say, 'Don't bother.'"

Dumbledore agreed, and we briefly discussed the ongoing Quidditch matches. It turned out that although he was a Chutely Cannons supporter, he could never work up much enthusiasm for the World Cup. So, he wasn't going to attend any of the games. With that, we went our separate ways.

The next few days were the typical round of my summer holidays. I spent the morning reading the *Times* and the *Prophet*. I fixed myself a light lunch. I went for a brisk walk at some park and I spent a little time writing these narratives. It was usually in the summer that I caught up on writing. In any case, eventually Friday came. I pulled my suit out of mothballs in the closet of my attic room. I hoped that I'd not enjoyed the cuisine of Hogwarts too much the last couple of years or I'd never fit into it.

The fit was snug but somehow, it didn't look awful on me. The Tube was pretty crowded with Friday evening pleasure-seekers. So, I stood most of the way.

When I arrived at Albert Hall, I found Dumbledore had already arrived and was standing in the lobby looking dapper in a dark grey suit that didn't somehow look out of line with his long nearly white beard. We approached the ticket window, and as we did, Dumbledore took my elbow and tugged me out of line.

"I just realized that I don't have any Muggle money with me. Would you stand me a loan?"

I just smiled and said, "Don't worry. I think I can afford two tickets, and we'll just pretend that this never happened. Even when it comes time for salary review. Really."

Dumbledore nodded quickly, and we got back in line. There was no problem getting a couple of seats together at the back of the Arena. The concert consisted of four works—Corelli String Trio, Czardas by Monti, Albinoni's Adagio and Libertango by Piazzolla. There was an intermission.

During the intermission we went out and got in line for something to drink. I anticipated the question, "Professor, let me treat you to something to drink." He acquiesced, and I asked him what he wanted.

"Oh, what are you having?"

I replied, "I'm having a Coke. I can never get them at Hogwarts, of course. I always try to celebrate my homeland's contribution to potables by having a couple during summer holiday."

Dumbledore stared curiously, "What in the world is a 'COKE'. It sounds illegal."

I couldn't help laughing out loud and attracting a few stares. "No. It's perfectly legal. COKE is short for Coca-cola. The company that produces it started out in Atlanta, Georgia in the States. It has a long and storied history. Back in the late 19th century, it was actually made with cocaine. It was truly addictive then. However, by the early 20th century, the recipe no longer included cocaine and already was available worldwide.

"The company became gradually more socially responsible as it aged. By the middle of the 20th century, its adverts featured morally uplifting songs, like, "I'd like to teach the World to Sing." Nowadays, it even features adverts with street toughs giving beggars rolls of bills, saving little old ladies from muggers, putting out fires and being an all-around good guy."

Dumbledore shook his head and said, "I'll just stick with my usual. A nice dry white wine."

"OK. But, I'm not sharing my can of Coke." I purchased the Coke and the wine, and we discussed the Corelli."

356

As we returned to our seats Dumbledore whispered, "Did you notice the two people who seemed to be paying special attention to us?"

"No, I just thought they were staring at me because I was laughing out loud."

"I'm not sure. I think they are wizards and I can't quite place the faces, but I think I've seen them before. I just can't place the connection."

We enjoyed the second half of the concert. As we were leaving the concert hall, Dumbledore asked me if I'd like him to give me a "lift" home.

"By disapparation?"

"What else?"

"Oh, I can think of a couple of dozen other possibilities, but taxi comes to mind. Would you like to share a cab?"

"No, thank you. When I take my life in my hands, I have other more interesting options."

"Well, in that case, I'm going as I came—by Tube."

We parted company, and I worked my way toward the Knightsbridge station. If Dumbledore had been familiar with the Tube, he'd have wondered that I bothered with the Tube at all. However, I enjoy riding the Tube, and any opportunity that I have to do so, I take. It affords me the opportunity to observe people whom I wouldn't run across in my day to day activities—like other Muggles. There was a fairly steady trail of concert-goers walking Kensington, apparently toward the same station as I. As we got further along, the crowd thinned as the faster walkers started to separate from the slower.

As we approached the station, I began to feel my skin crawl a bit. That wasn't entirely unusual while walking alone in late-night London. At first I just paid closer attention to the surroundings just in case the feeling had an objective basis. Everyone that I could see seemed to be normal concert-goers. As I entered the station, the crowd divided into Eastbound and Westbound. I was going Westbound and there were few of us. If you were going west on the Tube from Albert Hall, you'd more likely have gone to the Kensington or Gloucester stations directly.

I and four other people got on. They were two couples who didn't seem to be acquainted with each other. One couple I thought had walked from the concert. I was pretty oddball for walking to this station.

Could another pair of people feel the same way? The creepiness factor notched up a rung or two. We approached the South Kensington station, and nobody left when we stopped. Then, we went on to the Gloucester station, which was mine. As we approached it, I got up preparatory to leaving, and one couple rose as well.

I made a split second decision not to get off at this station, so I went to the route map, as if I weren't sure which stop to get off on. The couple who had risen returned to their seats! That sealed it; I wasn't getting off without somebody other than the spooky couple no matter how far I had to go.

The Gloucester station came. Nobody got off, and we went on. I decided that I needed to stay with the second couple until I found a populated public place where I could phone for help. My mind raced. I'd have to start talking with the second couple to establish a reason to stay near them for a while after we got off. I got up again and approached the route map and thought furiously. I could ask the couple for help finding my destination, but suppose I picked one that was different from theirs'. Then I had an idea. It was one that was close enough to the truth about me that I might just be able to make it fly. I approached the second couple and said, "Excuse me." I added hesitantly, "I don't usually approach strangers on the subway." I used the American word to help establish my bona fides.

The couple got that expression of polite but *distant* interest that told me that this would be difficult, and I'd better sell my story quickly. "But, I'm an American tourist and this is my first day in London. I came to town thinking that I'd find a hotel after I arrived. But I picked up a paper and saw that there was a string quartet performing at the Albert Hall tonight. If I went straight there, I could just make the concert."

I added, "By the way, the Silesian String Quartet was wonderful in the Corelli String Trio. I probably wouldn't have done that on the spur of the moment, but they are one of my favorites. Anyway, it's late now, and I don't have an idea of where to stay the night. You couldn't suggest a place could you?" It was oh so tempting to add that it would be just peachy if it happened to be close to their ordinary stop, but I thought that my real intent might be too obvious if I said that.

The man asked, "Really? Just in the country?"

"No, I came down from Edinburgh on the train. It's wonderful how you can travel by train in this country rather than fly. In America, you feel like you've got to fly wherever you go. I really don't like being in the air without any visible means of support."

The man introduced himself, "I'm George and this is Petunia. We only know the big hotels. But if you don't mind spending a packet, we would recommend the Hotel Earl's Court." He was a little stout. His suit was not the latest cut but clearly had been recently cleaned and pressed. She wore her greying blond hair pulled back in a small twist at the back of her head. She wore a blouse and jacket of a tan tweed and a skirt that was mid-calf length. They looked to have been on a night on the town and were returning to the suburbs.

I began to hope this might work, "That's not a problem. I'd probably just move to a cheaper hotel in the morning."

"Well, you'll want to get off at the next stop, which we're just slowing for."

Petunia interrupted, "Oh, George, you know how hard it is to get from the Earl Court station to the hotel. Maybe, we should get off and help him find it."

"Oh, it's not hard at all. You just get out on Earl's Court Road and go to the right and then turn left on Pennywert and it's just a long block to the corner where Earl's Court Hotel is."

His wife looked at him reproachfully, and I tried to look my most innocent as I added. "It would be wonderful if you'd help me that way. I'd be happy to stand your cab fare home if you'd do that."

Petunia said, "Ridiculous. We can catch the next train which will probably just be arriving when we get back to the station."

By this time the train had fully stopped, and the doors opened. All five of us were up and leaving. I looked back and found that the other couple was only a couple of paces back. I noticed the man reach in his jacket pocket, and in an instant I knew what was going to happen. I took the first step of a sprint for the barrier, hoping to take them by surprise.

Instead, I was surprised when all my muscles seized up, and the first step turned into a painful fall to the floor. My two companions bent over me and asked if I were all right. I was totally paralyzed and couldn't say a word. But I heard a man's voice say, "I'm a doctor. Please, you and your wife, go call for help."

George reached in his pocket and pulled out his cell phone. I could not see what was happening but I heard him say, "Bloody Hell! I don't have any signal here. Let's go up to the street level, Petunia and call there." I heard his hurried steps recede.

Then my stomach turned inside out, and I tried to throw up but the muscles of my esophagus were as paralyzed as the rest of me. It was one of the least painful things that happened for some time, but at the time it seemed my throat was on fire. I knew from the disorientation, the attempted retching, and the change in lighting from the bright Underground to a dim room in which I couldn't see the walls, that I had just disapparated.

Then for a brief eternity, every cubic centimeter of my body cried out in pain. I'd had my wisdom teeth pulled once. Three of the teeth came out fairly easily. But one had broken into several pieces. Extracting those pieces was somewhat painful, but the additional Novocaine that the dentist injected directly into the nerve had caused me the most intense pain for about one second that I'd ever experienced—up until that moment. Every part of my body screamed in pain, and again I tried hard to wretch but my muscles were still frozen solid.

Shortly after the pain ended, my paralysis did as well. Then, amazingly, I didn't wretch. When I found that I could move, I slumped and felt my whole body to see if anything were broken. A voice said, "Get up, Muggle, quickly or I'll give you another little touch of Cruciatus."

I slowly raised myself to my feet, amazed that I could do so without wrenching pain. The curse must directly hit the pain center of the brain without affecting the rest of the body. The man who was speaking went on. "Don't think that I've taken mercy on you. We just realized that it's not nearly as fun watching someone who is paralyzed being tortured as someone who can writhe and scream."

And at that point, my body was wracked again. My back arched trying to get me away from the white-hot searing touch of whatever was driving me insane with pain. I don't know whether I screamed or not. I must have. It ended.

I slumped to the floor, and I whimpered and begged, "Whatever you want, I'll give it to you. Just tell me what you want." I didn't care if he heard the desperation in my voice.

360

The woman spoke for the first time, "Yes, you're right; you will give it to us. As a matter of fact, you are giving it to us already. What we want, Muggle," she almost sneered the word, "is for you to suffer and then to die."

The third round of pain hit. My jaws clamped together so fiercely that I thought I would break teeth, and I passed out. As I slowly came around, the two were arguing. I didn't catch it all, but what I did catch worked out to be an argument. The man insisted that the woman be more careful—they might kill me before I'd given them all the pleasure that I could. She was whiny and said that I'd just passed out. I could pass out many times before I would be close to death. Then they turned to another topic.

The man said, "Another thing. We want him to be able to open his moke-skin pouch before he's too far gone to be able to. There might be something valuable in it."

She sneered, "That will be a long time from now. Let's have some more fun, first."

He insisted that it was important not to take chances. They should get the contents before doing anything more to me. Eventually she agreed. The man came over and kicked me with a heavy Wellington-booted foot and said, "Come on, get up. You must be conscious by now."

I did, slowly. The conversation had given me an idea. But, I wanted to seem like I was more damaged than I really was.

He held up my purse and said, "What's in this? Be careful you don't lie."

"What will you do, if I do lie, torture me?" Before the words were completely out of my mouth, I regretted that I'd said them. For the briefest instant the woman had cursed me and I'd doubled in pain and after many false heaves finally wretched. Neither said anything. They knew the point had been made. There was nothing that would make me openly defy them again.

He simply said, "Well?"

"There's gold."

He smiled and asked, "How much?"

I gasped out, "I don't know—maybe 100 galleons, maybe more."

She said, "Not bad. Give it to us."

361

Now, we were coming to the point. I reached out my hand for the purse. For a moment he just held it. Then she said, "You be careful. No tricks. You know how much you'll regret it."

I just nodded but the man said, "Come on, Elek, he's a Muggle, even if there is a wand in there, what could he do with it?"

She just stared at me a moment and repeated, "No tricks."

Then he handed me the purse, and I slowly opened it, buying time to think. My Glock and bullets were in it, but it wasn't loaded and even if it were, I could maybe get a shot off at one of them, but I doubted that I could manage two.

Then, a miracle happened. A doorbell sounded, and the man cursed. Then he said, "Elek, go see who that is."

But she didn't move. I went ahead and pulled most of the galleons out and stretched out my hand with them. She said, "Put them on that table. I'm going up to answer the door."

I slowly, apparently painfully rose and dragged a foot slightly as I went to the table and spilled the galleons out on it. The man came closer but had his wand firmly gripped in his hand. He asked, "What else have you got in there? I heard rattling in the purse."

I truthfully said, "More galleons."

"Well, what are you waiting for, pull them out." I slowly reached my hand in, and he moved a bit closer and said, "Hurry up, we don't have all day."

In that instant, I felt the Glock and twisted it in my hand, bring the heavy butt around so that I was grasping the gun by the barrel and the butt extended forward from my right hand. I pulled it out trying to conceal what it was with the purse. I had been slowly twisting away to the left from the man as if I were trying to protect the contents for a moment more from him. He didn't move, but stretched his neck a little to get a better view.

Then I swung around with all my strength, bringing my hand around like a backhand tennis stroke and his head was the tennis ball. He saw the motion and tried to dodge, but the butt of the gun caught him on the jaw and stunned him for an instant. I swung as quickly as I could with a forehand stroke and caught him squarely on the side of his head. He went down. I was on him. I got the wand out of his hand and snapped it. He was coming around but he didn't realize for a second that he no longer had his wand. That realization slowed him another second and let me deliver another blow—to his forehead.

That felled him. I immediately searched for the purse, which had flown somewhere. In the dim light, I scanned the room. I swore, trying to figure what direction it would have gone. After an eternity, I saw it, grabbed it, reached inside and found the magazine of the Glock. I hurriedly forced it into the Glock, advanced a round into the chamber and got back to the man, who was just beginning to come around. I got behind him and pressed the Glock into the back of his neck—hard.

He groggily said, "Wha??"

"Listen carefully. If you make any move that I don't expect, you brains are going to be spattered on that wall over there. Understand?"

He just said, "Huh?"

I repeated it again, slowly and said, "Tell me what I just said?"

He said, "If I move, my brains are going to be gone, right?"

"Good enough. Now, when your wife comes in, it's going to be important for her to understand that if anything happens that I don't like, you're going to be dead."

"Not my wife. Sister."

"Doesn't matter."

Then I went to the table and grabbed a handful of the galleons that I'd left there, and we waited.

We heard her before we saw her. I whispered to him, "Don't say anything until she comes in. But start talking fast then. And I'd better like what you say."

The door opened and he started talking even before either of us saw her. "Elec. Just drop your wand. RIGHT NOW. Toss it across the room."

She gasped and said, "I'll save you."

He screamed, "No. This Muggle'll kill me if you don't toss the wand in RIGHT NOW."

There was silence for two seconds, and then the wand skittered across the floor. Then I said, "Come in very slowly. Keep your hands clasped above your head."

Slowly, she came in and scanned the room.

I tried not to give her time to think. "OK. Now, turn around slowly. Stand there for a moment." I got up and dragged the man with me to where her wand had landed. I ground it into the floor with my left foot.

"OK. The next thing that's going to happen is that you're going to lead us up and out of this building. As we go, walk slowly. If anything happens that I don't like, the last thing that you feel will be your brother's brains splattering against the back of your head. And then, yours will splatter against the wall in front of you. Do you understand?"

"Yes."

"Repeat it back to me."

"If you don't like anything I do, you'll blow our heads apart."

"Good enough. Let's go. Tell me what you're going to do before you do it. If you do anything that you didn't tell me about beforehand.-.-." I let my voice trail off.

"I know." She said. "OK. We're going to walk out this door and turn to the right and walk to the end of the hall."

"Do it."

We thus slowly walked out into the hall. I was really concerned when we turned the corner into the hall. I was terribly afraid of having Elek out of my sight for even a second, but nothing happened. We walked down the hall and then reached the door.

I asked, "OK. What's on the other side of the door?"

Neither said anything for a moment. Finally after the application of a little more pressure from the Glock, the man said, "It's the showroom of Borgin and Burkes."

For the first time that day, I was tempted to laugh. "Does he know what you two have been using his store for?"

Neither said anything.

"Is anyone in the room?"

They said nothing. I said, 'OK. We can play it that way. I'm getting tired of dragging you two around anyway. I'll take my chances on my own."

He answered, "Nobody's there. It's too early for the store to be open on a Saturday."

I went on, "OK. Lady, let's open the door. Sloooowly. And then walk out into the room slowly. Just keep moving straight until you run into something. Understand?"

The response was a tight "yes."

364

"Do it."

She opened the door slowly, and light flooded in. I hadn't thought to ask what time it was, but I didn't want to risk even a glance at my watch. So, as we walked slowly forward I asked, "What time is it?"

"Fuck you."

I was reaching the end of my tether. I simply barked, "It's not too late to redecorate in here with brains."

The man said, "It's Saturday morning, maybe 10. " Then he added, "What are you going to do with us?"

I hadn't actually thought that far. I said, "Nothing until we're out on the street. I think the Aurors might be interested in you. Walk directly to the main entrance. Tell before each turn." The room was full of display cases. I had no attention left for the contents. What little I'd heard about Borgin and Burkes led me to believe that I wouldn't be interested in them whatever the circumstances. We walked among the display cases, and at the end of each aisle, the woman gave a simple direction—left or right."

We reached the main entrance, and the woman said, "Let's make a little deal. Do you know what street Borgan and Burkes is on?"

"Sure, Knockturn Alley."

I could tell whether she was smiling when she said what she said next without seeing her face. "It's a kind of 'dodgy' place. You're going to have a hard time keeping us with you if someone comes up and says hello. How about this? We don't make any trouble with passersby. When we reach Diagon Alley, we part company, and nobody needs to get hurt. You'll be on the main street with plenty of friendly foot traffic and we pop back down Knockturn Alley and everybody's happy."

I didn't like letting them go, but I had to admit that it was tempting. Maybe too tempting. It would be easy to let vigilance down. I said, "That sounds easy-peasy but if you try something, I WILL scatter brains around." I pressed the Glock even harder into the man's neck. He gave a little yelp and said, 'Watch it, you're going to break something."

"Oh, that would be too bad. OK. Let's go. Same drill. Open the door nice and slow. Walk out slow and announce turns in advance." This time I didn't ask if she understood, I just said, "Do it." And she did. We walked out into the full light of day, and my eyes took a second or two to adjust. We turned left and strolled up the alley toward what was really full light of day. The three hundred uphill meters to Diagon Alley seemed like Mount Everest to me as we slowly mounted them. I couldn't see any traffic on Knockturn Alley, but it felt like every window had unfriendly eyes surveying me. We finally reached the top and paused there for a moment. We were still standing in Knockturn alley with the sister just shy of walking into Diagon Alley.

I said, "And now the time has come the Walrus said to speak of many things. OK. You lived up to your part of the bargain. Here's how I'm going to live up to mine. We're just all going to about-face. Lady, you'll turn to your left and face down into Knockturn Alley. At the same time, your brother and I will sidle around so that we're still behind you, and we're all facing the same direction. Then, I'll back away from you slowly, but I'll still have my gun pointed at you both. You'll count to ten slowly, and then you'll walk down into Knockturn Alley.

"You'll not turn around unless you want to help me do some target practice and see whether all the hours I've spent on the shooting range helped any."

The way the muscles in the back of the man were tensing, I knew that he didn't intend to wait for a slow ten count, but would he try turning on me or would he just run down into the alley? I decided not to give him any warning, and I just silently, and as quickly as I could, backed away keeping my Glock pointed. He broke into a run down the alley but the woman kept her position for what could have been a ten count. I was well into Diagon Alley, and I kept backing toward what I thought was Gringotts, which should have been directly behind me.

When I hit the other curb, I turned and tried to sprint up the steps into the lobby. It was more of a quick scramble, but I reached the door and practically fell through. I regained my balance and went to the Reception Desk, stuffing my Glock into a pocket. The goblin on duty there stared at me. Finally, he croaked, "What can I do for you?"

I glanced down at myself and found my be-draggled Muggle suit. It was stained with some of my blood and maybe with some of the blood of the Deatheater. At least, it seemed to me that he and his sister must have been Deatheaters or fellow travelers anyway. I tried to compose a coherent answer. "I know that I look pretty awful. As a matter of fact, I'd like to send an owl for someone to come and help me get home. Can you help me with that?"

He frowned and said, "We're not a messenger service."

I tried to crack a smile and said, "I'll pay gold for the service."

The goblin cracked a smile himself, and scratched his chin. "I suppose I could get a secretary out here to send an owl for you. Where is your note?"

I stared for a moment and said, "Do you have a piece of paper that I can have and a quill to borrow?"

He had turned blase now, "It will be a galleon extra."

All I said was, "Of course." He signaled to another goblin—a young one—who ran over. The goblin whispered in the young one's ear. Then the young goblin ran off. In the meantime, the receptionist got out a quill and a piece of parchment and held out his hand. I reached in my pocket and pulled out a galleon and handed it to him. I wrote a simple note, "Minerva, I'm in a lot of trouble. I'm at Gringott's in Diagon Alley. Please come soonest to rescue me. Love, Wendt" I folded it over and put it in the envelope that the goblin, Warzak according to his name tag, had sold me for another galleon.

In the meantime, a wizard came up. I thought he looked familiar but when he got close enough to talk to, I realized that he was one of the Weasley's. I said, "You're .-.-. uh.-.-. a Weasley, right? Is it Percy?"

He made a little face and said, "No, I'm Bill. They told me that you want an owl posted, but you look like you're what the dragon dragged in."

I nodded and said, "Yeh, I had a really rough night. It's a story that I'd tell you if I trusted my legs to hold me up." I looked around and asked to no one in particular, "Is there a chair around here that I could use?"

Bill walked over to a guard station and pulled a folding chair back to me and said, "Go ahead and sit down. I'll get this letter off to.-.-. " He glanced at the address and said, "Oh, yes. Professor McGonagall. Good choice though if I were you, I'd probably have chosen Madame Pomfrey. It looks like you need a healer most of all."

"That's OK. I'll take Minerva." He strode off with my letter and I closed my eyes, fairly confident that I was safe here if I would be safe anywhere in London.

I must have passed out because, the next thing I realized I was hearing the voice that I love the best saying, "Well, what kind of mischief have you gotten yourself into this time?"

I looked up and said, "It's a long story. Do you think you could get me back to my place and I'll be very happy to tell it to you."

She harrumphed, "I certainly will not. You're on your way to Saint Mongo's immediately." She didn't say anything else but took my hand firmly. I felt like I was going to wretch again, but there was nothing left. We were standing in a large vestibule. She led me through a door into a large waiting room and dragged me to some sort of Reception Desk. The witch behind it asked, "What kind of malady?"

Minerva was clearly exasperated, "Do you not have eyes, girl? Don't you see the blood all over his clothes. He has multiple lacerations and .-.-." She turned to me, apparently wanting me to fill in details.

I obliged, "Well, I was cursed with the Crusiatus curse several times and the petrificus totalis and I think I may have broken something when I fell after one or more of those curses."

The receptionist stared at me and said, "Surely, not."

"Yes."

She turned to Minerva and said, "Take him up to the Fourth Floor immediately; I'll let them know you're coming. We'll have an Auror there as quickly as we can."

Minerva dragged me over to an elevator, and we went up to the fourth and found someone waiting for us. He led us to an examination room and pulled out his wand and silently passed it over my body. All the time, he muttered to himself, "Yes. Yes. Ah, broken tibia." And so forth. Finally, he asked, "Is this woman your mother?"

I glared at him and said, "She's my, my.-.-. " I stopped and considered what to answer, but she broke in and said, "I'm his superior. He's a professor at Hogwarts and I'm the Assistant Headmistress. Anything that you want to say to me, you may say with him present."

I puzzled that a moment and said, "I think you have that backward. You said that anything that he said to you, he could say to me. But that's backward; you meant that anything that he says to me.-.-."

She broke in, "Don't pay any attention to him. He's delirious. Just go ahead and tell me what's wrong."

The healer said, "Well, I suppose that's all right. He has had several lacerations. I'll treat them with Dittany. Then, I'll heal the couple of broken bones.

"The bad one, of course, is the Cruciatus curse. It doesn't have permanent consequences if it has not been prolonged enough to cause severe mental distress that sometimes leads to insanity." He then turned to me and asked, "Are you insane?"

I stared at him and asked, "Would I know if I were?"

He nodded sagely and said, "He's perfectly fine. That is a cogent response.

"However, in cases of suspected or confirmed exposure to the unforgivable curses, I'm required as a registered healer to hold the victim until Aurors can come and interview him. Otherwise, I could treat him and release him within an hour."

Minerva said, "The receptionist sent for them. They should be here shortly."

He nodded and asked me to undress so that he could treat the lacerations. He asked Minerva to leave but she snorted and said, "I've seen him much more undressed than this. Just get on with it."

After he'd finished treating me, he glanced at his wrist and asked rhetorically, "Where are those Aurors." We waited another ten minutes and two men walked into the Exam Room and bowed slightly. They introduced themselves as Herbert Lamb and Jacque de Vrie. They pulled out folds, flipped them open, and announced that they were from the Auror Office and needed to speak to the Cruciatus victim.

I raised my hand. They wanted to interview me alone, but the healer insisted on staying to see to my medical safety. Minerva insisted on remaining because.-.-. well.-.-. because she was Minerva and was going to stay.

At the end of the interview, Herbert summarized, "So, you were kidnapped from the Muggle tube station, whatever that is, in the presence of two Muggles whom you can't identify. You were taken to a place that you believe to have been the shop of Borgin and Burke."

I objected, "I'm sure it was Borgin and Burke's."

Herbert continued, "That remains to be seen. There you were subjected three times to the Cruciatus curse. Do we have any verification of that?"

369

Here the Healer said, "Yes. I examined him and there's no doubt that it was the Cruciatus. The magical detritus of that curse are clearly present."

"All right, then you somehow subdued one of your captors and threatened the other that you would kill him if she didn't cooperate. You forced them to help you get to Knockturn Alley, through Knockturn Alley, and on to Diagon Alley. Then you weren't able to restrain them further, and they escaped. You don't know their names, other than the woman was called, 'Elect'"

"No, the name was more like "E L E K" or maybe ending with a "C"."

"You could perhaps identify them if we have photos of them."

"Yes, perhaps."

"Well, we'll ask you to come to the Auror Office to go through photos of criminals that are not in Azkaban to see if you recognize any of them. So, don't leave England, and be ready to come when summoned by owl."

With that, they handed over a written version produced by a Quick Quotes Quill that they had me review, correct, and finally sign when I was satisfied. We were preparing to leave when the door to the exam room opened and someone came in. I looked up and discovered it was Professor Dumbledore. He glanced at me and seemed to take it all in. "I hope the other fellow looks worse."

About the Author

William Wilkin lived in a small Southern Ohio town until he began his college career. He has a Bachelor's degree in Physics from The Ohio State University and a Master's degree in Physics from The University of Chicago.

He has a career in corporate Information Technology.and currently lives in Nashville, TN.

He enjoys music, both "serious" and "classic Rock". He reads classic Detective fiction and Science Fiction & Fantasy as well as trying to stay current in Physics.

He began writing seriously about 2005. He has a blog, in-mid-world, where he writes about Science Fiction & Fantasy and remotely related topics.